BREAKING GODS

✦

D. J. MOLLES

SPECIAL THANKS

I'm once again indebted to a whole crew of people, without which this book might not have even happened.

First, to Dave Fugate, my agent, who was instrumental in every phase of this book, from concept to completion. It started out as a cool idea, and would have languished in that state, never becoming a full story, if it hadn't been for his knowledge and guidance in all things fiction.

Much thanks to my beta readers, who were always ready to lend me their excellent and informed opinions as experienced consumers of fiction: Brad Molles, Josh Gibbons, Jon Carricker, and Coty Bradburn. I'm almost sure that I'm forgetting to name someone, and if that's you, please know that it's because I'm scatterbrained, and not because I'm not grateful!

Last, but not least, thanks to you, the reader, for taking a chance on me and on this story. I hope that you will find it well worth your time and attention.

[VIII] And the gods perceived a great wickedness in humanity, and that every inclination of the thoughts of the human heart was only evil all the time, [IX] and that they would never be satisfied, and that they wished to swallow all the stars. [X] The gods saw what the human beings were building, and all that they had become, and all that they intended to become, [XI] and the gods said to themselves, "Come, let us go down to them and destroy everything they have built so that they will not swallow all the stars."

Translated from the *Ortus Deorum*

2nd Song, 3rd Stanza

CHAPTER 0

✪

BEGINNINGS

HE SITS IN PRISON and his sentence is death.

He does not know who he is, or what he is capable of.

And yet, destiny hurtles towards him whether he knows it or not.

Before we see who this condemned man is, let us look back to who he *was*, just a few days before. Let us go back to a battlefield, and a scavenging crew, and a series of events that will place this young man on a path from which he can never come back. A path to discovering who—and what—he really is.

If, of course, he manages to survive that long.

CHAPTER 1

✿

SCAVENGERS

THE TRUTH AND THE LIGHT were murdering each other in droves.

Perry and his outfit waited on a dusty escarpment to pick over their dead.

It was the month of the Giver of Death. At night, the Deadmoon waned, and the days were short. The battle had begun later than usual today, and already the sun leaned westward. If it ran long, the crew might have to scavenge after dark. Boss Hauten did not like to scavenge after dark, and so he stood off to the side, fidgeting impatiently as he waited for the slaughter to be over.

Perry sat away from the ledge, his back against a comfortable rock. Around him, the rest of the outfit waited, holding quiet conversations and occasionally laughing at a joke. At twenty years old, Perry had already been on the crew for three years. That made him a middleman, with only a few others having more seniority than him.

First, there was Jax. He was a crotchety, white-bearded old fart that had been on Boss Hauten's crew since time immemorial. He held the job of "chief primer," and he guarded it jealously because it was easy work and he was ancient.

Second, there was Tiller.

Tiller was an ass, and he got along with nobody. Least of all Perry.

Lastly, there was Stuber.

While the rest of them waited, backed away from the edge of the cliff, hoping not to catch a stray round, Stuber stood at the edge in his battered armor and looked down at the battle that splayed out in the valley below. He watched the violence, always with an element of yearning, like a captured animal pines for the ferocity of the wilds.

The clasps on the back of his spaulders still had a bit of Stuber's old *sagum* cape.

The cloth was now sun-faded. Almost pink.

But it had once been a bright red.

Red for The Truth.

Staring at the ex-legionnaire's back, Perry felt a mix of unpleasant things rising up in his throat like gorge. Fear. Hatred. Loathing.

All things best kept hidden. It wouldn't do for anybody to guess Perry's past.

Stuber turned like he felt Perry's gaze on him. Those predatory eyes of his stared out from the rocky promontory of his face. A broad grin split the dark growth of his short beard.

"Shortstack," he beckoned with one massive hand. "Come watch."

Perry shook his shaggy, brown head. "Nah. I'm good."

Stuber's face darkened. "Come watch. Don't be bleeding vagina."

Perry grunted irritably, but rose up from his comfortable rock. It was probably the best seat on this ridge, and he was being forced to give it up. He dusted the back of his pants off and took a few steps forward, hunching his head down as he did, thinking about stray rounds from the battle below.

"You remember what happened to Hinks?" Perry griped, remembering how the poor girl's head had just seemed to cave in, like an invisible hammer had struck it.

"Hinks was an unlucky bitch," Stuber said dismissively. "She'd barely come back from the ants the day before." He snapped his fingers impatiently. "Come on. You're going to miss the best part."

Perry glanced behind him. Back to his comfy rock.

Tiller had already slid into place there. He crossed his booted feet and stretched himself with a great, dramatic sigh of pleasure. Then he smiled at Perry and mimed jacking off, completed by flinging an imaginary substance at Perry.

Perry's fingers twitched, and his brain tried to dip into the place where it always went when conflict was imminent—a place of flowing, red momentum that existed deep in Perry's brain—but the second that his body tensed to react to Tiller, a huge, callused hand grabbed Perry by the back of the neck and pulled him up to the edge of the cliff.

Stuber's hands were like iron wrapped in sandpaper.

"Look," Stuber commanded.

"I've seen it before."

"You've never seen *this* before."

"I have. Many times."

"Every battle is different."

"They look the same to me."

"That's because you're a peon. Here it comes."

Down below them, three or four miles away, the two armies prepared to converge. Blue on one side. Red on the other. Their *sagum* capes brilliant in the afternoon sun. Smoke coiled and wreathed them. Flak burst like black blooms in the sky above them.

Mortars launched with a constant thumping rhythm and were shot out of the sky by the autoturrets. Gales of tracer fire scoured back and forth, lancing the crowds of men. Every once in a while a mortar shell would get through and a hole would appear in one battleline or another. Stuber didn't seem to care which side it was—when the bodies blew apart, he laughed.

The two armies were within a hundred yards of each other now. Their front lines were shielded phalanxes that inched towards each other, gaining ground stride by stride while bursts of bullets clattered back and forth, searching for a chink in the wall of shields. A body would fall, and the fire would concentrate on that hole, trying to kill more of the men behind it, but in seconds another shield would appear to plug up the hole, the dead soldiers trampled under their comrades' feet.

The two armies had closed the gap.

"Foreplay," Stuber said. "If the battlefield were a whore's bed, this is the part when you finally get to stick your dick in."

Below them, the gunfire intensified.

The mortars silenced, the two sides too close now for the shelling to continue. The autoturrets turned their focus on the front lines. Hammered shields. Created holes.

The space between red and blue was filled with bright muzzle flashes and glowing tracers and billowing smoke. It crescendoed, madly, and then, all at once, there was a break. A release.

The two sides crushed into each other.

"Haha!" Stuber thrust his hips. "Yes!"

Perry thought of the dead, crushed underfoot in the melee, in the stabbing, in the contact shots that would blow them open from the big .458 rounds. He thought about the way the mud would be a slick red-brown as he sloshed through it later, the dusty world watered by thousands of gallons of blood, but it would never be enough to bring the earth back to life.

At the rear of the two armies, further back than even the autoturrets, two armored command modules hovered on their turbines above blocks of troops waiting in reserve. On the deck of the modules stood the paladins.

Demigods.

They wore the colors of their side. Watching. Commanding.

Perry had never seen one of them die.

***

"Dogs and ants and spiders!" Hauten yelled at them.

Their buggy trundled its way down the rocky slope towards the carnage below. A warm wind blew crosswise, buffeting in Perry's ears and making him squint against flying dust.

He could see the redness below. The floor of the valley had become a butcher's house. Bodies strewn about. Both The Light and The Truth left their dead where they'd fallen.

How many dead in six hours' worth of fighting?

Perry guesstimated that there were about a thousand bodies below.

Each body containing five liters of blood.

Draining.

Five thousand liters of blood in that valley.

"Dogs and ants and spiders!" Hauten bellowed over the wind and the rumble of the buggy's tires, and the struggling whine of the electric drive.

The buggy teetered at a steep angle that made Perry's insides feel watery and he clutched the roll bar nearest him.

"Keep your eyes peeled!" Hauten continued. "Watch what you grab! Watch where you put your feet! Don't die, because I can't afford to bury you!"

"What does he mean?"

Perry, still clinging to the rollbar as the buggy now listed to the right on what felt like a forty-five degree slope, looked over his tense shoulder at the girl riding next to him. Her name was Teran. She was new to the outfit. She'd come on with them at their last stop in Junction City. She claimed to have experience. Perry had discovered that that was a lie.

Perry doubted that Hauten had been fooled. Probably he kept her on because he thought he had a chance to fuck her. She was what they called "outfit pretty." Which was to say, in a town amongst other women, you wouldn't look twice. But in an outfit full of guys…yeah, you would.

"The crows come first, but they won't do anything," Perry answered, his voice wobbling with the shaking of the buggy. "Then the dogs. They smell the blood. They're mean, but they won't attack you unless you're alone. Then the ants come up from underground. Don't step on their hills—they'll tear you up. Almost lost a girl a few months back because of that."

Poor old Hinks.

"What about the spiders?"

8

"The spiders sometimes make nests in the shell casings. They jump out and catch the flies. But they'll catch a finger too."

Teran blinked a few times, facing forward. "Aren't we supposed to collect the shell casings?"

"Yes."

She processed this with a frown, and then seemed to hunker down. Her lips flattened into a grimly-determined line. The wind whipped a bit of her sandy hair into her eyes. She pulled it back and tucked it behind her ear, where it promptly came loose again.

The buggy lifted itself over a rock, and then started to tip.

Stuber, who rode on the backend of the vehicle slid to the left side and leaned out as a counterbalance.

Perry clenched down hard, knowing that if the buggy started to tumble, he'd be meat by the bottom. They all would be. Except for Stuber, who'd simply hop off the back.

Why did Hauten have to drive like such an idiot? There were a million other routes off the damn ridge, but of course, he had to take this one, because it was the shortest, and he was in a rush to make a profit.

All four tires touched the ground again.

Perry let the air out of his chest slowly.

A moment later, the ground began to level out.

"Why are you doing this anyways?" Perry asked her.

He half-expected a sharp response from Teran. Most women that he'd seen come onto the outfit knew that they were the outsiders and that

Hauten was probably trying to fuck them. Hauten rarely hired a female that wasn't outfit pretty. They were always a bit defensive, and Perry couldn't blame them. That didn't make them very pleasant to be around, but then again, there weren't too many people on the outfit that were.

But Teran just shrugged. "All the places to make an honest living in Junction City were full up. So I figured I'd get on an outfit. This happened to be the outfit."

"You gonna ditch us when you find a steady town job?"

It was loud enough with the wind and the tires rumbling, and other peoples' shouted conversations that Perry wasn't concerned about being overheard. He didn't really think Hauten would care anyway. Turnover on the outfit was high amongst greenhorns, and nothing to balk at.

"Depends on how much Hauten pays," she replied.

"You ever goin' back to Junction City?"

This time she did look at him. "I dunno, Perry. You ever going back to what you did before?"

Perry stared at her. He didn't care for the way she said it. Like she knew about Perry's past. But that was impossible. No one knew. He'd never told anyone.

He quickly changed the subject. "When we get to the bottom, stay with me. Do what I tell you and watch where you put your feet and your hands."

The smell of blood was palpable now.

Perry could taste it on his tongue.

It was more humid down here in the valley than it had been on the ridge.

Despite it being the Deadmoon, out here where the earth had been scorched, the sun shone hot, no matter the time of year. And when it baked a pond made up of five thousand liters of blood, then it turned the valley into something of a steam room.

"Dogs and ants and spiders!" Hauten reminded them one last time, and then began to slow the buggy. As it rolled to a halt amid a cloud of dust, he looked back at them from the controls. "Work quick and we won't have to mess with any of that shit, yeah? Alright. Get to work."

Perry slid out of his seat and over the horizontal bar of metal. The black paint on it was hot to the touch. Flaking off. Rusty underneath. He went to the back, and Teran followed.

"Jax! Tiller!" Hauten called out, exiting his driver's seat. "Get some guns."

At the back of the buggy, Stuber had dropped to the ground. His Roq-11 .458 rifle was strapped to his back at the moment. He pulled a long, battered, black case out to the edge of the buggy's cargo bed. He undid the locks and lifted the cover.

Inside were two shotguns nestled next to each other, and a large, silver pistol.

The Mercy Pistol. Stuber left that where it was, but he grabbed the two shotguns in each of his meaty paws and turned, just as Jax and Tiller trotted up.

Tiller made it a point to shoulder past Perry.

Stuber shoved the shotguns in their hands. Jax ran his sunken, blue eyes over his, charged a round into the chamber, and then shoved his arm through the braided sling. He turned and walked off.

Tiller had the shotgun in both hands and he tried to pull it, but Stuber held on.

11

Tiller stared up at the ex-legionnaire, confused.

Stuber held the shotgun in his right hand. With his left, he jabbed an index finger like a dart into Tiller's chest. Tiller let out an offended yelp and glared.

"Don't be an asshole," Stuber growled.

"I won't," Tiller grunted indignantly. He jerked hard and Stuber let him have the shotgun.

Tiller checked his action, just like Jax had, although the movements were not as sure. Tiller did most of what he did in an attempt to look as experienced as Jax.

When Tiller was satisfied that he had a loaded shotgun, he gave a baleful look over his shoulder at Stuber, and then marched off. He made another attempt to shoulder Perry, but Perry saw it coming and slid out of the way.

"'Scuse me," Tiller said anyways. Kept walking.

Perry felt that flowing river deep inside of him.

The blur of red.

As much as Perry enjoyed watching Stuber mess with Tiller, it only meant that Tiller was going to be more pissy than usual today.

"Come on," Hauten hollered, reaching the back of the buggy. "Buckets. Work quick. Quick, quick, quick. Lezgo lezgo lezgo."

There was a stack of buckets. They hadn't made it down to the valley in their original, stowed position. Perry grabbed two from the jumbled pile and gave one to Teran. He started towards the battlefield.

"We're here for the brass. Don't try to loot the bodies: some of the legionairres booby-trap themselves before they die. Besides that, we've got a delicate understanding with several other scavenging outfits—they let us have the brass, we let them have the armor, or the tech, or whatever their flavor of scrap is. All you gotta do is pick up brass. If it's severely dented, leave it. If you can see a spider web inside it, leave it—those things are poisonous. Don't try to move anything that already has an ant mound on it. If you notice anybody that's still alive, don't touch them, don't move them, and don't talk to them. Just call for Stuber."

The very first body they reached was still alive.

A man with half his face blown off.

His chestplate rose and fell with hitching breaths. His massive shield lay still attached to his left arm, dented and dinged, the edges chipped from thousands of projectiles that had skimmed by him.

But one had found him. And one was all you needed.

His blue *sagum* identified him as a legionnaire of The Light.

The dying legionnaire reached a hand towards them. He tried to speak, but couldn't.

Perry first eyed the man's right hand to see if he was still armed. Both sides left the bodies, but they were careful to retrieve the weapons. Funny how they did that.

Perry saw no weapons. He turned his head to project his voice back over his shoulder, but he kept his eye on the dying soldier in front of him.

"Stuber!"

13

The soldier knew what was next. Whatever he wanted, he forgot about it, and his outstretched arm fell to his side. He sat there with his chestplate heaving, his one good eye still looking straight at Perry.

Perry heard the sound of retching behind him.

He glanced over his shoulder, and saw Teran, doubled over with a thick rope of yellowy stomach juices issuing from her mouth and nose.

He turned back to the dying legionnaire.

The man's one remaining eye was a pleasant hazel color. The eye was nice and round. Thick lashes. He might've been a popular man with the ladies, Perry thought, though with half his face missing, it was difficult to tell if he was handsome. Maybe he just had nice eyes.

Stuber came over. Perry gestured to the dying soldier.

Stuber knelt before the man, as he would so many times that day. He put his hand on the soldier's forehead and he said the words that Perry didn't even need to hear, he knew them so well by now.

"In the eyes of the gods, it matters not the color of your banner, but the courage of your heart. Under the watchful gaze of Nur, the Eighth Son, all warriors are brothers. As your brother, I bear witness to Halan, the Eldest Son, that you have fought your fight. Be at peace. Accept this mercy, and go to The After."

The dying man closed his eyes as Stuber put the large, silver pistol against his head and gave him mercy.

And, as he always did, Perry watched, and thought, *That could have been me.*

And that made him think of the Tall Man.

14

CHAPTER 2

✿

PERRY

PERRY WAS TWELVE YEARS OLD when he first saw the Tall
Man.

What he remembered most was how the Tall
Man had seemed to appear out of nowhere.

It was evening at the farming freehold outside
of Touring. The sun dipped into the horizon line, and
the sky was burning umber, and the millet shuffled
and whispered in the hot breeze coming out of the
south.

They'd run the well pumps the hour prior,
and the dusty ground in which the fields of millet
clawed for life was still moist, and it caked onto the
bottom of Perry's sandals and got under his toes as
he played a violent game of battlefield with the other
boys his age.

He was, of course, smaller than them. He
endured the nominal amount of ribbing that is
mandatory among male peers, but the boys knew he
was ferocious on the field, and gave him his due
respect for that—he was never picked last.

His most common assignment was to take the
legs out from anyone that tried to rush their
battleline, which he accomplished with the reckless
abandon of youth—complete and utter disregard for
the breakability of bones. The only precaution that
the boys took was to not slam each other's faces too
hard. You could hide bruises on your torso, but
broken noses and busted teeth would get you in

trouble once the game was over and you had to face your parents.

Perry didn't have parents. He had an uncle. But, as Perry's only surviving relative, the uncle fussed over him enough to account for both missing parents.

The boys churned through the empty field, their gangly young bodies straining, showing hints of fatless muscles that seemed to pop up anew every day. Dirty knees and elbows and chests and backs. Calling commands to each other like demigods. Heedless of their foolishness. Lost in the game.

It was playing "battlefield" with the other boys of the freehold that Perry first became conscious of that blurry red river inside of his brain. Something he eventually came to think of as The Calm. Conflict and violence didn't upset him, despite his diminunitive size. He sank into The Calm, and when he was there, it was all just a rush of colors, like a current carrying him.

One might think that calm and violence did not go hand-in-hand, but for Perry they did. There was the jitteriness that accompanied the *anticipation* of violence, but once he was in it, it was all just frictionless momentum.

When he was in that place, the world made sense to him.

It all flowed easily in the red.

Perry remembered throwing a vicious block, sending the other kid cartwheeling into the air, and himself sliding face-first into the moist dirt, nearly knocking the wind out of his chest.

He coughed into the dirt. He remembered the taste and texture of grit in his mouth, the smell of moist dirt and sweat. And when he looked up, sucking air, he saw the figure standing there at the edge of the field, where no one had been only moments ago.

The fields all around them were flat and featureless. Not even a boulder to hide behind. The millet only grew to four feet. And this figure was easily seven feet tall.

It seemed that all the boys at play noticed the figure at the same time.

"Holy shit," exclaimed the boy that Perry had just blocked, as he staggered up onto his feet. "Where'd he come from?"

The Tall Man was dressed like a desert nomad. Swathed in sand-colored cloth from head to foot, dust goggles over his eyes.

But desert nomads didn't grow this big eating bugs and wild dogs.

The Tall Man stood there, watching the boys for one long, terrifying moment. All the boys were considering whether to run and scream for the nearest adult. The only thing that kept them there was the fact that their macho friends were watching.

Perry pulled himself out of the dirt, his eyes never leaving the robed figure.

After a long moment, the Tall Man began to walk towards them.

At first, none of the boys moved. None of them made a sound. They were all too scared to be thought of as scared.

When the Tall Man was about twenty feet away from the cluster of boys, Perry got the distinct impression that the figure was striding directly towards him. His eyes left the figure for the first time, in order to glance from side to side at his friends.

They moved for the first time. Melting backwards from Perry, like oil separates from water.

"You," a voice rumbled.

It was deep. Like gravel being rubbed on the top of a massive drum. In the background of Perry's mind, he registered the abnormal rasp of it. As though the stranger were obscuring his voice.

Then he realized that the dark, mirrored surface of the dust goggles were directed straight at him. He realized this because he could see his own stunned face in the reflection, gazing back at himself.

"Me?"

"You have an uncle."

"Uh…"

"Take me to him."

***

Perry waited in the waning twilight outside of the mudbrick hut that he shared with his Uncle Sergio. He sat there, watching the last sliver of a crimson sun dip below a distant horizon beyond which he knew nothing.

As the sunlight disappeared, the quiet hum of the power inverters disappeared, no longer feeding power from the solar cells that sprouted from all the mudbrick huts like weeds. The ground-mineral reactors slugged to life beneath Perry's feet. The warm glow of electric lights came on, house by house.

Somewhere a few houses down, a conical windmill with a bad bearing creaked a steady rhythm in the evening breeze.

Perry perceived all these things absently, but in his mind he could only picture Uncle Sergio's face.

Perry had expected curiosity when Uncle Sergio had opened the door to their hut and found Perry standing there with the Tall Man. He had expected suspicion. Perhaps even some fear, because the Tall Man was mysterious.

But he hadn't been prepared for the expression that infiltrated his uncle's demeanor.

Uncle Sergio bore the face of a man staring at his own death.

And now Perry couldn't stop thinking about it. Couldn't stop thinking that he'd made a terrible mistake by leading the Tall Man to Uncle Sergio. A misstep from which he would never be able to recover.

He couldn't shake the conviction that he would forever see his life divided into two parts, and the knife that cut them was the appearance of the Tall Man.

He was not wrong.

It was fully dark by the time that the hut door opened again, and the Tall Man exited, pulling his dust goggles down over his eyes before Perry could see anything about him. Masked and hooded again, he stepped over the threshold of the hut, and out into the dusty alley.

Uncle Sergio stood like a statue in the doorway. The only evidence that he wasn't petrified was the sudden bob of his Adam's apple.

The Tall Man stopped in the middle of the alley.

The head turned. Perry wasn't sure if the eyes behind those mirrored dust goggles were looking at him, or at Uncle Sergio, or simply determining which direction to go.

The Tall Man never spoke to him again.

He strode off, disappearing into the dark, just as he had seemed to materialize out of the day.

Neither Uncle Sergio nor Perry moved until the darkness into which the Tall Man had disappeared did not betray any hint of movement.

Uncle Sergio stirred. His sun-leathered skin looked pale and sallow. Gray whiskers sparkled on his cheeks like silver dust. The crown of white hair that circled his bald pate seemed mussed. Like Uncle Sergio had tried to pull it out.

"Get inside," Uncle Sergio husked.

"What was—?"

"I said get inside!" Uncle Sergio moved out of the doorway, and thrust his arm in with a commanding finger. "No more questions."

Perry obeyed, his heart drumming, his throat dry. Uncle Sergio followed, closing the door behind him.

Uncle Sergio's odd outburst of temper was gone as quickly as it had appeared. His eyes seemed unfocused. When he spoke, it was with a strange numbness. "Gather your things. We have to leave this place."

Perry was about to ask another question, but a flash of fire from his uncle's eyes shut him up again.

They did not have much to gather. They owned very little, and it all fit into a single large pack, which Uncle Sergio put onto his old back. Perry thought of protesting and taking the bag, but still didn't dare to open his mouth.

They snuck out at midnight, on foot, like escaping prisoners.

They had been walking for nearly an hour in silence when Perry heard a rumble in the distance behind them, like a thunderhead had formed. But the night sky was clear and cloudless and showed a million stars.

Perry looked behind him and glimpsed a dangerous orange glare in the distance, burning like fever in the night sky. Uncle Sergio gripped Perry's head and forced it forward again.

"Don't look, Perry. Keep your eyes on the road."

By dawn they had arrived in Touring.

Uncle Sergio took them to the coach house there, and chartered a buggy with gold that Perry had never seen before and didn't even know that his uncle possessed.

"Keniza," Uncle Sergio told the driver in a hollow voice.

The driver accepted the payment, but cast a scrutinizing glance at Perry. Up and down. As though sizing him up, and finding him wanting. But he shrugged. Faced forward again. Drove the buggy out of town, out across the plains.

Perry spoke for the first time since they'd left the freehold.

"Keniza?"

"Yes."

"Why? What's there for us?"

"The Academy."

"Hell's Hollow? Are we going to work there?" Perry was dumbfounded. He and his uncle were peons. He could only picture them in the kitchen, or perhaps cleaning the lavatories, or, if they were lucky, working the greenhouses where the food was grown to feed the next generation being trained at Hell's Hollow to be legionnaires for The Light.

Perry hoped it would be the greenhouses.

Uncle Sergio stared out through a dirty pane of clear plastic that shivered in the desert wind as they plunged across the dusty wastes. He took a long, slow breath, as though steeling himself.

"You'll be attending."

Ahead of them, the driver snorted, then covered it with a cough.

Uncle Sergio glared at the back of the man's head.

Perry waited for further explanation, figuring that "attending" meant something different than his initial impression. Because his initial impression was impossible. Perry was too small. He would barely rank in a peon outfit. He would certainly never be accepted into a legion. And people did not attend Hell's Hollow unless they were on track to be legionnaires.

Uncle Sergio must have meant something else.

But an explanation was not forthcoming.

And with a growing sickness in his gut, Perry began to realize that Uncle Sergio had said what he meant, and that "attend," actually meant "attend."

Perry's mouth worked without words. He tried to find adequate ones. But they collided in his throat. And then none of them managed to get out.

Finally, a single thought escaped: "I'm too small."

Uncle Sergio didn't meet Perry's eyes. He didn't react as Perry had hoped he would—by either admitting it was a horrible, idiotic idea, or by finding some way to comfort him and convince him that he could survive Hell's Hollow.

"Do you remember your father?" Uncle Sergio asked, his voice barely audible above the rumble of the buggy's tires.

Perry had no clear memory of his father. Nothing that bore any linear logic to it, as an adult's memories do. But he had snippets. Images.

Here is all he recalled of his father:

Large. Smiling. Intense. Hard.

Sitting on his father's hip, and feeling his father's hands holding him, and feeling how they were almost painful there, not soft like his mother's touch. His mother made out of gossamer and down. His father, made out of stone and sinew.

Perry revered his father, in his own small, infantile way. But also feared him. How you might both love and fear a benevolent, but all-powerful god. A god who could crush you if the whim came upon them, but you trusted and hoped that they wouldn't.

When his father spoke it was the booming of thunder. Joviality was clear in his recollections of his father. But also sternness. Command.

Uncle Sergio had told Perry things about his father.

That his father's name was Cato McGown. That he'd been a legionnaire for The Light. That he'd died when Perry was three years old. Killed in glorious battle against The Truth. His mother, who loved Cato so much, died of a broken heart.

"I remember some things," Perry said. "And what you've told me."

Uncle Sergio kept his eyes fixed forward. At the time, Perry thought that there was some adult reason for this. But many years later he would realize that it was because his uncle couldn't meet his gaze.

"I've told you that your father was a legionnaire. But the truth is, he was more than that. Your father was a *legatus*. A general. He commanded legions."

Perry sat, small and insufficient under the weight of this revelation. He was well-acquainted with the fact that, as a runt and a peon, he would never follow in his father's footsteps. But now those footsteps seemed infinitely less attainable.

And yet, that's exactly what Uncle Sergio was telling him, wasn't it?

That he would follow in the footsteps of his father.

"They'll never accept me," Perry said, his voice higher, more squeaky than he would have liked in the midst of such a serious conversation.

"They way has been paved," Uncle Sergio remarked, bitterness in his voice. "You will go. They will accept you."

Perry stared at his uncle's weathered profile. "The Tall Man."

Uncle Sergio winced, but said nothing.

"Is he a legatus too?"

Uncle Sergio finally turned his head, and met his nephew's gaze. His eyes looked hollow and haunted. He said the words, but it didn't escape Perry that they came out through clenched teeth. "He was...a friend...of your father's." Then he looked back out the window, as though Perry's gaze was too hot to hold for very long. "No more questions now. You should sleep."

But Perry did not sleep that night.

***

That cataclysmic night had been eight years ago.

Perry had spent five of those years in Hell's Hollow.

And then he'd spent three of them on the run, working for Boss Hauten on the outskirts of society, never mentioning his past, and associating only with men who knew better than to ask.

In those three years, Perry had avoided the authorities in every town they went to, knowing that if he ever got caught, they'd find out that he'd deserted, and he'd be executed as a heretic.

Oddly enough, it would not be heresy that would eventually lead him to the gallows.

CHAPTER 3

✪

BRASS

PERRY GUESSTIMATED that 1.5 million rounds had been fired on the battlefield.

Give or take a few hundred thousand.

Boss Hauten's crew collected the brass.

The brass went into the buckets.

The buckets got emptied into the hold, which was a large, metal container that bulged under the deck of the buggy like the potbelly on a pig. The hold was full when there was roughly 100,000 spent shell casings.

Another crew had arrived late to the scene, and had carefully skirted the battlefield, keeping a good, non-threatening distance between themselves and Boss Hauten's crew. They started on the opposite side of the field of dead. Hauten watched them like a hawk until he'd determined they were not taking any of his brass—just bits of military tech that had been shot up and left behind.

Hauten's crew left the battlefield as dusk crept up on them and the crows took flight and the dogs got bolder in the darkness. They'd worked over a sixth of the sprawling, blood-soaked valley. There was much more to harvest, but not much time to do it in.

By then, the smell of blood had curdled into the reek of death.

The ants had already begun to mound up around the dead bodies, and the spiders were busy making their nests.

The risk-versus-reward would sway out of favor of making a return trip by tomorrow night. If Perry knew Hauten—and three years on this outfit made him think he had a pretty good idea of the man—they were going to return at first light. They'd work all day. If they were lucky, they might harvest as much as they harvested today.

Hauten returned them to the ridge that they'd begun on. He liked this spot. He liked a high overlook. Things could get dodgy out here. Occasionally another outfit would show up who had bad blood with Hauten, or maybe they were just new to the game and overly aggressive. And there were always the Lokos to keep an eye out for.

But despite the dangers, work didn't end at dusk. It had just begun.

With the buggy parked and chalked, the lights came on, and the workbenches came out.

Their little camp was now bathed in stark, white worklight.

Stuber faded into the shadows, disappearing like he was sinking into brackish water. He took one of the shotguns and his Roq-11. The other shotgun and the Mercy Pistol were locked up for the time being.

Tiller started up the tumbler and began feeding brass into it. The tumbler made an aggressive racket. But it could clean and polish a massive amount of shells.

As they waited for the first batch of shells to be cleaned, Perry took Teran aside so that they could speak over the din of the tumbler.

"You obviously have no idea what you're doing."

She looked at him guardedly. "Sure I do."

"Right."

This was their third day out of Junction City. Their first that they'd actually harvested brass. So far he'd had to tell her how to collect the brass, and she'd puked at the sight of the carnage. Not just at the wounded man either—he caught her retching two other times, and gagging throughout the day. She looked drained because of it.

Perry pointed to one of the press stations. A big gray chunk of metal that was affixed to a thick, sturdy workbench. "What's that?"

She stared at it. Blinked. Her eyes went back and forth between Perry and the press.

"It's...a...reloading press," she said.

"Yeah. What type? What's the operation? I'll give you a hint—it's the first press operation in the whole process. The very first thing you do, right after you clean and sort the brass."

She stared at it even longer. Like she was going to conjure the answer. Or perhaps she thought she could take a wild guess and somehow get it right.

Perry admired her stubbornness.

"That's the resizing station," he said. "Resizing and depriming."

"Oh. Right. I just..."

Perry rubbed his temple, squinting at her. "Why do you have to resize brass, Teran?"

"Uh...because..."

"Because brass expands when it's fired. Gods in the skies, you really have never done this before."

Teran shot him a look. Her arms were stiff at her sides. Her fists clenched. Her jaw muscles bunching. She lowered her head like a bull about to charge. Perry almost wanted to take a step away from her.

"You gonna tell Hauten?"

"Easy, now. I'm not gonna tell Hauten. But you need to learn quick."

"I can learn quick."

"I'm sure you can."

"So teach me."

Perry took her by one shoulder and turned her back to the buggy and the operation that was now laid out in the lights. He outstretched his hand and pointed to each station, starting with the tumbler. "Crash course. The dirty brass goes into the tumbler. Clean brass comes out. Then it gets sorted. After it gets sorted, it's resized and deprimed in that press right there. When it's resized, the shell casing lengthens. It has to be trimmed back to spec. That's the trimming station right there. When it's trimmed, a new primer gets seated. After the casing is primed, it's charged. After it's charged, the bullet is seated, then crimped. And you have a brand-new cartridge. You with me?"

"Who does what?"

"Don't worry about who does what. All you need to worry about is sorting the brass. That's what most of the greenhorns do." He guided her towards the workbench. "Brass gets laid out on the table. You got four buckets in front of you. This is your 'uglies' bucket. If the brass is discolored, corroded, or misshapen, you put it in the uglies bucket. Get rid of your uglies first. Then you sort by calibers. There should only be two calibers, either ten-mil, or four-five-eight. The ten-mil are the smaller pistol rounds. A little over an inch long. The four-five-eight are the big rifle rounds. They're about three inches long. After you get rid of the uglies, separate your ten-mils and put them in the pistol bucket. After that, you should only have four-five-eights. You have to sort these individually."

The tumbler switched off. Tiller gathered the grated container and pulled it from the body of the tumbler, shaking it several times to get the polishing beads out of the shells. Tiller dumped this into a bucket that waited in the arms of one of their greenhorns, a guy named Pebbles.

Pebbles hoisted the bucket of brass, straining at it. He was a wiry kid, but strong. He waddled over to the sorting workbench and grunted the bucket of brass up onto the bench. Then he turned it over and spilled the brass, shaking it out in a long line along the bench. Like you might fill a hog's trough with slop.

Perry grabbed one of the four-five-eight casings. Upended it. Showed Teran the bottom. "See the manufacturer's marking? This one says 'BMM.' That's shit. That's peasant stuff. The armies hand it out to the peons. So put it in the peon bucket." Perry hunted around, checked the bottom of a few shells, found what he was looking for. "Here," he said. "See the maker's mark on this one?"

Teran eyed the shell. "The cross thing?"

"Right. The cross is one. The other just looks like a triangle. Those are the good brass. High quality. Consistent. You put that in the good bucket. Make sense?"

Teran nodded. She pointed to the buckets, each in turn. "Uglies. Pistol. Peon. Good."

"Yeah. You got it."

"Okay."

"Word to the wise?"

"Yes?"

"Work fast, but more importantly, *sort correctly*. Hauten doesn't like mixed up brass. He takes it personally."

"Okay."

"One more thing."

"What?"

"The four-five-eight shells? Rap them on the table like this." Perry tapped the open end on the table. "In case there's a spider in there."

"You said they were poisonous."

"They are."

"What am I supposed to do if one pops out?"

"You squash it."

"Won't it bite me?"

"Not if you hit it hard. If you hesitate, it'll jump on you, though. They're mean. Trust me. Move fast."

Pebbles and the other greenhorn, Ernie, were already at the workbench, their deft fingers picking through the brass, extracting the uglies. Tossing them into the bucket. Another sound to add to the racket— the *plink-plunk-plink* of brass going into the buckets.

***

The work was organized chaos.

The three greenhorns—Ernie, Pebbles, and Teran—stuck to the sorting table. The rest of the outfit had multiple responsibilities. The brass made its way through the process as orderly as soldiers in formation. But the hands that crafted it back into a cartridge hustled back and forth to this station and that.

It was a familiar madness.

It was easy to get the hang of after a while.

Perry being third senior man, was in charge of the resizing and depriming. He cranked those presses, round after round, until a pile of spent primers lay at his feet. And by that time there was a stack-up of cases that Jax and Tiller had primed, and so Perry switched from the resizing press to the charging station, metering out EDT540 Powdered Propellant into each case.

When they were charged, they were stuck in a special rack. The rack held twenty .458 cartridges. The rack kept them separate so that whoever was at the charging station didn't double-load a casing. Once you put a casing on the rack, you didn't touch it.

Twenty casings filled a rack, and then you slid it down to the last station, the bullet press. Bullet pressing was one of the quicker processes. There were only two presses that were set for that usage. Slider, one of the low middlemen, would be along shortly to start seating them.

It was in the middle of this orgy of unorganized and semi-cogent chemistry that Perry realized that Teran was at his side.

He glanced over his shoulder at her, abruptly irritated.

He had a case in the powder meter.

Had he already charged it?

He had to take it out and look into it to see.

Yes, there was powder in it.

He set the casing in a half-full rack.

"What?" he snapped at Teran, as he grabbed another case.

"What are you doing?"

"Powder charge. Go back to your station. Hauten'll dock you."

"How much powder?"

"Forty-one-point-six," Perry said. "Not to be rude, but seriously, fuck off."

"Question."

"Gods. What?"

"How long have you been doing this?"

Perry froze in his movements. But only for a second. His eyebrows twitched towards each other and he gave Teran an uncertain glance before he went back to his work. Slipped a new cartridge in the collar. Charged it with propellant.

"Five years," he lied. "Why are you asking me these questions? 'Perry, what'd you do before this?' 'Perry, how long have you been doing this?' Why you keep asking shit like that? You're making me nervous."

Teran raised her hands, looking put off. "I just want to know how long I have to be on before I'm not considered a greenhorn anymore. Why would that make you nervous?"

Perry fed another charge without answering. It was about the hundredth time he'd worked the powder meter. Sometimes the set screw on the powder collar would loosen up. End up over- or under-charging the cartridges. Either would be disastrous.

He set the full casing on a scale and it told him all was well. The appropriate amount of powder was still being dispensed.

When he finished that, he whirled on Teran. Stood close to her so that he didn't have to shout. "You ever think about the type of guys that get on a reloading outfit?"

Teran narrowed her gaze. "I'm aware."

"Well, there's a lotta guys that don't wanna answer a buncha questions about their past. Okay? So stop. Before someone takes it the wrong way. Now get back to your station before Hauten see's you." He didn't wait for any reply from her. He raised his head up and hollered, "Slider! You jackass! Seat some bullets!"

"Yessir, Sergeant Shortstack, sir!" Slider yelled back, somewhere on the line.

Perry forced a grim smile, as though everything was fine.

When he glanced over his shoulder again, Teran was already moving back to her station.

He was replaying the conversation over in his mind, wondering if he was just being paranoid, when a smattering of gunshots rattled through the night, and everyone stopped what they were doing and looked up in the direction that the gunshots had come.

For the span of several heartbeats, there was only the sound of the tumbler.

Then Stuber plunged out of the darkness and into the light, running at a dead sprint. "Lokos! Kill the tumbler!"

CHAPTER 4

✪

LOKOS

"GODS IN THE SKIES," Hauten spat as he killed the tumbler.

Perry's ears hummed with the memory of the noises. The air seemed to press at his eardrums. Heavy, for a moment. Like he'd dropped altitude.

Stuber stamped to a stop at the back of the buggy. "Breakin' out Charlize."

"You'll make me a poor man," Hauten griped.

"Better a poor man than a dead man."

Perry looked down the line and found Teran. She stood back from the sorting table with her hands tensed at her sides, like she wanted to be doing something, but didn't know what.

"Teran!" Perry called out.

She snapped her head in his direction.

He waved her over. He was already pulling the black tarp out to cover his station. They didn't want any brass that Stuber was about to fire mixing in with the casings that were being reloaded. It would make a mess of things.

"Help," Perry ordered.

She grabbed the other side of the tarp. They hauled it lengthwise across the station.

"You ever had a run in with Lokos?" he asked.

"Once or twice."

"Once or twice is enough." Perry straightened the edge of the tarp. "Come on."

He felt responsible for her. Hauten had made him the mentor, and her the mentee, after all. That meant that he had to look out for her.

Out in the darkness there rose a sound like someone laughing. A shrieking, whooping cackle.

Perry made for the buggy. Ernie and Pebbles were already on the deck. The others scrambled up inside. Tiller and Jax had the shotguns again. Hauten had his own pistol, the huge, black revolver that he always carried.

Perry grabbed one of the rollbars and vaulted himself in. He turned to help Teran, but she was already in.

"We get guns now?" she asked.

"Hell no."

She looked incredulous. "How we supposed to fight 'em off?"

"We get pikes."

The pikes were strapped in bundles of five. One bundle on each of the long rollbars that ran the length of the buggy on the right and left. Monty, the guy with the flattened nose, was yanking the straps off the bundle that was right in front of Perry's face, so he helped.

The pikes came down.

Eight-foot-long pipes with the tips cut at angles, like a hypodermic needle.

Perry handed one to Teran.

She looked at it. "What the hell am I supposed to do with this?"

"You skewer 'em."

Out in the darkness, the mad laughter came again. It was answered this time, by another voice, coming from the other side of them.

"Here," Perry went down to a knee. Propped his pike up on the siderail. Tucked it firmly under his armpit. The sharpened tip lanced out from the side of the buggy.

Teran knelt to his right and copied him.

That same look—the flat-lipped, gray-grim determination.

To Perry's left, Stuber took up his position. He hefted a Boren LRG with a grunt. The thing weighed almost as much as Perry himself. He dropped it on the rollbar and the anchors auto-locked in place. He gave the thing a violent shake to make sure it was solid.

"How many did you get eyes on?" Hauten asked, standing in the middle of the deck. The buggy was now a porcupine—pointy things jutting out at every angle. Jax and Tiller ready with the shotguns. Stuber ready on the LRG. Hauten inside of the circle that they all created.

"Half dozen," Stuber answered. He powered the LRG on. It emitted a low, constant whine.

"Half dozen?" Teran whispered.

Perry took that to mean that Teran had never seen that many. "Clans get a little bigger the farther out you get from civilization."

"Give me the Roq," Hauten ordered Stuber.

Stuber unslung it from his back and shoved it into Hauten's waiting hands.

Hauten put his back to Stuber and covered the opposite direction.

There was no more hysterical laughter coming from the darkness.

Just short, sharp yips, here and there.

And then after a moment, not even that.

Just the silence.

Just the night wind whipping through the valley. Scraping over the ridge.

Some of the legends said that the Lokos were people who'd gone mad when so many of their family had been slain on the battlefield. Other legends said that they'd simply been cursed by the gods in general, or sometimes by Batu the Trickster specifically, depending on who was telling the story.

Perry knew that none of that was true.

The Lokos existed because, when you lived out on the plains, surviving like an animal…

Well, eventually you became an animal.

"Call 'em when you see 'em," Hauten called out.

The lights blazed out from the buggy, creating a ring-like glow. Like all the world was nothing, and only their buggy existed in the night. They were surrounded by emptiness.

"I think…" Teran whispered, then stopped.

Perry's eyes searched the darkness. He tried to keep them moving. If you let them sit in one spot for too long, the darkness itself would appear to move. But he tore his eyes away for a brief glance at Teran.

"What?"

She peered into the darkness, the way a cat looks at midnight. But she didn't say anything else.

Night. Night. More night.

The wind moved something out beyond their lights. Low sage, probably.

It was about the only damn thing that grew out here where the earth had been scorched.

Perry stared at it for a moment, but it didn't move again.

Just sage.

He felt the flow of red, but he found it difficult to sink into it.

The fear, the adrenaline, sometimes they pushed him out of it. Snapped him back into reality. He hadn't always been fearful, but time and bad experiences build that up in us all, like the charry residue after multiple fires.

He breathed to fight the fear.

Tried to sink into The Calm.

A voice lilted to them over the wind, high and wavering and not at all sane.

"Vultures!" the voice warbled. "You pack of vultures! You know your choices! Submit or be skinned!"

"We'll take our chances," Hauten belted back, and then under his breath: "You fucking psychopath."

There was no other talking.

Just the night, and the wind.

And then it happened, and when it did it was quick, and it was violent in the way that only the insane can accomplish.

All around them from the darkness the cries went up, the weird, yip-yap-laugh. And figures began to pulse out of the night. The sage brush that the wind had moved came alive and burst into the light.

You could hardly call it a person anymore. Their clothes were tattered patchworks of cloth and skin and gods-knew what else, and they moved in a hectic, blur of motion. He or she, Perry had no idea. He felt his heart lodge itself in his throat and he bore down on his pike and reared it back, waiting for the Loko to get close enough...

The LRG roared.

The Loko seemed to disassemble.

Its limbs went every which way. Head and torso, and one leg still attached, fell flat into the dust, writhing through a cloud of its own vaporized blood.

A cluster of hot, smoking brass rattled against the side of Perry's head, and one or two went blistering into his collar, but he had to ignore them—he didn't dare take his hands off his pike. He'd been burned by hot brass before. It had to be better than being skinned alive.

Out of the hands of the dead Loko tumbled its weapon: what looked like a pipe with a rusty spike lashed crosswise to the end of it.

Stuber traced his fire left, where two of the Lokos ran, side by side, throwing their knives at him from an ineffectual distance as he terminated their lives with a belch of fire and lead.

To his right, the darkness birthed another shape that ran at them, crying its war cry, its face and body coated with white mud. This was a woman, Perry thought, because he saw the shriveled breasts under the mud.

She had a knife in one hand, and a gun in the other.

Perry pivoted his pike in that direction.

The Loko woman raised the gun. It looked like some rusted 10mm that she'd swiped from a battlefield long ago. She fired wildly at them, still charging.

She was close.

Perry reared back with his pike, his cheek close to the cold metal, sighting down along it, ready to plunge it into the Loko's brain, sinking into that red blur…

Someone bumped him.

He registered Hauten cursing at him, telling him to get out of the way.

The Loko woman danced past the point of his pike.

Shotguns roared, which meant that the Lokos had made it through the pikes on the other side.

The LRG screamed into the darkness.

Hauten was at their side, firing the Roq-11.

Perry watched a burst of big .458 rounds pound the woman's midsection. But she didn't stop coming. Her eyes were wide and wild and Perry saw the whites of them as they rolled around in a sheer madness.

She was still coming.

And then a pike went through her skull with one quick, efficient plunge.

The Loko woman's legs kept running for what would have been another two big strides, her arms loping, like she was treading through waist-deep water. Her breasts still swaying, now hitching with dying breaths.

For good measure, Boss Hauten leaned over the siderail and gave her another burst from the Roq, which obliterated her head and caused her body to slump from the pike that had skewered her.

Just like that, it was over.

Perry traced his eyes up along the pike that had killed the woman, and found Teran on the other end, her mouth twisted up, her nose curled like she'd smelled something bad.

"Good work," he mumbled.

Someone was shouting.

It took a moment for Perry to re-center himself and make sense of the words being said.

"They got Slider!" someone called.

Stuber yelled over them, "Everyone calm your tits! There might be more!"

Perry felt the adrenaline hit that peak in his body were it was like falling over a cliff. It went down, down, down, and there was nothing left in him but a fast-beating heart and the start of a hot, poking headache behind his eyes.

He leaned back away from the rail and craned his neck.

Hauten rushed to the front of the deck and knelt down.

Perry barely saw Slider before Hauten blocked his view. Just a glimpse.

Slider, young and lean and dark-haired, lying on his back. He looked right back at Perry, his eyes wide open, and he looked like he saw everything in that moment. Like Slider had been granted an understanding that the rest of them would never know.

He was seeing The After.

Then he coughed and blood burbled out of his mouth.

And then Hauten blocked Perry's view.

He felt something hit him in the side. Jerked, for a moment thinking *another Loko*, but it was Stuber, kicking him. Pissed because Perry was distracted.

"Watch your godsdamned lane, peon!"

Perry went back to staring down the length of his pike at the darkness, but the six dead Lokos that surrounded their buggy were the only ones that attacked them that night.

***

The ground was too hard to bury Slider.

So they erected a little cairn over his body.

Just enough to keep the dogs off of him.

Perry had liked the guy. Felt sad looking at that lonely pile of rocks.

When Hauten asked if anyone would like to say a few words, Perry glanced around, wondering if Slider's friends would speak up. Chester and Bigs were the ones that had come on with him. They'd known him the best.

But Chester and Bigs just stood there, their hands clasped at their crotches. Their eyes were affixed to the dusty ground. Dry.

Perry stepped forward. "I liked Slider. He seemed like an okay guy. He had a bit of a temper when he drank, but then again, he did brain that guy in Dry Gulch. Did it with a beer bottle. I do believe he saved my life, or at least my teeth. I never did pay him back for that." Then, to the spirit that had gone on to The After: "Slider, I still owe you one."

All of the crew, including Boss Hauten and Stuber, knelt and picked up a small stone. Then they all tossed them onto the cairn they'd already made. The clatter was dim and forlorn.

It was customary to give an offering of something old or well-aged to Halan the Eldest, to escort the deceased into The After. But out here where the earth was scorched, and men were poor, and carried little to nothing of value, the oldest things to be found were stones.

Scavengers maintained that Halan understood their predicament.

If he didn't, then they were all headed for the Dark Side of The After.

45

They wouldn't know until they died and found out.

After that, everyone went back to work.

***

Guesstimation: Boss Hauten's outfit probably cleared in the neighborhood of 5,000 rounds that night. What with all the distractions.

They ate dinner far passed midnight, and at first light Hauten sent Ernie, Pebbles, Chester, and Bigs down to the rot-stinking battlefield to harvest what they could. Hauten took them down in the buggy, which still had the LRG anchored to the side of it. Hauten intended to be their coverage. Stuber remained up on the ridge with the rest of them while they continued sorting and reloading.

By the end of that second day they had netted about 15,000 rounds. Well below their average, but no one commented on it. Not even Boss Hauten. A man had died, and it wouldn't serve to make it sound like interring him had been the cause of their backlog.

They had a full hold of brass, though.

Hauten decided to head for Karapalida, with the intention of reloading on the way and arriving with no less than 30,000 rounds. Which, at eight bits for a rack, stood to net each of the outfit about a hundred whole-pieces—with Hauten taking his usual twenty percent.

Setbacks and all, it was not a bad haul.

The outfit set out for Karapalida, where another one of them was to die.

CHAPTER 5

✪

KARAPALIDA

K<small>ARAPALIDA WAS</small> T<small>HE</small> L<small>IGHT</small>.

It had been that way for as long as Perry could recall the place.

There were certain towns that swung to one side or the other. "Battleground towns" they were called. There was no "front line" in the war that had raged for the last five centuries, but these unlucky battleground towns simply found themselves consistently being taken over by one force or another.

When they were taken, a new pontiff was appointed by the conquering paladin, and the pontiff would create a press gang, and then they'd rally up a bunch of young men and march them off to war in a peon unit. Off to die for The Truth, or The Light, whichever had won the town.

Then all the townspeople would declare their allegiance to the conqueror, and they'd hang the appropriate banners about town. At least until another battle happened, and another paladin came in, and swung them to the other side once again.

Karapalida did not swing.

It was The Light, and likely it would always be that way.

Blue banners with white suns in the center.

Blue and white pennants.

Boss Hauten drove the buggy into the Old Section of Karapalida. The New Section was bright and buzzing and the people were in celebrations.

Something about a massive victory won for their side. Thematic music boomed from loudspeakers, echoing through the streets. A stately voice rumbled and the people cheered.

From between a line of buildings as Hauten drove them into the Old Section, Perry looked out from his seat in the buggy and spied the glowing light of one of the jumbotrons that graced the center of town. On it, there was a glimpse of a battlefield. A valley.

"That where we just came from?" Teran asked from beside him.

Perry nodded. "Looks like it."

"Wasn't aware there'd been a winner."

The jumbotron passed out of view.

Perry looked ahead again. "Me neither."

From somewhere behind Perry, Monty whined: "Why we gotta go to the Old Section? Can't you take us to the New Section for once?"

Boss Hauten didn't even look around. "You're welcome to go."

Monty took in their clapboard and mudbrick surroundings. Dirt streets. Heavy-gauge power wires running to and fro, spliced into whatever reactor hub they were stealing electricity from. Various cobbled-together technology sprouting from people's windows and rooftops.

He sat back in his seat. "Nah. Drinks are cheaper here."

Hauten nodded. "M-hm."

The city was more crowded than usual. The year was coming to a close, the Deadmoon now at three-quarters turned, so everyone was flocking in from the smaller outlying cities and freeholds to take part in the Festival of Primus.

Teran gawped at the amount of people flowing around them. The vendors and the merchants crowding the sides of the streets. The river of workers, agitated with the desire to get some wild release from their monotonous lives.

"There's so many," Teran said.

Perry frowned at her. "Junction City isn't that much smaller than Karapalida."

Teran gave him a sidelong glance. Seemed to recover herself. "Yes. Right. I guess it's just been a while since the paladins declared the last godsmoon."

Perry watched her suspiciously for another moment. It sure as hell seemed like she was trying to cover something up. Was she even from Junction City? Or had she lied about that, too?

And why lie about a thing like that?

Perry looked away from her, back out to the passing throngs. "Last godsmoon was three years ago," he mused. He remembered that distinctly—it'd been the same year he'd deserted from Hell's Hollow. "Every one of these poor fucks is so excited, they're going to blow through the year's wages by the time the month is out." He shook his head, but smiled ruefully. "I swear, the paladins give us a month-long festival every few years, just to keep us poor."

Teran snorted. "They don't *have* to spend all their money. Besides, half of them think this'll be the last Festival of Primus ever." She waggled her fingers and made her voice spooky: "Omens and signs and portents!"

A month-long festival would have been enough to supercharge the atmosphere in Karapalida.

But when the Deadmoon had turned full, not one week ago, it rose as red as blood.

The paladins chose not to speak of it. But the people whispered.

A blood moon was always cause for speculation, but no one could recall blood ever appearing on the face of the Giver of Death. It was inherently ominous.

And then for that to happen on a year when a godsmoon—a thirteenth month—had been declared?

Well, that was just too much for everyone.

Theories abounded as to whether this was an ill omen, or a good one. But everyone seemed to agree: It was an omen of *something*.

"You know," Perry said. "Hauten hired you the night after the blood moon. Maybe *you're* the ill omen. Maybe *you're* the harbinger of doom around here."

Teran gave him a secretive smile. "Maybe I am."

Jokes aside, Teran was right: The people were steeped in a fever pitch of festival atmosphere and superstitious religiosity, and the air in Karapalida felt distinctly dangerous.

But, dangerous or not, it didn't dissuade Perry from wanting to be a part of it.

It was the kind of danger that came from drunk and rowdy people. And Perry intended to be one of them.

It was the kind of danger that made you smile and order another drink—just to see what might happen.

Hauten parked the buggy at the loading docks of the Common Market. Stuber stayed with him, as he always did. The rest of them piled out and began surveying the scene.

Chester and Bigs looked particularly antsy to get a drink in them.

"Jax," Hauten called to the lean, old piece of gristle. He pulled a handful of whole-pieces from one of his pockets and slipped these into Jax's hand. "Get us some suitable lodging. First place along this road that'll house all of us. And for godssakes, take baths."

***

"Suitable lodging" at a cost which Hauten was willing to pay meant a crewhouse.

A crewhouse was not a hotel.

More like a barracks for rent.

This particular crewhouse—Little Billy's—had room for four crews. Which meant that it had four long halls, the walls of which were lined with double bunks. One on top, one on bottom. Twenty beds per room.

Plenty of space for the Hauten outfit.

Teran carried a small haversack with everything that she owned in the world. This was customary. Perry had a similar sack, as did every other member of the outfit.

She plopped her haversack on the bunk above Perry's and gave him a nod.

He nodded back.

Over the course of the past week, she'd stuck close to Perry. When they rolled out their beds at night, hers was next to his. She seemed to understand the precarious footing of a woman who has joined an outfit. She seemed also to understand that Perry felt some responsibility for her. She used it to her advantage, and Perry didn't blame her.

As it turned out, bathing became more of an issue than the sleeping arrangements.

The nine of them, dirty and smelling, tromped up to the front to request a bathhouse.

The front was manned by a chubby, balding clerk with a mean glint in his eyes.

Jax had the boss's cash, so he did the talking.

"Bathhouse, please. Got nine filthy souls in need of cleansing."

"The temple's down thataway," the clerk said with a snicker.

No one laughed.

The clerk scanned their number. "You'll fit in one. That's two and four bits."

"Just enough for that and a two bit tip. Keep the change."

"How generous."

"I'm a generous guy."

"Oh, hey…"

"What?"

The clerk gave Teran a greasy look. Licked his top lip.

"You gots a lady in your outfit, sir."

Jax threw a look over his shoulder. He stared at Teran, and his face flashed with irritation. He looked back to the clerk with a frown. "She'll be fine," Jax grumbled.

The clerk leaned on his elbows. "Now, I couldn't allow any indecency in my establishment. 'Specially nearing on the festival season."

Jax sucked his teeth, pursed his lips like he was about to spit, but held back. "Awright. How much for two bathhouses, then?"

"Well, it's two and four bits more."

"No package discount?"

"I still gotta turn the pumps on," the clerk said. "Cost me just as much whether one person's bathing, or twenty."

"Shit. I ain't got that much." Jax turned to Teran again. "What about you? You got two and four bits so we can get you a separate bathhouse?"

Teran's jaw tightened. "I don't. Haven't been paid yet."

"Yeah. 'Course not."

Perry, growing irritated, stepped forward and started to rummage in his pocket for the few spare bits that he kept there. "I got four bits on me." He looked about at the others. "What about y'all?"

There was some mumbling and shuffling of feet, and excruciatingly slow movement towards some pockets.

Perry felt a fire rise up in him, because he knew damn well that between the eight men present, there was plenty more than two and four bits.

"She can pay you back after Hauten pays her," Perry said, trying not to sound too angry because he didn't want to seem self-righteous to the others.

Teran stepped forward and pulled Perry's arm back from placing the four bits on the counter. "It's fine," she declared.

Perry shook her hand from his arm. "You been a week on the plains like the rest of us. You need a bath."

"I'll have a bath," she said, her tone light and airy, but Perry saw that it was strained. She was putting on a brave face. He'd seen her do it before.

Teran directed herself to the clerk, raising her chin. "I'll bathe with these gentlemen. I'm a part of the outfit after all. We piss and shit and sleep together. Why not bathe?"

"Teran," Perry mumbled.

Because there was a difference, and he knew it.

She knew it too.

"'Sides," she said with finality, and glanced sidelong at Perry, as though to settle him. "Any of them try to touch me I'll kick their balls up into their throats."

There was some murmured laughter at that.

Tiller in particular was amused. He guffawed louder than everyone else. But his laugh was not the same as the others'.

Most of them laughed in a manner as though to say, *tough broad.*

Tiller laughed in a manner that said, *just try it, sweetheart.*

Jax turned to the clerk. "There. That's settled. Can we get a godsdamned bath now?"

The clerk shrugged. "If the lady insists. I'll turn on the pump. You're in bathhouse two, on the right. You got twenty minutes."

Jax marched for the bathhouse.

Seeing Teran unclothed was probably the furthest thing from Jax's mind. The man cared more for whiskey than women. Come to think of it, the only time that Perry recalled ever seeing the old codger get sweet with a woman was the barmaids that brought him whiskey.

But Perry looked around him at the other men in the outfit, as they shuffled off to the bathhouse, and he saw the distracted look in their eyes. Like they were already picturing it.

"This is stupid," he mumbled to her. "These aren't gentlemen. Neither am I."

"You got my back," she said, sure of herself.

Despite himself, he pictured her, naked and clean, backed up against him.

He swore under his breath.

Outfit pretty only counted when the clothes were on. When the clothes were off…well, that was a different story. If you gotta climb a tree to get an apple, you pick the nicest looking one you can reach. If the apple's dropped into your lap, you ignore the spots and eat it.

They went to bathhouse number two. Under the floorboards, they heard the pumps rattling on and the water groaning in the pipes.

The bathhouse was tiled. Perry hadn't been expecting much, but it was nice and clean. The faucet heads rumbled, and then spewed out water that looked rusty at first, but then cleared and began to steam. The faucets were positioned over four big barrels. They filled up quick, a head of suds growing on top.

The men stripped down with abandon. The sort of excitement for bathing that only came when you were truly filthy. It smelled significantly worse in the room as the clothes came off and they piled them up in their individual stacks, to be given to the launderers later.

To the credit of the men present, there was a concerted effort to ignore Teran. This was led by Monty and Bigs and Chester, who started speaking loudly of all the wreckage they would cause tonight.

All the drinks they would drink. All the women they would score. All the men they would beat down.

It got them thinking about something besides the woman in the room who was undressing.

Whether they did this as a sign of respect for Teran, or because they didn't want to be caught with an erection, Perry wasn't sure.

By unspoken agreement, the men divided themselves up amongst three of the barrels, and left the fourth to Teran.

Jax and Tiller scrubbed at one.

Perry joined Monty and Bigs at another.

Chester, Ernie, and Pebbles were at the third, hollering back and forth to Monty and Bigs.

Perry remained quiet.

He started sloshing hot, soaped water over his body. He watched dirt flow off of his skin. The water that ran off of his feet was brown.

Don't think about it.

He had his back to the corner of the room. It allowed him to see everyone else. Mostly, he was concerned about Tiller. But even while he tried to focus on cleaning himself, he could see a small, flesh-colored shape at the top of his peripheral vision.

Don't look.

But then he looked.

Teran stood at the side of the barrel in a posture of self-conscious modesty that almost made Perry laugh. One arm positioned across her breasts to cover her nipples. The other hanging down to cover her crotch. Almost funny. But it made him a little sad, too. She had not wanted to be in an outfit full of rough men. She'd probably wanted better for herself. But she would plunge forward, brave as ever.

She had a good body.

He didn't want to notice this, but he did. A man can't *not* notice.

At a glance: Firm; lean. But curved in that pleasant way that short women are curved.

Sandy hair, wetted to a light brown, just past her shoulders.

She looked like she was trying to decide whether to stand behind the waist-high bucket, which would mean that her exposed breasts would be facing eight men, or to stand with her back to them, concealing her front, but exposing her backside.

All at a glance.

He looked away.

Looked to his left, to where Jax and Tiller bathed.

Tiller was staring at her. Not trying to hide it.

Out of the corner of his eye, Perry perceived that Teran had decided to put her back to them and wash herself. So maybe she didn't notice it. Maybe it wouldn't make her uncomfortable. But based on how hard Tiller was looking at her, Perry figured she could feel his eyes on her.

Jax, on the other hand, was focused on picking at something between his thigh and his low-hanging nutsack.

Looking at Tiller, any warmth that the sight of a woman had brought to Perry went out of him. The other man stood there, displaying a half-erection, like he wanted Teran to notice it. He had the look on his face like he was thinking about doing something.

"Hey Tiller," Perry called.

The man turned to look at Perry like he was an interruption.

Teran glanced over her shoulder. Went back to washing herself.

"Why don't you wash up?" Perry said.

Tiller glared. "Don't tell me what to do, Shortstack."

"Just a friendly suggestion. Seemed like you forgot what you were doing."

"Oh, I know what I'm gonna do."

Perry rinsed himself. Thinking about soap on his feet. Thinking about traction on these tiles.

There is something about smaller men—they can't rely on brute strength. If they want to win, they have to be clever. They have to be faster and smarter.

"Yeah, I know what you're gonna do, too," Perry said. "You're gonna wash your shitty ass. Now, maybe I *am* telling you what to do."

"Ain't how it works, Shortstack. I'm senior—"

"Don't really give a shit if you're Hauten himself," Perry said. He worked his foot on the tile. It didn't slip. He felt the river of calm accepting him. The tension ebbing out of him. Sinking into the red flow. "You focus on washing yourself before someone in this bathhouse gets hurt. Lotta soap on these tiles. Easy to slip and bust your head."

Tiller started to walk around the barrel towards Perry. "Small man. Big mouth."

"Big man," Teran suddenly announced, turning to face Tiller. "Little dick."

The bathhouse became dead silent.

Teran stood exposed. Not bothering now to cover herself. She looked at Tiller's eyes, and then down to his dick, and then back up, and her expression was one of pity.

"Seems like you're the one who should be called Shortstack," she said.

Tiller smiled, and started walking towards her. "This is gonna be good."

Perry moved in a flash.

Tiller must have heard him coming. He turned, but not before Perry yoked his left arm up and around the man's neck, which required him to jump to get that much altitude, but when he came down, Tiller wasn't ready to carry Perry's entire weight on his neck, and he bent in half.

Rushing. Flowing.

The Calm.

Perry had already planted his right leg behind Tiller and he twisted his body, throwing the bigger man over his hip and landing him with a bone-aching crunch on his back on the tile. Tiller grunted hard, but still fought.

Beyond the current of rushing calm, Perry heard everyone shouting at them, felt the hands grabbing Perry's upraised arm, keeping him from pummeling Tiller's face, and likewise restraining Tiller.

Perry managed to snake his left arm free, which he used to grab a hold of Tiller's throat in a death grip, and he pulled himself close, just long enough to hiss in Tiller's face: "Touch her and I'll fucking kill you!"

Then the two of them were ripped apart and hoisted to their feet.

Teran's breath was hot against the side of Perry's face. He hadn't realized she'd been one of the ones grabbing him up. "I could've handled it!"

"Sure," Perry spat. "But I wanted to."

Jax was between the two men now. Like an ancient referee between two boxers. Chester and Bigs held Tiller back by his arms. Monty and Teran held onto Perry. Ernie and Pebbles stood staring.

"Letting a woman hold you back?" Tiller called over the top of Jax's head.

In truth, neither Perry nor Tiller were straining to be free. With Jax in between them, the fire had gone out of the moment.

"Gods in the skies, you buncha ijits!" Jax bayed. "Get one girl in the mix and everyone loses their godsdamned heads!" he pointed a gnarled finger at Tiller. "You keep your cock to yourself. You know you gotta pay for pussy." He turned the finger to Perry. "And you keep your hands to yourself, Shortstack. Quit tryin' to prove how tough you are."

Jax eyed them each in turn. Old, sunken, blue eyes meeting their gazes. Evaluating whether they were fit to be released. Then he waved a hand and the arms that held Tiller and Perry let go.

"Now warsh yerselves so we can go drinking."

CHAPTER 6

✿

TRUE COLORS

THEY ALL WENT TO THE CLEMENTINE to drink.

It was an ancient establishment that had once been built of wood, but could no longer afford to maintain itself with that material, and after so many years of rowdy business, was equal parts wood, metal, and mudbrick.

It smelled of booze and piss and sweat.

But the millet whiskey was cheap, plentiful, and relatively palatable, and so far as anyone had heard, no one had died from drinking it. So The Clementine's customers were loyal.

Tiller took a single shot of whiskey, and then looked around like he'd suddenly realized what filth he was amongst. He sneered, met no one's gaze, plopped down a single bit on the counter, then turned on his heel and left.

The black cloud of tension went with him.

The eight remaining crewmembers were scattered amongst a few tables and the bar. Each segregated into their own particular group that they preferred the company of. Pebbles and Ernie at a small table against the wall, hovering over tepid beers and casting anxious glances about them, as greenhorns were prone to do.

Chester and Bigs and Monty were at another table, drinking whiskey and water. They raised their cups to Slider, and poured one out for the dead man. They left the glass sitting at the corner of the table where the ghost of Slider could stare at it with impotent longing. Comfort for the living and torture for the dead.

From the bar, Perry tipped his own glass of whiskey towards them in salute to the fallen. Bigs saw him do it and nodded back. Perry drained his glass, which was not his habit, but mourning the fallen was a special circumstance. He put it down on the bar and asked for another.

"Open a tab?" the barkeep asked. An old man. Bushy white eyebrows. Bushy white mustache. He seemed suspicious. Like he wasn't sure whether to trust this rough-looking outfit to be able to pay.

"That'd be fine," Perry said.

In truth, the four bits he kept in his pocket had already been spent. He had nothing on him until Stuber and Hauten returned with their cut of the sales.

"You good for it?" the barkeep asked. Perry couldn't see his mouth, but his mustache moved like a shaggy white rug with a rat caught underneath it.

Perry smiled what he hoped was a reassuring smile. "We're all good for it, sir."

Sitting to Perry's left, Jax gave the barkeep a knowing nod and a wink. A signal between the two silver foxes. Don't worry, Old Boy, I got control of these pups.

The barkeep appeared mollified. He opened the tab. Gave them a bottle of whiskey to pour themselves.

"Should you go after him?" Perry asked, measuring a finger into his cup.

"What?" Jax griped. "Tiller? Fuck 'im."

"Gonna get himself shot in his current mood."

"That's his problem. Not mine."

Perry shrugged. Set the bottle in a neutral location on the bar where any of them could grab it when they needed it. Teran sipped slow, but at least she drank whiskey. And she didn't shudder or cringe at it either. A mark in her favor.

"What were you planning to do?" Perry asked her.

"What do you mean?" Teran swirled the whiskey, stared through it.

"Calling him out in the bathhouse."

"Ah." She didn't answer for a moment. Took a small sip. Swirled the glass again. "Gonna kick his nuts into his throat, I figured."

"Solid plan."

"I'da been fine."

"You ever fought a grown man before?"

She quirked an eyebrow at him. "Have you?"

Perry was taken aback by the question.

Teran saw him stumbling for a proper answer and gave him a glare. "Seems like a lot of guys like to talk about how tough they are. But maybe the actual real world experience falls a little short of what they claim."

Perry had an urge to be defensive. That was the chip on his shoulder talking. All small men have one. But he took a moment to sip his whiskey. Let it burn him down a bit.

He had nothing to prove. The night was still very young. Best not to get riled so early.

"Yeah," he finally said. "Suppose that's common enough."

Teran released him from her glare with a measure of smug vindication. "You gotta be more specific."

"How's that?"

"Well, men lie about generalities. But they're truthful about specifics. So you ask a man if he's ever fought another man, to him he hears 'have I ever had conflict with another male.' Then he's likely to claim he's had any number of hellacious battles, because in his mind he's counting the male dogs he's shot off his property, or any time he's had raised voices with someone and maybe even got to the point where they bumped chests. Men are slippery when they're talking about how tough they are."

"Hm."

"But," she said after a sip. "They also have a great deal of shame. So when you pin 'em down to specifics, then they won't lie. Well, most of them won't. Because everyone knows it's more shameful to pose than to be inexperienced."

"Alright. I'm with you."

"So." She skewered him with a look again. "Have you ever gone toe-to-toe with another man, in a square fight, where he was just as capable of harming you as you were him? And if you did, how'd it turn out for you, Shortstack?"

Perry squinted up at a bar lantern over the rim of his glass, taking a long, slow sip. When he set his glass down, he cradled it in both hands, thinking.

Teran began to smile as though she'd proven her point.

"Don't be hasty," Perry said. "I'm thinking. I wouldn't want to tell you a lie and bring shame upon myself."

"Has it ever happened?" Teran pressed. "Even once?"

Perry met her gaze. She had brown eyes that looked almost black in the dim saloon lighting. He didn't care for the way they looked at him.

"Yes," he said.

Teran raised her chin. "More than five?"

"Yes."

"Ten?"

"Maybe."

"Maybe?"

"Some drunken recollections, Teran. I can't pin an exact number."

"Okay. And how did they turn out for you? The ones you can remember?"

"Well, most recently, I was about to get my teeth broken in by a big fella when Slider smashed him in the head with a bottle and got me out of it. I'm pretty sure I would've lost that one. 'Nother time it was a few guys didn't like something I said and they whooped me in a back alley. I went down swinging, though. Think I may have even connected a few times. I was laid up for a bit after that. Then there were a few times where I came out on top. And once where I left a man in an alley like they left me, and to this day I don't know whether he was alive when I left him or not."

Perry realized he hadn't even counted all the fights at Hell's Hollow. Perhaps because they hadn't been true fights. Sure, he'd given it back as good as he could, but when you're surrounded by six guys and outsized by every last one of them, is that really a fight?

No. It's a beating.

He had to give Hell's Hollow it's due, though. Mostly, it was five years of being indoctrinated (which never took for Perry) and learning how to march in formation, how to create phalanxes with shields, and a lot of other theoretical, strategic bullshit. Firearms-specific training largely took place at the legion-level, after you were already commissioned. The only combatives they taught were endless hand-to-hand training, and drilling with wooden swords and shields.

But between the hand-to-hand training, and the almost daily beatings, Hell's Hollow *had* taught Perry how to handle himself, and he figured he could safely say he was above average in a fight.

But Teran didn't need to know about the Academy. She didn't need to know that Perry was a deserter. That was something best kept locked away.

Teran stared into her whiskey.

Perry swallowed, and pushed the unpleasant memories away. "So, I've won just enough to make me keep fighting," Perry said, turning in his seat to face her. "Now, answer my original question. You ever fight a grown man? I suppose I don't need to be more specific since exaggeration is solely the territory of the male and a woman will always answer the spirit of the question."

Teran gave him a single sidelong glance. Brought her glass to her mouth. Her voice was hollow and muted in that glass. "No." Then she drank. Set her glass down. "Talked 'em off. Shot at 'em. Gunned down a couple Lokos. But no. Never gone toe-to-toe with a grown man."

"Do you want to?"

She frowned at him.

"Because Tiller isn't gonna just stand for you calling him out like that," Perry said. "He'll want a go at you another time. Maybe not tonight. But eventually. And when that happens, you tell me right now how far you want me to let you take it. Do I jump in immediately? Do I wait until you're almost unconscious? How many teeth would you like to keep in your face? I'll try to keep a count while he's smashing them down your throat, but it'll be hard with all the blood."

"Shut the fuck up."

"Answer the godsdamned question, Teran."

She glared. "I don't write checks I can't cash."

Perry snuffed at her. Shook his head. "Alright then."

A raucous shout went up behind them. Pleasant. Joyous. Irritating.

Perry looked behind him and found that Ernie and Pebbles had joined a game of skulls with some strangers. Ernie had just managed to sink a knife in the dead center of the wooden skull's left eye socket. He removed his knife with a flourish while Pebbles backslapped him and their two opponents sneered.

Perry didn't like the look of those two strangers. Sullen and watery-eyed.

A scheming set of drunks.

He turned back to the bar.

Jax slammed back whiskey and began to hum along with the two-man band as they skittered through an up-tempo jig.

Perry and Teran drank in silence.

They were about halfway through that bottle of whiskey—which meant they were well in debt to the barkeep already—when Stuber lumbered through the saloon doors. He was not carrying his Roq-11, but Perry knew the man likely had several other weapons hidden about his body. A few pistols. A few knives. Probably something that Perry didn't even know could kill a man.

Stuber held a battered lockbox. It had once been green. Now it was the color of rust. The green varnish had been chipped away, but it was still there in a few places, like patches of verdant leaves in a dying forest.

Usually one did not waltz around town carrying a lockbox that so obviously contained valuables. However, one also did not make a habit of robbing an ex-legionnaire, still suited in his armor.

The only times Perry had ever seen the man out of his armor had been when he slept with a whore in town. Out on the plains, he slept in his armor. And when he was in town, he only ever slept with whores.

He slapped this lockbox down on the table that Monty, Bigs, and Chester occupied. They made room for him. Stuber looked around, searching for Ernie and Pebbles. He found them and ordered them over. They excused themselves from the knife game.

Their opponents watched them leave, then began to eye the big legionnaire.

"Shortstack!" Stuber grouched at him. "You comin'?"

Perry shook himself out of watching those drunken strangers with their mean, beady eyes, and he touched Teran on the elbow, beckoning her to come with him.

Jax slid out of his stool, already a tad loopy. He was hitting the drinks pretty hard.

The crew gathered around the table, created a sort of privacy booth with their bodies standing shoulder to shoulder, and Stuber in the center, a head taller than the rest of them. He jangled the rusty lock mechanism open, muttering curses at it because it was far too small for his hands.

When he got it open, they saw that it contained one less satchel than it should have. He supposed that Tiller had already met up with Stuber and been paid. That was good. With full pockets, he'd hopefully stay out of their hair until tomorrow.

Stuber plucked the satchels out and slid them, each to a person, like a dealer slinging out cards. "Number's ninety-eight a piece."

It was neither exciting nor disappointing.

Everyone in the outfit had already done the math in their head and knew it was going to be around a hundred per hand.

"Hauten wants to move out tomorrow," Stuber said, taking the last satchel from the box and tossing it closed with a hollow *clang*. "So we only got one night to blow through this shit." He turned to the bar. "I'm fuckin' gettin' started."

He slapped a whole piece down on the bar top. "Whiskey!"

The barkeep gave him a whole bottle, then offered to replace the half-empty one that sat between Perry and Jax, magnanimous now that he knew they had money. Perry declined. Jax demanded more. A new bottle came.

Ernie and Pebbles didn't return to their knife game.

They drank rapidly and then thundered towards the exit, talking of whores, of which there weren't many at The Clementine, and those that were there were already indisposed.

Perry watched them leave, starting to feel it now himself, and relishing it.

At the door, the two sullen strangers that Ernie and Pebbles had beat at skulls threw a few words their way.

Already drunk, Ernie shouted something unintelligible at them, concluding with "Go fuck yourself!"

There lasted a tense moment of three or four seconds.

Then Pebbles strong-armed Ernie through the bar doors and out into the street.

The two weasel-eyed strangers watched them go, mad and unsatisfied. Violence unrequited. But they were looking for it. Of that, Perry was certain.

"Think we should go before those two do anything?"

Perry looked at Teran. "What's that?"

She nodded toward the strangers. "Those two. Look like trouble."

"Yeah."

"Should we go?"

"Nah." Perry sipped. "Trouble isn't a person, it's a cloud that hovers over you. If its trouble you have in store, it'll find you no matter where you are."

"You're poetic in your cups."

"In vino veritas."

"Huh?"

"In wine there is truth."

"And what about whiskey?"

"Angry exaggeration."

"Ha."

Jax had begun to sing louder by then. He got appreciative looks from the band. Not for his singing so much as his enthusiasm. Encouraged by their smiles, he raised his glass to them every time they looked in his direction, and then finally trundled off to sit closer to them.

He took the bottle of whiskey with him. It still had about a third left.

Perry didn't say anything. Let the old man go.

Stuber, who still had a decent amount left, slid over into Jax's seat and pivoted himself to face

Perry and Teran. He filled their cups without being asked, then filled his own.

Stuber was a generous man. He liked to spend his money on things and then give them to others. He liked to pour other people drinks from his own bottle. He liked to pay women up front and then send them to whichever crew member was looking down.

Perry thought that it was because Stuber liked to show off. But then sometimes it seemed that Stuber genuinely enjoyed it. Which was strange coming from the man, because he seemed so hell-bent on being violent.

The two concepts never could jive in Perry's mind.

How a man could appear to care for others, but also want to kill them all the time.

For a long time, Perry had tried to refuse Stuber's generosity. But Stuber was not the type of person to take 'no' for an answer. He could get pushy. Demanding even. He had an overbearing personality. So Perry had learned to accept it.

Stuber, half on and half off his stool, loomed over Perry and Teran, one elbow on the bar, the other arm seizing Perry by the shoulders. "Tell me something, Shortstack."

Perry eyed him over the lip of his cup as he sipped.

"Shortstack. Do you dislike it when I call you Shortstack?"

Perry hated being called Shortstack.

"I don't care," he said. "It's a name."

"Perry is just so…" Stuber looked at the rafters and swirled his cup as he searched for the right word.

"Effeminate?" Teran offered.

Perry shot her a look.

Stuber snapped his fingers. "Yeah. Effeminate. I hate to use it because it sounds so *effeminate*."

"Shortstack is much more masculine sounding," Perry responded dryly.

The closeness of everyone's attention caused him to drink faster.

It started to burn in his belly.

Stuber started poking Perry in the chest with a finger. Perry thought about shoving him off, but decided to let the big galut go on. "Always appear to be less than what you are."

He said it like a proverb, well-loved and many-times rehearsed.

"Hmm," Perry said, grabbing more whiskey from Stuber's bottle.

Stuber scooted very close to Perry. Lounging on him like a piece of furniture. That was another thing. Stuber liked to touch. He liked to paw at people. He was very handsy.

"Teran," Stuber said. "Teran, Teran."

"Yes?"

"You know why I like this guy?"

"Why?" There was a smile in her voice.

Stuber yoked his big, callused hands on the back of Perry's neck and shook him like you might rough a favored dog. Perry was trying to take a sip at that moment and it sloshed and spilled a bit. He grit his teeth together, waiting for the love-throttle to be over.

Stuber leaned on Perry now. Perry smelled his whiskey breath. Felt it on the side of his face, warm and humid.

"'Cause he's a fucking warrior, that's why." Stuber shook him again. His vice-hands forced Perry to turn his head to look Stuber in the face. "He don't look like much at all, but there's a godsdamned fire burning in him, and I see it every day. Look at it. Look at it!"

Stuber grinned.

Perry all but glared back. He disliked the manhandling. Disliked how it made him feel small.

"Oh, look at that," Stuber marveled. "Such hate and contempt. I love it. Teran, Teran, I wish you could see what I'm seeing right now."

"Why don't you let go of his neck?" Teran offered.

Stuber shook his head, but released the grip.

There was a solemnness to his smile now. A sadness in his bright eyes. It came on him suddenly, as though someone had mentioned the name of a dead friend. He leaned away from Perry.

"All I'm saying is that you have the fight in you. I see it."

Perry didn't have much to say. His mouth opened, hoping that something would come to him. He felt flattered and annoyed. How you feel after a particularly well-delivered backhanded compliment.

"Thanks, I guess," is what he said.

Movement drew his eyes over Stuber's shoulders.

"Head's up," he murmured.

Stuber slid back into his seat and tracked Perry's eyes by spinning halfway around and facing the two sullen-eyed strangers. They stared balefully at Stuber. Both tall and skinny. One blond. The other with a wrinkly old felt hat.

"Legionnaire," the blond one said.

Stuber did not reply, outside of a quirked eyebrow.

"I saw your spaulder," Blondie accused. "I saw your *sagum*. You trying to flaunt it in our faces? You think you're immortal?"

Stuber stared at the man with no real expression on his face now. He brought his glass around. Put it to his lips. Took a long, slow sip, holding that eye-contact with Blondie, then smacked his lips and set his glass down.

"I'm not immortal," Stuber said. "And I don't flaunt."

The bar had grown quiet.

Blondie, perceiving an audience to be won, turned himself to address them. "He's a Red. He's a Truther. Look at his *sagum*! A fucking Truther! Here in my godsdamned town!" Blondie had turned back around to face Stuber. His drunken eyes flared. "You Truthers. It's your fault we live like this. It's your fault we can't use the god-tech. Your fault we scrabble in the dirt for enough to feed our children. Keep us primitive, you say. Keep us subservient, you say. Isn't that what you believe, legionnaire? Don't lie about it. We all know that Truthers lie!"

Stuber was at the edge of his barstool now. Almost standing. He looked nothing like the man of only moments before. He seemed to have sobered. He looked calm and self-possessed.

"What you see," Stuber replied. "Is not a *sagum*, sir. It's only the remnants of one. I fight for no man but myself now. I'm no legionnaire."

"You lie!" Blondie shrieked.

"Let me buy you both a drink and we can speak of friends lost."

"Red *sagum*!" Blondie insisted.

74

"Only tatters."

"You're a traitor to the human race!"

Stuber placed his hand near the whiskey bottle. "You speak unwisely, friend. Come have a drink."

"You think I'm afraid of a has-been traitor like yourself?"

"Yes," Stuber said. "I think that you are."

"Take a weapon then!"

Stuber smiled now. "But I am one."

Blondie fumbled under his coat.

Perry saw the butt of a pistol tucked into Blondie's waistband.

He never did get it out.

Stuber smashed him in the side of the head with the bottle of whiskey. It shattered and slung glass shards and blood and liquor in a cloud.

As Blondie pitched towards the floor with a vacant expression, his friend in the felt hat drew a knife from the sleeve of his shirt, and he pulled it back in order to plunge it under Stuber's armor.

As he pulled the knife, he sidestepped to the right, out of Stuber's visual range, and then he lunged forward.

"Stuber!" Perry shouted, and all he could do was kick out with a single foot, which caught the man in his knife-wielding elbow, and stopped the advance of the knife.

Stuber spun. Jabbed out with the hand still holding the shattered neck of the whiskey bottle. It gouged the man's eye out, and Stuber left it protruding from the bloody eye socket.

The man screamed and lurched backward, but Stuber had already seized hold of his knife-wrist, and he held him there with one hand while the other drew a pistol from under his armor and he placed it, almost thoughtfully, to the bottom of the man's chin and fired upward.

The felt hat flew off.

A little volcano of blood spurted up from the crown of the man's head.

His screaming stopped.

The body hit the floor, sounding like a sack of stones.

Stuber stood there with a smoking gun in his hand.

There was the very distinct *rack-rack* sound of a shotgun chambering a round.

Stuber turned, holding the pistol down at his side.

Perry stood up from his seat on tingling feet.

Shit. It had all happened so fast he was left wondering if it *had* really happened or if it wasn't a moment's absent-minded daydream.

But it had happened. He could smell the gunsmoke. He could hear the dribbling of the man's perforated skull, still emptying its contents onto the wooden floors.

The barkeep stood on the other side, a shotgun held level at Stuber's face.

The barkeep didn't look angry. He bore the expression of a janitor having to mop up a nasty mess.

"Now, I saw them boys pull on you first," the barkeep said. "Everybody saw that?" he said, raising his voice.

There was a demur chorus of affirmative grunts from those that watched.

"Alright then," the barkeep nodded. "No need to call the guard then. You been coming here for years as I remember, and I know you ain't a legionnaire no more, but them boys had a point, now didn't they? You mightn't want to wear that *sagum*, tatters or not, anywhere 'round this town. Karapalida's Light as ever will be Light."

Stuber gave the shotgun a hollow smile, and slowly holstered the pistol in his hand.

"I'll find another place to drink," Stuber said, quietly. Then he finished what whiskey was left in his glass. "But I won't take the pieces of *sagum* from this armor. They remind me of lessons I've bled to learn."

"Suit yourself."

Stuber nodded. "I will."

Before he left, he turned and looked at Perry.

"Thank you, Shortstack," he said, and then walked out.

CHAPTER 7

✿

SIXTEEN BITS

PERRY AND TERAN didn't stay long after that.

Chester, Bigs, and Monty didn't stay at all. They'd watched the whole thing from their table with cool aplomb, as though they had infinite faith in Stuber's ability to defend himself and there was no need for them to intervene. Or maybe they were curious as to whether or not this would be the fight that finally got the best of Stuber.

They hadn't moved to help, and when the bodies were on the floor and Stuber left, they shrugged and mumbled to themselves. Then they finished their drinks and departed, no longer feeling welcome, since they were obviously associated with Stuber.

Perry stayed rooted to his barstool for a few minutes longer, staring at his glass. Then he finished his drink, just as two men came into the bar from the back entrance and began to collect the bodies. The barkeep watched them work and directed them to take the bodies out back.

Perry stood up from his seat. The room faltered, but righted itself.

"You stayin' or goin'?" he asked Teran.

The woman had finished her drink some time ago. She sat now with her hands clasped before her. When he asked her this, she separated them and pushed herself up off the bar.

"Suppose we're going."

Perry nodded. He stepped over a puddle of brains on his way to the door.

The other patrons watched them leave.

Outside, it had turned dark. No trace of dusk leftover in the sky.

"What time is it? Do you know?" he asked.

Teran shook her head. "Don't have a watch."

The two of them walked. An even, unrushed pace.

They reached the corner of the bar. Perry looked right, to where the intersecting street led over to the New Section, with all its bright lights and clean lines. The massive temple stood, its observatory higher than any other building, so that the timewheel could be seen from most places in the city.

The statues of the Nine Sons of Primus, all having turned and rotated away with the passing of the months. Along with them, the Giver of Strength, and the Giver of Wisdom had also turned their faces. That left only the Giver of Death, his grinning skull three-quarters turned.

His longstaff was raised high, but not quite vertical.

"Twenty-two hours and some change," Perry said, then crossed the road.

"Maybe time to turn in."

"Nah. You can go if you want."

The air was cool. It felt good on his face. He hadn't realized how sweltering the bar had been. Hadn't realized that the back of his shirt and the seat of his pants had become moist with sweat.

"Where are you going?" she asked.

"Find another place to drink."

"Gods. You people."

"That's the life, Teran." He turned to her. "Why don't you go? Get some sleep. When you wake up in the morning, don't come with us. Go and find a better job."

"You tryin' to get rid of me?"

He shrugged. Kept walking. "You do what you want, Teran."

"Think I'll stay on a little longer," she remarked at his back, and then trailed after him.

"The gods know why."

"I'm learning."

Perry didn't respond to that. Wanted something biting to say back, but came up blank, so he let it lie. It drifted behind them like leaves in the wake of a breeze and was soon forgotten.

They went to another bar, and they drank there. Teran switched to beer. Perry said nothing of it and kept on with the whiskey. They did their drinking at a small, dark, corner booth. It felt intimate to Perry. Made him feel awkward.

"Why you so adamant about this shit anyways?" he asked her.

"About what?"

"Staying on. Learning to reload."

"Maybe I wanna start my own outfit one day."

"That why?"

She shrugged. "Maybe."

He shook his head. "You're not telling me something."

"Maybe not."

"Well, I won't ask you about it."

She frowned at him.

He leaned forward. "Some people like to have secrets because they like people to wheedle them out. Makes them feel important. Well, I'm not going to do that. You keep your secrets. I'll keep mine. Everybody'll be happier that way."

She smiled in a righteous sort of way and raised her glass. "Well, that suits me just fine, Perry."

He clicked her glass with his, a little hard.

He drank. Set it down. Poured another.

He was getting drunk. He felt it coming up from his chest now. Tingling his face. The precipice where the good meets the bad. Best not to step over, and yet, he knew he would.

Teran looked away from him. Peeved. "What sort of an attention whore do you think I am, anyways?"

"Never said you were one."

"Yeah, you did."

"No, I didn't. I said that *some people* are like that. Never said that *you* were. In any case, I won't ask you. And if you're not an attention whore, you should be happy that I'm not gonna ask you about it." He sniffed, triumphant. Took a heavy drink that emptied his glass. Poured another. "Tell me this, though." He held up his glass with his index finger pointing at her, his eyes squinted down into a knowing leer.

"What's that?"

"You Truth or Light?"

She hesitated in her answer. Then said, "I'm not sure I believe in either of them."

"You're not sure?"

She didn't answer.

"If you're not sure, then you're a heretic."

"It's that black and white, then?"

"According to them, it is."

Her face soured some. "Never any room for middle ground. You're either a friend or an enemy. You're either a Truther that thinks the demigods' job is to keep humanity primitive so the gods won't destroy the world again, or you're a Light-sider that thinks we should use the god-tech to fight back against the gods—when and if they ever return." Teran shook her head, her nose wrinkling. "And since we can't agree on that, we're going to fight to the death. Forever."

Perry nodded. It was an accurate summary of the last five hundred years of human history.

"You ever think about them?" She cast a glance skyward.

"The gods?"

"The original ones. The ones from the Ortus Deorum."

Perry made a disinterested face. "I didn't read from the Ortus much when I was growing up. And whoever they were, I doubt they're coming back."

"The Ortus says they're watching, all the time."

"Yeah? I wouldn't know. But if they were watching, don't you think they'd swoop down and destroy the Light for planning to use the god-tech against them?"

Teran shrugged. "Maybe you're right. Maybe they're gone. Maybe they're never coming back."

"Yeah. Then we'll just be stuck under the thumb of the demigods they left behind. For the rest of eternity."

"Careful," she smirked. "You're sounding like a heretic yourself."

If you only knew, he thought.

"What I've never understood," Perry said, scraping a fingernail along the rim of his glass, watching it progress with a sort of resentful intensity. "Is how it's more heretical to refuse to fight, than it is to join the Light and rebel against the gods. And how, when a town changes sides, whoever takes over doesn't punish the populace for their rebellion. But if you desert from either side, then either side will kill you."

Teran squinted at him. "Now...no one mentioned anything about desertion."

Perry's eyes shot up to hers.

He was saved from having to respond by the doors to the bar slamming open.

A man entered, hanging on two hookers and hollering, "Barkeep! Get me some fucking *whiskey*. I'm about dry in the fuckin' mouth."

It was Tiller.

"Sonofabitch," Teran mumbled. "Guess we chose the wrong bar."

"No. He did," Perry said. "Just ignore him."

It was hard to do.

Impossible, as it would turn out.

Tiller got to the bar where they had whiskey waiting on him. He downed a glass of it. There were two other glasses. He insisted the whores drink. One did, readily enough. The other tried to decline. Tiller glared at her until she finally choked it down and coughed.

Tiller laughed. Slapped her on the back the way you would a man.

"There you go! Another round!"

"Let's just go," Teran mumbled.

"Thought you weren't into writing checks you can't cash," Perry ribbed.

"I'm also not into picking fights. Let's go."

But Perry wasn't interested in going.

He'd come to this bar. He'd arrived first. He was sitting quietly in a booth, minding his own business. He was not doing anything wrong. He was not being boorish. He was not going to be the one to leave.

Tiller made the two whores drink again.

This time the unwilling one gagged, but managed not to puke all over the bar.

Tiller slapped her on the back again.

She didn't appreciate it. Told him so.

Tiller stared at her with eyes that were unfocused and mean. He leaned in close to her and he took a hold of her elbow in a grip that Perry could tell, even from across the room, was harder than necessary. He said something into her ear, but Perry couldn't hear it.

The woman jerked away from him, breaking his grip on her arm. He was drunk, and his reactions were slow. He stared at her for a moment, like he couldn't believe it.

Then he pointed to the door. "Well, then get the fuck out, whore."

"You gonna pay me for my time?"

"Fuck you, cunt. Get out of my sight."

"You cheap shit!"

"Dirty bitch!" He swung a haphazard boot at her skinny rear as she made for the door. He missed and almost fell. "Dirty fuckin' whores. Godsdammit." He turned to the other whore. "What about you? You needa go somewhere?"

"Nah, baby," she purred. "I just wanna be with you."

Tiller sneered at her.

She snaked an arm up around his shoulder.

He pushed it off of him.

"Get the fuck out of my face," he snapped.

The whore managed to look hurt for a second.

"Go on with your bilge pussy. Get outta my *face*!"

She jerked back from him like he might hit her, then glared. "Some man!"

"Oh, shut up," Tiller slurred and waved a hand at her. "Go on. Get out. You ain't getting any of my money, you nasty, bilge-rotted pile of roast beef drapes. Gods in a stinkin' sky, I can smell your yeasty pussy from here. I ain't payin' you a damn bit. Get the fuck outta my sight!"

The whore stomped away. At the door she turned and addressed the barkeep. "You better kick this shithead out. He's nothin' but trouble, you know. Nothin' but trouble, you stupid limp-dicked cheap fuck!"

She disappeared through the door as the glass that had been hers shattered right where her face would have been.

"Fuck you, *CUNT*!" Tiller screamed at her. "Dick don't get hard for your moldy shit!"

"Hey!" the barkeep shouted. "You can't be breakin' my glasses! Now chill out or take a walk, mister!"

"Awright, awright, awright," Tiller said, holding up his hands and bowing his head in the utmost penitence—or at least as much as could be expected in his current state. "I'm sorry. Sorry 'bout the glass. Here. Take this." He pulled his little leather satchel of money out and fished around inside of it. "Sorry. Hold on. I didn't mean any harm. You know how those...you know...you know..."

He located what he wanted and pulled it out, swaying on his feet. He slapped it on the counter. Two whole-pieces.

"For the glass. And the disturbance to your customers. Okay?"

The barkeep took the two pieces, but kept a careful eye on Tiller.

"Now get me a godsdamn bottle of whiskey, wouldja?"

The barkeep pocketed the two pieces and gave Tiller a curt little nod. He turned to the bottles to get the man's order. As he did, Tiller turned to face the room, sweeping his arms in a grand gesture.

"I apologize for the disturbance. So sorry. You know how it is."

As he addressed the room, his eyes fell on Perry and Teran.

"So sorry, everyone," he continued to say, more absently now as he stared at Perry. "Please…accept…my humble 'pologies."

The barkeep set the whiskey down with an audible thud.

Tiller turned and grabbed the bottle. Then the glass that was still in front of him. He held them there with his head bowed, and Perry couldn't see his eyes, but imagined they were not staring at much of anything in that moment.

Tiller swayed on his feet.

Then he popped up.

He turned with a smile on his face.

"Would anyone like a round on me? Anyone at all? I have the bottle."

No one cared for any of his whiskey. It seemed like everyone wished he'd just be quiet or leave. They forced themselves back into conversations with others, deliberately ignoring Tiller now.

Tiller didn't seem to care. He wasn't even looking around to see if he had any takers for his apparent generosity. He just looked at Perry.

Teran made a noise across from Perry and shifted in her seat. "Told you we should have gone."

Perry didn't reply. He sat very still with his mostly-empty whiskey glass in his hand. Watching Tiller approach him.

Already feeling the first tinges of red.

Tiller stopped at the edge of their table.

He stared at Perry for a second. Then he turned and looked at Teran.

"Well," he said, slapping the bottle and glass down. "Fancy meeting you two here."

He poured himself a glass. Then he poured some into Perry's glass.

Perry made no move. Just sat. Watching.

In that mental space where he hovered, just above the rushing flow of The Calm.

"We were about to leave," Teran said and then started to stand up.

"Sit down," Perry said.

Teran looked at him.

He didn't look back.

He was locked in with Tiller.

"Sit down," he repeated.

Teran started to protest.

"We were here, having a drink," Perry said. "We were here first. You do not have to get up, Teran. You sit back down and finish your beer."

Tiller started smiling. He turned to Teran. "Yeah, Teran. Sit down."

Teran was in the process of sinking back to the seat. Now she stopped.

"Don't tell her what to do, Tiller," Perry said, in that same ice-cold, steady voice.

"Okay, fine. Teran, do what your *pimp* tells you to do."

Teran's eyes narrowed to fiery little slits. "I'll stand, thanks."

Tiller laughed. Drank some of his whiskey. He looked at Perry. "You gonna take that, Perry? You gonna take that shit from your whore?"

"Why don't you get gone, Tiller? Things are gonna shape up badly for you."

"Yeah? That right? Okay." Tiller leaned away from the table, started rooting through his pockets again. He smirked. "You know what Jax said in the showers. It's so true. You remember what he said, don't you?"

"No."

Tiller pulled his leather money sack from his pants pocket. "He said everyone knows I gotta pay for pussy. Ha! Ain't that the godsdamn truth? Funny man. So funny. And so true. But I guess that's why it's funny. So my question to you, Shortstack…"

"Shut up and walk away while you can, Tiller."

"…Is how much?" Tiller begun plucking bits out of his satchel. "How much for your whore? I wanna fuck her. But you know, it's me, so I gotta pay. That's just how things are. No woman'd touch me without getting paid first, ain't that right? Alright. That's fine. How much? How much do you want for her, Shortstack?"

"I'm leaving," Teran said, exasperated. "The two of you ingrates can figure this out."

With a quantity of bits in his palm, Tiller opened his fingers and counted them. "Five…ten…fifteen…sixteen. I got sixteen bits."

Teran tried to edge passed him.

Tiller stood there, impassible.

Teran looked like she was about to start swinging.

Perry was as still as stone.

Tiller reared back. "Sixteen bits for your fucking whore!"

Then he threw them at Perry's face.

They clattered across the table.

Tinkled like chimes against Perry's glass.

Perry launched himself out of the booth. He took Tiller in the midsection, and he put everything he had into that one thrust. He lifted the bigger man off his feet and he drove him as far and as fast as he could, blank in the mind, only red, nothing but rushing red.

They hit the ground.

Tiller's head cracked on the floorboards.

Perry still had his whiskey glass in his hand.

He posted one hand down on Tiller's throat, and with his right hand, he held the glass by the base, and started hammering it down on Tiller's face.

Tiller reached his hands up, blocked the first few blows, growling and spitting like a dog in a fight, trying to buck Perry off of him. But Perry wasn't going. He was latched on. He kept hammering, and the blows came down hard and fast and the glass cracked in his hand and the splinters of it went through his palm and they went through Tiller's and Tiller began screaming but Perry didn't utter a sound, he just kept hammering away.

The sounds around him were drowned out by the river of red in Perry's mind.

Tiller's voice, distantly: "Wait! No! Stop! Perry!"

Perry kept hammering.

Hammered the hand out of the way.

"Stop! Wait!"

Hammered into that face. Shards. Glass on bone.

Screaming. Muted, behind the red.

Perry let what was left of the glass fall out of his bloody hands and then he grabbed Tiller by the sides of his head and he began raising Tiller's head off the floorboards, the other man caterwauling now, bubbling blood out of his mouth and spewing it every time he tried to yell.

Perry rammed his head down onto the floor. Repeatedly.

The banging of the head on the floor became soft and wet.

Someone was yelling at Perry. It sounded like Teran.

Then something hit Perry in the back of his head and he was out.

CHAPTER 8

✿

CHOICES

PERRY AWOKE TO A WORLD OF HURT.

It was like the surface of his consciousness was coated in burning pitch. He felt the pain even as he swam up to it, and he wanted to go back down, away from the pain, but the pain wouldn't let him.

His mouth was dry. His head throbbed with the pounding of his heart. He felt sick to his stomach.

That was just the whiskey.

The back of his head ached, then spiked. Back and forth between the two. It felt like every follicle of his shaggy hair hurt.

His hand stung from lacerations. He didn't want to move it. Didn't want to move his fingers. When he drew his hand up to his chest he saw that it was covered with a bloody bandage. Hopefully, someone had pulled the pieces of glass out before bandaging it.

That was all just physical.

There was a sudden mental anguish as well.

Because when he opened his eyes, he saw that he was in a cell.

He moaned under his breath, let out a slurry of curses.

When he spoke, he heard someone move.

He'd already closed his eyes again. Didn't want to open them.

What did you do?

Shit. You know what you did.

Tiller had it coming.

But now you're in jail, aren't you?

He didn't want to think any more about it. He knew the truth. Dreaded confirming it. But he knew it. He just didn't want to deal with it. Because he couldn't handle it right now. The pain robbed him of any fortitude.

"Shortstack, you ass."

Perry still didn't want to open his eyes.

He knew who it was.

"Look at me," Boss Hauten commanded.

Perry gritted his teeth against the pain, but that made it worse. Tiller must have got him a few times in the jaw when they had fought.

Finally he forced his eyes open.

Just painful little slits, like they'd been cut open by razor blades.

Perry lay on a thin mattress on the floor. His feet were to the rusty iron bars. On the other side of those bars, Boss Hauten stood, looking down at him with a grimace on his face and a curled nose, like he sensed a foul odor.

"I'm lookin' at you," Perry rasped.

"Do you even remember what happened?"

Perry considered it. Then he nodded. "Did he die?"

"You killed him, you idiot."

Perry felt like he was going to vomit. He swallowed and breathed.

"I'm locked up for..." Perry left it open for Hauten to fill in the blank.

"Fucking murder!" Hauten cried. "What'd you think?"

"He was gonna rape Teran."

"That's her problem! Not yours! Gods, man! She wants to come work for an outfit like this? You better be wearin' a godsdamn chastity belt or have some good hand-to-hand skills. Any woman comes onto an outfit like this takes that shit in her own hands! It ain't your responsibility! You are not the protector of the weak!"

"He threw the money at me," Perry said. "Threw sixteen bits at my face. Said he was paying me to fuck her."

"And?" Hauten demanded, his voice pressing like a vice at Perry's head. "*Aaannnnd?* So you *kill him*? Are you even listening to yourself right now?"

Perry looked at his boss and felt a wash of desperation. If he could've gotten on his knees in that moment, he would've. The reality rammed into him like a runaway train car.

"You gotta get me out of here."

"Get you out of here?" Hauten gaped.

"Please! Pay my bond! You can take it out of my pay! With interest! I'll work for free to pay you off whatever you want!"

Hauten stared, shaking his head.

Perry was going to beg again, but then snapped his mouth shut. His face flushed and he averted his eyes.

"You ain't got a bond, you dumbshit," Hauten said with a note of pity in his voice. "They don't give bonds for murder."

Perry lowered his voice to a hiss. "A golden prayer then. Please. I'll pay it off."

Hauten just glowered at him for a moment. "I won't be paying the pontiff for you, Shortstack. Not out of my pocket. And even if I was of a mind to, he don't strike me as the type of pontiff that would go for something like that." Hauten's eyes glanced around darkly. "This fuck'd send his own son to the conscriptors."

Perry was silent for a while.

Staring at the wall. Unable to meet Hauten's gaze.

Locked up for murder. And it was only a matter of time before they discovered he was a deserter. Not that it mattered now. Executed for murder, or executed for desertion—he'd wind up just as dead either way.

Finally, he said, "Why are you here, then?"

Hauten raised his hands, let them flop to his sides. "Beats me. Guess I was hopin' you had a better reason for killin' the man."

"No," Perry said, forcing himself to go cold inside. To feel nothing. No guilt. No sadness. "He had it comin'. He earned what he got."

Hauten scoffed. "Well. That's just great."

"They gonna hang me?"

"I suppose so."

"When?"

"Soon, I guess."

"And there's nothing you can do for me."

"No, Perry. There ain't shit anyone can do for you." Hauten paused. "'Cept maybe the Light."

Perry frowned. "What do you mean?"

Hauten shook his head sadly. He put one big hand up and grabbed one of the rusty bars, as though he needed to support himself. He pointed at Perry with the other one.

"Pontiff can offer you conscription."

"Shit."

"It's better than danglin' from a rope."

"Is it?"

"At least you have a fighting chance."

Perry leaned up, ignoring the pain. "Does it look like any of those bodies had a fighting chance, Boss?"

"Not all of them die."

"The conscripts do."

"Well."

Perry laid back down. Stared at the ceiling. It didn't matter anyways. Hauten didn't know he was a deserter. Conscription wouldn't be an option for him—not when the pontiff discovered that he'd deserted from the Academy at Keniza.

Murderers and rapists could be conscripted.

But not heretics.

Perry and Hauten were silent for several painful breaths.

"It's dawn," Hauten said, and his voice sounded to Perry like a judge's gavel. Final. Resolute. "We're leavin'."

Perry didn't look at him again. "Okay. Do what you gotta do."

Hauten let out one more exasperated sigh, as though to tell Perry without words what a worthless waste of life he was. And then he was gone, and it was just Perry, and the jail cell, and his thoughts, and a fear that he wouldn't let creep up too close to him, but he let it prowl around the edges of his mind, like wolves at the edge of firelight.

***

The pontiff was a tall, erect man, who wore a conscript's chest plate. It was not as big or as thick as a legionnaire's armor. It had no spaulders. No *sagum*. It was only there to protect the vital organs, and a point-blank shot from a .458 would pass through it.

The pontiff's chest plate was blue with a white sun.

The symbol of the Light.

His name was Canis, which was a taken name if Perry had ever heard one. The mark of a true believer.

He had straight, black hair that he wore slicked back with grease. He was clean-shaven. His face angular, and imperial, and judgmental.

He stared down the length of his equine nose at Perry, who still lay on his thin mattress in his cell.

Perry hadn't moved much. There didn't seem to be much point in it. Plus it hurt.

"You're a doomed man," Canis announced. He affected the clear, accent-less diction of the demigods.

"Yeah," Perry murmured. "So I heard."

"This doesn't upset you?"

Of course it upsets me.

"It is what it is. Life for a life and all that."

Perry gauged the pontiff after he said this. To see if Canis would point out that it wasn't just murder that he would be hung for, but desertion as well. Heresy. The only crime you can't come back from.

But Canis gave no reaction to it. He continued on like he didn't know that Perry was a deserter. "Most men in your situation beg and plead."

"I imagine there's not much point to that."

"No, there is not."

"Well, there you go."

"You don't care about your life?"

Perry leaned up again, propped himself on an elbow with a grunt and frowned at the man on the other side of the bars. "What are you trying to do right now?"

"Excuse me?"

"You trying to break me down? Trying to make me cry? Trying to make me beg? You get off on that shit? Or are you just trying to soften me up for your conscription pitch?"

Canis smiled. "You're savvy. I won't say 'smart.' I don't think 'smart' men commit murder in front of witnesses. But you are savvy. I'll give you that."

Perry said nothing back.

"Where do you come from?"

"Western parts."

"How did you come to be here?"

"Travelling with Boss Hauten's outfit."

"And what did you do prior to that?"

"I grew up on a freehold." Perry kept his words even and deliberate. "Wandered around for a bit. Got hired by Boss Hauten. Now I'm here. Suppose I'll die tomorrow."

Certainly an abridged version of events. He left out the part where the freehold had been firebombed while he and his uncle had fled in the middle of the night. And the five years at Hell's Hollow. And his desertion.

Canis leaned towards the bars, and his face looked earnest. "Fight for the Light. And you will save your body. And perchance, in the process, you might save your soul."

Perry stared back at the man, feeling off-kilter. "You're still offering me conscription?"

Canis's eyes twinkled. "Why would I not?"

He had no idea why Canis had not uncovered his desertion, but he certainly wasn't going to volunteer the information. And in that moment, with the certainty of his execution looming over his head, he actually considered it.

He thought of it all.

He thought of signing his life away. Indoctrination. Boot camp. The yelling. The screaming. The long days filled with crawling through mud and slogging heavy armor up and down endless hills. The forced starvation. The beatings for trivial infractions. The bowing on his knees in the presence of legionnaires.

He would only be a peon. He'd be trained to kill as many as possible before he died, likely in his first battle.

And who would he be killing in that first battle?

Stupid peon conscripts like himself.

He imagined that battle. He thought about the morning lying clear and cool all about him. He thought about the sick nerves that would be huddled in his stomach like a den of rats. He thought of the sun coming up over a ridge and seeing the forces of The Truth laid out on an opposing hill, and then the carnage would begin, and the bullets would fly, and Perry and his unit would march, and they would die as they took yard by yard, step by step, standing shoulder to shoulder, shield to shield, sweating, bleeding, cursing, crying, shooting, dying.

And in the end, as Perry was trapped in that crush of bodies, perhaps Stuber would be up on a rocky ridge, looking down on him, and smiling, as a flurry of .458 rounds obliterated Perry's midsection and left his mangled remains to die.

Die staring up at a sun-scorched sky.

Or die, lying in his own blood and filth and the blood of others, much later on, when the thirst had taken over his body, and the pain was just a distant throb, and the ants came up from underground. Perhaps Pebbles or Ernie or Monty would find him out there and they would call for Stuber, and the ex-legionnaire would come stand over him, blotting out the setting sun and stroking the blood-soaked hair from Perry's eyes as he placed the Mercy Pistol to Perry's temple and said, "Accept this mercy, and go to The After."

Perry saw all of this.

His heart pounded him through it like a locomotive.

A vision of struggle. A vision of pain. Death begot at the hands of others for reasons unknowable.

And all of this was the exact reason why he'd deserted in the first damn place.

When the bloody, terror-filled vision cleared and he realized he was still staring at Canis, he shook his head.

"Just hang me."

CHAPTER 9

✿

GALLOWS

"Is it quick?" he asked Canis the following morning.

Canis sat in a chair outside Perry's cell, watching Perry eat his last meal. Perry didn't get to choose what to eat. But he wasn't complaining. He was glad that he wasn't going to die on an empty stomach.

Perry looked up from a bowl of millet porridge.

Canis ran a finger over his upper lip. "If you don't tense up."

Perry chewed slowly.

Not much appetite.

It was hard to tell between sickness because he was so damned hungry, and sickness because he was terrified.

The porridge was very salty.

It'll all be over soon.

"Do you want to know about it?"

Perry swallowed. Felt like the food was stuck in his throat. He waited for it to clear a path. Then he stubbornly shoved more in his face.

"Sure," he mumbled.

"What do you want to know?"

"Do you drop or suspend?"

"We drop."

"That's good." Perry felt like he was talking about someone else's execution.

"It should snap your neck."

Perry felt like he might vomit. He stopped eating. Looked up at the pontiff.

"So, does that kill a man? Or does it just paralyze him?"

"Oh, it'll kill him."

"Instantly?"

Canis shrugged. "Not sure how instant it is. Never had a chance to talk to a hanged man."

Perry offered a brittle smile. It felt strange on his mouth.

"You seem very at peace with this," Canis pointed out.

"I'm not."

"It may be cleansing for you to allow yourself to feel. You do not have much time, and there is not much purpose for stoicism now."

"Do you enjoy watching men break?"

"No. But I feel much better when a man dies with some..." he waved about for the right word. "Catharsis."

"Catharsis."

"Yes. Catharsis is acceptance."

"Well," Perry placed his bowl down, no longer interested. "Seeing as how this all happened kinda quickly, I don't see myself coming to terms with it."

"Sometimes it rips the man's head off."

"What?"

"The drop. Sometimes it rips the man's head off."

Perry kept his mouth tight for a moment, until it stopped sweating. His stomach clenched once, but now he was determined not to puke or show any sort of emotion in front of Canis. The bastard just wanted to see him weep. That's all this was about. Or maybe it was a last ditch effort to try to get him to conscript.

Either way, Perry was a dead man. The only difference is that he could die quickly at the end of a rope, or die slowly, after months of misery.

"Sounds like that would be the fastest way," Perry said without a trace of emotion.

Canis looked surprised. "You *want* it to decapitate you?"

"I want it to be over with," Perry said. Then he stood up and brushed his pants off. The back of his head still throbbed. The cuts on his hand stung. But that wouldn't last much longer. "I suppose I'm ready when you are."

Canis watched him for a time and Perry thought that the man was going to make the conscription pitch again. But he didn't. He stood up and stretched his back so that it cracked.

"Well then. If you're so ready to die a meaningless death, I won't hold you back." Canis smirked. "If you'll allow me a moment to fetch my men, we'll be on our way."

Then the pontiff turned towards the door.

As he put his hand on the door latch, the entire door detached from its hinges, flew away from its berth, and crushed the pontiff against Perry's cell bars.

The shockwave hit Perry immediately after.

He toppled backwards, the air going out of him.

Bits and pieces of the concrete doorframe clattered around in the jail cell, pinging off the bars like hammers on a xylophone.

Perry found himself curled in a fetal position, his arms wrapped around his head.

He didn't hear anything except for the ringing in his ears. Like he was stuck inside a bell and someone was ringing it with a sledgehammer.

His head felt overstuffed and his ears felt broken.

He pulled his hands away from his head and opened his eyes.

He smelled high explosives.

He looked around and realized that his vision was a little delayed in its tracking. He couldn't quite think in words yet. Like his brain had forgotten them. All he could do in that moment was feel. Crazy-panic-hope.

The interior of the jail was smoky.

The light poured in from the doorway. Bright, dawn light, caught in smoke and dust.

A dark shape loomed up, hunched, aggressive.

It flowed like a wraith. It ripped the door from the pontiff. The pontiff's hands raised up, pleading for mercy. A rifle protruded from the dark figure, and it fired three rounds. These reports barely made it into Perry's brain. They sounded like someone thumping on a wall.

The one factoid in all of this that came to him was the knowledge that the pontiff's chest plate was a peon's chest plate, and could not withstand a .458 round.

And it was a Roq-11 .458 rifle that shot him dead.

"Stuber?" Perry mumbled, not believing it.

The big legionnaire bent over the pontiff's dead body and stripped it of two items: the big pistol the man wore on his hip; and the keys that he had on his belt.

Stuber slammed the keys into the jail cell lock and ripped the door open.

Perry was still on the floor, trying to sort up from down.

"Catch!" Stuber threw the pistol at Perry.

Perry fumbled for it, missed. The heavy metal object clattered off his face. He was saved by the fact that he still couldn't feel much.

"Oh, gods, you fucking peon!"

Perry rolled, scrambled, grabbed the pistol with both hands.

He tried to get to his feet, like a newborn fawn.

Stuber lifted him up and placed him there. Kept a hand on him until he steadied.

"Come on," Stuber ordered. "Can you hear me?"

"Kind of."

"Good. Shoot anything that's got a gun and isn't me."

Stuber hauled him toward the exit.

When they came out of the doorway, they were in the middle of the street. Stuber kept hauling him. He seemed to know where they were supposed to be going. Perry, on the other hand, goggled about like a drunkard.

They were surrounded by people.

There was a dead body off to the side that wore a similar outfit to the pontiff.

Stuber held his Roq-11 with one hand, the stock tucked under his armpit. He let loose a rattling string of fire that kicked the concrete at the feet of the onlookers. The ricochets bit a man's legs out and he fell to the ground, screaming.

"Peons!" Stuber bellowed. "On your knees when you see a legionnaire!"

Some of them ran. Most of them hit the ground.

Stuber hadn't stopped moving, and Perry was finding his legs again.

"Put your face in the concrete!" Stuber ordered them. "If you put your eyes on me, I'll shoot them out of your skull!"

They rounded the corner of the jail.

A civilian lay there, face on the concrete, hands quivering over his head.

Stuber kicked him in the face for no apparent reason, then laughed.

Perry detached himself from Stuber. "I can walk," he said. "I can walk."

"Don't walk," Stuber said, picking up the pace. "Run!"

They ran. Down the alley that existed between the jail and some other brownstone building. There was a small, four-man buggy at the end of the alley.

Behind them a wail rose up, and for a brief second Perry thought that it was the cry of the people, but then he realized it was an alarm. It rose up, up, up, earsplitting.

Stuber laughed. His eyes blazed. "That's not good!"

They reached the buggy.

It was Teran in the driver's seat.

And no one else.

"Front seat!" she ordered Perry, who was still not lucid enough to do his own thinking. He obeyed and tumbled into the front seat.

The chassis rocked as Stuber vaulted into the back.

"Get us out of here, bitch!"

Teran stomped on the accelerator. "Don't call me a bitch!"

The buggy took off, tires grinding for traction. At the end of the alley Teran pulled a hard left. Perry caught himself on the roll cage and kept himself from falling out. The tires skidded across concrete layered with fine gravel. The buggy caught purchase and raced down the street. Civilians dove out of the way.

The Roq-11 chattered behind Perry.

He turned and looked.

Two scramblers pursued them. The riders wearing blue chest plates.

Stuber squatted down, bracing the front-end of his rifle against the back roll bar and firing three bursts. The first two missed, but the last one caught the rightmost scrambler, destroying the front tire, and then catapulting the rider from his seat.

The scrambler wobbled, then veered and crashed into a bystander, flipping him into the air like a ragdoll.

"Reloading!" Stuber called out.

Perry heard the ping of bullets striking the roll bars.

"Shortstack! Heads up!" Stuber yelled.

The whine of a scrambler's electric drive reached Perry's ears. He looked to his right and realized that the other rider had drawn abreast of them and was aiming for Teran.

Perry twisted in his seat and started cranking off rounds. Only on the third or fourth round did he

109

think to aim, and when he fired the seventh round, it struck the rear axle of the scrambler.

The rider had to give up his shot on Teran in order to stabilize himself.

"I'm up!" Stuber roared. Then leaned out from the back of the buggy, his rifle now only a few feet from the rider, who had just recovered control of his scrambler, and Stuber put four rounds into his head, vaporizing it and leaving just the stump of his neck and a bit of his lower jaw, squirting up a ribbon of blood that trailed behind the scrambler as it listed to the left, clipped the back end of the buggy, and then went tumbling end over end.

Stuber let out a horrendous cry that Perry had never heard from him before. It caused him to jerk in his seat and look up at the ex-legionnaire with wide eyes.

Stuber beamed like the sun. "I forgot what it was like to be alive!"

"Perry," Teran called.

Perry tore his eyes off the maniac behind him and looked at Teran. She had an expression on her face like she was bearing down on some terrible abdominal pain.

"I need you to take the wheel, Perry," she said, sounding out of breath.

It was at that moment that Perry saw how she held her stomach. How the blood came out from beneath her fingers. Soaking her stomach and waist and legs.

"Oh shit! Stuber!"

"What?"

"She's hit!"

"Then take the wheel from her!"

"Perry, I need you take the wheel!"

The buggy swerved in the narrow thoroughfare.

"Seriously! I'm gonna pass out!"

Stuber loomed over them. "Don't pass out, *you bitch*."

"Godsdammit!" She cried out.

Perry negotiated himself half into the driver's seat and took the wheel with both hands. "Okay! Slide over!"

She struggled to pull herself out of the driver's seat. Stuber expedited the process by grabbing her under the armpits and lifting her like a sack of grain, and then placing her in the passenger's seat with surprising gentleness.

Perry slid down into the driver's seat. He kept taking rightward glances at her. "Teran. Teran! Don't pass out."

Her skin had already gone ashen. Greasy sweat coated her face.

"Nope," she said, barely audible over their whining motor. "It's gonna happen."

"Shortstack! Right!" Stuber ordered.

Perry stomped on the brake, which managed to widen Teran's eyes for a second and give him a hope that she wasn't going to pass out after all. He hung a hard right, and when they straightened out, the city of Karapalida disappeared behind them, and they were in open country, and the paved road of the city turned to hard-packed dirt.

"Don't let me die," Teran said.

"We're not gonna—"

Then she moaned and passed out.

CHAPTER 10

✺

OKSIDADO

THEY HALTED THE BUGGY in the middle of open country.

It was neither plains, nor desert. Just a vast, scrubby flatness. It extended like an ocean to the east, but to the west and the north, there were gray peaks and rocky hills.

A cloud of their own dust swept over them, making Perry squint and hold his breath as he searched for the parking brake and engaged it. He twisted to look at Teran.

Her hands and feet twitched like a dog that dreamt of chasing a rabbit. Her chest rose and fell in an unnatural rhythm.

Perry reached across, pulled her hands from her midsection. "Help me with her!"

"I'm working on it," Stuber replied, pulling his bulk under the top roll bar of the buggy. He pulled a canvas satchel from his belt. It had once been black, but now was sun-bleached to gray.

Perry found the hole in her midsection. It was up and to the right of her navel a few inches. Just the exit wound, though. He bent her forward in her seat. The right side of her back was dark with blood. He pulled up her shirt, revealing pale skin, capillaried by tiny rivulets of blood that followed the patterns of the fine hairs on her skin.

The hole was obvious enough.

An angry little pucker, like a shrew's mouth, right there at her lowermost rib. A bit of meat protruded from it, but it wasn't bleeding all that bad.

"That's a good thing, right? That she's not squirting blood?"

Stuber bent over the top of the raggedy vinyl passenger's seat and grabbed the woman by the hips and shook them back and forth.

Perry heard it: a horrible, sloshing sound.

Stuber dropped his canvas satchel between the two front seats and ripped it open. The zippers separated and the thing opened like a clamshell. Inside were all manner of outdated medical equipment, their clear sterilized packaging gone yellow with age.

"Well, that's not a good sign," Stuber said, pulling a big package out and ripping it open to reveal a large bandage.

"What?"

"The sound. The sloshing. All that blood's on the inside."

"Shit. How is that possible?"

"It's called internal bleeding."

"I know it's called—!"

"Did you know you can drain all your body's blood into your abdominal cavity?" Stuber said conversationally.

Perry stared at him.

Stuber glanced sideways as he started balling up the bandage and pressing it onto the hole left by the bullet. He smiled, and nodded. He was taking Perry's flabbergasted expression to mean that he found the medical factoid hard to believe, rather than that he found it hard to believe Stuber was saying such bullshit at a time like this.

"Oh yeah," Stuber nodded. "Every ounce of it. Hey. Help me out here. Use your little rat hands to hold pressure there. Okay."

Perry felt himself getting indignant, but there wasn't much time to vent it. What was wrong with Stuber? Didn't he know that Teran could die? Did he just not care?

Perry grabbed the wad of bandage from Stuber and pressed.

Teran moaned, low in her throat, but didn't wake.

Stuber, with dirty, bloody fingers, began rummaging through his medical pack, leaving streaks of red behind. He came up with another set of bandages. He ripped them open. Started getting them ready.

"Keep holding it there. I'm gonna lean her back."

Teran was tilted back onto the seat. Her head lolled. A bit of drool came out of her mouth. Perry kept pressing the wad of bandage against the wound.

Stuber applied another wad of bandage to the exit wound. Held it there with one hand, then took what looked to Perry like a thin sheet of plastic, and pressed it firmly down over the exit wound-bandage and all. The material glistened, then shrunk slightly, adhering to her skin and sealing the wound. Stuber did the same thing to the entry wound, then leaned back to inspect his work.

"The occlusive dressings have localized vasoconstrictors. But it's still just a stop-loss, Shortstack," Stuber said. "She's gonna need to get to a doctor. And I'm not gonna lie to you. It's not looking good."

"What is wrong with you?" Perry cried.

Stuber looked at him with genuine surprise. "What?"

"She could die!"

"Yeah. I know. I just told you that."

"Well, stop being so casual about it!"

Stuber gazed at him with inscrutable eyes. Perry wasn't sure whether he saw wanton violence in them, or that same old sadness that he'd seen in the bar a few nights ago.

Maybe it was both. Hand in hand.

Stuber looked back at Teran. "Huh. Right. You had a thing for her."

"I didn't…" Perry let it go with a growl. "We need to get her to Jax. ASAP. He's the only one on Hauten's crew with medical experience."

Stuber cleared his throat. "Yeah, well, that's not possible."

"What?"

"We're not exactly welcome back."

"Not welcome? What do you mean? Why did Hauten send you to bust me out then?"

"Yeah, no. Hauten didn't send me to bust you out, Shortstack. They, uh, they don't want you anymore. Had a big roundtable about it and everybody agreed on 'fuck Shortstack.' It was pretty much unanimous."

"Unanimous?" Perry breathed. He was shocked how much that hurt. He'd been with those people for three years. There wasn't a single man among them that had voted to try and save Perry? Not even Monty?

"Well, you know, except for me and Teran." Stuber finished.

"I don't understand," Perry mumbled. Which was silly, because he *did* understand. He just didn't like it.

"Well, me and Teran voted to spring you, but we were outnumbered. The issue was settled. Except for…" Stuber cleared his throat again. "Except that Teran has a thing for you, I guess, and she came to me when the others were asleep and insisted that we try to spring you."

"Why would you agree to that?"

Stuber glowered. "I dunno, Shortstack. I guess I was bored. Now shut your mouth and start driving."

"Where are we going?"

"Well, Teran had a place for us to go, but she's not talking. So let's pick a different place, shall we? I know someone who can do some doctoring. Go west. And step on it. 'Cause your girlfriend here doesn't have a whole lot of time."

***

Oksidado was a tumbledown patch of shanties in the middle of nowhere. Not so much a city or a town as an isolated commune. One of those places where people coalesced and hunkered, figuring this was as good a spot as any to take their dreams out back and shoot them in the head.

If you were to ask anyone who lived in Oksidado how they came to be a resident, you'd hear similar stories. This is where they ran out of money. This is where their buggy broke down. This is where they exhausted their supplies.

It was like a tar pit for people's aspirations.

Everyone was a sad wooly mammoth who'd simply given up trying to get out.

And here came three new victims of desperate circumstances.

Perry and Stuber carried Teran. Stuber could have carried Teran by himself with minimal effort, but Perry insisted on lending a hand.

Stuber had been adamant that they leave the buggy out in a little grove of sage.

"They're gonna be looking for this buggy," Stuber had said.

"Who?"

Stuber had only shrugged. "We have to assume *someone* is looking for you. And me. Maybe not Teran. But definitely you and me." He smiled, as though at a private joke. "Can't just go about breaking people out of jail and not expect to be wanted by *someone*."

So they left the buggy there, parked between two clumps of sage that did a poor job of hiding the vehicle. But it was the best they had.

As they hauled Teran's pale and motionless body into the east end of Oksidado, Perry griped between struggling breaths: "You coulda killed me with that explosion."

Stuber, who was only just beginning to sweat, looked at him with confusion. "What?"

"When you blew up the door to the jail."

"Oh. That."

"Yes. That. You could have killed me."

"Yes."

"Did you think about that?"

"Yes."

Perry didn't have much else to say on the topic. He stewed, his jaw working, trying to find something else to say.

Stuber watched him in glances, his eyes going back and forth between the alleyway they walked and Perry's face. As he watched Perry's silent anger, Stuber's face clouded over like rolling thunderheads.

He stopped them in the middle of the alley.

Teran made a pitiful noise.

"Why are we stopping?" Perry snapped.

"Listen to me, you little peon fuck," Stuber ground out, all semblance of friendliness gone.

Perry glared back, but inside, his testicles drew up into his stomach.

"You were either definitely dead at the end of a rope, or possibly dead because of an explosion. It was a risk I was willing to take. Trying to rescue you when you were on the gallows platform or otherwise out of the jail presented too many tactical difficulties and would have likely resulted in everyone dying. As it stands, right now, in case you hadn't noticed, we're all still alive. And that's a pretty damn good job, in my very educated opinion. So I think some thanks are in order from you, because you should be hanging from a rope right now, except that you have exactly two friends in the world—me, and this bitch bleeding out in your arms."

Perry felt a fire burning on the back of his neck. If there was one thing in the world he hated more than anything else, it was being talked down to. If there was a second thing, it was when someone made him feel beholden.

So here was a nice one-two punch.

"Thanks."

Stuber shook his head, but started moving again.

"Most insincere thanks I've ever heard in my life," he mumbled.

At the mouth of the alley, they intersected with…another alley.

Were these supposed to be roads? Perry wasn't sure. They were very narrow.

To either side of them were stoops created by stacked stone and concrete blocks. The right stoop was unoccupied. On the left stoop stood an old lady in a brown sack-dress, smoking a reed. She was watching two men carrying a bloody body. She eyed them with suspicion, but no apparent surprise.

Stuber smiled at the old lady.

"Looking for Doctor Remming," he said.

The lady squinted at them. Took a long drag.

Perry shifted his grip on Teran's feet and took a breath to belt out a string of curses at the old crone, but finally the woman lifted two fingers, reed pinched between them, and pointed to their right.

"Down that way," she husked, cancerously. "Four doors. On the left."

Stuber nodded his thanks and they continued on.

Perry felt like he was dying by the time they reached the door. His arms were on fire from carrying Teran. His face was a constant grimace. Even Stuber was starting to show a bit of strain.

"Should've just driven in here and hidden the buggy afterwards," Perry said.

Stuber climbed the two steps to the door and knocked. "Yeah. Well, that would've been a great suggestion twenty minutes ago."

"You're the professional. You're supposed to think about these things."

"Sorry, I had a peon bitching at me the entire time. It was hard to concentrate."

"Peon this. Peon that. We get it! You're a legionnaire!"

The door opened.

A striking red-headed woman looked down at them.

She looked at Stuber first, and then at Perry.

To Perry she said, "This guy? Oh no. He's an *ex*-legionnaire. Don't give him credit. He's a deserter."

Stuber gave a brittle smile. "Petra, my love. We have a situation."

"I can see that," the woman said. "Who is she? And where is your crew? What the hell happened?"

Stuber shifted his grip on Teran. "Time is of the essence, my love."

"Hey!" Perry was on the verge of dropping Teran's legs. "Her name's Teran and she's gonna die if she doesn't see the doctor. Could you *please* just take us in to the doctor?"

Petra looked at him with cool, blue eyes. "I *am* the doctor."

"She *is* the doctor, you ass."

Perry nodded—almost bowed. "Then please. Help us."

Petra looked Teran over with a clinical eye, then stepped aside and waved them in. "Come on." As Stuber passed her, she said, "I can only imagine why this man is here right now, but it can't be good."

As the door was closed behind him, Perry grunted, "You're right. It's not."

CHAPTER 11

✦

OLD LOVE

THE SURGEON WAS ANCIENT, but Perry hadn't expected a brand-new model in a piece-of-shit town like Oksidado. It took up nearly the entire back room of Doctor Petra Remmer's house. Just the styling of the machine told Perry it was at least fifty years old.

On the plus side, it looked well-maintained.

Petra hovered alongside Stuber and Perry as they pulled Teran's body onto the bed of the Surgeon. The maw of the active portion gaped, lit with red scanners waiting to diagnose. The arms of the machine stood, poised and ready, not unlike the legs of a spider that's expired on its back.

Newer models weren't quite so frightening looking.

Petra crossed over a power column to get to the other side of the bed and pulled Teran onto it. "How long ago was she shot?" Petra looked up at Stuber. "I'm assuming this is a gunshot wound."

Stuber nodded. "Maybe an hour ago."

"Well, if she hasn't died yet, I'd say that's a good sign," Petra remarked.

She took her red hair and bundled it atop her head, tying it off with a flick of her fingers. Then she slipped into a pair of aquamarine gloves and grabbed an IV starter line from one of the waiting spider's legs.

She swabbed Teran's arm, turning it a burnt umber. Then she looked up at Stuber and Perry as though just remembering they were there. She pointed with her chin towards the door. "Out. Let me work."

Stuber bowed his way back from the side of the Surgeon and then turned for the door, taking Perry by the shoulder and ushering him out.

Perry looked over his shoulder as he was pulled for the door. Looked at Teran's inert form, lying there, still breathing oddly, her skin pale and waxy and glistening.

Perry's heart was still pounding, his breath still risen from the exertion. His arms still ached from carrying Teran.

"Is she going to live?"

"Couldn't tell you that, Shortstack." Stuber kept a hand on his shoulder, guiding him away from the door. "But I trust Petra."

Perry felt like he was floating.

This is nothing. Why are you tied up in this?

Berating himself seemed the only logical response to his emotional involvement.

Buck up, you idiot. Did you get all assed up when Slider bit it? No. You boxed it up and you moved on. Just like you did with all the others. You're not a stranger to this.

But he felt sick.

He felt on the verge of losing something important.

So he minimalized it. He trivialized it.

You're acting like a teenager. You saw her ass, and you think you're in love.

You don't love anyone. You look out for yourself, and that's it.

He felt dirty after that. But it helped to distance himself.

When he finally felt like his feet were touching the ground again, he was standing on a balcony. He vaguely remembered Stuber pulling him up a rickety indoor staircase to the second level of the doctor's house, swiping a bottle of whiskey from a liquor cabinet—very fancy for Oksidado—and pushing him outside onto the balcony.

The balcony faced east.

Back the way they had come.

Perry leaned on the railing, which was made of old wood. It creaked, but held. Perry imagined himself falling off and dying. He didn't much care. That was nice.

Out east, the emptiness stretched, interminable.

He tried to see if Karapalida was visible, but it wasn't. There was a smudge on the horizon that might've been the pall of smog that hung over the city, but he couldn't be certain.

He still could not figure out why Canis hadn't known he was a deserter.

Everyone else that deserted was hunted down and executed.

Why would Perry be any different?

Unless Canis hadn't checked the system. But Canis hadn't seemed like the type of guy to be lackadaisical about his duties. He would've checked Perry's DNA immediately upon taking him into jail.

Something didn't add up.

In the square of Oksidado, he saw the top of the jumbotron. Not as a big as the one in Karapalida, nor as loud. But he saw enough of it to recognize the exact same footage that he'd seen in Karapalida. The same battlefield—the one that he and Boss Hauten's outfit had picked over—and they were saying that it was a great battle, and a glorious victory.

Except they claimed it was a glorious victory for The Truth.

I guess it all depends on your perspective.

Oksidado might not have a very impressive jumbotron, but across from it, poking up above all the rooftops, was a sizeable bronze statue. The jumbotron and the statue were likely the only things that the demigods had seen fit to give this sad collection of mudbrick hovels.

Perry recognized the stern, bearded face of the Paladin Primus, the Father of Demigods, the First God of Men, and the Savior of Humanity. He stood, three stories tall, his empty, bronze gaze directed at the heavens. His left arm reaching, as though accepting something from the sky. His right arm held down, as though offering something in his hand to those below him.

It was absurdly large, given the size of the town. Like the town perhaps had been created around the statue, rather than the statue erected for the sake of the town.

These statues and monuments were meant to invoke awe and piety.

They did no such thing for Perry.

But then again, Perry was a deserter and a heretic, so…

He sighed, deeply.

His heartrate had finally levelled.

His breathing was normal.

He was above it all. Considerations of death were beneath him. The consequences of killing Tiller, and then being sprung from jail, and who would be hunting him, and what they would do to him when they found him—all just a bunch of nonsense that could wait for another time.

That was good.

That felt like homeostasis.

He felt a nudge on his arm.

He looked down.

Stuber held a glass full of whiskey towards him.

"Helluva fuckin' day," Stuber said, shaking the glass. "Let's get ripped."

Perry took the glass. His stomach turned just looking at the liquid. But he took a sip, and at first it felt like the gorge might rise, but after he swallowed and waited a moment, it settled him.

He didn't want to think about Teran.

So he turned his attention to Stuber.

He nodded at the bottle of whiskey. "You're awfully liberal with her stuff."

Stuber glanced at the bottle. Then shrugged. "Well. We have some history, her and I."

Perry eyed Stuber up and down.

The ex-legionnaire stared out into the east and leaned on the railing. It groaned in agony.

Perry knew that he should be thankful, but it was too difficult with Stuber.

If Stuber stopped and thought for two damn seconds, rather than shooting and exploding his way through life, then things might turn out better for him and the people around him.

But no. Stuber's brain worked in only two gears. Gear one: Are we friends? Let's drink! Gear two: Are we enemies? I'm going to obliterate you.

Drunken love and violent hate. That was about all that Perry had ever seen out of him.

Except for that sadness.

127

Perry grunted at his own thoughts and looked away from Stuber.

"Petra's a pretty lady," he said, looking east again. Wondering if he could see the little dried up oasis of sage where they'd hidden the buggy.

Stuber gave Perry a sidelong glance, as though evaluating the threat level.

Gear one or gear two?

But he just smiled and looked back out again. "Yes, she is."

They drank in silence for a time.

In the silence, Perry cooled. Then felt bad.

You only hate him because you'd be dead without him.

Perry sucked his teeth, angry at his own inner voice.

You only hate him because he is what you could never be.

My father would have been proud to have a son like him. But he got a runt like me instead.

He took a long, bracing breath. The type of breath that you take when you are getting ready to admit that you are wrong about something.

"Thank you for getting me out of jail, Stuber."

Stuber waved it off. "Meh. Don't thank me. I'da let you swing. Teran's the one that convinced me to go. She's the one with the silver tongue. Thank her. You know…if she lives."

"Could I get more whiskey?"

Stuber seemed pleased. "Of-fucking-course."

He filled Perry's glass. Three or four fingers' worth.

"You know, I've known you for three years, Stuber. Still don't know why you deserted."

Stuber filled his own glass again. Capped the bottle. Set it down at his feet. Leaned on the railing again. Looked into his glass like the answer was floating in it. Finally, he raised the glass to his lips, and just prior to taking a drink of it, he said, "Difference of opinion."

Perry turned towards the ex-legionnaire, propping himself thoughtfully on an elbow. "Lemme guess. A superior officer told you *not* to rape and pillage an entire town, so you beat his skull in. Then you had to go on the run or be shot for treason."

Stuber belted out a laugh. For a moment his face shined with merriment. Then it grew dark again. "Not exactly."

"Really?" Perry wasn't sure he believed that.

Stuber gave him another look. "You don't know everything about me, Shortstack. You should open your eyes and see the whole elephant."

"Hmm." Perry frowned, not understanding the reference.

"Look."

Perry glanced up, saw that Stuber stood more erect, pointing out to the east. He followed the man's finger to where a skein of clouds parted, and three objects made tiny by distance descended.

A few heartbeats later, the sound of distant thunder reached them.

"That's not…" Perry trailed off.

Stuber nodded. "Most likely."

Perry gripped the rail and felt momentarily hopeful. "If Karapalida is The Light, then those skiffs will be blue as well. They won't come to a red town." As he said it, he realized that might not be the case. "Will they?"

"You see a garrison?" Stuber asked, then finished his glass of whiskey in a single gulp and grabbed the bottle to pour himself another. "No. Each of those skiffs carries a squad of legionnaires. They could wipe Oksidado off the map in an hour."

Perry frowned at him. "And this doesn't concern you?"

"They haven't found the buggy yet."

"It won't be that hard to find."

Stuber shrugged. "When they find it, I'll be concerned."

"Will you even know if they found it?" Perry squinted into the distance but he'd already lost the skiffs in the clouds.

"Yeah." Stuber pointed again. "The copse of sage. It's right there. You see it? About a mile out."

Perry squinted harder. Couldn't see what Stuber was talking about. "You messing with me right now?"

Stuber chuckled. "No. You have peon eyes. Good for doing peon shit, like working in the dirt two feet from your face. It's not an insult. It's just genetics."

Perry ground his teeth. Swallowed a retort.

The door to the balcony creaked open behind them.

Perry turned and saw Petra standing there, her eyes addressed to Stuber.

"Help yourself to my whiskey, Franklin."

Stuber turned and raised the glass with what Perry was sure he considered a charming smile. "I already did, love. Thank you."

What shocked Perry was that the smile seemed to work. Petra shook her head, but favored Stuber with a wry smile. Her hair was down, and her smile made her blue eyes twinkle, and Perry realized that she was far more than just striking. He was very attracted to her.

Petra stepped out and closed the door behind her. She turned to Perry and grew professional. "Teran is doing as well as we can expect. She had a bad reaction to the SanguinEx, but the Surgeon is acclimating her to it right now and the worst of the reaction has passed. It looks like her body will accept it. All her vital signs say that she's out of the danger zone. She had about three pints of blood in her abdomen. However, aside from the vein it clipped, the bullet didn't hit anything else valuable accept for a two inch section of small intestine. Went ahead and removed that."

Perry nodded along with the medical diatribe. "So she's going to be okay?"

"She'll have some pain at the wound site for several more days. Probably feel weak. Have dizzy spells. Pain when she urinates. That type of thing. But it'll pass. She'll heal."

"Is she awake?"

"She's still under anesthetic."

"When will she wake up?"

"Sometime in the next few hours," Petra said. "This evening at the latest." Then, as though that covered everything that needed to be covered, she turned herself to Stuber, and again, her demeanor changed out of its professional mode like you might shuck off a jacket. She strode over to Stuber and took the whiskey glass from his hand. "You give me that," she said. "You can drink from the bottle like the reprobate that you are."

Stuber shrugged. "I have no problem drinking from the bottle."

"I do. It's not ladylike." She took a sip, and then pointed to the door. "Shall we go inside?"

"I think its best that we stay out here," Stuber said.

"Keeping watch, then."

"Yes."

"Alright." She pointed to a set of weathered wicker chairs that were jumbled to the side of the balcony. "Then let's sit at least."

When they'd sat, Petra looked at Perry. "I never did get your name."

"It's Perry, ma'am."

She smiled. "You can call me Petra."

"Thank you." Perry wasn't sure why he'd thanked her. She was very attractive, and Perry was not accustomed to being around women of her caliber. "How do you and Stuber know each other?"

Petra looked at Stuber, whom she'd addressed as Franklin earlier. "You drag the poor kid into the gods-know-what situation, wind up at my door with a half-dead girl, and you don't even tell him who I am?" She shook her head. "Are you ashamed of me, Franklin?"

Stuber seemed mellowed by her presence. His usual abrasiveness appeared to have been sanded smooth. "Of course not, darling. Just the opposite. I figured you were ashamed of me."

"What nonsense," she said, then drank. When she lowered her glass, she looked at Perry. "Franklin and I are married."

Perry sat there. Waiting for the punchline.

"Were," Stuber corrected.

Petra looked at him. "Do you see another man in my house?"

"I hadn't checked under the bed."

"There's no other man."

"Or in the closet."

"There's no one," she said, this time with more finality. "Hasn't been. Ever. You should respect the effort that's taken on my part."

"I figured they'd be lined around the block. Especially in a town like Oksidado."

"I've run them all off several times."

"You're a paragon of fidelity, my dear."

"Wish I could say the same about you."

Stuber didn't respond. Looked away from her.

"So you're serious?" Perry asked, leaning forward. "You two are actually married?"

"Twenty years," Petra replied. "This past winter."

Stuber perked up. "Did you get the brooch I sent you?"

"I did." She smiled. "It was very lovely."

Stuber seemed satisfied.

Perry recalled the brooch. He was there when Stuber had bought it. Spent damn near two week's pay on it and wouldn't say why. He'd been very urgent and shady about the whole thing. At the time, Perry had assumed it was to bribe some high-priced whore. Now Perry realized he must've sent it here.

Realization and acceptance are two very different things.

Perry looked from Petra to Stuber, and he marveled at the man sitting there. Marveled, and also felt dismay. He couldn't see Stuber for anything but the man in the bloody legionnaire's armor, his expression of manic joy lit by the strobing muzzle flashes of his Roq-11 while he gunned down Lokos, or gouged men's eyes out with a broken bottle.

This man?

This man?

The one who stood and watched the battles, heedless of the stray rounds that sometimes pocked the rocks around them? The one who insisted that the battle was a whore's bed and the clash was when you got to stick your dick in? The one who would thrust his hips every time those two tides of humanity crushed against each other?

Perry looked at Petra again.

This woman?

Beautiful, intelligent, and refined? A doctor? A healer of people?

Perry laughed. He couldn't help himself.

"Sorry, I know this is going to sound bad," Perry said, stifling the rest of the laughter. "But how does a guy like Stuber end up with a woman like you?"

Stuber flashed his eyes in Perry's direction. That old familiar violence. Like he was considering how likely Perry was to die if he was thrown from the balcony.

Petra laughed at the question. A bright, wonderful noise. "Well, he wasn't always the gruff asshole you see sitting before you now."

Stuber rolled his eyes.

Petra looked at him and it took Perry a moment—because he couldn't believe it—to realize that she was looking at Stuber with genuine affection. "Once upon a time, Franklin was actually a very kind-hearted boy. Shy, even. Sensitive."

"Bullshit," Stuber grumbled. "Lies."

"Franklin," Perry said, mystified. "A boy. A *sensitive* boy."

"Oh, gods in the fuckin' skies…" Stuber shifted in his chair. "Don't you want to know why we're here?"

Petra slid her empty glass towards him. Her face grew serious again. "Actually, yes. I do."

Stuber filled her glass. The bottle was nearly empty.

Gods, how much had the man already drank? Perry had only had two glasses so far.

Stuber nodded his head in Perry's direction. "Young Shortstack here got into a bit of trouble over in Karapalida. Was supposed to be hung this morning. The young lady apparently has something for him. She convinced me to help her break him out before they took him to the gallows." Stuber drank from the bottle. He sighed. "In all the hullaballoo, she got shot. She was supposed to take us somewhere, but her being unconscious and all kind of kept her from doing that. So I brought her here."

Petra listened, circling her glass on its bottom rim, causing a light scraping sound on the table. A thoughtful, cyclical sound. Like a slow fan moving. She looked up at Perry.

"You chose the gallows?"

Perry pursed his lips.

Suddenly, he didn't want to answer that question. Even though it seemed that Petra already knew. Still. To admit it to her seemed like shame. He felt his face growing hot.

Had he really given up on life?

But then he remembered *why* he'd made that decision.

"I didn't want to die for The Light," Perry mumbled. "Bleeding out in some desert valley while the ants built a colony over my legs and stripped me while I was still alive." He shook his head. "I've seen it all happen before. So yes. I chose the gallows."

Petra sipped. Considered.

"That makes you a heretic."

"Well, that's nothing new," Perry remarked.

Out of the corner of his eye, he detected Stuber giving him an evaluating look.

Perry almost told Stuber about his own desertion. But then he clamped his mouth shut. When you live so long with secrets, it gets harder and harder to let them out.

"We'll be out of your hair as soon as Teran wakes up," Stuber said to Petra.

Petra looked at him. For a brief flash of the eyes, she seemed sad. But then she blinked and it was gone. "Yes."

Stuber seemed suddenly seized by a whim. He leaned across the table and took Petra's hand. "Come with us."

Petra didn't pull away. In fact, she squeezed his hand back. But she also shook her head. "Don't do this, Franklin."

"Come away with me. We can go east. Or south. We can find a new place. A place where I'm not a fugitive. We can build another life."

"And where is this place?" Petra asked, humoring him. "Where's this place where The Truth and The Light don't exist?"

"There must be. They can't own the whole world."

Petra smiled wanly. "That place doesn't exist."

They sat there, looking at each other, still holding hands.

That's why they're not together, Perry thought. *Because Stuber is a deserter. A fugitive. The longer he stays, the more danger he puts Petra in.*

And you're a deserter, too.

You have something in common with him.

"You'll need to move tonight," Petra said. "When the girl wakes up."

Stuber sighed, long and depressed.

"You should get some sleep."

"Yes," Stuber agreed. "Sleep."

Petra smirked.

Stuber stood up, still holding her hand. "Perry, if you will, keep watch on the horizon. Let me know if they find the buggy. I need to...have a private word with my wife."

Perry smiled mirthlessly and drank from what was left in his cup. He said nothing. Didn't trust his mouth not to be snarky in the moment. And what was this? Jealousy? How petty of him.

But seriously. A drunken boor like Stuber with a beautiful woman like that.

She smiled bedroom eyes back at Stuber.

She stood up as well.

"Right," Perry remarked. "I'll keep watch."

CHAPTER 12

✿

GLORIOUS VICTORIES

THEY WERE LOUD.

Perry sat on the balcony and stared out to the horizon where the sun began to angle itself. The pontiff's pistol dug into his back where he'd shoved it into his waistband and he had to adjust it. He'd forgotten it was there. He finished his glass of whiskey and set it down next to his chair, and then folded his hands across his stomach.

He didn't so much mind Petra's voice. A woman making love is a beautiful sound. But then Stuber would pipe up and it was like the cymbal player in an orchestra clashing away at inappropriate times. It made the whole thing unpleasant.

They quieted down after a bit.

In the following peaceful silence—because Oksidado was one of the quietest damn towns that Perry had ever been in—he kicked his feet up on the railing and leaned back in his seat. The whiskey glowed across his body like a blanket. The afternoon sun cradled him.

The jumbotron mumbled in the distance, the same old news.

His eyes grew heavy on lack of concern, which was strange, considering the stakes. But he had not slept the night before, and he still felt like he was in a dream, and that none of this was really happening to him.

So he fell asleep.

***

They came to him in his dreams, as they often did.

Their faces loomed up over him, monolithic in memory. He could feel their heels in his ribs, their fists against his face, beating him senseless as he lay naked on the tile floor of the bathhouse at Hell's Hollow.

His classmates.

It was their faces that he always remembered.

Their faces that showed the strain of effort as they beat him, but never anger.

They were just scared. Scared that a runt like Perry would graduate from the Academy. Scared that he would be assigned to their battleline. Scared that he would be the weak link that would get them killed.

And behind them, in the corner of the bathhouse, the granite face of their *Praeceptor Legionarius*, watching the violence with blank boredom, his blue *sagum* hanging on the edges of his crossed arms.

***

"Hey."

All it took was a word.

Perry rocketed out of his chair.

It was dark.

He grabbed the rail while his head spun. A single throb went through it. He stared out to where the black land met the navy blue sky.

"Oh, shit! Are they coming?"

His heart pounded.

"What?"

He realized the voice was neither Petra's nor Stuber's.

He wheeled around.

Teran stood there in clean clothing—tan trousers and a white blouse. They were Petra's. The clothing hung loose on her.

She looked pale and about ready to fall over.

Perry stepped to her side and grabbed her arm to steady her. She held out her other hand for balance, and it shook in the air.

"I'm fine," she said, though her voice was weak. "I'm okay."

"You don't look fine," Perry said. "Well, I mean, you look good. Better than dead. But you look like you're about to pass out."

"No. But I do feel like I might throw up."

"You probably don't want to do that."

"Why not?" She sounded worried.

"I don't know. It just seems like something you shouldn't do."

"Where the hell are we?"

"Oksidado."

"What?"

"It's a town. Stuber took us here. He said he didn't know where you wanted to go. And he knows the doctor that fixed you up."

"Oh."

"You should sit."

"Okay."

Perry guided her to a wicker chair. She walked like a person treading water. Still high from the anesthetic. Sat down. He grabbed another chair and brought it over next to her. Glanced at the horizon again.

He hadn't missed anything, right?

He sat down, facing her.

For a minute or so, neither of them said anything.

Perry looked out towards the center of Oksidado. The jumbotron cycled through the same news again. A great battle. A glorious victory.

"Why'd you save me?" he asked her.

Teran kept staring out into the gathering darkness. "I need you," she said.

Perry didn't know how to respond to that. He fumbled around for a moment. "Look, Teran…I like you too. But you've only known me for a week, and…"

She snapped a frown in his direction. "Not like that, you ass!"

His eyebrows went up. "Oh."

"Look at that." She gestured in the direction of the jumbotron. "You've watched it. You saw it in Karapalida. Glorious victories. For The Truth. For The Light. It doesn't matter." She spat. The glob of spittle sailed over the railing and into the darkness. "Fuck that. How many people do you think died that day?"

Perry knit his fingers together, thinking of them all, thinking of that valley soaked in blood. The dirt turned to mud from the emptying of so many humans. "A thousand. Give or take."

"A thousand dead," she said. "For what?"

He couldn't answer her. He didn't know.

"Did you see more red cloaks than blue cloaks in that pile of bodies?"

"No."

"More blue than red?"

"I saw the same amount of both."

142

"Exactly. Does that sound like a glorious victory for anybody?"

He shook his head.

She sat forward, wincing as she did. "How many people in this shitwater town are watching that jumbotron? How many young people that think they want glory? How many people that have no idea what they're fighting for?"

Perry pulled his hands apart. Rubbed his palms on his thighs. "I get it, Teran. I do. The whole thing—"

"Do you?"

He nodded. "I just don't know what it has to do with me."

Teran opened her mouth to say something else, but then stopped.

It was not so much a sound, as a sensation.

A deep, basal rumble. Almost like an earthquake.

Both he and Teran looked up into the darkness.

But there was nothing.

Even the blue ribbon of sky had disappeared.

Now it was just black on black.

The only light came from the jumbotron.

Glorious victories.

"The hell was that?" Perry breathed.

From inside the house there came a crash of something glass, and the sound of Stuber cursing. Petra said something, but Perry couldn't tell what it was. There was an urgent cadence to her voice. There was the thud of feet on floors. The creak of an opening door.

Petra and Stuber tumbled out onto the balcony.

143

Petra was buttoning her blouse.

Stuber was affixing his armor. He had no shirt on beneath it.

"Did you feel that?" Perry asked. "What was that?"

"Why didn't you wake me?" Stuber demanded.

"What?"

"Did you not see the…?" he trailed off. "You fucker."

"What?" Perry almost yelled.

"You fell asleep, didn't you?"

"Uh…"

"Godsdammit." Stuber tightened the last strap of his armor. "We gotta go. We gotta go *now*."

Petra nodded. "You need to get out of here. All of you."

"What was it?" Teran asked. "What was that rumble?"

"They've landed," Stuber said. "They're coming."

CHAPTER 13

☼

HERETICS

THEY TUMBLED DOWN THE STAIRS to the ground level.

Stuber was in the lead. He had his Roq-11 up and ready.

Petra spoke urgently to her patient: "Drink as much fluids as you can. Try to rest as much as possible. You're going to feel like crap for a few days. Try to eat. If you start running a fever or if you have any redness or swelling at the wound sight, you probably need to get some antibiotics."

"I think I'm gonna throw up."

"Okay."

They'd turned the corner of the stairs by then. They were almost to the back room where the Surgeon sat.

Teran bent over and retched.

"Come on, Sweetie," Petra prodded while Teran issued out a gruel of stomach juices and stumbled along. "We gotta keep moving. Hey! You!"

"Me?" Perry looked at her.

"Yes. You need to make sure she gets food and water and rest. Don't push her too hard. I'm holding you responsible for this."

"What about Stuber?"

Petra gave him a stern look. "Stuber's responsible for keeping you both from getting shot. I hold him responsible for that. You worry about Teran, okay?"

Perry felt a weed of resentment shoot up from the fertile soil of the bitterness he held deep down in himself. She was telling him he needed a legionnaire to protect him. She was telling him that he had to rely on the very same type of person that had beat the piss out of him in the Academy on a daily basis.

It was something that Perry simply couldn't live with.

He could take care of himself!

He didn't need anybody, and nobody needed him!

Accept that…

He *did* need Stuber. He'd be dead without him. Stuber had what Perry lacked: combat experience; and all that firearms training that Perry had never received because he'd deserted before being assigned to a legion.

And, he realized, Teran needed *Perry*. She'd said so herself.

Perry swore. "Okay, fine. I'll take care of her. Don't worry."

Petra shuffled them to the back door of the house. Stuber held up a hand. The rest of them became quiet. He addressed his weapon to the door. Reached forward. Ripped it open.

A gust of cool night air chilled the sweat on Perry's face.

Stuber plunged through the doorway.

"Stay," Petra whispered.

The three of them did not move.

Stuber reappeared. "It's clear. Let's move."

Perry drew the pontiff's pistol from his back with one hand, and took a hold of Teran's arm with the other. He shuffled her out the door. She'd stopped puking. Now she was coughing and spitting the bile out of her mouth.

Petra stood in the doorway, watching Stuber.

He smiled at her. "Come with me, my love."

"And leave Oksidado without a doctor?"

"They'll find a new one."

But Petra shook her head. "You know I won't go with you, Franklin."

"You break my heart every time."

"I'm sorry."

"Me too." He stepped down to the ground and blew her a kiss. "Until next time, then."

"Stay alive," she ordered him.

He smiled, cocksure. "Of course."

Then she looked left and right, stole one last glance at Stuber, and closed the door.

Stuber stood there for a second. His jaunty, careless countenance melted.

But then he straightened up.

"Godsdamned hard-assed bitch of a woman," he griped. "I love her." Then he pulled the Roq-11 tighter into his shoulder and with his support hand, pointed to Teran and Perry. "You two follow me. Do what I tell you to do. And keep your mouth shut."

Perry snaked his arm under Teran's and pulled her torso against him. She let her arm hang over his shoulder, gripping his shirt in her fist.

Stuber turned his back on them, rifle to his cheek.

And at that point, all the lights went out.

Perry thought it had been dark before. But there'd still been a smattering of lamps that burned on people's porches, and of course, the glow of the jumbotron.

It all went dead.

The faint, background rumble-hum of working machinery went silent.

Now there was nothing.

Darkness.

The stars over their heads cold, silent witnesses.

The town of Oksidado was an invisible black maze.

Perry could just see Stuber's armor. His bare arms just visible in the starlight.

"They're here," Stuber whispered, and in his hushed words there was a strain that Perry thought sounded like excitement.

Stuber moved forward in the darkness.

It was so quiet that Perry felt like he couldn't breathe. His lungs ached. And when he let himself take a gulp of air it sounded like a roaring wind in his head.

Stuber was heading *into* town.

"Shouldn't we be going the other way?" Perry hissed. "*Out* of town?"

"Shut your trap, peon. We're not running."

Perry was caught in a tug-of-war with himself: half of him wanting to follow Stuber because he knew the man had better combat skills than he did; the other half wanting to break away because he thought Stuber was being too brazen.

In the darkness with them, around any corner, there were going to be legionnaires.

Not *ex*-legionnaires.

Not washed-up has-beens, like Stuber.

Active-duty legionnaires that slaughtered massive amounts of people on a regular basis.

Perry felt that old, familiar fear taking root inside of him, the fear of legionnaires that had been built up inside of him from five years in Hell's Hollow, and it seemed that when it came, he could barely feel the flow of The Calm anymore.

But his feet followed Stuber, and Stuber led them further *into* Oksidado.

They crept down an alley.

It smelled bad. Like rotting meat.

Stuber reached the mouth of the alley.

Perry'd given up trying to control his breathing. He hung his mouth open wide. It made the breathing quieter than the hiss of his nose. Teran struggled along next to him, but she seemed to be taking more and more weight for herself.

At the mouth of the alley, Stuber checked both directions.

Somewhere in the town a dog started barking.

It barked maybe a dozen times.

Then it stopped.

Nothing else.

Stuber held the rifle in one hand, and with his support hand reached back and waved them forward.

Perry and Teran shuffled up.

"What?" Perry whispered.

"Across," Stuber replied. "Straight across. Move quick."

Then he checked again—right, left—and sprinted across.

Thud, thud, thud, thud.

There's really no way to sprint quietly.

The noise made Perry's heart lurch up into his throat.

Stuber disappeared into the inky blackness on the other side.

Was Perry supposed to follow immediately? Or was there some sort of signal? Because they hadn't covered that.

The pale flash of Stuber's arm, waving them on.

"Ready?" Perry whispered to Teran.

She nodded.

They hobbled across the street.

Two people in a three-legged race where you were dismembered if you lost.

They were halfway across, when the alley ahead of them blazed.

Stuber's shape became a silhouette.

An angel from hell appeared to have erupted from the ground in the middle of that alleyway. Its armor seemed to burn, a shimmering *sagum* swirling around it that was somehow both black and bright, and two red eyes showing out from the face of the helmet, its horse-hair crest high and aggressive like the raised hackles on a wolf.

A deep, devilish voice: "Heretics! Kneel!"

Perry and Teran skidded to a halt.

All of this occurred at once. Perry registered this terrible sight, even as the being in the alley ordered them to kneel.

Stuber, however, did not kneel.

He danced.

He slipped left, as nimble as a featherweight boxer.

He used his own rifle to parry the muzzle of the other that was pointed at his chest, knocking it off to the side so it struck the building to the right. A burst of reactive fire spat out of it, tearing the wall to shreds.

Stuber didn't stop there.

He drove into the demon, fearless where mortals would have cowered at the mere sight. He smashed a hand up beneath the helmet. The devil-voice grunted, and Perry realized it was a synthesized voice, designed to invoke terror.

Stuber's hand ripped up, yanked that helmet off.

The devil-voice turned into the normal voice of a man.

A man crying out, because he was getting more than he expected.

Stuber had put the devil on its heels.

Stuber leaned his body out and hooked the man behind his neck, which forced his already-off-balance opponent to bend backwards. Stuber made a violent whip motion with his body.

There was an audible crack.

The body went to mush in Stuber's arms.

As he fell, paralyzed by a broken neck, Stuber speared him to the ground by putting his own muzzle into the man's mouth. When the body hit the ground, Stuber gave him a single round and scattered his head across the dirt.

The armor went dark.

Stuber righted himself. Spun and looked at Perry.

"Get out of the fucking street!"

Perry and Teran tumbled into the alleyway, all wide eyes and open mouths.

"Holy shit," Perry said.

"Young buck," Stuber growled. "I've forgotten more than this turd has learned." He bent, grabbed the dead legionnaire's rifle, and shoved it into Perry's arms. "But...we've got a bit of a problem."

"Yeah, no shit," Perry snapped, pressing the pontiff's pistol into Teran's hand.

Stuber took Perry by the back of the neck and made him look at the dead body on the ground. "You see red or blue anywhere on him?"

151

"I can't see shit. It's dark."

"There isn't," Stuber said.

And, now that Perry thought about it, in the moment when he'd seen the armor lit up in the alleyway, he recalled the swirling *sagum*—not red or blue, but a shimmering black.

Perry felt the realization hit him like something was caught in his throat.

"Not legionnaires after us," Stuber said. "These are praetors. Which is a tad more serious." He glared at Perry. "There something you not telling me about yourself, Shortstack?"

There was a lot that Perry hadn't told him.

And now wasn't going to be the time when he did.

"We should be going," Perry said.

Stuber stared at him for another half-second, then whirled around. "Come on."

Down the alley.

Perry put his head down and hauled. Teran was no longer interested in the three-legged race, but she still clung to his shirt.

Bricks exploded next to Perry's face.

He yelped, tried to skid to a halt.

The alleyway shimmered in the strobe of muzzle flashes.

At the other end, a dark figure firing at them.

Incoming bullets whined past their heads.

No light this time. No more calls for heretics to kneel.

Now it was death on sight.

Stuber fired back.

The shape at the mouth of the alley took a round and staggered.

Stuber leapt to his right, hit a door with his shoulder, and barged through.

Perry dove in after him, letting out a string of fire from the heavy rifle in his hands. He had no idea where those rounds went. He wasn't watching.

The interior of the house was dark.

A pale spear of light shot through the black.

Stuber's weaponlight blazed like a particle beam in the dusty air.

A man and a woman crouched in the corner on a dirty mattress. Both of them starting to yell and scream.

"Silence, peons!" Stuber roared at them, then raced through the first room and into what appeared to be the kitchen, with another door out. Stuber yanked the kitchen door open and started to lean out.

The doorjam disintegrated.

He jumped back with a shout, looking irritated.

He growled, dropped to a squat, went low around the corner, and rattled off a long string of fire.

When he looked up over his sights, he spat in the direction of whatever he'd been shooting at. "Go in peace, you fuck."

Perry and Teran watched this from the main room where the man and woman still whimpered, holding onto eachother.

The door behind Perry blasted open.

The woman screamed, high-pitched.

Perry swung around, rifle coming to his shoulder.

Teran fired the pistol rapidly at a shape that jumped to the side of the door.

"Out! Out! Out!" Stuber yelled.

A hand flashed through the door. Something sailed through the air, hit the ground and rolled to the foot of the mattress where the man and woman stared at it in terror.

Perry grabbed Teran's arm and rushed for the kitchen. He tripped over his own legs and they both went down in a pile of limbs, just inside the wall of the kitchen.

The main room exploded in a gout of dust.

The man and woman were silenced.

A smoking foot tumbled to the floor in front of Perry.

A dark cloud of dirt and smoke swirled all around them, choking them. A figure loomed up in the gloom, coming from the main door.

Perry and Teran both started firing.

It was a panic of gunshots. No calculation. Just fear demanding that they pull the trigger as fast as possible.

The dark shape grunted, and disappeared.

Teran screamed, but Perry's perforated eardrums could barely hear it. She rolled, her face in Perry's, eyes wide. "Did we get him?" she shouted.

"Don't know," Perry said, his own voice sounding like it was underwater. He hauled himself up and backwards and pulled Teran along with him. "Let's go!"

The two of them tumbled through the kitchen, out the back door, and into another alley.

Stuber loomed in front of them. "You got one?" he asked, incredulous. "Well, good for you, killers. Come on. We're almost there."

Stuber took off at a run this time.

Stealth had gone out the window.

Dogs barked. People shouted.

154

Perry tried to go into The Calm, but the fear was a blockade in his mind.

They rounded another corner.

A praetor lay, moaning and twitching on the ground.

Stuber kicked his helmet off and then stomped him in the face. Perry's hearing had returned just enough to perceive a mushy crack. The back arched, then the body slackened into death.

Stuber crossed the street at a brisk walk, his rifle up, scanning for threats.

They got to the other side. Stuber didn't wait. He hit another alley and ran for the end of it. Perry and Teran struggled to keep up.

As he neared the end, Stuber slowed.

Peeked around the corner.

Turned back to them.

He smiled.

"What is it?" Perry whispered.

"Skiff," Stuber replied. Then he went around the corner.

Perry and Teran followed, and there, right in between two buildings, so close that its gunpods were nearly scraping the front stoops to either side, was a skiff.

It was an open platform. Ship controls at the aft. Gun controls at the fore. Very no-frills. Designed to ferry a squad of praetors from point-A to point-B, and to give them some minimal air support if needed.

But they'd left it sitting unattended.

So confident were they.

They either didn't know that an ex-legionnaire was one of the heretics they hunted, or they didn't put much stock in his abilities. A mistake that both they and Perry had just been corrected on.

155

Stuber clambered on board and made for the gun controls. He pointed behind him to the ship controls. "One of you fly this thing!"

Perry staggered up to the big metal boat. It swayed as Stuber stomped around on it. He glanced at Teran. "You know how to fly one of these things?"

Teran shook her head. "I'm sure I can figure it out, though."

"Go for it."

The deck was about three feet off the ground. Perry climbed aboard on hands and knees, feeling like an idiot, and then reached down and pulled Teran up. She stumbled to the aft and looked relieved when her hands grabbed the controls, steadying her.

Stuber was already harnessed into the gun controls.

A crackle of rifle fire.

Perry saw the muzzle flashes out of the corner of his eye.

Felt the rounds ping off the deck, very close to him.

He ducked, scooted back a few steps, then raised his rifle and let loose. He couldn't even see what he was aiming at. But he was pretty sure that whoever had shot at him had been down the alley that they'd just come from. So he kept firing down there, into the dark.

The skiff lurched. A newbie at the controls.

Perry fell to his knees to keep from flying off.

The skiff spun and Perry thought the centrifugal force might hurl him from the deck, but then it jerked to a stop.

Facing down the alley they'd just taken fire from.

Hovering now at about twenty feet.

Perry stood up and craned his neck.

There.

Down the alley. Two praetors.

Then two missiles streaked out from the skiff, one from each gunpod.

The area where those last two praetors stood turned into a fireball.

Stuber disengaged himself from the gun control harness, and he bowed with his head, and said, "Go in peace to The After." Then he turned and looked at Teran. "Didn't you have a place you wanted to go, Teran?"

Teran's eyes were wide and blank. "I have no clue where we are."

Stuber pointed in the direction they were already facing. "Then let's just go that way until you recognize something."

"I can't recognize anything in the dark."

Stuber gave her a death's-head grin. "Pick a direction, Teran. Or would you rather we take on the whole platoon that's on the way?"

Teran gripped the controls tighter. "Point taken. Everyone hold on."

CHAPTER 14

✿

PULLING WEIGHT

"You recognize anything?" Stuber asked.

Teran took her time in reply. She looked out, squinting against the strong morning sun that was already beginning to heat up the day.

The skiff had run out of power just before dawn. Stuber had been driving at that time, in order to give Teran a chance to rest.

With the battery alarm screeching, Stuber had landed the skiff in a dense copse of brush about midway up a ridge. He'd cut the power and then they'd been surrounded by the shocking silence of a wide open space.

Teran had looked about, still half asleep, and announced, "I don't recognize any of this. Where the hell are we?"

Stuber shrugged. "I don't know."

He walked over to a compartment on the side of the control module and opened it. He pulled out a medical satchel, which he slung over his shoulder. Then four, tan water bags, each containing a gallon. They had a slit for a carrying handle, and he threaded the strap of the medical satchel through these in order to carry them without his hands.

Four gallons at roughly eight pounds apiece.

"Let me carry some of those," Perry said, pointing at them.

Stuber shook his head. "You need to help Teran so I can keep my gun up."

Stuber had pirated the small amount of remaining ammunition from the weapons that Teran and Perry had swiped in Oksidado. Just pieces of dead weight now, they left the empty weapons in the skiff.

Stuber looked up to the top of the ridge above them. "We're heading up there to get a look around."

By the time they reached the top, nearly an hour had passed and the sun was yellow and blinding.

Now they lay amid the scrub brush that was just high enough to hide them. Teran looked around to see if she could recognize something.

"There," she said, stretching a hand out and pointing into the east, just below the sunrise. "That little double ridge."

"You're familiar with it?" Stuber asked.

"Maybe."

"Where are we going anyway?" Perry asked.

"My clan."

"You have a clan?"

"Yes."

"I thought you said you were from Junction City."

"I lied."

Perry looked from Teran to Stuber. The ex-legionnaire was nodding along as though he already knew all of this. No big deal. Not a revelation. When he saw that Perry was looking at him, he shrugged.

"I would've lied too," Stuber said. "Outsiders are forbidden."

"You're an Outsider?" he gaped at Teran.

She quirked an eyebrow at him. "Technically, at this point, so are you."

Perry opened his mouth, then shut it with an audible snap.

He was, wasn't he?

Back to Stuber. "And you knew about all this?"

"Oh, yeah."

"This doesn't make any sense." He rubbed his face with a dirty hand.

"You'll see," Teran said.

"I'll see? What's that supposed to mean?"

"It means you'll see." Teran struggled to her feet. "When we get there."

"Why not just explain it to me now?"

"Because you'll argue with me."

"So?"

"So I don't have the energy for that right now," she growled. Took a breath. Brushed her hair out of her face. "Just wait. Then you can see it with your own eyes and I won't have to expend all the effort to convince you."

Perry and Stuber were both on their feet now too.

"Alright. Fine." Perry cast a hand out into the wilderness. "Lead the way then."

They began by walking along the ridge. At first it headed north, but then it curved to the east, making a long, crescent shape towards the double peaks that Teran had pointed out. They walked in silence, and Perry brooded.

Teran made it about fifteen minutes, and then stumbled to a stop. "Hey, I think I'm gonna pass out again." She bent over to put her hands on her knees. Her face looked sweaty. Perry saw her eyelids flutter and her body start to rock forward.

He managed to grab her before she face-planted into the ground. He laid her down as gently as he could, but he was off-balance himself and

161

nearly fell on top of her. She mumbled a few incoherencies and then was out cold.

"You were supposed to be helping her," Stuber pointed out.

"I did help her!" Perry felt defensive. "I helped her not hit her face. She didn't want me to help carry her. She said she could do it by herself. This isn't my fault."

Stuber held up both hands. "Slow your roll, Shortstack. I'm not comin' down on you. Just...you know...observing."

"Well..." Perry pointed away. "Observe *that* way."

Stuber ignored him and bent down over Teran, putting a few fingers to her forehead. "She feels hot."

"You think she's got a fever?"

"She could have an infection."

"Well, give her something then."

Stuber squatted down, his elbows on his knees, the Roq-11 cradled in his arms. He squinted at Perry. "Could you stop doing that?"

"What?"

"The thing where you don't know what to do so you get mad at me. It's highly counterproductive. And frankly, kind of bitchy."

"Counter..." Perry trailed off, making a snorting sound. He looked away, too mad to speak anything coherent for a moment.

Stuber shifted so one knee was on the ground. "You seem to have a problem with me."

"I don't have a..." Again, Perry trailed off. There were a lot of things he wanted to say, but his level of anger had removed any filtering from his brain, so it all hit him at once, and he knew if he let it out he'd end up sounding like an idiot.

"No," Stuber insisted. "You seem to have a very big problem with me."

Out of all the things he *wanted* to spew out at that moment, Perry selected something that put him on the high ground. He thrust his hands out to Teran, still lying on the ground.

"Can we focus on the real issue right now? Like our friend who's dying?"

Stuber held Perry's gaze for a moment, and that old, incongruous sadness flashed over him again, but then he looked down at Teran and he focused himself and the look was gone. "Well, I don't think she's dying. Not *right now* anyways." He slung the medical pack around and opened it up. "But, if we don't give her something she might."

He selected a small rack of ampoules, all attached together by a plastic link. He read the label on the ampoule, and appeared satisfied. "This should clean her out pretty good. If it is an infection."

"Any bad effect if it's *not* an infection?"

"Uh...liver failure I think. Something like that."

"What? Liver failure *you think*?"

"You're doing it again."

Perry closed his eyes. Pinched the bridge of his nose. "Stuber. I do not want her to die of liver failure."

"Would you rather she died of an infection?"

"I'd rather her not die of anything."

"Well, that's just not how these things work. You have to play the odds. Unless..." Stuber perked up and looked around them, searched along the ridge, back in the direction they came, and then in the direction they were heading in. He sold it so convincingly that Perry started to look with him and almost asked what they were looking for. "Is there a Surgeon around here?"

Perry rolled his eyes. "Okay."

"No seriously. I could've sworn we passed one a mile back or so."

"Alright."

"If we can just backtrack to that Surgeon that someone left out here in the wilderness, then maybe we can diagnose exactly what's wrong with her."

"Alright!" Perry shouted.

They were silent for a moment.

Stuber put the remaining rack of ampoules back in the medical pack, then uncapped the one in his hand, revealing the needle end. "Unfortunately this is the situation we are in. We have to play the odds. Far more people have died of sepsis after gunshot wounds and surgery than they have of liver failure from taking this shit."

And with that, Stuber lifted Teran's shirt to expose her belly, pinched a fingerful of flesh just next to the healing wound, and stuck the needle in.

Perry crouched there watching it and he felt sick to his stomach thinking about Teran dying of liver failure. Then he shook his head and looked away, and he chided himself.

You don't know her. Harden the fuck up, boy.
Right.
Yes.
That's what he'd always done.
That was best.
He didn't need anybody, and nobody needed him.

But that had begun to feel like a lie.

Stuber dug out a handful of the loose, sandy dirt that they stood on, dropped the spent ampoule inside, and buried it. So that anyone on their trail wouldn't find it, Perry assumed.

Then Stuber stood up and started hoisting off the medical pack with the water bags attached to it. "Here. You can take this, and I'll take her."

"No." Perry waved him off. "I'll carry her."

"We've got another ten to fifteen miles to go, Shortstack—"

"I got it," Perry said, and he grabbed Teran by the arm and the leg and hoisted her up onto his shoulders, then straightened up into a standing position. She was light. Still wouldn't be pleasant to haul her fifteen miles over rough terrain, but Perry wasn't just going to let Stuber do all the hauling because little Shortstack Perry couldn't pull his weight.

"I'll carry her," Perry repeated.

Stuber smacked his lips, sighed, and situated the medical strap back onto his shoulders. "You and the chip on your shoulder. Gods in the skies. Okay then," he said, turning back around. "Let me know if you need to rest."

They walked for maybe two miles.

Perry's shoulders burned. His legs shook. Every slight incline following the ridge seemed like a mountain itself. Every slight downslope made his knees wobble. He had stitches in his sides.

"Let me carry her for a while," Stuber said.

"No."

They kept going.

Four miles perhaps.

Perry was at crawl. He had to stop often and lean against whatever there was to lean against.

Sometimes a small, scraggly pine. Sometimes a boulder. His willpower was waning. Stuber would march on up ahead, realize that he'd lost Perry, then stop and look back, and wait for him to catch up.

A trembling ball of lactic acid, Perry reached Stuber, trying not to gasp too much. He kept going. Ha. That would show him that Perry was indomitable. It wasn't just big men that could carry shit. Perry didn't need any damned help.

"Let me carry her."

"No."

Mile five.

It'd been about two hours.

Perry couldn't go on. He stopped. Stood there. Shaking.

"What's wrong?" Stuber asked. He was just now beginning to breathe heavily.

Perry had to speak through clenched teeth. "I gotta stop."

"Okay," Stuber nodded. "Put her down."

"I can't."

"You can't?"

"If I try to bend down I'm gonna drop her."

"Oh, I got it."

In a wash of humiliation, Perry allowed Stuber to help him guide Teran to the ground. About halfway down, Perry's legs gave out and he let himself fall back onto the rocky ground. Stones jabbed him in the back. He'd never been so relieved to be off his feet.

Stuber took the full brunt of Teran's weight without batting an eye and laid her down. "Probably about time for another dose anyways. Let's rest up a spell."

Perry heaved air. He lifted a weak arm and gave a thumbs up. That was all he could manage.

Stuber gave Teran another dose. Felt her forehead. Looked mildly concerned. He knelt and sat back on his heels. He regarded Perry for a long time, while Perry regained his wind.

"We'll stop here for the night."

"What?" Perry raised his head off the ground. A muscle in his neck cramped. He had to twist to relieve it. "It's not even noon!"

"You're spent."

"I'm not spent."

"Okay. *I'm* spent. Need to rest."

"Dammit…" Perry hauled himself into a sitting position. Now his abs cramped. He had to arch his back, glaring at the ex-legionnaire who sat in front of him in that almost meditative pose. "Don't be an ass. We have plenty of day light."

"I'm not being the ass here," Stuber replied.

"Hey." Perry jabbed his chest with his thumb. "I carried my weight."

"Sure. And exhausted yourself. And now we're not gonna make half the distance that we could have made."

"I can walk."

"Yeah. But you're so fucked right now you'll turn an ankle. Then I gotta carry both of you. That ain't happening."

"Stuber!"

"We'll rest here." Stuber pulled one of the water bags from the strap of the medical satchel and shoved this into Perry's hands. "Hydrate yourself, you pcon. And next time fucking listen to me."

Perry drank what he could stomach. Sullen and silent.

Stuber dropped the water and the medical pack. He was still only wearing his armor and his pants. Where the spaulders touched his bare shoulders, the skin looked red and chafed, as did his neck, where the strap of the medical pack had been.

He stretched his back, shouldered his Roq-11, and nodded up to a tall outcrop of boulders. "Gonna go have a look-see."

He headed up the hill, lithe and able as a mountain goat.

Perry watched him go, sipping water.

He abruptly decided that he was not going to sit on his ass any more. Sitting on his ass, admitting that he'd exhausted himself—that was what Stuber *expected* to see. Because Perry was a "peon."

"No," Perry mumbled to himself. "I'm not that easy."

He stood up. Threaded the half-empty water bag back onto the medical pack. Then he shouldered the whole ensemble, which weighed somewhere around thirty pounds. After carrying Teran for five miles, his back and shoulders immediately began to protest.

But his legs weren't shaking anymore. That was good.

When Stuber came back down the mountain, he found Perry standing, loaded, ready to go. Perry nodded to Teran. "I took her about halfway. You take her the other half. Let's not waste daylight."

"You—"

"I got plenty of rest."

"I—"

"What? Are you more tired than me?"

Stuber pursed his lips. Scratched at his whiskers, making a coarse, rasping sound. Then he shrugged. He walked over to Teran and scooped her up. He carried her over both shoulders, just like Perry had. Then he set out at a brisk pace.

"Keep up," he said over his shoulder.

"You sonofabitch," Perry mumbled, jogging to catch back up.

With the lighter weight, Perry caught his second wind about a mile in. He pushed past Stuber, who was huffing by that time, and Stuber didn't retake the lead.

That gave Perry an extra boost of energy.

By the time that they reached the double peaks, Perry had not stopped once. He was in a march. A groove. One foot in front of the other. Not thinking about it anymore. When he looked up and saw the peaks above him, he stopped and turned around and realized that Stuber was a few hundred yards behind him.

Perry took a seat on a rock and enjoyed the following few minutes as he waited for Stuber to catch up. He felt like he was glowing. He'd never felt so vindicated in his life. If someone were to paint his picture at that moment, his head would be surrounded by a beatific, heavenly radiance.

Stuber arrived, puffing hard. Breathless. Beneath his short-cropped hair, his scalp was flushed and glistening with perspiration.

"We should stop here for the night," Perry said, casually. "Don't want you twisting an ankle."

Stuber appeared to be too tired to give him much of a joust. The corner of his open mouth twitched up and he nodded as though to admit that he'd been had.

"You got a set of wheels on you, peon. Good work."

"Keep up next time," Perry replied.

They found a small flat area under the overhang of one of the peaks. Since they didn't know where they were supposed to be going once they reached these peaks, they figured they would have to get comfortable and wait for Teran to wake up.

They built a fire for Teran's benefit, as she was more at risk of exposure during the cold desert nights, since her system was already compromised. They kept the fire low—they needed the heat, not the light, and a fire on a hillside can be seen for a long, long ways.

But Perry was grateful for that small comfort.

The medical pack from the skiff contained two emergency ration bars.

They tasted exactly like what they were: starch, fat, and amino acids.

Still. It was better than millet porridge in a jail cell.

Teran lay on her back, closest to the overhanging rock, where the stone would reflect some of the heat of the fire back to her. She mumbled a few times in her sleep, but otherwise remained still and quiet.

It worried Perry.

He didn't want to worry, but he found himself doing it anyways.

Perry sat beside her, looking into the flames, his muscles sore but glad to be resting.

Stuber sat, leaning forward on his upended rifle. Like an ancient soldier might lean on his spear. He kept his back to the fire. Eyes out, watching the darkness.

Perry's own eyes grew heavy.

The last bit of cobalt disappeared from the western sky.

Just the darkness and the fire, and the three humans around it.

The fire bathed his face and chest in warmth.

Perry thought he could use a rock for a pillow, and be the most comfortable he'd ever been. He looked at Stuber's broad back. "How long have you been awake?"

Stuber stirred. "Two days, I believe. I'll need to sleep tonight."

"We'll take it in shifts."

"I can stay awake for a while longer." Stuber's voice seemed quiet and distracted.

"Okay," Perry said, and lowered himself to the ground. His head was close to Teran's. "Wake me when it's my turn."

He curled an arm under his head as a pillow.

He lay there, staring at the flames, letting his eyes droop.

"It wasn't because I was bored," Stuber spoke into the darkness.

Perry's lips twitched. He sighed.

Couldn't the big lug see he was trying to sleep?

"What are you talking about?" Perry mumbled.

"I told you that I'd gone with Teran to get you out of jail because I was bored. But that wasn't why."

Perry frowned. More awake now. "Then why'd you help her?"

Stuber waited a minute. Sniffed. Adjusted his shoulders.

"The guy with the knife," he said. "In the bar. He had the drop on me." Stuber's head turned. The firelight was orange on the side of his face, but Perry still couldn't see his eyes. "You had my back in that bar. Figured I should have yours."

Perry watched the other man for a moment.

Regardless of Perry's reasons for hating legionnaires, Stuber had stuck his neck out to save Perry. He'd put his life on the line. Multiple times. And now they were on the run from praetors. And Stuber didn't even know why.

Didn't he deserve to know what he was risking his life for?

Hadn't he earned the right to know the truth about Perry?

"The praetor," Perry began.

Stuber shifted, but still didn't face Perry. "Yes?"

Perry's hands clutched each other. The fingers began to wrestle.

How to explain these things?

"There are…some things about me…that I haven't told you."

"Like how you're a deserter from the Academy at Keniza?"

Perry started. Felt an electric tingle go through his limbs. "How do you know that?" he demanded.

Stuber finally shuffled around and faced Perry. He looked amused. He nodded in the direction of the woman sleeping next to the fire. "I think Teran might know a tad more about you than you think."

Perry shot a look at the unconscious form. "How…?"

Stuber leaned forward. "If you're thinking the praetors are after you because you're a deserter, I can assure you, they're not. Praetors answer to paladins. And I don't see a paladin getting themselves in a tizzy over one deserter."

Perry's mind flashed in a dozen different directions. He'd been sitting there struggling with how to give Stuber some answers, and now was suddenly faced with a new slew of questions.

"How did Teran know that?" he stammered.

"You'll have to ask her when she wakes up."

"Well, what did she tell you about me?"

Stuber gave a small shrug. "That you went to the Academy at Keniza. That you deserted the night before your commission as a legionnaire. And that you'd been on the run for the last three years."

Perry gaped. Stunned into silence by the abject nakedness that he felt.

Who the hell *was* Teran, and how did she know all this about him?

And how dare she expose all that to Stuber!

"If I were to take a guess," Stuber said, casually. "I'd say that her clan of Outsiders has been looking for you for some reason. And I'd also guess that whatever that reason is, it's the same reason why there are praetors after you."

Still in a daze, staring at the flames, Perry couldn't come up with anything.

Stuber's brow furrowed. "Who exactly are you, Perry?"

Perry's eyes flashed up to Stuber's. "I'm nobody, Stuber. I'm just a runt. I'm the son of a dead legatus who couldn't fill his father's shoes."

Stuber's lips pursed. He continued to watch Perry, and it seemed that behind the man's eyes he was making a lot of connections, seeing Perry in a new light.

Perry looked away. He drew his knees up to his chest, and folded his arms over them, like he was trying to cover himself against the exposure that he felt.

"Your father was killed by The Truth." It was half a question. Half a realization.

Perry nodded.

"Well. That explains your exceptional saltiness towards me, a former legionnaire for The Truth."

Perry didn't confirm or deny it. He didn't need to.

Stuber let out a long, heavy breath. "I doubt you had an easy time at Hell's Hollow. Even amongst all the academies on both sides, it's got a reputation for…harshness. Or so I've heard."

Perry was pulled back into dark memories.

His classmates, practically begging him to quit, almost as though they were tired of beating the pulp out of him.

Please, Runt. Just quit. You're a liability. You're going to get us all slaughtered. You're going to be the first one of us to die, and it'll open a hole in our battleline and we'll all be crushed by autocannon fire, because of you, Runt. Please, Runt, do it for your own good, if not for ours!

Perry would fight back. He would *always* fight back.

They'd stop short of killing him—they weren't allowed to kill each other. Although, truth be told, Perry tried sometimes to kill them. But he was always outnumbered. Always outsized.

And when he was left bleeding and bruised on the floor, *Praeceptor Legionarius* Pike would lean over him, looking disappointed, and say, "Fight harder next time, Runt."

Perry remembered all of this, but spoke none of it. Some secrets we try to keep, even from ourselves. Especially the ones that are our deepest sources of shame.

For Perry, he felt shame because, after five years in the Academy, the voices of his classmates had finally gotten into his head. After five years, he believed them. He was certain that he was going to die. And he stopped fighting.

He ran away instead.

Because he was afraid.

Stuber took a breath. It was the sharp inhale that drew Perry back to the present. He looked across the fire at the ex-legionnaire. Stuber looked pained, uncomfortable. And Perry suddenly realized why: Because Stuber was being sincere.

"This war..." he looked skyward. Grimaced at the stars over their heads. "It's like a tax on our wholeness as humans. We all have to pay it. Some pay more than others. But in the end, it takes from us all. Bits and pieces of who we are. In the end, we all lose."

That old sadness washed over Stuber, the corners of his mouth turning down. He looked away from the sky, and if Perry didn't know any better, he might've believed that there was just the slightest shimmer at the bottom of Stuber's eyes. But just as quickly as he thought that the firelight had betrayed it, Stuber blinked, and it was gone.

Stuber looked at Perry. His face stern again. "I don't know how much it's taken from you. And you don't know how much it's taken from me. But I will tell you this: I didn't kill your father. And I was not at Hell's Hollow. I am not your enemy."

Perhaps it was the warmth of the fire. Perhaps just the pure exhaustion. But Perry couldn't hold onto his anger. He'd seen a glimpse of a man under that armor. A man who could never go home. A man who could never be whole again. A man who had lost things, just like everyone else.

And when he thought of that, he felt a hint of regret.

"I don't hate you, Stuber," Perry said.

Stuber seemed to suddenly comprehend how vulnerable he'd let himself become.

Old habits die hard.

He nodded curtly. Cleared his throat. A big, dismissive *harrumph*. "Well. Go to sleep. I'll wake you when it's your watch."

CHAPTER 15

✿

OUTSIDERS

THIS IS HOW PERRY WOKE UP, and this is what he saw when he did.

There was shouting. That was the thing that pulled him from sleep first.

He was upright and his eyes were open before he was fully conscious. He was in that confused, semi-delirious state of a sleep-starved man being yanked from the first tenuous threads of true rest. He wasn't sure where he was, why he was there, who was with him, or what was happening.

It was still dark.

There were people.

A man.

Right in front of Perry.

That man pointed a rifle at something across from Perry.

"Put him down!" the man yelled.

What the fuck is happening?

Perry turned to his left and saw that Teran was awake. She sat up, and her hands were held out in front of her, her face a mask of fear and urgency.

"Easy! Easy! Easy!" she shouted.

Stuber had a stranger by the neck and he was using him as a human shield, his Roq-11 held to the back of the man's head. The man looked terrified. Stuber looked pissed.

"You wanna wear your buddy's brains," Stuber ground out. "Then keep pointing that thing at me."

"Everybody calm down!" Teran shouted. *"Lutzen la verdeit! Lutzen la verdeit!"*

Perry stared at her. He knew she was an Outsider, and that Outsiders used Pallesprek, but it still surprised him to hear her speak it. He didn't understand a word of it, but whatever she'd said, it had a powerful effect.

The man pointing the rifle at Stuber tore his eyes off of his target and stared, surprised, at Teran. "What did you say?" he mumbled in shock, his feet shuffling in confusion.

Teran nodded, her hands still upraised. "It's me. It's Teran. Simon's daughter. Do you remember me?"

The man frowned.

The other man, the one with Stuber's rifle pressed to his head, squeaked out a high-pitched question: "Teran? Is that you?"

Then, a third voice appeared, along with a jumble of footsteps: "Whoa, whoa, whoa! Teran! Everybody cool your shit! Teran! Is that you?"

The third man stumbled into the dim light of the dying fire. He held a rifle, but it was pointed at the ground and he was focused on Teran.

"It's me," she said. Then she looked at Stuber. "Stuber, let him go."

"Not until he stops pointing his gun at me."

The third man held up a hand. "Wait a minute! Nobody moves! Why is there a legionnaire with you?"

"He's not a legionnaire," Perry grumbled, drawing a few looks. Defensively, Perry pointed to Stuber. "You see a *sagum* on him? He deserted. Years ago."

"Why's he wearing legionnaire's armor?"

Stuber made a raspberry noise. "I don't know, jackass. Maybe to protect my vital organs from bullets. Who is this fucking guy?"

The third man pointed to Teran. "Teran, are you vouching for this man in the legionnaire's armor?"

"Yes," Teran said without hesitation.

The third man nodded. "That's good enough for me." he looked to the first man and nodded. "Lucky, lower your weapon." Then he turned to Stuber. "Let go of my guy."

Stuber glared. Then he gave his hostage a little shove, and the man yelped, and stumbled, but caught himself before he tripped into the fire.

There was a tense moment when Stuber kept his rifle upraised for a second and Perry thought that the whole damned thing was going to blow up again.

Then Stuber lowered his rifle. He pointed at the man he'd used as a meat shield. "You walk like an elephant, peon." Then to the third man, who appeared to be in control. "He should never be allowed to try to sneak up on someone again."

A fourth stranger emerged from the night, directly behind Stuber. Tall and lean-muscled with a haughty smirk on his face. Perry immediately hated him.

"What about me?" the lean man said softly.

Stuber looked over his shoulder at the man. Then nodded. "Nope. You're pretty quiet."

The lean man looked past Stuber to Meat Shield. "Don't worry, Temps. I had him dead to rights the whole time." Then he slipped around Stuber and looked down at Teran. "Teran. I apologize. I didn't recognize you with your hair. It's grown so long."

Teran smiled up at the lean man.

That made Perry hate him even more.

"Good to see you, Rope," she said. "Still the resident technology expert?"

The lean man smiled. "I keep the lights on." Then he drew his head back. "But do I still look Rope-y to you? I've actually outgrown that name, Teran."

"Pussy Foot?" Stuber suggested from the side.

The Man Formerly Known As Rope turned a challenging glare on Stuber. He grabbed a red scarf that hung around his neck and held it up for Stuber to see. "They call me Sagum now. Because I wear this memento of a legionnaire that I killed."

Stuber leaned forward. Inspected the bit of *sagum* that now served as a man's neckerchief. "Wow. Good job." Stuber leaned back. "I mean, I just single-handedly killed four praetors last night. Didn't bother getting a memento because it's not that big of a deal for me. But, you know. Congrats on that one guy. I think I'm going to call you Smegma instead."

Sagum's haughty look soured.

Teran had pulled herself to her feet. "Hey, if the men are done comparing dick sizes, can we get the hell out of here?" She pointed at Perry. "I think I've found him."

***

I think I've found him.

Found *him*.

That seemed very specific, in a way that Perry didn't care for. As an individual who had been

180

on the run for three years, he didn't like the idea of being "found" by anyone.

But…

Teran was a friend, wasn't she? Maybe a friend that knew too much about him, but a friend nonetheless. She'd sprung him out of jail. And now she was taking him back to her clan of Outsiders. And Outsiders were considered heretics because they refused to fight in the war, so why would they hold it against him if he was a deserter?

The party that had accosted them at night hadn't taken them prisoner, per se, but they kept Stuber and Perry isolated from each other. Teran was up front, speaking in hushed tones with Sagum and navigating the treacherous footing of the brushy slopes by moonlight.

Perry was in the middle of the column. Stuber trudged along a few paces back.

Perry peeked at the Outsider directly behind him.

"Lucky, right?" Perry quizzed him.

The man jerked, as though surprised he'd been spoken to. The expression that he gave to Perry was strange. In fact, the demeanor of all of the Outsiders had become strange since Teran had said "I found him."

"Yes," Lucky mumbled. "That's right."

Perry lowered his voice. "Where the hell are we going?"

"To our clan."

"Right, yeah, I know that." He glanced around, but no one seemed to be paying him any attention. "I mean…why am *I* going there? Why do you guys want me? There's nothing special about me."

Lucky shook his head with the vehemence of a man denying the devil's temptation. "Can't tell you about it."

"Well, who *is* going to tell me about it, Lucky?"

"You'll have to talk to Sabio."

"Who the hell is Sabio?"

Lucky looked guarded. Didn't respond to that.

Perry took another tack. "You speak Pallesprek?"

Lucky nodded.

"The thing that Teran said…"

"*Lutzen la verdeit.*"

"Right. What's that mean?"

Lucky looked at him with import. "It means 'illuminate the truth.'"

Teran looked around at them, and Lucky clamped his mouth shut.

"Ssh," he hissed, like Perry was getting him in trouble.

Perry couldn't be sure in the moonlight, but he thought Teran's eyes lingered on him for a moment before she turned back around. She said something to Sagum, who then looked over his shoulder at Perry for a brief second, then said something back to Teran.

Teran snickered.

Perry glared at the back of Sagum's head.

Yes, it was true.

Perry hated Sagum.

***

Dawn had started creeping into the sky when they reached their destination.

In the crook between two cliffs, the party rounded a bend and came to the mouth of a cave that sat a few yards up from a dry riverbed.

The two cliffs were the entrance to a box canyon. On the walls of the canyon Perry saw not just the single cave opening that he'd noticed when they'd rounded the bend, but a network of them. A warren of caves, where ancient waters had found weak points in the rock and carved them out over centuries, leaving a place where, eons in the future, the outcasts of a society would hide.

Perry saw the glimmer of firelight coming from one of the cave mouths that was a little higher up, and the figure of a man with his back to the fire, watching the entrance to the canyon.

In the lead of their little procession, Sagum raised a hand and made a call that sounded so much like a desert bird that Perry had to blink and squint at him to confirm that the sound had indeed come from his lips.

The figure in the mouth of the upper cave appeared to return the sound, and then stood up, and disappeared into the cave.

Their procession had stopped there at the mouth of the canyon, and they went no further.

Teran turned and looked at Stuber. "Good behavior, please."

Stuber reared his head back and rested his hands on his Roq-11. "I'm a model gentleman. Tell that to your savage friends."

A few heads turned to look at him. Perhaps some miffed feelings.

Teran smirked and turned back around.

Perry wanted to be up there with her. He wanted to be in the know. He wanted her to at least *say something* to him, but she'd just looked right over the top of his head and addressed Stuber.

Gods in the skies, Perry hated being small.

The padding of footsteps across the rocks.

A man—probably the one that had been on watch—turned the corner and went directly to Sagum. The two men embraced with great aplomb and Perry sneered at them, resenting their fraternity while he stewed in the back.

"You show your emotions on your face too easily," a voice rumbled next to him.

Perry jumped and looked to his left.

Stuber had crept up to his side and was looking down at Perry.

"I don't…" Perry trailed off. He'd been about to deny it out of reflex, but if Stuber had remarked on it, then perhaps it *was* obvious.

"You should work on that," Stuber suggested.

Up front, the newcomer had finished his embrace of Sagum and turned his smiling face to Teran. "Teran," he said warmly. "You've been gone a very long time."

"Yes, I have, Dino. It's taken me a long time to find him."

Dino stiffened when she said this. His smile faltered, overtaken by surprise. "You…?"

Teran nodded. Then gestured back at Perry. "I believe so. Only Sabio will be able to say for sure."

Dino stared at Perry for a long time. Then collected himself. "Strange. I knew he was supposed to be short, but…"

Sonofabitch…

Dino approached, with Sagum tailing. Teran remained where she was.

Sagum seemed dubious of Perry. Dino, on the other hand, despite his comment about Perry's height, acted like he was in the presence of a demigod.

"You are Percival?" Dino asked him.

Perry frowned. He'd never heard the name Percival in his life. But he couldn't help seeing the similarity between 'Percival' and 'Perry.'

Stuber snorted. "Percival."

Perry shot him a look. "Franklin."

Stuber shrugged. "I'll stick with Shortstack then."

Perry whipped back around and fixed his eyes on the woman who'd brought them here. "Teran, do you mind telling me what's going on?"

Teran only replied, "You need to speak to Sabio."

"Fine." Perry threw up his hands. "Fine, I'll speak to Sabio."

He agreed, and then regretted it. And then realized that it didn't matter whether he agreed to it or not. He got the sense that they were going to make him regardless.

Dino nodded, oddly formal. Almost ceremonial. "Follow me, then."

Sagum gave Perry one last cynical look, and then stepped out of Perry's way as he began to follow Dino.

Teran fell into step with Perry. She held her stomach and breathed hard, but kept pace.

The group walked around the entrance to the box canyon, and towards a small cave opening that was level with the ground. Now a few other people were visible, standing from different cave mouths at different levels in the warrens. They watched the procession with fixed stares.

Perry leaned into Teran, keeping his voice low. "You got the wrong guy."

Teran glanced at him. "What?"

"You got the wrong guy, Teran. I hate to break it to you, but I'm not Percival. I've never gone by that name. I don't even know anybody by that name."

Teran had adopted that stubborn, grim look of hers. "We shall see."

They walked into the entrance of the cave. At first it seemed darker than outside, but as they got a few paces into the cave, Perry started to see lantern light. Both torches, and electric lights. It got brighter the deeper they went.

The air was cool. It smelled of people. The scent grew mustier as they went. Not the funk of fresh sweat and body odor, but the more palpable thickness of a place that has been lived in for a long time.

They passed more Outsiders. They lurked around corners, watching the strangers closely. Several times, they grumbled under their breaths when Stuber came into view. Once, a child yelped and began crying. Perry smiled at that.

The passageway began to climb.

Beside him, Teran huffed.

"You okay?" he asked her.

"Yeah," she grunted back. "I'll be fine."

He reached out to take her by the arm, but she shook his hand off.

"I'll be fine," she repeated.

At the top, the passageway opened into a massive cavity in the rock. The ceiling vaulted over their heads, and there were several levels below their feet, crude stairways chiseled into the ruddy orange rock.

There were a few people in this area, and Dino turned to one of them as he descended the stairs towards a central area. "Where is Sabio?" he asked.

The person—a boy, busying himself with stacking firewood near an oven carved in the rock—gestured towards one of several passageways that led away from this main chamber. "Praying, as usual," the boy said.

Dino nodded and continued on.

Perry followed, feeling the adrenaline of his own curiosity subsiding and giving way to the first sense of misgivings. He wanted to know why this mysterious Sabio was looking for him...but he feared he wasn't going to like the answer.

They crossed the main chamber and Dino stopped at a narrow opening. He turned to face the group, and gave them a glance that said, *you are not needed anymore*. Then he gestured to Perry.

"Just you," Dino said.

Perry hesitated. He looked at Teran. Then at Stuber.

Teran nodded.

Stuber's eyes were shrouded by suspicious brows, his lips pursed and tight. But he didn't say anything.

Perry faced Dino, and proceeded forward.

Dino allowed him to enter first.

The room on the other side was small.

It smelled intimate and smoky.

Like tallow candles and sweat.

The room contained only three things: A straw mat for a bed; a shrine cut into the wall, at which a collection of candles lit the room; and an old man, hunched on his knees before that shrine. The old man's head was bowed in prayer. In the shrine, surrounding the flickering candles, were statuettes of the Nine Sons and the Three Givers.

The small, boyish figurine representing Chak the Youngest was set forward, in front of the others. The god of wayward youths. It was to Chak that the old man appeared to be praying.

"Sabio," Dino said softly.

The man's voice was phlegmy as though he'd just woken up. A bit crotchety. "I believe I've asked not to be disturbed during my morning prayers."

"Yes, but…" Dino leaned over the man's shoulder and whispered: "Teran has returned. And she thinks she's found him."

The old man sat upright with a single, springy movement.

He spun, the robe that was draped over his shoulders swishing across the dirty floor.

Perry felt his fingers and toes go numb. Felt the breath catch in his chest. He had two words to say, but he choked on them.

"Perry," the man uttered, with all the hush of a prophet's fulfillment.

Perry's mouth worked several times, and finally his clamped throat opened. He managed to speak the two words: "Uncle Sergio."

CHAPTER 16

☼

UNCLE SERGIO

PERRY STOOD, staring at a ghost from his past.

While Perry stared at Uncle Sergio he saw no change at all, except that the man looked bedraggled. His beard was longer and less kempt than it had been. His hair was whiter. His clothing worse for wear.

But it was Uncle Sergio.

On the other hand, Uncle Sergio seemed barely to recognize Perry. There was an expression of shock across his eyes and mouth. Perry supposed he had changed a lot in the last three years. The stamp of time and cruelty is always more evident in the young.

"They call you Sabio," Perry said, unsure how else to start.

Sergio's jaw worked. "Yes. They do. It means 'wise'. They adorned me with it. It was not my choice. But…" his eyes grew strained. "But you. You're so much larger than I last saw you. You've turned into a man."

Perry had to look away. "Still a runt, uncle."

"Stature is not always about size." Uncle Sergio reached his hand up as though to touch Perry's face, then faltered and fell away. "There is so much to say, I don't know where to begin. I had a plan for how to start but now that I'm standing in front of you, it's fled my mind."

"Why don't you start with how long you've been looking for me?" Perry shifted his feet, glanced over at Dino, who was still in the room, looking enthralled as though Perry and his uncle were actors on a stage in some great and consuming drama. "And why? Why didn't you just let me go?"

Sergio nodded, his mouth opening and closing with unsaid words. Then, with a sudden resolution, he turned to Dino. "Thank you Dino. You may go. This is something that must be handled between us."

Dino looked stricken, but he nodded respectfully, and left the room.

Perry swallowed hard around a knot of apprehension. He did not like the way his uncle was approaching this. It had all the bad omen of a dangerous subject. A life-altering subject.

When other people needed to leave the room, and you lost track of how you were going to broach the subject because the person in question is finally standing in front of you—that usually means the person standing in front of you isn't going to like what you have to say.

Perry was getting antsy. "And why're you here?" he gestured about, but he lowered his voice. "With Outsiders? With heretics?"

Sergio chuffed. "And you're so innocent?"

Perry looked away. "I just meant that it's dangerous. But you're right. I'm a deserter. Which is the same as a heretic. And now I'm an Outsider too, I guess. They're all the same damn thing."

"I had no choice but to leave Keniza when you deserted." Sergio winced and held up a hand. "I am not blaming you for that. I'm simply...dammit, this is very hard."

"Just say the truth."

"Yes." Sergio's voice was hollow. "The truth."

He nodded again. Then he lowered himself to the floor, folding his legs under him. He sat with his back to the candles, and they glittered over his shoulders. He motioned to the ground in front of him.

Perry did not like sitting on the ground. It made him feel like a child. But Sergio was seated the same way, so he supposed that made them equals at the moment.

Sergio's nostril's flared as he took a deep breath in through them. He held it. His eyes became stern and resolute again. Calm. Determined. "These people call me Sabio, though that has never been my name. You know me as Sergio, and that is the name I was born with...but for a very long time in my life, I was called Sirvien."

Perry frowned. There must be something more than that...

His uncle, a patient man, waited for the dots to connect in Perry's head, and after a moment, they did.

"Sirvien," Perry said, as though testing the flavor of it. "That's a taken name." One connection foretold another, even less pleasant one. Perry's eyes narrowed. "You were in a legion?"

Sergio shook his head. "No. But I worked for a legatus. I was his manservant."

Sergio hesitated.

Perry waited.

"It was your father," Sergio finally said. "He was the legatus that I served." Sergio drew himself up, then hung his head. "I'm still getting my thoughts twisted up."

Perry put his hands together. Clenched them. "Why would you hide that from me?"

Sergio reached out and grabbed Perry's hands. "Be still," he breathed. After a moment, he removed his hand from Perry's, and folded it in his lap. "There are many things that you do not know. I am trying to be gentle, but each revelation has its own barbs. Each truth that I've hidden from you will require its own time for you to swallow."

Perry matched his uncle's resolute expression. "What I want is an explanation. Why did you send Teran to find me? What could be so godsdamned important that she would risk breaking me out of jail? And why in the hell are praetors coming after me?"

"It's complicated," Sergio said, seeming bitter…more with himself than with Perry.

"Why am I here, Uncle Sergio? And why are they coming after me?"

Sergio closed his eyes as though he needed to meditate. And for a moment, Perry thought that was just what he intended to do. Perry was about to spring to his feet, the impatience more than he could bear.

But Sergio spoke, his tone low, his eyes closed. "I hid my name from you because I was ordered to do so. I took you to Keniza because I was ordered to do so. I compelled you to attend the Academy because I was ordered to do so."

"By my father."

Sergio opened his eyes. Calm now. "No. By the man who killed your father."

"He died in battle," Perry heard himself say, as though from a different room.

Sergio shook his head before Perry could even finish. He spoke in that same, almost trance-like voice—the voice of a person who has decided to back-float on the treacherous waters of a conversation, rather than expend the effort to swim against the tide. "No, Perry. That is the story I have told you. That is the fiction that I built to shield you from your own past. The truth is far more complex. And far more unpleasant."

CHAPTER 17

✡

THE MANSERVANT

THE CHILD SAT ON THE FLOOR, playing with blocks.

Sirvien watched him.

The room was spacious and well appointed. This was the child of a legatus.

Sirvien sat on a square box that was used as a chest for loose toys.

In the other room, the voices of the legatus and his wife could be indistinctly heard.

Sirvien did not eavesdrop. His master, Cato McGown, relied on his complete discretion. And the better part of discretion was knowing when to listen, and when to close the mind's ears.

It was clear to Sirvien that Cato was troubled. And he knew it had something to do with the boy playing with the blocks before him. But other than that, Sirvien was unsure.

Sirvien would not eavesdrop, but there was nothing to stop him from watching the boy, and wondering, and trying to piece together what exactly about this three-year-old Cato found so concerning.

The boy stacked the blocks. His chubby, toddler's fingers were nimble. Where another child might've clumsily toppled the blocks, the boy placed them with careful attention to their balance.

He was also creating a pattern. The blocks were his favorite, and he liked to create patterns with them, which Sirvien thought was delightful and indicative of the boy being so intelligent. The boy laid the blocks like bricks, so that the block of the second layer straddled the line between the two blocks below it—staggered, just as you would expect a brick wall to be.

When the boy stacked blocks, or when he encountered anything that was a challenge to his toddler brain, rather than become noisy and angry, it seemed that the boy went quiet. He went somewhere in his head, almost a trance, and he sank into the challenging thing until he succeeded at it.

When he was in this state, it was like the rest of the world was lost to him. It was difficult to get the boy's attention when he was like that. For a while they feared that he was deaf, but they'd discovered that wasn't the case.

He was just…someplace else.

One of the more disconcerting aspects of this trait was that the boy spoke very little. His vocabulary was small, and rather than getting frustrated with his inability to communicate, he simply seemed to prefer to *not* communicate.

The boy was also very small, which seemed an unfortunate fluke of genetics, given that both of his parents were of normal height.

And, of course, there was the fearlessness.

Most toddlers get frightened by everything.

Sirvien didn't believe he'd ever seen the boy cry out, or become upset because of fear.

And if you didn't know any better, given all of these negative aspects—the lack of speaking, the trancelike behavior, the small stature—you might begin to think that Percival had been born *subnormal*.

Sirvien had begun to fear that perhaps Cato thought that of his son.

Sirvien had no children of his own, but that did not mean he had no experience with children. He had a peon brother with a brood of his own in an outlying town not far from the installation where Legatus Cato lived.

What Sirvien had learned was that every child developed differently.

So Sirvien looked at the boy and figured that he was a bright young boy that enjoyed keeping his own company. Sirvien considered this a rare sign of self-possession, and he wanted to extend to Cato that same gentle wisdom, but he feared that he was not getting the entire picture about what was bothering Cato, and he chose to remain silent until the circumstances were clearer.

Family issues always eventually clarified.

"Percival," Sirvien called.

The boy ignored him.

Sirvien smiled wryly. Then he clapped his hands and raised his voice: "Percival."

The boy looked up at Sirvien. His gaze was steady. Calm. He held eye-contact—which was good. By Sirvien's way of thinking, that meant he was a confident boy.

Sirvien grinned at Percival.

Percival only stared back. His eyes coursed over Sirvien's grinning face, like he saw something else. The shadow of a frown went across the boy's features.

Not surprising. The boy was very serious.

Aloof, even.

That was best, though. A good trait for a general's son, Sirvien felt.

"Percy," he said. "How old are you?"

The boy continued watching his guardian for a moment. Not appearing inclined to answer.

"How old are you?" Sirvien insisted.

The boy looked down at his hands. Then back up at Sirvien. Then he brought his hand up and displayed three fingers.

"That's right!" Sirvien proclaimed, smiling even broader now, though he noted that the child had chosen not to use words, but rather a gesture, which was typical.

Being correct caused the corners of Percy's mouth to twitch upward—almost a smile, and a twinkle in his eye to boot—but then he turned back to his blocks, as though to say that he was glad the conversation had reached a satisfactory conclusion, but would like to return to his previous activities and not be interrupted again.

Sirvien chuckled to himself.

Yes. He was simply a fearless and self-possessed boy.

Within an hour, Sirvien would have reason to believe that things were more serious than that.

***

The conversation that had been murmured in the other room was concluded, or had dropped to a level that Sirvien could not hear. Which he found troubling. Because no one had emerged from the room, and Legatus Cato and his wife, Fiela, were busy people. It was not like them to be in their quarters when time was still left in the day.

It was, however, growing close to evening time.

Sirvien was getting concerned because of his duties, and the evening meal would need to be planned and executed. Taddly, the mistress of the house, would already be preparing.

Sirvien knew Percival would remain absorbed with his blocks, and so he left him in his room and bustled over to the kitchen. The clanging of pots and pans and the rapid-fire *tap-tap-tap* of a knife on a cutting board greeted him.

Taddly glanced up from mincing an onion as he walked in. "Ey, ya talked tada mastah yet?"

A frown flashed across Sirvien's brow.

Taddly was possessed of an incredible ability to harbor two very different people in one stocky, buxom body, and she switched between them as fluidly as a professional interpreter switched languages. When she was in the presence of Cato or Fiela, she was saccharine and buttery-tongued. But if there was a wall between her and them, her mouth was loose, heavily accented, and often foul.

"No, I haven't." He looked around the kitchen. Taddly was in command of the cutting board, but her girl—Sirvien struggled to remember this one's name—simmered something on the stovetop.

House-help had large ears.

Sirvien stepped around the kitchen island to Taddly's side, watching her dice the onion with frightening precision. He lowered his voice. "I'm not sure what's going on with them. Have you..." He hated to be a rumor-monger, but this factored into his job. "Have you seen them?"

"Oh, ey yah," Taddly said, without looking up. Her bosoms quivered with the quick movements of her hands. "Mizz Fiela's none too happy."

"No?" Sirvien found his hands tightening down on each other. "Did you see her?"

"Only in passin'." A glance up at him, true concern behind her nonchalant attitude. "Saw her back as she was goin' to her private. Closed the door 'fore I could see her face, but the way her shoulders was…Well, ya know."

Sirvien did not know. He watched Taddly, awaiting further explanation, and knowing that she was the type of person compelled to fill silences.

Taddly took the quiet for a few beats, then glanced around and stopped chopping the onion. She turned to face him, their heads close together, and their voices even lower.

"Shoulders a'shakin. Stooped. Ya know? Stooped like she'uz carryin a weight on 'em. Like she couldn't stand up straight." Taddly turned back to hacking at the vegetable. "Somethin's askance atween 'em. Believe you me. Somethin' serious."

Sirvien straightened from the conspiratorial huddle.

His hands were still clasped at his waist, and despite the heat and steam of the kitchen, he felt like his fingers were cold. He watched a drip of sweat meander down Taddly's chest and slip into her cleavage, like it was trying to hide.

When the master and the missus were in conflict, the household suffered.

Everyone suffered.

This was not good for anyone.

"Well." Sirvien released his hands from their deadlock. Touched his temple. "I suppose I should speak to Master Cato and see what his wishes are." He cleared his throat, then felt the need to clarify. "For dinner, that is."

The onion had started to make his eyes water.

He turned away.

"Careful in ya inquiries," Taddly remarked. "Matters is sensitive, if you was to ask me."

Yes, well I didn't, Sirvien thought, the concept of taking cues on social graces from Taddly briefly horrifying.

He was quick when he'd exited the kitchen, but as he approached the master suite through the dining room, and then the lounge, his pace slowed. His feet fell softer. The gentle padding of a good servant. Not to be obtrusive.

Speak softly, walk lightly, knock gently.

He listened on the other side of the door for the briefest of moments.

There was a rule when you were a servant: Even if you approached softly, you might be heard. And you wouldn't want to be heard approaching the door and then standing silently outside, snooping.

But then again, you didn't want to knock when Cato and Fiela were in the middle of things, either.

So a brief ear to the door was called for.

Two, maybe three seconds.

And then a gentle knock.

Rap-rap-rap.

A pause of a few more seconds.

From the other side: "Yes. Enter."

He did not like the sound of Cato's voice.

Sirvien pushed the door open, slipped through, let it close behind him.

The master suite was spacious. A bed. A small sitting area. A nook that opened out into a veranda that overlooked the military installation— not the most beautiful of views, but beyond the scrabble of huts and buildings was the desolate beauty of the deserts.

Cato stood in the open door that exited out to the veranda. Straight and erect, as though he were about to take the veranda to issue a speech to troops gathered below, though there were no troops gathered. His back was to the room, his gaze fixed outward, far beyond the installation, and in the distance the sun struck hot, molten gold from a ridge of cold, blue mountains.

Sirvien glanced around for Fiela, but she was not there.

He crossed the room and stopped a few paces behind Cato.

"Sir, how will you be taking your evening meal today?"

Cato didn't seem to react to the question. He remained still, as though the striking sunrise had him transfixed.

Sirvien swallowed. He felt tense and disordered. Like things were out of place. Tension sat in the air like a bank of gunsmoke hugging a valley floor after a battle.

After a few more seconds, Sirvien took another tentative step forward. "Sir."

Cato twitched, like he hadn't realized Sirvien was behind him.

He turned and looked at his manservant. "What?"

"Yes, sir," Sirvien nodded. "I was just asking how you will be taking your evening meal?"

Legatus Cato stared at his manservant for a long stretch, and in that time, Sirvien glanced away. He did not like the look in Cato's eyes. It was far beyond troubled. There was rage simmering there.

He didn't think he'd ever seen anything like that in Cato. The man was usually a hurricane of joviality.

Now, he looked like he could kill just for the sake of killing.

Cato seemed to see what affect his demeanor had on Sirvien. He blinked and looked away. "I'm sorry, Sirvien. I do not think Fiela or I will have much appetite tonight." A breath. "Please apologize to Taddly. I know she's probably already begun preparing."

"No need to apologize, sir. A beverage perhaps?"

"No," Cato replied, looking across to where a tray in the corner of the room bore a decanter filled with whiskey. "I'll serve myself, thank you."

Sirvien bowed at the waist. "Very good, sir. If you should change your mind..."

"Yes, I'll call," Cato said absently.

Sirvien turned to exit the room.

What has happened? His mind reeled through different possibilities, something that could fit with the evidence before him, that Fiela was locked in her private room and Cato was gazing out at nothing, and no one wanted to eat their evening meal.

Could this much discomfort come from Percy?

The thought that kept popping up in his mind was that perhaps Fiela had been discreetly pregnant and had miscarried a child, Sirvien thought, and that seemed like a good explanation, but it didn't fit with what he'd seen in Cato's eyes, which was not grief, but anger. And besides, the doctor had not been in...

"Sirvien," Cato said, just as the manservant reached the door.

Sirvien turned. "Yes, sir?"

"Come here."

Sirvien managed to only hesitate for the tiniest of seconds. It was the look in Cato's eyes that caused the hesitation. The look that said he could lash out and start taking lives, perhaps even Sirvien's, simply because the man was present.

But he crossed the room and stood by the legatus.

The legatus turned back to the open door to the veranda, and he pointed out. "What do you see, Sirvien?"

Sirvien chose the most obvious. He was not dense, but he also knew that a servant's job is not to speak his mind. "A lovely sunset, sir."

Cato laughed, but it had a stabbing, rasping quality to it. "No. Below that. Scrabbling in the dust there."

"You mean the base, sir?"

"Yes."

Sirvien looked sidelong at his master, feeling ever more uncomfortable. What the hell did Cato want him to say?

Cato shook his head. "Stop, Sirvien. Stop being a manservant, and be a friend. Because I consider you a friend. I don't know what you consider me, but I don't think I'm amiss in believing that over the years we have acquired something deeper than simply a master and a servant. So I ask you, Sirvien: speak as a friend."

Sirvien swallowed hard. Heat rose up his neck and engulfed his head.

A good servant doesn't speak frankly.

"You want to know what I see, sir?"

"I want to know…godsdammit. I know what you see! We see the same damn thing. A cluster of boxes in the middle of a wasteland five hundred years fried. No, I'm not asking what you see. We both see a military installation—*my* installation. But what does it make you feel?"

Sirvien stared. Parsed words in his mind. Tried to find the least offensive, and then became frightened that the least offensive would be insulting to Cato. So he steeled himself and he drew himself up and he chose the truth, because Cato had asked for the truth, and a servant obeys.

"I see a lie that will take the life of many of the people below," Sirvien spit out. Then, haltingly: "Perhaps even the life of the man up here."

Sirvien feared wrath.

But Cato only nodded solemnly. "Generals rarely die in battle."

"It is not always the battlefield that takes a soldier's life."

Cato looked at his servant. "You would speak heresy?"

Sirvien's face flushed, and for a brief, mad moment, he considered backtracking and denying everything that he'd said. He was foolish to have said it, to have spoken heresy in the presence of a legatus…

"Sometimes heresy is truth," Cato said.

Sirvien stood frozen. Denials waiting in his chest like loaded bullets.

Cato turned to him, and his eyes were no longer filled with that inexplicable rage. Now they seemed sad and pleading. "You trust me enough to speak heresy?"

Sirvien realized his hands were locked together again. Sweating and cold all at the same time. "I trust you with my life, sir."

The smile that Cato gave him was grim and heartbroken. He put his hand on Sirvien's shoulder and squeezed. "I may have need of that trust soon."

CHAPTER 18

✦

THE FALL OF LEGATUS CATO

Percival played on the balcony. The blocks again, although this time outside. Sirvien felt the boy needed some fresh air. Usually Cato or Fiela made such decisions, but Cato had been gone too much and Fiela was distracted.

The entire past week she'd wandered the house like a ghost, her watery eyes gazing about at things as though it was the last time she would see them. She looked like a woman walking to the gallows, rather than the wife of a legatus in her own house.

Sirvien sat in a chair just inside the door to the balcony. The door was open, so that he could watch the boy and hear him. A warm wind came in off the surrounding wastelands, but it was dry, and it didn't carry dust with it like it so often did, so the effect was pleasant.

Sirvien had one leg crossed over the other, and his hands clasped together in his lap, watching the boy thoughtfully. The house was quiet. The boy was quiet. He heard the rumble of troops in formation somewhere out in the installation, and the distant hum of skiffs. He heard Taddly clanking away in the kitchen, cleaning the lunch dishes, or preparing the dinner dishes.

Out on the balcony, Percival again pursued the laid-brick pattern with his blocks. But this time he pursued perfection. Having seen that the pattern could be created, he had been obsessed with creating it more accurately. Today's pattern, at least from Sirvien's perspective, looked exact. Not a single block out of order.

"Marvelously smart, isn't he?"

Sirvien jumped and looked to his right.

Fiela stood there. Hair down over her shoulders, flax-colored, some of it in braids. Fine features, though not traditionally beautiful. A dress that seemed fit more for an evening at an officers' ball than to slink around the house.

She seemed at first to be stock-still, but then he saw her thumbs wrestling with each other, the diminutive representation of some much larger struggle, like seeing a battle occur from a long way off where entire legions just looked like small blotches in a valley.

Sirvien stood up. "Pardon, ma'am. I didn't hear you walk up."

"Please sit," she said.

The way she said it. Not the graceful allowance of a servant to relax. Almost as though she was pleading with him. Pleading with Sirvien not to react to her presence. It wasn't enough that she drifted like a ghost, she apparently wanted to be invisible to her staff as well.

Sirvien eased himself back into the chair.

Fiela's eyes never came off her child.

Sirvien felt compelled to answer her question. "Yes, ma'am. Surprisingly bright."

"And yet he won't speak."

Sirvien shifted. He did not like sitting while in her presence. Did not like these observations that seemed to carry so many pitfalls with them that he had to search for a smart response.

"The talking will come," Sirvien said, mustering a good-natured tone. "Every child is different. And don't worry, once he starts, you'll wish you could make him stop."

He had hoped that the little joke would garner him a smile.

It didn't.

Fiela remained where she was, as though transfixed and yet, on some level...disgusted.

But he didn't think she was disgusted with the boy.

No.

Perhaps disgusted with herself?

Sirvien frowned at her, then wiped the expression from his face, lest she turn and catch him making it.

"I wish I could see it." It was barely more than a whisper.

Sirvien stood up from his chair, unable to bear sitting any longer. He turned to the lady of the house and allowed his concern to show. "Why would you say such a thing? All mothers witness these things in time."

A bloodless smile flashed over her lips. It frightened Sirvien.

"I don't believe that I will, Sirvien." She held up a finger between them, halting him from speaking further. "Sirvien, you have always been faithful. You have always been trustworthy. Cato believes in you. And so do I. It is one of the few things we can agree on lately."

Sirvien's mouth worked, wanting to speak, but the finger maintained its request for silence.

"Love the boy," she said to him. "Love him as I would have. And please...please tell him that I did. I loved him as much as I could. As much as a broken woman is able."

Sirvien felt his throat thickening against his will. He fumbled with words. "Ma'am, I don't…You're confusing me. Please. I wish you would tell me what is troubling you. You and Cato."

Fiela looked at him with pity.

She may have been about to speak.

But the sound of an approaching skiff—close, and moving fast—came screaming through the open balcony doors.

Sirvien spun and looked, catching only the tail end of the skiff, heading towards the front of the house. Out on the balcony, the wind rushing in from the skiff's passing billowed over the boy and knocked over his blocks. The boy looked up, only betraying a slight irritation in his expression, and covered his ears with his hands. Then he looked back at Sirvien, and then at Fiela, as though just noticing that she was there.

But Fiela's eyes had gone hard. "It's time," she said. Gone was the softness of her tone. The nuances of grief and pain. Now it was cold command. "Sirvien, take the boy."

The boy.

Not "Percy" or even "Percival."

"Yes, ma'am." He rushed through the open balcony door and scooped the boy up. Percy made a rare noise, as though indignant about being separated from his blocks, but otherwise didn't fight it. He kept his hands over his ears.

The front door of the house slammed open, the sounds of an idling skiff and running boots clattered down the main hall towards them.

Sirvien's mind raced, believing for a moment that the house was being invaded, and all his mind could come up with for a perpetrator was The Truth, because that was the only enemy he was capable of imagining.

He rushed in, intending to attempt to protect Fiela, perhaps to shove Percy into her arms and then rush her out of the house. But she stood where she was, apparently unwilling to move, and when Sirvien drew up at her side and looked down the hall, it was not the red capes of The Truth that swirled towards him, but the blue *sagums* of The Light.

Cato marched towards them. And behind him followed four legionnaires.

For a moment, the intensity of everything made Sirvien think that Cato meant violence to his wife, and here Sirvien's decency wrestled with his duties, which were to Cato first, and Fiela second. But when Cato reached his wife he took her face in his hands and he kissed her, briefly, but passionately.

When he pulled back, there were tears in both of their eyes.

"It's happening."

"Were you able to do it?"

Cato looked stricken. "No, I didn't have time."

Fiela's countenance withered. A flower caught in a drought.

"You have to leave," Cato said. "You need to take Percival and you need to go. Sirvien will accompany you. You will go to—"

"I'm not leaving."

Cato bared his teeth. "Fiela. You *will* go."

Fiela drew herself up, lifted her chin. "I will not. I will remain by your side. A legatus's wife dies with him."

His face twisted in anguish. "Fiela—"

"They're here!" one of the legionnaires called out, putting his big rifle to his shoulder.

Cato spun. "Barricade the main door. And leave if you will. I won't hold it against you. This is my battle and my battle only."

One of the legionnaires slammed the large front door closed and dropped the steel bar across it. Even so, Sirvien knew that it wouldn't last long. He wasn't sure who was coming for Cato, or why, but he was sure that he saw imminent death in Cato's eyes.

The legatus knew he was going to die.

With the door barricaded, the legionnaires turned to Cato. "We stand with you, sir. We will all remain by your side."

"And I," Fiela said.

Cato didn't have time to express any appreciation to his legionnaires, though Sirvien saw a welling of emotion on his face. He turned to his wife and lowered his voice far passed the level of a commander. Down to the level of a supplicant. The gentleness of a lover.

"Please, Fiela," he whispered. "Please leave."

Fiela shook her head. "I want to look him in the eye," she replied. "Don't deny me that."

There was the sound of a skiff outside.

And then another.

And another.

Sirvien fidgeted. "Sir. Ma'am. The boy."

Percy held to Sirvien, unperturbed by what was happening around him.

Cato's face appeared to tremble. Like tectonic shifts were occurring behind the flesh that covered his skull. He held eye-contact with Fiela for another long, breathless moment.

Then he released his grip on his wife.

Stood up straight.

Faced the manservant.

"Sirvien," he said, reaching into a pouch at his side that was half-hidden by his blue *sagum*. "Take Percival. Take him far away from here. Go through the cellar maintenance tunnels. I do not think…" he halted, as though he didn't want to say a particular name. But then he said it. "I do not think Selos knows about it."

"Selos?" Sirvien stammered. "Is he the one that is coming?"

"Sirvien!" Cato's voice was stern and demanding. "It is Selos that is coming, and you must never let him find you or the boy. He will kill you both, and you must not let that happen. I am putting everything I have into you, Sirvien. All the trust I have. All the faith I have."

"It is misplaced!" Sirvien blurted. "I can't…"

Cato cuffed him across the face. Not very hard, but it still stung.

It also centered Sirvien.

Cato put a finger in Sirvien's face. "You can. I know that you can. And my trust is not misplaced. Hide Percival. Take him far away. Never let Selos find you." Cato extracted an object from a pouch at his side, then pressed it into Sirvien's hands. "Give him this. It contains a message. Only he will be able to open it." The object was a small, round piece of metal. A decorative clasp for a *sagum*. "Do not give it to him until he is a man, you understand?"

213

Sirvien did not understand at all. But he nodded.

"There are things in the message that a boy will not be able to handle. He must be a man."

There was a shout at the front door.

A huge, thunderous bang.

Cato winced at the reverberating sound of it, but then refocused on his manservant. "These are my last orders to you, Sirvien. You are bound by them. Tell them back to me."

Sirvien's mouth worked for a moment. "Hide the boy. Never let Selos catch us. When he is a man, I will give him this clasp. It has a message that only a man will understand. Percival will be the only one capable of opening it."

Cato reached out and gripped his manservant by the shoulders and gave them a single, hard squeeze. "All my faith I've put in you." Cato then reached one hand out and touched the top of Percival's head. Grief and pain came to his face again. "My boy. Whatever the circumstances, you have always been my boy." He pulled Percival's head in close, so their foreheads touched. "Always do the right thing. Never shy away from a fight. And remember that your mind is your greatest weapon."

Then the legatus kissed his son on the head, and pressed Sirvien and the boy away. "Go now. Do not look back."

Sirvien fled.

In the end, Sirvien was right. Cato's trust had been misplaced. Because Sirvien was destined to fail Cato's orders.

The first was that he did look back.

At the entrance to the cellars, he stopped and he turned around and looked through the tiny window in the cellar door, back into the house that he had served in for the last fifteen years of his life, and he watched and heard and felt the front doors blast open, fire and brimstone chasing the shattered parts.

In the face of this gale, Legatus Cato and his wife, Fiela, stood, side by side, and hand in hand, only bowing their heads against the wash of dust and debris.

There was a brief, violent battle in the main hall, and Sirvien watched it occur when he should have been running, should have been carrying this boy to safety, but it was like these people were a tether that would not let him go.

The four legionnaires fought bravely from the alcoves of the main hall, but their attackers were prepared, and they entered the smoky breach with their shields in hand and they inched forward under withering fire and cut their fellow legionnaire's down with point-blank shots and with the sword.

The black capes of praetors swirled behind them.

Taddly emerged from the kitchen, screaming, and out of pure fright, she hurled what looked like the lid of a pan at one of the invading praetors. The praetor fired three rounds into her from his rifle and obliterated her upper body in a spray of gristle.

Then the invaders simply marched up to the legatus and his wife, and they surrounded him, standing steady behind bullet-pocked shields, like stone monoliths in the smoke.

From the hall emerged a tall figure.

A paladin.

Easily seven feet tall, and lean, even with the armor that he wore and the helmeted head that hid

215

every bit of his face and plunged his eyes into darkness. He carried with him the longstaff that all paladin's carried. As tall and as cruel as the demigod himself, with its thick, oddly-shaped base, and it's long, rifle-like body, and the bayonet that was like a long, sickle blade.

A paladin.

A demigod.

The very same one that Legatus Cato had sworn fealty to.

Paladin Selos.

The paladin stalked past the dead legionnaires and he didn't spare a glance. He headed straight for the legatus and his wife. His blue *sagum* billowed behind him. Any expression was unreadable beneath his helm. The impenetrable forcefield around him sizzled as particulate hovering in the air touched it.

He gripped his longstaff in both hands now.

"Selos!" Cato cried out, as though challenging him.

But no respone ever came.

Selos swung the longstaff in a single, malevolent arc, and the sickle bayonet crackled with the sound of flesh hitting terrible heat, and he cut Cato and Fiela both in half in a single blow.

Sirvien watched their bodies tumble apart. His breath was barricaded in his chest, unwilling to go in or out, his diaphragm fighting as though chained. Tears flooded his eyes and blurred the picture before him.

Cato and Fiela were not dead.

The halves of their bodies moved. Their mouths let out groans and cries.

Selos had no words for them. He looked briefly between them, and then leveled the longstaff, one-handed, at the upper half of Cato's body. The muzzle of the longstaff flared with a terrible flash of green light and Cato's head ruptured open like something inside of it had suddenly grown.

The demigod then turned to Fiela.

And here he paused. Not for long. It couldn't have been for long, although Sirvien struggled for breath and his eyes sparkled with lack of oxygen, and every second stretched and dragged like wounded animals.

There seemed in that moment, a hint of regret in Selos, as he stared down at Fiela. If such an emotion were possible from a paladin.

And it certainly did not stop him.

He pointed the longstaff's muzzle at her head and killed her just as he had Cato.

The praetors remained silent, awaiting.

Selos's head panned around, as though taking in the residence.

He spoke for the first time, his voice low and gravelly through the modulator.

"Find the boy. His name is Percival."

It was at that point that Sirvien finally got his legs to move and his eyes to tear themselves from the destruction of the house he had served. He ducked away from the door and fled down the stairs into the cellar, and from there, into the maintenance tunnels that Selos did not know about.

Sirvien knew that he had violated an order already.

Cato had told him not to look back, but he'd been unable to obey.

Now he felt the pressure of that mistake building up in him, causing his panic to mount, because he should not have wasted the time.

"We'll get away," Sirvien muttered to the little boy in his arms, who had begun to grow heavy, the further into the maintenance tunnels he got. "It's okay, Percy. Everything will be okay."

The calm and fearless boy clung to the manservant and gave no reply.

Sirvien was destined to make a second mistake.

To disobey another of Cato's orders, although, this one was not for lack of trying.

He *tried* to stay ahead of Selos and his praetors. And he succeeded for a time.

But eventually, Selos would find them.

CHAPTER 19

✪

THE CAVES

PERRY. PERCIVAL. PERCY.

How fluid names become in the shadows of the past.

A young man of twenty years now.

He sat in hard-clenched grief in a hovel in a cave, in the flickering light of candles, the yellow glow dancing across his uncle's haggard features.

Not his uncle at all.

Perry realized that his hands were tight on each other, turning the skin white where the pads of his fingers pressed. His legs were tense. Inside of his boots, his toes were flexed.

But he didn't shake.

"You told me…"

"I told you a great many things." Sergio took a breath. "I told you what you needed to hear. Because…" he struggled.

After all of that, there was more truth stuck in his throat?

"You have more secrets?" Perry's voice was soft at first, but then it began to grow harsher. "You're not my uncle. My father didn't die in combat like you said. My father and my mother were both murdered. By their own paladin. What else could you possibly have to tell me? Isn't that enough? How much more is there?"

Sergio nodded, his brow crinkled, pained.

Perry shoved his face in his hands. "Gods in the skies." His voice was muffled through his palms.

He removed them. "Why? Why did you lie to me? Why…" he latched onto some new offense. "Why did you send me to Hell's Hollow? Why send me right back into the same system that killed my father? What were you thinking?"

"I had no choice in it."

"You had no *choice*?" Perry rose to his feet. "What if Selos had found me at the Academy?"

"Selos *did* find you!" Sergio nearly shouted. "He was the one that forced me to send you there!"

Perry blinked rapidly, as though flipping through a codex of memories in his mind. Back to the Academy. And then further. Back to the night before they arrived in Keniza. Fleeing from the firebombing of the freehold. And before that…

"The Tall Man," Perry breathed.

Sergio rose. "Perry, I'm so sorry." There were tears in the old man's eyes. "I beg your forgiveness. I failed your father and I failed you. My failures have been the reason for all of this." His head hung now, unable to meet Perry's gaze. "His faith was misplaced."

Perry was suddenly on the fence, not knowing whether to continue to be angry or to console the old man. But he never had an opportunity to decide.

A whistle was heard.

It sounded like a bird call. Two short chirps, one after the other.

If Perry hadn't known there were no birds in these caves, he might've been fooled by it.

The whistle was then repeated, louder and closer.

And then repeated again by four or five others.

And again by ten or twenty—they all began to meld into one crescendo.

Stuber burst through the door of the room, trailing Dino who grappled at the legionnaire's mass like a child trying to barricade a parent. Stuber looked at Sergio, and then at Perry, and his gaze was lively as it was when death was in the wind.

"Problem," Stuber announced.

"What?" Perry said.

"They're here." Stuber grabbed Perry by the shoulder and started pulling him for the door. "Two skiffs. Full landing party. At the mouth of the canyon."

Behind them, Sergio spoke. "*He's* here."

Stuber and Perry both looked back at the old man.

"Selos," Sergio said. "It will be Selos and his praetors."

"Why is he after me all of the sudden?" Perry demanded.

Sergio's eyes flicked between Perry and Stuber. "He has been after you since you deserted the Academy. Except, that he had no way of knowing where you were while you were on the run. Something must have happened. Something must have put you back in his sights."

Perry felt his face flush. "I may have been arrested for murder in Karapalida."

Sergio looked shocked. "Murder…?"

"We need to get *moving*," Stuber barked.

"Wait," Sergio demanded, and then he dove behind him into a small trunk of hardened polymer that looked out of place here in these austere environs.

"Oh my fuck!" Stuber threw up an exasperated hand. Then he started clapping them together. "We gotta *go*, we gotta *go*, we gotta *go*!"

Sergio didn't bother to turn around. "Keep your mouth shut and do the fighting like you're supposed to, legionnaire! There are bigger things at stake here than—Ah! There it is!" Sergio spun around, holding something out to Perry. "You need to take this!"

Perry grabbed the object from Sergio's hand without looking at it. "Okay, fine! Now let's go!"

Far away, perhaps at the mouth of the tunnels, there came the rumble of an explosion.

"Put it in your pocket," Sergio insisted, refusing to move his feet until Perry had done so. "There. Good. Keep it safe. I have to tell you the rest of the story." Sergio began shuffling for the door. "I'll talk while we move."

"Save your breath for the moving, old man," Stuber remarked and shouldered his Roq-11.

Sergio ignored the legionnaire. He caught Perry by the shoulder and held him there, preventing him from going out of the little chamber and into the tunnels. "You must know the truth. Or everything is lost. And if I die, the truth dies with me. Please, my boy, keep me alive long enough to tell you."

Perry's only response was "Shit."

"Alright, we'll keep you alive," Stuber hollered, then positioned himself behind the pair and shoved them out of the room, using his rifle as a baton. "Which would be a helluva lot easier if you would get a *fuckin' move on!*"

Perry, Sergio, Dino, and Stuber came tumbling out into the tunnels.

It was already chaos. A tide of bodies flowed past them, and like rain swelling a river, it rapidly grew thicker.

Teran and Sagum rushed up to them. Teran looked worried. Sagum looked pissed.

"Same guys from Oksidado," she called. "We gotta go."

"Yeah," Stuber kept pushing Sergio and Perry. "I'm tryin'."

Sagum had locked onto Perry. "We're in these caves for decades! You're here for one hour and the demigods have already found us! What did you do?"

Perry rolled out of Stuber's incessant pushing and squared up to Sagum, fists balled, jaw jutting, feeling the red...

Teran shoved an arm between them.

Stuber grabbed Perry by the back of the collar. "Easy, Shortstack! You and Smegma can slap-fight later."

Perry was dragged backwards down the tunnel, staring at Sagum, who was jogging along behind him, smirking. Perry felt that his position was undignified, and his cheeks flushed. He writhed and freed himself from Stuber's grip but turned himself around and moved forward.

At the lead of their column, splitting through the crowd like a plow through earth, Stuber yelled and shoved and sometimes picked people up to move them aside.

"Move! Get the fuck outta my way! You! Go to the back and die like a man, you useless prick! Maybe the praetors will trip on you! Move!"

Another explosion sounded, this one closer, reverberating through the tunnels, and the way it echoed made Perry think that it had come from inside the cave system this time. It sent a shockwave of scared whimpers through the crowd.

"Hey!" Stuber slowed and turned his head to look at Sergio. "Can I ask where we're going right now?"

"You're in the lead!" Sergio pointed out. "We're following you."

"I was going with the flow. But where is everybody going?"

"There's an exit a mile down the tunnel. Empties out into the desert."

Stuber stopped. He frowned at Sergio. "How big is this exit?"

Sergio shrugged. "It's a single tunnel mouth. Small. One person…" he stopped, realizing what he was saying.

"Yeah," Stuber grabbed the old man and pushed him against the wall of the tunnel to get them out of the flow of bodies. He motioned for the others in their group to do the same.

"Why are we stopping?" Sagum demanded.

Stuber fixed the boyish man with a smirk. "What're you scared of, Smegma? I thought you could kill legionnaires."

"They're praetors," Sagum stammered, appearing off balance.

"Same difference," Stuber spat.

Sagum made no reply.

Teran looked irritated. "Stuber! What are we doing?"

Stuber had managed to scrunch the group together on the wall of the tunnel. The people rushed by them.

Stuber looked at Teran. "There's hundreds of people, all running for a single bottleneck. I can tell you how that's gonna work out. Half the peons will die in the crush and plug up your little secret exit. The other half will be mopped up by a single praetor when he finds them all crammed in there like fish in a barrel. We need to find a different way out."

Teran's face registered horror. She spun and opened her mouth, eyes wide with fear for her fellow Outsiders. "Wait! Don't—"

Stuber grabbed her by the face, his palm over her mouth, and he hauled her back and shoved her against the wall, pinning her there with her mouth covered.

"Hey!" Sagum advanced—brave, but ultimately stupid.

Stuber popped him once, his fist lightning-quick, straight into the jaw.

Sagum's head rocked back and he stumbled into the wall, hands holding his nose.

"Sit, bitch," Stuber commanded him. Then he looked at Teran who was fighting to be free of his hand. "Shut up and be still! You want to create a panic? You want everyone to start following us around? You try to lead this herd of sheep, they're all gonna die anyways, except in your version of events, we all die with them. Me? I'd prefer to let the sheep do what sheep do, and I'll live to fight another day."

She shook her head forcefully enough to free her mouth. "You can't just let these people die!"

"They had a horrible exit strategy," Stuber said, as though that was all the explanation needed. "Not my fault."

Teran started to shout again, stubborn as ever.

This time it was Sergio that stopped her. With a hand on her arm, squeezing her wrist. The touch surprised her and she looked to the old man.

"Teran, please," he said. "There is a bigger picture here. We have no choice now. It is most important that Perry escapes. You know this."

Her face seemed to shake. Then she bared her teeth, like she was biting down on a leather strap while some bonesaw operated. There were tears in her eyes. She stamped a single foot. Took a breath.

"Fine," she said. "We'll take the west exit."

"Which way is the west exit?" Stuber inquired.

Teran pushed off of the wall and started cutting through the flow of cave dwellers, cold in her spirit, as though they were already dead to her because she knew she could not save them.

The rest of them followed.

There were shouts far down the tunnels in the direction that everyone was fleeing from. Then a chatter of gunfire and when Perry turned and looked in that direction, he saw tracer rounds punching through people and impacting the walls.

A scream went up.

The crowd of escapees turned their worried jog into a panicked sprint.

Perry's party of six lunged for the opposite side of the tunnel, making it past just before the crush of screaming bodies reached them.

"They're right behind us!" Stuber called.

"I know!" she answered.

They ran along the tunnel for another fifty yards and came to a four-way intersection. One of the ways was not even passable. More of an air tunnel than a passage, it was dark and narrow and angled sharply upward.

Then there was a tunnel that ran left, and a tunnel that ran right.

The river of people was going left. Teran led them right.

"If you got any other secrets," Perry said as he ran along beside Sergio. "Now might be the time to tell them."

Sergio was flushed in the face already. Growing out of breath. He was having to take two strides for every one of Perry's. His old hips wouldn't allow a longer gait than that.

"The clasp that I gave you," Sergio huffed. "It contains a message, Perry. From your father."

"A message?" Perry almost stopped in his tracks. "Well, what's it say?"

Teran interrupted with a hiss. "Can you two quiet down back there?" Her own voice was a straining whisper. "Voices carry in these tunnels. You're going to give us away."

They kept moving.

Sergio lowered his voice. "I don't know what it says, Perry. I can't open it. But I suspect…"

"What?"

"Quiet!" Teran ordered them.

Perry looked at her. She'd come to a stop at the crook of a turn in the tunnel. She was close to the wall, looking over her shoulder at them, eyebrows pinched down into anger. "We're close to the mouth of the tunnel now. If there's a praetor guarding it, you're going to give us away. Me and Sagum will sneak ahead and see if there's a guard. Stuber, stay with them in case the praetors come."

227

Stuber nodded, and put his back to the tunnel wall so he could pay attention to both directions.

Sagum and Teran slipped silently around the corner.

Sergio, Perry, and Dino stood against the wall.

The old man's chest heaved. Sweat broke out on his brow. He spoke in a threadbare whisper. "Perry. Listen to me. Have you…" he seemed to falter, to not know how to say whatever it was he needed to say. Then he plunged forward. "Have you ever been to a place in your mind where your focus is absolute? Where the rest of the world seems to melt away?" Sergio held up a hand. "It's not a normal place. You know this, if you've ever been there. You know that other people don't have this place. You don't know how you know, you just do. Am I making sense?"

Perry stared at the old man, feeling his chest constrict, his blood pounding.

The Calm.

But how would he know about that?

Perry nodded once.

Sergio looked both relieved and disturbed. As though a great confirmation had just come to him, and it was a relief to finally know, but a horrible thing to discover. He reached a hand out and found Perry's shoulder, which he clutched in his fingers.

"The clasp," the old man rasped. "The clasp with the message from your father. Perry, I believe that it is god-tech."

Something clanked down the tunnel.

Stuber stiffened.

The object rolled into view: A small, metal ball.

"Ah shit…" Stuber muttered, then he lunged forward, kicked the thing, and dropped himself to the ground as it flew through the air, shouting, "Hit the dirt!"

CHAPTER 20

✿

THE CLASP

PERRY DOVE FOR THE GROUND, hauling Sergio down with him.

The metal ball caromed off the domed ceiling of the tunnel and bounced in an unnatural fashion—more like it was made of rubber than metal—but at that point Perry decided to bury his face in his arms and he saw nothing else but darkness and shadowed tunnel floor, and he heard nothing but the huff of his breath.

Then there was light.

The shockwave rammed into him, like running into a wall at a dead sprint. Someone cried out. Perry's ears rang like gongs.

He got up unsteadily, only aware of the fact that he should be moving and not lying there. His woozy vision panned to his left. Stuber was hauling himself off the floor, teeth bared, and Perry couldn't tell whether he was grimacing or grinning—probably a bit of both.

Sergio got up much slower than Perry. Perry grabbed him and pulled him to his feet.

There was another body. It was Dino, although you wouldn't recognize that anymore. He had been the closest one to the blast, and he'd soaked up the brunt of the shrapnel.

"Well, they know we're down here now!" Stuber hollered. He ran ten steps, reaching out to grab Perry by the sleeve and haul him along. Perry kept his grip on Sergio, creating a human chain.

Stuber whipped them like he was trying to send them scuttling down the tunnel, and he spun on a foot and raised his Roq-11 and let it spit fire down the hall.

Perry kept running. He wanted to fight, but a weaponless man in a gunfight is just another body at the end of the day. So he ran, towing Sergio behind him like an uncooperative trailer with a busted wheel.

"Come on, Uncle Sergio!" Perry gasped.

"I'm trying," Sergio wheezed.

They got fifty yards further into the tunnel before Perry had to stop. Sergio had become dead weight. He whirled on his so-called uncle, angry again.

"What are you doing?" Perry demanded.

He noticed that he couldn't see Stuber.

Further down the tunnel, there were bright flashes and pumping rifle reports.

Sergio was bent double. Hands on his knees. He craned his neck to look at Perry, his mouth hanging open.

There was blood on his lips. It dribbled out of his open mouth in a thin stream.

Perry's anger dissipated again. Replaced by panic.

Perry seized Sergio by the shoulders and hauled him upright, supporting his weight now. Sergio sagged in his arms, his head lolling as he worked for air. Perry scoured the old man's body and saw that the wound wasn't hard to find. The entire front of his tunic, from the mid-point of his belly and down to his knees was soaked in dark red that was almost black.

"Oh, shit!" Perry stammered. "What do you need?"

"They got me," Sergio mumbled. "The grenade got me."

"Don't…" Perry didn't finish. "Let me see it."

The two of them hobbled to the wall of the tunnel.

Down the tunnel, the firefight drew closer.

Perry eased Sergio down into a sitting position against the wall, and then he ripped the old man's tunic up, and struggled not to show what he saw on his face.

There was no jagged hole where a piece of shrapnel had gone in.

The shrapnel had instead opened Uncle Sergio's abdomen as cleanly as a cut from a saber, and his intestines bulged out.

Perry dropped the tunic back in place. It was heavy and sopping wet with blood. He stared at Sergio with fear and reckoning.

Sergio had no more fear in his eyes any more. He seemed to know.

"That bad, is it?" he asked.

Perry didn't answer.

From the exiting end of the tunnel, Teran and Sagum rushed back up to them.

Teran came sliding in on her knees. "Oh, gods, what happened?"

"They got me," Sergio repeated.

Teran reached for the tunic, but Perry stopped her, shaking his head. Teran looked like she might fight Perry on it, but when she saw his eyes, she relented.

Sagum was all but dancing beside them. "We don't have time for this, Teran!"

"Shut your mouth!" Teran barked at him.

"We've got a clear way out, we need to use it!"

Perry spun on him and held up a finger, but was too angry to speak.

Perry felt a rough hand touch the skin of his face and turn him away from Sagum. Sergio, pulling Perry's attention back.

"No time. This is all I can give you, Perry. I've suspected for a very long time, but..." Sergio frowned, and then looked pained. He managed to shake his head, as though refusing something of himself. "No. No, I won't do that to you. But listen to me, Perry. The clasp is god-tech. I'm almost certain of it. And you will be able to operate it."

Perry shook his head. "I can't use god-tech! I'm not a demigod!"

Sergio seized the back of Perry's neck. His eyeballs strained, bloodshot. "You can!" he hissed. "And you must. You must. You can no longer only look out for yourself, Perry. You can no longer run. Now you have to stand and fight."

Sergio squeezed his eyes shut for a second, and tears came out of the corners.

Perry's mind spun like a dervish going out of control—pins and nuts and bolts sheering loose, about to fly free and tumble into its destruction. He felt his entire body shaking with questions, but he kept his mouth shut so that Sergio could spill the truth.

Sergio's grip on the back of Perry's neck became loose, almost slid away, but then tightened once more. His eyes looked stern again for just long enough to speak his next words. "Always do the right thing. Never shy away from a fight. And remember that your mind is your greatest weapon."

Footsteps pounded in the tunnel. Stuber hauled ass around the bend in the tunnel. He juggled two spare rifle magazines in his hands that Perry assumed he'd swiped off a dead praetor.

Stuber's expression became one of surprise when he saw them, and then anger. He staggered to a stop, breathing heavily, and stuffing the two stolen magazines into slots on his chestplate.

"What the fuck, peons?" he bawled at them. "I hold six preators off for five minutes, thinking that you're getting free of this shit hole, and here you sit like lambs in a slaughterhouse!"

Perry had no words.

He looked back to Sergio, but in that lost moment, the old man had gone slack in his arms.

Shots from down the tunnel. They struck the wall, leaving deep gouges.

They all flinched—Stuber included.

Perry didn't have time to be angry with the ex-legionnaire for interrupting Uncle Sergio's final moments. He was too confused to feel much of anything at all.

Teran slapped him hard on the shoulder. "Let's go, Perry!"

He thrust himself up.

They ran.

There was the sound of feet, and it felt jarring, all the way up through his body. His mouth was open and he felt the air going in and out past his lips, drying them, drying his tongue, and he was a million miles away, going through the motions like you do when you're dreaming, like your life is on a track and all you can do is go along for the ride.

They reached the mouth of the tunnel. Sunlight poured in. Stung his eyes.

Stuber went through first, weapon up, clearing the exit, and Sagum followed close behind them, not to be out-warriored. Perry took up the rear and didn't care. Why would you care about the outcome of a dream?

He was in open sunlight. Crossing sand now. Dodging between scrub.

Stuber allowed Teran to take the lead, and he hung back, coming up beside Perry. "You with me, Shortstack?"

"Don't call me that."

"Fuck you, Shortstack," Stuber whispered back. "I'll call you whatever I gotta call you to get your head out of your ass."

Perry spun and tried to grab Stuber by the throat. It was awkward, because they were both still jogging along behind Teran and Sagum, and of course, the ex-legionnaire was about two feet taller than Perry.

Stuber batted his arms away with a look of minor annoyance on his face. "Cut it out, peon," he said, shoving Perry away from him and causing the smaller man to stagger sideways.

Perry was suddenly, and literally, spitting mad. Flecks of foam issued from the corners of his mouth as his face went red and veins bulged as he yelled without truly yelling. Little more than a whisper, though he pressed it out of his throat with all his might.

"Stuber, you arrogant piece of shit! Don't fuck with me right now! Can't you give me one fucking second without your bullshit?"

Stuber appeared to either not hear him or not care. He kept scanning as they kept jogging. "There," he said, self-satisfied. "Glad you're back."

"What are you two doing?" Teran demanded.

"Nothing," Stuber said. "All good back here. Where are you taking us?"

Perry steamed and trembled, but looked to Teran to see her answer to this. Because Stuber was right. This wasn't a time for Perry to go into mental hiding. They were still in danger. And yes, he also wanted to know where the hell they were going.

Teran motioned with her head. "We've got a place. Underground."

"Shit. Again?"

"You wanna go overland?"

"Not particularly."

"Well then shut up and follow."

Stuber did as he was told with a wry smile.

Perry had run out of humor, so he just scrambled along, feeling that little clasp in his pocket as it tapped against his leg and seemed to grow heavier with each passing stride.

They traversed some sort of canyon. Perry got the sense that they were not at ground level, that this little canyon or ravine stood higher in the cliffs than the box canyon in which they had entered the system of caves to begin with. The red rock cliffs did not tower over their heads here like they had in the box canyon. Here, the way was narrow, and to either side the walls of rock only appeared to rise up about ten or fifteen feet.

The floor of the small canyon was sandy in spots, and treacherously rocky in others, and so narrow in certain places that they had to straddle the walls of rock, or turn their body sideways to get through. Perry didn't like tight spaces, and whenever he felt both sides of the canyon touching him, he felt his heart work into his throat.

Ahead of him, Stuber squeezed his bulk through with quiet curses at Teran, as though she had designed this obstacle course specifically to screw with him.

In the distance, Perry registered the muffled sound of gunfire. The faraway noise of a skiff taking off. Once, a skiff flew so close that they thought for certain it was going to overfly the narrow canyon they traveled, and they all stopped and stared skyward, but the skiff peeled off and went another direction before ever revealing itself.

They went on this narrow path for about five hundred yards before Teran finally stopped, white-faced and breathing harder than the rest of them.

"You okay?" Perry huffed.

Teran was doubled over, hands on her knees. She spat on the ground, a rope of saliva dangling from her chin. She nodded and the string of spit swung around and attached to her chest. She noticed it and wiped it away like a minor nuisance. She pointed straight ahead.

"We're here."

Perry followed the direction she pointed but didn't see anything. "I don't..."

"Yeah, I don't think I'm gonna fit in that," Stuber declared.

Sagum had already approached whatever it was that Teran had pointed to, and as he stopped and looked over his shoulder at Stuber, smirking haughtily, Perry saw what it was, and what Stuber didn't think he could fit into.

There was a cleft in the base of the canyon. The kind of crevice that you might peer into as you passed by and drop a rock down out of curiosity to see how deep the hole went.

Sagum lifted his chin to Stuber. "Guess you'll have to stay out here then. Good luck with that, Fat Boy."

Then, Sagum squatted down, grabbed either side of the cleft, and slipped in. First his legs, and then his hips, and then he was gone, like the ground had swallowed him up.

"What?" Perry shook his head. "I'm not going in that thing. You gotta be kidding me!"

"I'm not kidding," Teran said. "And you will." She stepped to the cleft and looked back at the two of them. "This is the way out, Perry. Take it and live. Or stay up here and die."

Stuber shook his head, but began removing his armor. "Never gonna fit through with this shit on. How long is it tight for? Am I gonna get stuck?"

"It's not tight for very far. You'll have to squirm. You should make it."

"Should."

Teran shrugged at him. Didn't appear to have energy for argument. She said nothing else. She dipped her body down into the cleft and was gone.

Perry watched, cursing up a storm.

"You first," Stuber said.

"You're such an ass," Perry hissed, more terrified than irritated.

"Actually, I'm being considerate," Stuber replied. "If I get stuck, I might plug up the hole, and you won't be able to make the getaway with your girlfriend. Now hop in there. Let's get this shit over with."

Just a few minutes of terror, Perry told himself. *She said it wasn't long. Just a few minutes. I can do anything for a few minutes. Just don't think about it.*

But he thought about it. He thought about it a lot.

He shuffled over to the cleft and peered down into it.

Reassuringly, the walls of the cleft widened as it went deeper. The mouth of it was the narrowest part.

Unreassuringly, he couldn't see the bottom.

"Alright. Okay. Shit." Perry treated it like diving into ice cold water. Best to commit yourself rather than easing your way in. He grabbed the sides of the cleft and dropped in.

CHAPTER 21

✸

THE UNDERGROUND

THE HOLE IN THE GROUND led straight down at first, and then at a forty-five degree angle.

Perry scrabbled his way through it. Above him, Stuber grunted and groaned and made a racket as he writhed his way gracelessly down the hole, sending dust and pebbles skittering onto Perry's head and into his collar.

As the entrance hole disappeared from view, the tunnel became inky black. Perry slid blindly along on his rear. But after about fifteen feet of scooting along like that, he noted that the darkness was not quite so thick anymore.

The further he got into the tunnel, the stronger the strange light became. A little further and he noted that he could see his hands and feet again, in a low, green glimmer.

Something down in the hole was glowing.

While he appreciated the illumination, Perry wasn't sure he liked it. By some inarticulable nature of the light, he knew that it wasn't from the sun, and it wasn't from electricity. Anything else that could emit such a glow seemed unnatural.

At this point the tunnel was wide and tall enough that Perry rose to his feet and went the rest of the way at a crouch. Behind him, Stuber no longer struggled through the confines, but he still grumbled and cursed.

And then the tunnel ended.

Perry stood up and stepped away from the mouth of the tunnel, momentarily blinded by his relief at being free of it.

When the blindness passed, he stood in stark silence.

Before him was a beach of sand. He couldn't tell the color of it, though it was pale. He knew that it was probably just dust from the rocks around them, so it must've been some hue of orange or ochre, but in the green light that seemed to be all around them, it looked like an alien landscape.

The sand under his feet was about fifteen feet to the water's edge. There, emerald water lapped and in its crystal-clear depths, things glowed. Many things. Large things. And sometimes it seemed that they moved, though Perry was not sure whether this was the undulation of the water.

They were in a massive cavern. A cathedral of rock. The ceiling vaulted high above, and for a moment as Perry's eyes coursed over it, he thought that the ceiling was pocked with holes and daylight was coming through them, but then he realized again that the quality of the light was not quite right, and that whatever constellations he was seeing on that black ceiling were specks of something that glowed the same odd green as whatever was in the water.

He stared at those fake stars above him, waiting for them to move, but he couldn't tell if they did.

"The hell is this?" Stuber breathed from behind him, strapping his armor back on.

Perry's eyes came down from the ceiling. Found Teran and Sagum, standing and watching them. Everyone's faces glowed strangely. There seemed to be no shadows cast, because the light seemed to come from everywhere, and yet the light wasn't strong enough to dispel the sense of cloying darkness.

"The Underground," Teran informed them. "Help us."

Perry frowned, until he realized that Teran and Sagum were both pointing at an object that Perry had first mistaken for a large rock sitting in the middle of the sand. When he looked at it again, he saw that it was a flat-bottomed boat that had been turned upside down.

Teran and Sagum were already moving for it.

Perry walked after them, his sense of surrealism only growing stronger.

"What's the glow?" Perry asked, glancing around again.

"The wyrms," Teran answered.

The four of them grabbed the boat and flipped it so its flat bottom was on the sand. Then they started dragging it towards the waters.

"The wyrms?" Perry watched the water growing closer, and found his pace slowing, and yet he was tugged along as the other three dragged the boat to the water's edge. "Is that what's down in the waters?"

"Yes."

The boat hit the water.

Teran and Sagum shoved it out a little bit.

The boat bobbed in Perry's grip. Half on land, half in the water.

"Where are we going?" Perry asked.

"Down the river," Teran nodded to where the glowing waters disappeared far ahead. Judging distance was disorienting. "Get in."

Perry put one foot in the boat, then stopped. "This is a river?"

"River. Or a long lake. Not sure. Get in. Time's wasting."

Perry put the other foot into the boat and sat down gingerly, his land-loving feet completely unacquainted with the feeling of buoyancy and finding it sickening.

The boat shoved out farther into the water. The feeling of floating became stronger as its connection with land disappeared. Teran and Sagum jumped in, causing the thing to rock, and Perry grabbed the side of it, feeling like he was about to be pitched overboard.

"Give us a shove," Teran told Stuber.

Stuber, apparently rendered all but wordless by the strange underworld realm, shoved them out with one push. Perry heard his feet splashing through the water. Then he hauled his bulk up into the boat and Perry's eyes widened as it felt like Stuber was about to tip them.

Then Stuber was in, and they floated gently on the water.

Perry wanted to look over the edge of the boat, down into the water. He got the impression it was clear all the way down to the bottom. But he couldn't bring himself to do it. He realized that he was terrified of looking into that water. Terrified of what he might see moving through the depths below them.

Teran had situated herself on one of the benches and with a soft groan, leaned on the side of the boat, and touched her stomach where her wound was. She took a few deep breaths, looking like a pregnant woman having her first contractions.

Then she fixed her eyes on Perry and frowned. "You okay?"

Perry realized he was gripping the side of the boat so hard that his knuckles hurt. His core was a solid rock of tension. His eyes were wide. "Uh. Yes. Fine. How are you?"

"I'll live," she said. "You've never been on a boat, have you?"

"I've never even seen this much water. Let alone floated on it."

"Just relax."

"If it's all the same to you, I'll stay tense."

"Suit yourself," she said. "But tense bodies make boats flip."

Perry evaluated that statement.

Stuber shifted around, heedless of how much he was rocking the boat. He loomed over Perry's shoulder to peer over the side. "Hm." He said. "I'll be honest. I am finding this a bit disconcerting."

Sagum lounged against the side of the boat, on the middle bench between Teran and Perry and Stuber. "You scared, legionnaire?"

"Scared?" Stuber appeared to legitimately evaluate the question. "No," he decided. "But I am working on inoculating myself to the concept of a watery death. I'd always assumed it would either be gunfire or liver failure. Drowning would be something new." He looked at Teran. "Tell me about the wyrms."

"You mean, are they dangerous?"

Stuber nodded.

"I'm not sure. Some of them are big enough to do damage, I guess. But I've never seen them attack anything before."

"What do they eat?"

245

Teran dismissed it with a shrug and a partial sigh. "I dunno, Stuber. I haven't exactly studied them."

Perry pointed to all the glowing dots on the ceiling. "What about that? Are those wyrms too?"

"Eggs. They hatch. Drop into the water."

"Who put them up there?"

Teran smirked. "The wyrms, I guess."

"So they can crawl up the walls?"

"There are other things down here that you should be worrying about more than that."

Stuber seemed intrigued. "Such as?"

"Nekrofages," Sagum put in.

Stuber rolled his eyes. "Of course."

Perry shook his head, like Sagum was trying to scare them with ghost stories. "Right."

"It's true," Sagum said, although his voice was still taunting. "They live down here. You know how the Lokos have lost their shit? Well, the nekrofages lost their shit centuries go. They're not even really human anymore."

Stuber took a breath and sighed it out. "Yes. When the gods destroyed the world, it was the poison from the blast that mutated all of the humans that had tried to fight back the hardest and turned them to nekrofages. Please, Smegma," he scoffed. "Tell us more stories from the Ortus."

"It's true," Teran said quietly from her spot at the front of the boat.

They all looked at her.

She wasn't looking at them, though. She gazed down into the waters, her face lit in ghostly green by the creatures moving about in the deep. "I've been down here before. With my father before he died. We used the river to ferry supplies to the

246

caves. And I saw them." She finally looked at them, and her eyes seemed watery and distant. "They glow in the dark. Just like the wyrms. My father said it was because they eat the wyrm eggs."

"Well." Stuber crossed his arms over his chest. "I think a young girl got spooked by the darkness and maybe saw some wyrms crawling up the walls or something." Then he shrugged. "But who's to say? Shit. I've never been down here. Thirty minutes ago I didn't even know that there was such a thing as wyrms."

No one spoke for a moment.

Just the big empty silence. Perforated by the very slight noise of the water lapping at the underside of the boat. Perry felt it when it did this, and he hated it. It felt like the water was alive. Like it was tapping on the underside of the boat, letting them know that it was in ultimate control, that, if it chose, it could tip them over and swallow them up.

Perry realized for the first time, as his heart rate began to level out, that it was chilly in this subterranean world. His stomach quaked, the first signs of shivering starting in his core. He wrapped his arms around himself and tried to peer far down into the caverns. But even though there was the eerie glow to everything, after about a hundred yards, the darkness still managed to consume what was ahead of them.

"How long are we going to be down here?" Perry asked, looking at Teran.

Teran didn't answer his question. Instead she looked to Sagum. The two of them had a silent conference, trading a few nods and shrugs.

"I was thinking we should go to the end of the river," Teran said.

247

"Okay," Perry raised an eyebrow. "And how far is that?"

"I don't know. I've never traveled that far."

"Oh."

"Been a long time since anyone has," Sagum said. "Fact, I don't remember *anyone* that has. But..." he turned his head to look into the darkness ahead of them, as inscrutable as the future. "That's because it leads to a place where no one wants to go."

"The Glass Flats," Perry said. Not a question. A realization.

Sagum nodded. "In Pallesprek it's called *Spiekel Diablo.* It mean's Devil's Mirror."

"Why?" Perry asked. "I mean...why would we go there?"

"Because it's the last place the paladins will be looking for someone."

Stuber wiped his nose with the back of his hand, shifted in his seat which caused the whole boat to rock. "I'd caution against presuming to know what the paladins will do."

"Would you rather us go to a city then?" Teran asked. She said it without much inflection, so Perry wasn't sure whether she was honestly asking Stuber's opinion, or pointing out that the Glass Flats were an obviously-better option.

Stuber met Teran's gaze. "I have no opinion on where we should go. I'm simply pointing out that we should never assume we've lost them."

It seemed like good advice, so no one countered it.

"So how long then?" Perry reiterated. "To the Glass Flats? Are we talking days? Weeks?"

"Not weeks," Teran said. "I'd guess three days. Maybe four. I'm unsure on that. But I know that if you follow the river, it takes you to the Glass Flats."

"Okay." Perry felt a bump of irritation in his chest. "And where do we go after that?" He tried to keep his voice even, but it was difficult. He felt like a pot that has suddenly started boiling over. He was fine two seconds ago, but the idea of dumping out of this subterranean hell, into yet another hell, with no apparent purpose to it, felt like too much to take.

Perry grabbed his legs, and addressed his anger at his boots for a moment. "Did anyone think about supplies? Food? Water? It's the Glass Flats. There's nothing there."

Perry looked up at Teran, and then at Sagum, and finally at Stuber.

They were all watching him steadily.

He tossed his arms up. "What?"

Stuber leaned forward on one elbow. "Shortstack, I believe we're all waiting to hear from *you* about where we're going next."

"From me?" Perry gaped.

Oh.

He suddenly felt foolish.

It was easy to get pissed at a lack of planning and decision-making when you thought someone else was steering the ship. But then you realized it was your own hands that gripped the wheel, and suddenly all those seemingly-simple decisions became paralyzingly complicated.

Teran watched this realization fall heavy on Perry's shoulders. "Perry, I don't know if you've fully realized this. But we've been searching for you for a very long time." She lowered her head, her eyes becoming sharp. "A lot of people have died to find you, Perry. Because your uncle made us believe that you could change things for us. We believed in it, because he believed in it. His hope was contagious. But we've all taken a leap of faith here."

Perry felt lost. "I don't…I'm not sure what I'm supposed to be able to do."

"Well," Sagum said. "For starters, you're supposed to be the only person that can operate the clasp that your father left you."

Perry's hand went to his pocket, felt a momentary alarm like maybe he'd lost it, but then when he slipped his fingers inside, he felt the sculpted metal curves of the clasp. Warm from sitting against his body.

A part of him didn't want to pull it out. Didn't want to look at it. Didn't want to accept this sudden, crushing responsibility, with these three people watching him and waiting for him to do something, to come up with a plan, their lives now firmly and inextricably in his hands.

Shit.

He'd been running for so long, looking out for just himself, that he didn't know if he could handle this.

He suddenly wanted to go back to running.

He wanted to rewind his life to the moment before he killed Tiller. Convince himself not to do it. And then maybe he would be back with Hauten's outfit. Hiding from reality. Hiding from his former life. Forever on the run, but at least it was simple. You steered clear of the law, and you spent your days picking through brass, reloading it, selling it, and then drinking and screwing your wages away.

What the hell was the clasp, anyways? A recording. A message.

What could it possibly say that Perry wanted to hear? Or even *could* hear? He barely remembered his father. Did they think that after the intervening decades, Perry would simply burst into loving tears at the first sign of a message from his long-lost father? That somehow that would reshape the path of fate that Perry had chosen for himself?

I'm not a warrior, Perry yelled inside his own head, though his mouth remained clamped shut. *I'm not a warrior, and I can't do anything special. I'm a runt, that's all. I'm a shortstack. I'm a less-than.*

Perry seemed to crumple under this deluge of bitter thoughts.

He ripped the clasp out of his pocket and looked into the deep waters and reared his fist back to hurl it away from him—to hurl away this abortion of everything he was.

A hard, rough hand enveloped his clenched fist, and, like stripping something from a baby's hand, the clasp slipped out of his fingers.

He whirled on Stuber, who held the clasp now in a clenched fist so big that the clasp was not even visible. "Give it back to me," Perry growled.

Stuber only shook his head. "You're about to make a rash decision."

"What the fuck do you care?" Perry shouted, and his voice echoed across the caverns. "This isn't something you believe in! You're no Outsider! You're not taking any great leap of faith! You're just here for the violence, right? You're just here because you enjoy stacking up bodies!"

Perry had risen up on his feet as he'd yelled at Stuber.

At first, Stuber watched him, and his face bore only that slight tinge of sadness that he'd seen many other times before. But as Perry finished yelling at Stuber, there came into the ex-legionnaire's eyes a mean glint.

A flash of a foot.

Not so much a kick, as a shove.

And then Perry was going over backward.

Wind-milling his arms.

Panic.

Deep dark water rushing up at him, the glow of mysterious creatures underneath, and the water, the water, its own entity, promising to swallow him whole—

SPLASH

His world was cold.

Discombobulated.

The rush of water in his ears.

The air coming out of his lungs in one long squeeze from a frigid fist of water.

His arms groped through the darkness, and when his eyes opened and felt the cold water on them, he could see so clearly in that water, he could see the things below him, and he swore they were rising to meet him, and he thought to scream but had no more air in his lungs.

Something poked him in the chest, and his hands seized it out of pure reaction.

He was being hauled towards the surface.

He didn't dare let go.

He broke the surface of the water.

Spluttering and gasping.

He was at the side of the boat, clinging to an oar, and on the other end of the oar, Stuber crouched, his brow beetled, his lips peeled back to show his teeth in something that was far colder than a smile.

Perry could almost feel the wyrms touching his feet. "Pull me up!" he begged. "Please!"

"Be still!" Stuber barked at him.

"The wyrms!"

"Fuck the wyrms! Be still!"

Perry didn't know what else to do. Stuber had him. He snapped his mouth shut and clung hard to the oar, wide-stretched eyes locked in with Stuber's glinting, furious ones.

"You feel the fear, Shortstack?" Stuber's face leered in the green glow. "You feel the panic nipping at your heels? You feel yourself at the ragged precipice of death?"

"Yes!"

"Good!" Stuber shouted in his face. "Now sit there, you fucking peon! Sit there and experience it! Let it soak into your soul. Let that fear go all the way through you. I want you to *feel* it."

"I feel it!"

"No you don't," Stuber's voice became a fierce whisper: "You don't know what fear is until you've sat in it, stewed in it, let it bore holes through your soul as you look around and realize that all that is keeping you from tipping over that razor's edge of death and destruction is nothing but chance! It's all just a roll of the dice! You have no control over it. Death simply waits in the wings and there's not a damned thing you can do about it if it decides to descend on you today. Do you believe me?"

Perry floated there, clutching the oar, but his body was still, his legs no longer thrashing.

The fear was boring holes through him.

And yet he lay there, eyes locked with Stuber.

Panic coursing through him.

And yet he was still.

Silent.

"You turn your fear and your panic and your insecurity into anger. You lash out because you're terrified. Because you buy into the stupid peon myth that you can somehow control when death comes to you, that you can somehow run fast enough to escape him. Trust me, Shortstack when he wants you, you'll know. Because you'll wake up in The After."

Stuber jerked the oar, as though he were about to try to wrench it free from Perry's grip, but then he held it still, and Perry realized he was trying to refocus Perry's attention.

"Now, do you feel the fear?"

"Yes," Perry said, quieter than before.

"And do you think I will let you drown? Or do you think the wyrms will get you? Or do you think I will pull you up into the boat again?"

Perry stared up at the ex-legionnaire and he realized that he had no idea.

"I don't know, Stuber."

"Exactly!" Stuber hissed. "You—don't—fucking—know!"

Then Stuber pulled the oar up, and Perry rose out of the water, dripping and shivering and looking below him at the streaks of dim green light that writhed through the depths below him.

Perry tumbled over the side of the boat. Felt Stuber's hands on his shoulders, propping him up. Perry wrapped his arms around himself. The water was frigid, but now being out of it felt even colder. He shivered violently and had to clench his teeth to keep them from chattering.

Strangely, in that moment, he felt a stillness in his soul. He felt the relief of being pulled out of the water, yes. But that relief was not as strong or as

BREAKING GODS

poignant as he'd thought it would be. It was overshadowed by something bigger. Something that was harder to swallow, but now that it had gotten past the lump in his throat, was like medicine that he desperately needed.

He raked his sopping hair back from his forehead. Wiped water out of his eyes.

He frowned, staring at nothing, and shivering, trying to organize his thoughts, trying to make peace with the oddness that surrounded him now, penetrated him. All of his attention was suddenly focused inward.

Seated beside him, Stuber liberated a foil emergency blanket from the medical pack that he'd taken from the skiff. He snapped it open, and then draped it, almost tenderly, over Perry's shoulders.

Perry took it, pulled it tight against him. Immediately felt better as the foil reflected his body's heat and began to thaw him out.

But still he didn't say anything.

"Well," Sagum said, leaning back and propping his elbows on the side of the boat. "That was interesting. Hey, legionnaire. As long as you got the oars in your hands, how about you paddle us along for a spell?"

Stuber sat there for a long moment, looking at Sagum with eyes that showed nothing. They might as well have been the eyes in a wax statue. Finally, as though awakening from his thoughts, Stuber plunked the oar that he held into the oarlock to his left, and then retrieved the other oar and put it to his right.

"Might as well," Stuber said. "Couldn't expect an adolescent boy like yourself to do men's work."

Sagum smiled. Didn't bristle at it. He relaxed even further into his reclined position. "An excellent point, legionnaire."

"Ex."

"Hm?"

"*Ex*-legionnaire."

Sagum frowned, the smile fading from his face. "I've wondered about that."

Stuber hauled on the oars and the boat lurched under the sudden strength of Stuber's pull. He reset the oars slowly, but when he pulled, it was with a massive stroke that sped the boat along. Stuber did this for about ten strokes, and then took a rest and leaned his elbows on the oars as the paddles skimmed over the water's surface.

Stuber smiled at Sagum, then Teran, and then even favored Perry with it, but Perry was still staring off into the darkness with a pensive frown on his brow.

Stuber turned back to the others. "It's dark, so we might imagine that it's nighttime. The glow from the wyrms is green, but we can imagine it as firelight. And nighttime around a campfire is always a good time to spin a yarn, isn't it?"

CHAPTER 22

✿

STUBER

FUCK THE BEER, I'LL DRINK THE LIQOUR
GIMME A WHORE, I'LL GIVE 'ER THE STICKER
NO COCK SHE'S FELT HAS EVER BEEN THICKER
I'LL OUT-FUCK AND OUT-DRINK AND OUT-KILL A
MAN QUICKER!

See the two red-faced men screaming this at each other with their noses practically touching?

Well, the one on the left is me. You can tell by my rugged good looks.

The ugly one across from me is my Decanus, which is a stupid, fancy, paladin word for Sergeant. His name is Pyler. No, that's not an assumed name. Typically only centurions and above assume demigod-approved names. Unless you're a real, hardcore believer. And let's be honest, most of the men that are out on the battlefield on a daily basis don't really give a shit. They're primary focus is on drinking, fucking, and fighting. They simply don't have time to be true believers. Faith takes effort.

See the rest of the men crowding around us, their eyes wide and bright, grinning like idiots as they watch us like hawks to see if we've shouted the lyrics without stumbling? That's the rest of our battleline—the paladins call it a *contubernium*, but who the hell can say that word? It's hard enough when you're sober. And we're never sober.

A battleline is twenty men. That's how we're arranged when we're marched off towards doom, in the thick of the autocannon fire, with the flak bursting over our heads. I stand in the middle of these men, shoulder to shoulder and shield to shield, and we inch our way towards death and destruction, and we laugh and we slaughter and we do our best to make sure it's the *other* side's death and destruction, but…you know how it is.

Death waits in the wings.

One day, chance will happen, and death will descend.

One of my shield brothers will stumble over a body, or slip in a mess of intestines, and he will dip his shield at just the right moment, and a .458 will plaster my brain through the back of my skull and that will be that.

You can't do anything about it. You just make sure that your own shield is up, and you make sure that you're picking your feet up high enough to avoid any snares, and you make sure that your blood-cleats are securely fastened to your boots so you don't slip, and that's really all you can do. You do what you're supposed to do.

And when you're not killing, you come and compound the sins of your murderous day's work with drinking and whoring, and you never, *ever* let it touch you, all the people you've left on the battlefield, stinking and rotting in the midday sun. You don't think about the wives and the families that you left in whatever city or town you came from, how many of them are widows now, and whether your wife will be a widow next.

Those thoughts are like bullets and mortar shells themselves.

You always keep your shield up, lest they wreck you.

Drinking and carousing is one of the ways you keep that shield up.

But, just like on the battlefield, sometimes a bullet gets through.

On this particular night, we are all very drunk. You know, there's a certain tipping point when it comes to drunkenness. A point in which you know things are going to go downhill. I think we had already passed that a few drinks back, but the whiskey was flowing, and the competition was keeping us distracted, so maybe we knew that the moment had already passed us by, but we didn't much care.

Now, Pyler is a hard drinking man. You know how I like to say that I can out-fuck, out-fight, and out-drink every man in the room? Well, Pyler is the exception to that rule. If he is in the room, then I can no longer say that and be an honest man. And I am always honest. It is one of my most shining qualities.

There have been rare occasions when I've seen Pyler actually *appear* to be drunk. But most of the time he drinks enough to kill an entire battleline, and still acts, walks, and talks like he's sober. Tonight, though, I get the feeling it will be one of those nights when even Pyler is drunk.

It was inevitable. You could see it in the men's eyes as the sun dipped below the horizon and the night chill settled on us. You could see the smoldering anger that needed to be either doused, or burned up. The wonderful thing about whiskey is that it does both.

It might've been different if we'd fought a battle that day. The bad energy might've found an outlet then, and gone off to wherever those things go. Dissipated into the ethereal realm. Or possibly just buried inside, waiting for a hooker to say something untowards, and then you black out and wake up with your hands wringing her dead throat...

I digress.

We *hadn't* fought that day, and that's the point.

We'd fought the *previous* day, and that is where the bad energy came from.

Our battleline, crowded around this table, acting like they don't care about death, there are only twelve of them now, myself and Pyler included. There are eight pewter cups at the far end of the table, splashed with whiskey and water, no hands to grasp them or mouths to drink them. They sit abandoned, and the ghosts of the men who should've been there getting drunk with them are the haunts that anger the rest of us.

You should know that we don't get angry whenever one of us dies. We wouldn't even get angry if a *lot* of us died.

It is not death that makes us angry. Rather, stupidity.

But I'll get to that in time.

Let me back up a bit.

We are drinking. We are shouting.

That is the object of this game. You shout the words as fast as you can. It is a race to see who can complete the entire lymeric without stumbling— hence the hawkish refereeing of our linemates, the close watching of our lips and the intense scrutiny of our words.

A dumb game, you say?

Perhaps.

But it gets you drunk quick.

Anyways, I complete the lymeric without stumbling, but I'm about two words behind Pyler. He shouts "QUICKER!" just as I'm tumbling through "AND OUT-KILL—Ah, fuck!"

Pyler thrusts his arms up in victory, his eyes wide and intense. "I can't be stopped! I can't be stopped!"

Everyone is shouting over each other now, including myself.

"He stumbled!" I yell, pointing an accusing finger at Pyler. "What the fuck was that? He stumbled when he said 'out-drink and out-fuck'!"

Pyler blows a raspberry and the spit speckles my face.

"You lie, Stuber! You lie like a dog!"

"Drink, peasant! Drink your punishment!"

"Say the words, Stuber! Say them right next time!"

"Say it with feeling!"

"Drink your punishment!"

I have my arms around two of my linemates. They are, perhaps, holding me up.

One of them thrusts the cup into my face. It teeters at my lips and dribbles out liquid that burns and makes me thirsty for it. I am still trying to shout in protest, but I am overcome with gales of laughter as they force the cup to my mouth and pour it in, all the while cursing me for a peasant, for being a peon that has no killing spirit and has never lain with a woman.

Despite my uncontrollable laughter, I manage to swallow the mouthful of grog. Then I belch, and bray and growl like a dog. I unwrap my arms from around my linemates and slam my fists on the table repeatedly, screaming as I do it.

Then I straighten.

"Again!" I demand.

A cheer goes up. They slam my chest with their fists, bolstering me out of drunkenness. They seize me by the shoulders and shake me hard. They scream in my ear to win this time, to win, to have killing spirit, to quit shaming my wife before she runs off with a better man.

Pyler observes that if my jaw wasn't so tired from sucking cock all day, I might be able to say the lymeric and stop heaping shame on myself.

They pour me a fresh cup. Up to the top this time.

Pyler waves a hand over the top of his cup. "None for me, thanks."

His cup has remained full for the last two rounds. The bastard.

"Actually," Pyler announces, with gusto. "Let's level the playing field here."

Then he takes his cup and drains it in one swift gulp. Slaps it back down. Demands to be refilled. The challenge set, all those present appropriately ooh, aah, and jeer their approval.

One of our linemates climbs up onto the table. His boots scatter mud across the wooden top. The table creaks. He crouches down drunkenly and holds his hand between us, taking it upon himself to be our starter for this round.

"Decanus Pyler!" he bellows, face flushed, veins protruding on his forehead. "Are you ready?"

Pyler leans across the table and nods.

I lean across as well, and this time I press my forehead against his.

He presses back, grinning.

Two bulls, locked in.

"Legionnaire Stuber appears to be ready!" our linemate-turned-starter proclaims. "On my mark, let 'em have it!"

A tense hush.

"Three…Two…One…"

"Centurion!"

There is a mad scramble.

Our starter drops a shoulder and combat rolls off the table, scattering cups everywhere.

I immediately disengage from Pyler and rock my body into something that might be called attention, if you are not inspecting it too closely. I have to lean forward on the table because I fear if I try to stand at attention on my own two feet I will pitch backward.

Looking out for me, one of my linemates comes to attention very close beside me, so that his hip creates another contact point with mine. Just in case I should start to fall out, he will keep me propped up. I think I'm okay, but I appreciate the cover.

We look down the length of our camp table.

The centurion stands there, looking at us. He is out of his battle dress. He wears only his breastplate, which no man had ever seen him out of.

His two guards stand beside him, eyeing us like we are pieces of shit that they have scraped off their boots with a stick.

Our centurion—our commanding officer—has a pose to him like he was just walking around the camp tables quietly and chose to stop out our rowdy table. A small smile plays on his lips, wistful, as though perhaps he is recalling his days as a legionnaire where he also spent the night drinking

263

with his linemates and refusing to think about death waiting in the wings.

The centurion's decorations glitter in the firelight.

One in particular catches my eye. A cross-of-gallantry. A new addition.

I glance sidelong at Pyler and I see that he is not at attention, he is leaning on the table, supported by an arm, while the other remains at his hip. He is not even looking at the centurion. He is looking down at his cup with his lips pursed and his jaw muscles locked.

Shit.

At the head of our table, the centurion's gaze seems to pass over Pyler, and for a half-second he frowns, as though wondering why this man is not standing at attention in his presence. But the hour is late, and if you choose to walk the camp at this time of night, you'll find many a legionnaire that couldn't stand if they wanted to.

The centurion nods to us. "I'm sorry to have interrupted you. I haven't heard that lymerick in a while. It warmed my heart."

Our linemate that took it upon himself to be our starter now takes it upon himself to speak, and I know what he is doing. He is speaking to the centurion so that Pyler doesn't have to. We can all feel the tension like a steel cable going through our chests, but if the centurion and his guards notice it, they don't show it.

"Yes, sir," our linemate says. "Of course, sir." Slight hesitation. "Would you like us to call it out for you, sir?"

The centurion laughs and shakes his head. He grins at us, but there is a sadness there. "No, but thank you for the offer. I expect it will…lack a certain verve if it is done under the eye of your centurion." He holds up a finger and looks at them under his brow in mock-sternness. "But, I expect to hear it loud and clear from my quarters."

There is a subdued chuckle amongst my battleline.

"Of course, sir."

The centurion nods toward us. "Carry on, gentlemen."

Then he turns to start walking again.

And that might've been that.

That moment, as I recall it, now and many days since, could have gone a different way. If it had, perhaps I would still be a legionnaire. Perhaps I would be a centurion myself by now. Or long dead on a battlefield. You never know.

But Pyler chooses that moment to pipe up.

"Is it heavy?" he asks loudly.

The centurion stops in mid-step. Rocks back to look down our rank and put his eye on the drunken man who couldn't be bothered to come to attention. He finds that Pyler is still in his state of repose, but now is looking boldly at the centurion.

"Pyler," I whisper under my breath.

"Is what heavy?" the centurion asks.

"The cross-of-gallantry. Is it heavy?"

Absently, the centurion reaches up and touches his latest decoration. "No. It weighs the same as the others."

It appears that the centurion is in a forgiving mood.

Or perhaps he isn't sure what is coming next.

We all hope that it will rest there.

But Pyler will not let it.

"I would think," Pyler says, slowly, confidently, his words not drunken at all. "That it would carry the weight of the twenty-two souls that died for it. I feel the weight of eight of them myself, and I have no decoration to show for it."

The two guards that flank the centurion dip their chins, their mouths flattening in distaste, and they step towards Pyler, our linemates between them and him spreading out of the way.

But the centurion barks, "Stand down," and they halt.

The centurion looks long and hard at Pyler, his eyes narrowed, contemplating the best course of action. After a breath or two, the centurion glances at our linemate who had spoken for us earlier and says, "I believe your Decanus is too deep in his cups for his own good. Perhaps you should put him to bed."

Our linemate almost melts with relief. "Yes, sir."

Two of our other linemates closest to Pyler take ahold of his arms, eager to set the situation right without the whole battleline having to be flogged for their sergeant's loose tongue. But Pyler is steeping in rage—has been steeping in it for the last two nights, and he's not about to choose the easy way out.

He shakes off the arms of his linemates and points a mutinous finger at the centurion. "You don't do a three-quarter turn in mid-field, you boot-fucking peon!"

The centurion's eyes go wide. In an instant, his face is flushed. Even in the dim glow of firelight, we can see his skin turning red. The veins under his eyes and on his forehead standing out. "Seize that little prick," he grinds out through his bared teeth.

The guards move like they are pleased to do it. They plunge through our linemates, and they give way before the guards, knowing damn well that it has reached the point of treason. Of execution, if they make one wrong move.

Pyler continues yelling at the centurion, heedless of the guards that are barging up to him. "You cocksucker!" He bellows. "The lowliest peon conscript knows not to do a three-quarter turn in mid-field!"

If you are curious by this point, the reason you do not do that maneuver is because when you are marching in mid-field, shoulder-to-shoulder, and shield-to-shield, it is damn near impossible to conduct a three-quarter turn in any direction without heavily exposing the line to enemy fire from one direction or another.

If they shift their shield to cover their sides from the main enemy line, they're open to the enemy flankers. If the block maintains their shields to the flankers, they'll be open to the autocannons.

And that is what happened.

And the autocannons chewed through twenty-two out of a hundred men before the centurion corrected his command. But he didn't give the command to dress their shields towards the fire until the entire block had already maneuvered into position to cover a breach in the main line.

A courageous action, above and beyond the call of duty. Something that might earn the centurion of the block a cross-of-gallantry.

Legionnaires know that they are likely to die a horrible, bloody death. But they do not want to die a horrible, bloody death just so that some centurion trying to suck a paladin's cock can get himself a medal.

Pyler continues to rave at the centurion, even as the guards seize him by both arms and slam him face-first into the table, scattering our cups. They silence him with a heavy blow to his gut, but in Pyler's defense, it takes them three tries before it finally knocks the wind out of him.

They clap manacles on his wrists, binding him behind his back, and then force him to his knees. They whip their rifles around, pointing them at the back of Pyler's head. They hold him down as the centurion approaches, shaking with rage.

He draws out a sap and with one swift movement cracks it across Pyler's face, breaking his jaw. "Now you'll have a loose jaw to go with your loose lips!" the centurion screams in his face. "And consider yourself lucky I don't have you shot!"

Then Pyler begins to laugh. Blood spewing out of his mouth, he laughs uproariously. Then turns his head towards the centurion and spits bloody saliva at him. His next words are his last, and they are garbled by his broken jaw, but we all understand them, and so does the centurion.

"I'd rather die than go into battle with you again!"

The centurion gazes at him for a few beats. Grows very calm. Then he nods at Pyler. "Suit yourself."

Then he draws his pistol and puts a bullet through Pyler's brain.

Pyler's body falls back. Dead as dead could be.

The centurion draws himself up in the burning silence. Holsters his pistol. And then he looks right at me. "Legionnaire Stuber!"

I can't say anything. I simply stand at attention, staring at the centurion.

"You are Decanus now."

CHAPTER 23

✿

DESERTER

THEY BOBBED ALONG IN SILENCE on an underground river.

Stuber sat there with the oars in his hands, staring at nothing in particular. That familiar sadness had overtaken his face again. He didn't row. Just sat there with the paddles skimming the water.

Perry huddled in his corner of the boat, still damp, but no longer shivering.

Teran and Sagum lay in positions of relaxation, but their necks were tight, and their bodies tense.

They all watched Stuber, and he watched nothing.

After a long moment, he seemed to rouse himself. He dipped the oars. Gave them another strong pull. The boat accelerated again. Then he rested again.

"So," Sagum said. "You became Decanus for your battleline."

Stuber grunted, still not meeting any of their gazes.

"Then how did you become an *ex*-legionnaire?"

Stuber hauled the oars in so that they rested on his legs, and he leaned across them, elbows on his knees. Finally looked up at Sagum, and gave him a humorless smile. "We met The Light in battle the very next day. My first day as Decanus. And the centurion positioned himself at the edge of our line, which was directly beside me. I suppose he thought that we might be mutinous, and so he wanted his presence there to…intimidate us, I suppose."

Stuber rubbed his short beard with a rough hand. "Well. We were midfield again. And again, he called a three-quarter turn." Stuber's small smile turned into a rictus grin. "I suppose to teach us a lesson. But…you could say the lesson didn't take. He called out the command, and I was supposed to call it out to the line, but I just looked across at him. He was to my right. Me, staring at him. Him staring right back at me. And I remember he had this stupid little smirk on his face, as though to say, *this will teach you*. Now, I'm not a hateful man, but I hated him passionately at that moment. He seemed to realize that I wasn't going to repeat his command, and his face turned to that same indignant rage that he'd shown to Pyler, just before executing him. And he opened his mouth to call out the command again, to *insist* on it. And I shot him."

Stuber's smile softened. Like he was remembering something pleasant. He even closed his eyes, as though trying to recall every detail. "I had my ten-millimeter already in my hand, and I just winged out a shot, straight from the hip. I don't think anyone saw me do it. All they saw was the centurion's face turn to mush. But…"

Stuber thrust the oars out again, and began rowing. "I knew that the paladins would know. They always know. They record the battles in detail. Where do you think all that footage comes from that they plaster all over the town jumbotrons? They would eventually see me murder my commanding officer. So, when our lines clashed with the lines of The Light, I allowed myself to become separated from my battleline. I took a fall, as though shot, and

I lay beneath my shield as legionnaires from both sides trampled over me, and their bodies fell on top of me. I nearly drowned in the bloody mud, but my concave shield gave me just a few inches of room from which I could suck air and survive. Air that smelled of blood and shit and piss and gunsmoke. And I lay there like that until it was all darkness around me and I heard the approach of the dogs, and then I worked my way out of the pile of dead bodies, and I escaped."

As he said this last part, Stuber's voice relaxed from the clench of his memories, and became casual again. He continued to haul at the oars with a steady, unhurried rhythm.

"The first town I came to was Dezkarriado, which was declared for The Light at the time. So I cut off my *sagum* and I went to a merchant and sold him my greeves and my spaulders and my helm, and all the rest of it. Except for my chest plate and my rifle. He knew I was from The Truth, but I gave him a good deal on the armor and my pistol, so he kept his mouth shut.

"Then I took that money to the first bar I could find and I attempted to drink myself to death. As you can see, it didn't work. The first night, I passed out before I could drink enough to kill myself. They threw me in the alley. I woke up around midday the next day, and, not to be deterred, I tried again, but this time I ran out of money first.

"I was considering robbing the barkeep for enough whiskey to do the trick. I guess I could've just blown my brains out with my rifle, but I'd kind of fixated on the death-by-whiskey concept. Anyways, I was about to do it when a gentleman by the name of Hauten offered to buy me a drink, and then offered me a job. He'd had to kill his last security guy because he'd tried to steal from Hauten. I understood and appreciated Hauten's position. Plus he was buying me drinks. So I decided I'd give it a try. And the rest, as they say, is history."

Perry frowned at the big man sitting in the middle of the boat. He shifted beneath the foil blanket. Let it slide off of him a bit. He was starting to feel clammy with it on. It was keeping him from drying out.

"In Oksidado," Perry said. "When I asked you about your desertion, I guessed that you'd killed your superior. And you said that wasn't it."

Stuber shook his head. "I believe my words were 'not exactly.'"

Perry waited, looking up Stuber.

"I said," Stuber continued, softly. "That you didn't know me like you thought you did. Perhaps now you see the whole elephant."

"What do you mean by that?" Perry asked. "The whole elephant?"

"Do you know what an elephant is?"

"Yes. From the time before the gods destroyed the planet."

Stuber allowed it with a nod. "Well, there's an old story I was told once about blind men feeling their way around an elephant. Each one felt a part of the elephant. So the one that felt its legs said 'this animal is shaped like a tree trunk,' and the one that felt its long nose said, 'No, this animal is shaped like a snake,' and the one that felt its tusks said, 'No, this animal is shaped like a spear.' But none of them were right because they couldn't see the animal in its entirety. It was all of those things put together."

Stuber pulled the oars a few more times in silence. They passed through a narrow tunnel, the rock walls on either side of them only a few feet past where the oars would dip into the water. The ceiling above them was cluttered with glowing eggs, and it was very close over their heads.

Perry looked up at them, disconcerted by their proximity. He thought that if he stood up, he might reach up and touch them. He felt both revolted and fascinated by the thought.

"On Boss Hauten's crew," Stuber said, his voice reverberating tightly in their close environment. "You only ever saw me as a killer. And I am. I won't deny it. But people are usually more complicated than they first appear." He rested the oars and looked pointedly at Perry. "What about you, Shortstack? I see a few aspects of you, but I also feel the entirety of a great beast that I haven't yet explored."

Perry tilted his head to stare at the ceiling again. He thought about Stuber's implications for a long time, and when he finally chose to speak, the tunnel was widening out again. The ceiling vaulting far above them once more.

"I don't even know myself," Perry said. He pushed the foil blanket away from him, and, moving slowly so as not to rock the boat too much, he stripped out of his jacket and shirt and spread them out on the side of the boat. Then took his soaking boots off and set them upside down to drain and dry.

Towards the front of the boat, Sagum leaned forward and quirked his head in Perry's direction. "We were told you were...capable of great things." He said it without malice, a simple observation.

Perry chuffed mirthlessly. "Who told you that? My uncle?"

Sagum nodded, watching Perry carefully, like you might watch a street performer—skeptically, but also expectantly. Hoping for a big reveal.

Perry looked away from Sagum. "Sorry, Sagum. I can't do great things. I'm not the warrior my uncle wanted me to be. I'm not the warrior my *father* wanted me to be." He took a deep breath. "I'm just a washout. My uncle put me in the academy and I deserted just before graduation."

"A deserter is not a washout," Sagum said. "A washout is expelled because he can't cut it. A deserter makes a decision to leave. They didn't expel you, did they? They were prepared to graduate you? Even someone of your...diminutive size."

"Fuck you," Perry said, but it had no heat behind it. Then he let out a snort of laughter. He looked back at Sagum and found the other man smiling.

"Well," Sagum shrugged. "Your uncle seemed convinced of your abilities. That must count for something."

Perry's expression soured. "He said the same thing to me, that he thought I could *do something*, but I have no clue what he's talking about. Did you ever consider that it's just some bullshit that my uncle made up to make me seem special, so you'd go out and find me?" Perry's eyes dropped to his hands. "Uncle Sergio always wanted me to fill my father's shoes. But...I'm not my father."

Teran, who no one had noticed was stewing silently as the rest of them talked, suddenly sat up and spoke. "And what do you think that has to do with it?"

Perry looked at her, surprised at the sudden volley. She glared at him, her brow creased in the center, her lips tight. The green glow from all around them cast strange shadows on her face, made her look even angrier.

"My father was a legatus," Perry replied. "*He* was the warrior. *He* stood his ground. *He* was the one I was supposed to be like. But I'm not. I'm not like him at all." He bared his teeth, and the words seethed out between them, the shame curdling them into bitterness. "I ran away."

"My father was a thief," Teran snapped back at him. "And my mother was *literally* a whore. She wanted to keep me when she had me but she was a drunk, and my thief of a father wouldn't let her, so he kidnapped me from her. He was already wanted, dead or alive. He fled and became an Outsider. And I grew up in the caves, hiding from everyone else in the world." She spread her arms out. "And yet, here I am. I'm not a thief, and I'm not a whore either."

"What are you saying, Teran?" Perry felt a twist of anger heating him up again. "That my father has nothing to do with this? That you all just went searching for me because I'm me? Because you wanted a coward and a deserter? Bullshit. You're only interested in me because Uncle Sergio was somehow convinced that I could be like my father."

Teran was not the type to be cowed by conflict, and Perry knew this about her, but somehow he was still surprised that his heated response hadn't got her to shut up. She leaned even farther forward, and she stuck her chin out towards him, as though daring him to take a swing at it.

"What I'm saying, is that your parents don't determine your fate. They determine your starting point. But in the end you're the one that makes the choices." She pushed both of her hands against her chest. "My parentage determined that I was born to ingrates and would grow up an Outsider. But I made the choices that guided my life to this point right now." She stabbed her finger down, as though spearing an imaginary timeline. "I believed in those choices when I made them and I believe in them now. I believe that I found you, and I believe that finding you was important." She thrust that finger at him. "Now the choice is up to you about where we go from here. You can either sit around and continue to have a pity party because your life up to this point sucked—which, hey, so sorry for you my friend, but *all* our lives have sucked up to this point! That's kind of why we're here—or, you can choose to *do something* more with yourself."

Perry groaned with exasperation. "What is it exactly that everyone thinks I'm supposed to do?"

Teran's voice lowered, but lost none of its bite. "Maybe you could start by honoring the sacrifice of your uncle and the countless others that died in those caves so you could get away, and listen to the message that your father left you."

His father. A man whom he'd never known.

A ghost that lurked in the background of his earliest memories.

I don't want to listen to what he has to say...

And sitting there on the cold metal bottom of the boat, Perry realized something.

The realization chapped his ass, and then it humbled him.

Stuber was right.

That was the bitter truth. The uncomfortable epiphany.

It's always difficult to take truth from a person who you have an antagonistic relationship with. Perhaps it was the dunk in the water that cooled him off. Perhaps it was Stuber's story of why he had deserted that had allowed Perry to see the whole elephant.

Whatever it was, the truth of what Stuber had said now hit him fully, and rearranged the landscape of his being: Perry always lashed out in anger to hide his fear.

He'd been doing it since the fear was born in him during his five years at the Academy.

Maybe it was hard to accept that from Stuber. But that didn't stop it from being true.

It wasn't anger that was going to cause him to throw the clasp into the water. And it wasn't anger at his father that caused him not to want the clasp in his hands again.

It was fear.

Perry was terrified of the truth, because the truth had not set him free. The truth had upended his life. It had put him on a course of fire and death, and he was scared to his marrow that whatever truths the clasp might reveal to him would not make things easier, but exponentially harder.

And…he was afraid of being *responsible* for these people.

Stuber shifted on his bench seat. Pulled the oars into the boat, letting the mild current of the underground river carry them along. He reached behind his chest plate where he had hidden the clasp earlier, and he pulled it out.

He held it there in the verdant light, between his massive thumb and forefinger. Eyeing it.

Perry watched the ex-legionnaire first, and then found himself staring at the clasp as well.

"You know," Stuber said. "I heard your uncle tell you that he thought this was god-tech. Did he ever say why?"

Perry shook his head.

Stuber's eyes shifted from the clasp, to Perry. "And did he ever say why he believed you'd be able to operate god-tech?"

"No." Perry held out his hand for the clasp.

Stuber held onto the clasp, and Perry's gaze, for a moment longer. "It would be very…interesting…if you were able to operate god-tech."

Perry took the clasp from Stuber's hands like it was a volatile compound that might explode if handled too roughly. He turned it over, studying it. "We don't even know that it's god-tech."

"Well, I can see why your uncle would think it was."

Perry frowned. "Why?"

Stuber pointed. "You see any buttons? Levers? Controls?"

Perry took a moment to continue looking it over. Then shook his head.

"God-tech has no manual controls. That's how the paladins maintain possession of their weaponry." Stuber tapped a finger to his temple. "It is something…in their minds."

Uncle Sergio's dying words skittered through Perry's head again.

His uncle's dying words. And his father's parting ones.

Always do the right thing. Never shy away from a fight. And remember that your mind is your greatest weapon.

He also remembered how Uncle Sergio had asked about The Calm.

The thing that Perry possessed, and others didn't.

Was that somehow the key to this thing?

"I don't..." Perry shook his head. "I don't know how."

Stuber sighed. "Well, neither do I, Shortstack. But as an experiment, why don't you just give it a shot."

A self-conscious titter came out of Perry. "You act like I have a clue what I'm doing."

Stuber quirked an eyebrow. "Surely there's something. Some idea that you have."

The Calm.

But that's ridiculous.

Still. It was the only thing he had. Maybe it was a stretch, but he couldn't think of anything else.

"Okay," Perry said, feeling nervous and not knowing why.

Perhaps nervous that his one idea wasn't going to work, and then what would he have?

Perry closed his eyes.

His nerves made The Calm seem dim and hard to reach.

Perry forced the nerves down. Breathed deeply and blew it out. Settled himself.

The red blur came up to meet him. He sank into it.

The rush. The momentum. Everything flowing.

He heard his own voice, as though from another room: "What now?"

Distantly, Stuber's grumpy response: "Gods, man, it didn't come with an instruction manual. Just…visualize it or something."

Visualize it.

No. That wasn't right.

But…

There was something in The Calm. Something that he'd never sensed before. Like he was not alone in his own head.

For a flash, the complete foreignness of it pulled him out of the red, but he kept breathing steadily. Sank back in. Determined now to see what this interloper was in his head.

It was not an entity. Not an actual being.

It was just an energy.

The clasp.

The god-tech.

As nerves gave way to curiosity, it felt to him that he moved closer to it. And he perceived that it was a part of him, somehow, and he a part of it. He could…

Connect

The thing in Perry's hands moved.

His eyes snapped open.

Seams suddenly appeared in the clasp where there had been nothing before. Seams that cut the circular shape into eight triangular pieces. A bright white light emanated from behind these seams, and then they spread open like the petals of a strange metal flower.

"Shit," Perry exclaimed, almost dropping it.

Stuber smiled at him, looking satisfied. "See? Just that easy."

CHAPTER 24

✿

THE GHOST

AS THE METAL FLOWER in his hand came into what looked like full bloom, the strength of the light became milder. For a moment, Perry stared into it, counting the seconds until something happened, wondering if something was *going* to happen, wondering if the thing had been broken somehow.

How the hell did I do that?

There was a mix of pride and fear.

The fear was like a tether, pulling him up from The Calm, but he deliberately cut the cord of that fear, forcing himself to maintain his focus.

It was challenging to stay focused both on reality and what was happening in his head, but he also felt a certain balance there, between the two realms, and he realized after a moment that he was capable of straddling the divide.

He sat very still, as though any movement from him would shatter the spell that he'd somehow worked.

The light coming from the clasp flashed.

Stay focused...

The next thing Perry saw was a man. The man materialized in the air above the white glow from the clasp, and he stood six feet tall and regal and floated there like a genie just issued from a bottle. Perry found himself reeling backwards from the image, as though it were a real man in front him, but he could see through it, like a ghost...

It *was* a ghost.

Staring up at the face of the man, stern and authoritative, Perry's deepest memories tingled with recognition and he knew that he was looking at Legatus Cato. He knew that he was looking at the man that had once been his father.

The image seemed to be looking back at him, and Perry found that his heart was hammering, and he could not determine what it was that he felt—fear, or a thrill, or pure longing for something missing that he had never even acknowledged that he'd been without.

"Percival, my son," the ghost said, its voice powerful and tangible and real. The voice, more than the image, caused Perry to feel a moment of vertigo, as though he were falling back through time to when he was three years old and that voice was his world, and it was the voice of a childhood god. "There are many things that I want to tell you, but I do not have the time. When you finally get this message, I will be dead for many years, and you will be grown into a man."

The face of the ghost seemed to writhe with momentary pain. The eyes looked up and away from Perry, at something far beyond any of their sight. Then they came back. Refocused themselves. "My time is very short, but it is not so short that I cannot tell you that I love you, and that your mother loved you, and if there was any way I could spare you from what I am about to ask, then I would. But that is not the hand that fate has dealt us. Sometimes we are called to do things we do not want to do. So please, forgive—"

Abruptly, a series of laser-like lines shot through the image of his father, and Legatus Cato's face froze in mid-sentence, as though he had been stunned. An unearthly, electronic tone seemed to come from his lips.

Perry blinked rapidly. The moment shattered. "What…?" he started to say, but then his father's voice reappeared in a wash of scrambled noise.

"There is so much more to say, my son, but not enough time to say it. I must be quick—"

Again, the eerie electronic tones interrupted his father's voice, the image of his face jerking through frozen bits of computerized memory.

Perry leaned forward, thrusting his hands up towards the hovering image, frustration clenching his features. "What's happening? What is this?"

Sagum leaned towards the image as well, his head tilted, eyes frowning. "I think it's corrupted."

"Corrupted?" Perry demanded. He vaguely recalled Teran suggesting that Sagum had some technical prowess. Something about him keeping the lights on for the Outsiders. Maybe he would know what he was talking about.

"The data," Sagum explained. "The recording. It's been there for a long time." He looked at Perry. "I'd guess the data got corrupted at some point."

Cato's voice boomed out again, interrupted by atonal screeches, like digital claws on an electric chalkboard: "I will be dead soon anyways, so my heresy doesn't matter. Listen to me—*eeeee-eeee-eeee-aaaaaaaaaa*—I do not know the full extent of their deception—*nuh-nuh-nuh-nuh-nuh-nuh-nuh-crrrrrrrrrrrrrrrrr*—something called The Source. I do not—"

Perry's eyes shot back and forth from the garbled image of his father to Sagum's face, washed in the blue glow of a decades-old recording. "Is there any way to fix it?" Perry felt like he was on the verge of panic.

What if the recording only played one time? What if it destroyed itself after this?

What if he would never be able to hear what his father had to say?

Sagum said nothing, only pointed up to the image, pushing Perry's attention back to it.

Cato McGown stared down at the son he would never know as a man. His eyes were serious: "—causes a shift in the formative DNA—" Another cacophony of corrupted sound. The image jerked to another part of the recording. The eyes were different here. They looked down at Perry with what seemed like anger.

"—And you *are* my son. No matter the blood that runs in your veins—in your veins—in your veins—in your veins—"

Perry stared up at this broken loop of recording, and wished that these words would only slide over him. But they didn't. They bored into him.

No matter the blood that ran in his veins?

What the hell was that supposed to mean?

Had Cato already been ashamed of Perry, even then? Had he already seen Perry's small size and known that he would be a failure?

But that seemed very different from what it sounded like his father was trying to convey—not a sense of shame in Perry, but of desperate pride.

Or maybe that was just what Perry *wanted* to believe.

He hadn't taken a breath in a few moments. His lungs started to burn.

"—in your veins—in your veins—in your veins—"

There was something else there, Perry felt certain. Something he wasn't seeing.

He breathed, and with a growing sense of pain, he drew his mind back with a jerk, and the image suddenly disappeared.

Sucked back into the clasp, the genie sent back into its bottle.

And yet the words continued to echo around in his head.

No matter the blood that runs in your veins.

Perry stared at the thing in his hands as the light from the center of it began to fade, and the petals began to close and seal themselves like a night-blooming flower come dawn. And then it was just a clasp that he held in his hand. Just a piece of metal that felt warm from some internal heat.

It took Perry several slow, heavy beats of his own heart to realize that he was doing the very thing that he had scoffed at only moments ago.

He was weeping for the ghost of his lost father.

***

No one spoke for some time after the message ended and the clasp had closed again.

Perry sat there with his back against the side of the boat. He hadn't moved from that position. He held the clasp in his hands, looking at it with a frown.

Stuber sat staring out into the dark distance, his bulky arms crossed over his chestplate, his lips pursed, brow furrowed in deep thought.

Teran studied her hands, and then Perry, trying to guage where his mind was at.

It was Sagum who broke the silence first.

"I'm pretty good with technology," he offered up.

Perry looked up at him. "What do you mean?"

Sagum put his elbows on his knees. Shrugged his slim shoulders. "I've been known to repair bits and pieces of tech hardware. I'm no good with software, but if there're wires crossed, I can usually uncross them." He offered a smile. "Holograms are delicate. But they're not particularly complicated. Could be a bit of dust caught in the wrong place. Could be changing temperatures cracked a diode."

"You think you could repair it? Get the whole message to play?"

"I could try."

Stuber took a loud breath through his nose, and stirred himself. "Might I make a suggestion?"

They all looked to Stuber.

"We are currently heading towards the Glass Flats—a highly inhospitable environment—where we intend to lay low for a while. As Shortstack has so aptly pointed out, we have no supplies. I propose we focus on getting the necessary items to keep ourselves alive, and perhaps when we feel we are in a good hideaway around the Glass Flats, then we can worry about mucking around with technology." Stuber held up a hand towards Perry. "I'm not belittling the importance of the message. Only pointing out where our priorities are. If we all die before we reach safety, then it doesn't much matter what it says on the message, does it?"

Perry felt no prickle of anger at this.

Stuber was simply being Stuber.

Good or bad, the man was pragmatic.

Perry nodded. He looked to Teran. "You mentioned you used to ferry supplies on this boat with your father. Is there any place to get supplies between here and the Glass Flats?"

Teran considered. Looked around them, as though their environment held some sort of landmark for her to gauge her positioning by.

Eventually, Teran nodded. "There's a town we can go to. Lasima. Last stop between us and the end of the world."

CHAPTER 25

✿

LASIMA

TERAN AND SAGUM stepped into Lasima proper.

You knew when you were officially in the city, because you passed under an ancient wooden arch, the timber so sun-bleached that it almost looked like bone. It seemed like this was the spot where there should be gates to the city. But there were no walls around the city, and therefore, no reason to have gates.

As though this strange wooden arch was sacred, not a single shanty or building had been erected prior to the imaginary line created by the standing of the arch.

"So," Sagum sighed, as they walked down the side of a dusty main drag, his eyes flitting over the people that gathered and bustled. "We're here for supplies. And yet we have nothing to buy them with."

"You have no money?" Teran asked him, but her tone suggested that she already knew the answer to that.

"Of course not. I ran out of the caves like the rest of you."

"You had money back in the caves, then?" Teran returned.

Sagum scoffed. "That's beside the point. What are we buying the supplies with?"

Teran's pace slowed, her eyes becoming circumspect. She trudged to a halt between two shopfronts, one of battered old concrete, half chipped away by wind and dust storms, and the other from nearly-petrified wood.

The space between the two buildings created an alleyway, and it was into this that Teran found a wall to put her back to. Not so far down the alley as to be suspicious, but in the shade, so that it seemed she was just escaping the burning sun.

Sagum sidled up next to her and mimicked her pose.

The two of them, backs to a wall, in the shade, watching the people out on the main drag of Lasima.

"Outsiders never have money," Teran murmured. "So how the hell do you think me and my old man used to score supplies?"

"You stole them?"

"No. We're not thieves." Teran sniffed. Swiped a finger under her nose. "We let other people buy them for us."

"Ah." Sagum nodded, knowingly. "So you run a con."

Teran shrugged, keeping her eyes outward. "Outsiders gotta eat too."

"Alright. How's it work?"

"Well, I'm gonna have to modify it a bit. But I think we can make it work." Teran squinted up the street, then down the street. "There," she said, indicating one of the hockers with a nod of her head. "That guy right there. Notice anything?"

Sagum stared. Tilted his head. Tried to see what he was supposed to see. But couldn't think of anything. "Uh…"

"I'll give you a hint, Sagum," Teran said with a small smile. "How's Lasima declaring right now?"

Sagum cast a glance around, and it became apparent from the red banners strung from nearly every shop awning and window, that Lasima currently declared for The Truth. "Well, it appears they are Truthers."

Teran nodded. "Lasima's a battleground town. Always has been, always will be. And whenever there's a switch, there's always a little core of true believers in whatever side they believe in, that don't want to make the switch." Teran indicated the hocker across the street again. "So, knowing that, look again."

Sagum looked again. A knowing glint came over his eyes. "I see. Our gentleman across the street declares for The Light, while the rest of the town declares for The Truth."

Teran nodded. "Exactly. We see his pennant holder over his shop awning…and yet, no pennant. Now why would that be, unless he begrudged the switch?"

"Okay." Sagum shifted his feet, made a little cloud of dust under him. "So how does this work?"

"Well, it starts with you taking off your shirt."

***

Barnabas was an honest man.

It is always said that you can't con an honest man.

That was about to be put to the test.

While honest in his dealings, he was not quite honest in his beliefs, although most around him knew that when Lasima was declared for The Light, he was outspoken, and he became somewhat sullen and silent during years when Lasima was declared for The Truth. However, when pressed, Barnabas would always say what he needed to say to avoid being lynched by a mob—that he wholeheartedly believed in The Truth.

Barnabas ran a small shopfront on the main drag of Lasima. It was little more than a stand with a cloth awning to shade it, and behind him, a very small building in which he kept his wares locked up at night.

Barnabas would sell anything that there was to sell, but what he specialized in was jewelry and other personal adornments—crafts that his wife and two daughters worked tirelessly to create.

Here is what Barnabas observed one day, in the middle of the hot afternoon sun:

A young man, jogging across the street towards him, appearing to come from the back alley of a saloon. The young man carried his shirt in his hands, his boots were unlaced and flopping on his feet, and he was buckling his trousers as he ran.

Obviously, he was running from a woman, post coitus.

Barnabas smiled at the hilarity of the image, until he realized that the young man was running straight towards him.

The young man stuttered to a stop in front of Barnabas's shopfront. "Hide me!" the young man urged, looking over his shoulder. He managed to buckle his trousers, and then looked to Barnabas with a flavor of panic gleaming in his eyes: "Hide me, and I'll make it worth your while!"

Startled, Barnabas moved around the counter containing all the bangles and necklaces and rings, but he stopped short of ushering the young man into his shed to hide him. "Are you running from the law?"

"No!" the young man nearly jumped in panic now. "Just some Truther-bitch-whore!" the young man hissed, lowering his voice so that others wouldn't hear him declaim The Truth. "Please! I'll make it worth your while! I swear to you!"

Well, that pretty much settled it.

Barnabas was a cautious man by nature, and he still had reservations, but the fact that this poor young man was being pursued by a Truther—the most despicable creature found on this scorched earth—had the shop owner's feet moving before he really thought about it.

"Come on," Barnabas mumbled. "Get inside."

The young man scrambled into the open door of Barnabas's small storage shed. He slipped around the corner and took up position in the dim interior, peeking out of a window to the side of it, while Barnabas stationed himself to the side of the door.

"Alright, you're hidden," Barnabas said. "Tell me how you're going to make this worth my while."

"Here she comes!" the young man hissed from the darkness.

Coming from around the same corner where the young man had appeared, a young woman stalked towards them. She was in a state of half-dress, much like the young man had been, and looked like she'd just pulled on enough to go into public without being arrested. She also looked extremely pissed.

"Be quiet," the young man whispered. "Let her move off, and I'll explain everything to you after she leaves."

Barnabas, uncomfortable, but now committed, stood by his storage shed door and crossed his arms and waited.

The young woman's angry eyes scanned across him, not stopping to take much note. She looked up the road. Then down the road. Then decided to break to the right, and went stalking up the street that way, with that special gait that women reserve for men who've done them wrong.

Barnabas gave it a few seconds, until he was sure she wasn't about to come stalking back. "Alright," he said, his discomfort with the situation getting the best of him. "You need to explain yourself or get outta my shed."

The young man shuffled around, getting his shirt on over his head now. "Well, I was foolish for a start. You never trust a whore. But…you know how pillow talk is."

Barnabas only harrumphed in response.

"I told her how I'd dodged the recent draft for the The Truth—not because I'm a coward, I swear—but because I refuse to fight for them. I will wait until Lasima turns back to The Light, and then I will be drafted. And I will fight for them."

Barnabas's simple heart swelled with that closeted pride that one feels when they hear the echoing of their own ideology. "I take it she doesn't appreciate your reasons."

"Apparently not," the young man scoffed. "She charged me double what she'd promised, and said that if I didn't pay, she'd out me to the pontiff as a draft dodger. I'd be hanged. That bitch!"

"What a bitch," Barnabas agreed. "But it's dangerous for you to be saying that around here.

Lasima is for The Light now. You shouldn't be so reckless with what you say."

"I saw your pennant hanger," the young man said.

Barnabas's head snapped around, and looked into the half-open door of his shed. Half shadowed, the young man's eyes glittered with conspiratorial knowledge.

"The pennant means nothing," Barnabas said, defensively. "My wife...she's repairing it right now. I'll hang it shortly. It wouldn't do to hang it with a tear in the seam, would it? That would be a dishonor to The Truth."

The young man shook his head, and spoke with searching earnestness. "You don't need to lie to me, sir. We're of the same mind. And in dark times like this, we need friends to stick by us."

Cautious as ever, Barnabas admitted to nothing. However, he did feel more at ease with the young man—a co-conspirator against the forces of evil that were The Truth.

But...Barnabas was also a sheisty man, as most hockers are, deep in their greedy little hearts.

"Right, well, friend or no," Barnabas began. "You said that you'd make it worth my while to hide you. So I guess you better explain that to me, or you can get outta my shed and let me return to my business. I'll let you escape out the back, and I'll have a clear conscious on it."

"Okay, okay, don't rush me," the young man urged. "Listen. It's...it's not entirely honest dealings, but I think that you'll be okay, considering who we're targeting here."

"You're talking about scamming her."

"I'm talking about scamming a whore and a Truther. And getting her to pay for her illegitimate lifestyle and her illegitimate beliefs."

"Sounds like justice to me."

"Exactly. Now listen. You seem like a savvy individual—I think most hockers are. I've got this ring, see here?"

Barnabas turned and looked again, this time seeing the young man prying a thick, silver ring from his finger and holding it for Barnabas to see.

Barnabas sneered at it. Turned back out to the street. "It's a piece of polished junk."

"Well, it's not *exactly* junk, but that's the point. In truth, it's only worth five pieces. But we're going to make it worth much more. At least in the whore's mind."

Barnabas pursed his lips in thought. "How much is it that you owe this whore?"

"Uh…well…four pieces."

Barnabas snapped his head around. "Then why the hell didn't you just give it to her to cover your cost and be done with the whole thing?"

"Because she's a cheat!" the young man cried. "She told me two pieces at the outset, and now she wants two more because she thinks she can blackmail me. Its robbery and extortion is what it is. I refuse to give it to her on principal."

Barnabas nodded along, tracking easily with the young man's pick-and-choose morals. "So, we're going to make her pay for it. I'm listening."

"Okay. So, I'll step out and allow her to find me here in front of your shop. She'll come over and demand her payment. I'm going to tell her that I have to get the money from a friend, but that I will let her hold the ring as collateral, with you here as a witness."

"Alright."

"Once I'm gone, I want you to inspect the ring. Being the respected jewelry expert that you clearly are, your opinion will count. You have to make her think that the ring is very expensive. Say forty whole pieces. She's an ignorant whore. She'll believe you."

Barnabas smirked again.

"Tell her that I clearly don't know that the ring is worth forty pieces, and then tell her that you think she can barter me down to twenty pieces for the ring. She will think that she can then turn around and sell it for thirty to another hocker for a ten-piece profit. She offers me the twenty pieces, I act like it's a tough sell, but accept. Then she walks away with my five-piece ring, and we split the twenty—ten pieces each." The young man grinned. "You've just made yourself ten pieces, and screwed over a Truther to boot."

Barnabas, being honest as a consequence of his simple nature, was very impressed by this plot. "Just that easy, huh?"

"I've done it before," the young man said. "For far more money. But I'm not trying to ruin the girl, you know. Just teach her a lesson."

Barnabas nodded. "She needs a lesson."

"Yes, she does."

Barnabas had been thinking through it all, and he couldn't find a reason *not* to do it. It required virtually no risk on his part. He was just a prop in this young man's con game, for which he was going to be awarded ten pieces. Easy money for easy work. Ten pieces was what he made in a day. This was guaranteed, for just a small amount of work.

And then Barnabas was already spending those ten pieces in his mind. Mainly on whiskey.

"Alright then," Barnabas decided. "Come on. Let's get this over with. I have a business to run."

"Of course, of course."

The young man stepped out into the sunshine again, and walked around so that he was in front of Barnabas's table, and visible to anyone on the road. It didn't take very long. A cheated whore has eyes like a hawk.

"You!" came the yell from down the street.

The young man made eye contact with Barnabas. "Remember. Get her to give me twenty pieces, once I walk away. You have to convince her it's worth forty."

Barnabas waved him off. "I'm a natural salesman, boy. Perhaps you'll learn something."

The whore came sweeping up to the young man, her palm extended, demanding money. "You owe me two pieces, you Light-side sonofabitch! Pay me now or I go to the pontiff!"

The young man groaned and pumped his hands. "I already paid you two! That was the deal!"

"That was before I learned you were a draft dodger! Plus, you came inside me and that costs extra!"

The young man's face flushed.

The whore's voice climbed. "Pay me now, or I call for the pontiff! I'll do it! Don't think I won't!"

"Alright, alright!" The young man's eyes shot around. The whore's shrill voice had already drawn the attention of several people. "Okay!" he hissed. Then he started taking the ring off his finger.

"Look. Look here. I don't have that much money on me. I gave you two pieces, and that was all I had on me. But I have a friend in town that will loan me two more. You have to let me go get it from him…"

"I'm not letting you out of my sight!"

The young man held up the ring. "With the gods as my witness, and this honest shopkeeper here, I will come back with your money. And here." He pushed the ring towards the whore. "This ring is worth five whole-pieces. You hold it as collateral."

The whore eyed the ring with suspicion. Then eyed her john. Then looked over at Barnabas. "You a witness here?"

Barnabas nodded, gazing at the ring as though he were distracted by its beauty. "Yes. Of course."

"And what will happen if this Light-side prick runs off without paying me?"

Barnabas gave her a greedy smile. "Well…then perhaps you can sell me that ring he's given you."

"No need," the young man said. "I'll be back for the ring."

The whore twiddled the piece of metal around in her hands. Finally, she nodded. "Alright, fine. Go get the money. And be quick about it. I don't have all godsdamned day. I gotta work."

The young man bobbed his head, looking pleased to have come to an agreement. "I will be quick." He pointed a finger at the whore. "I swear to the gods, if you make off with my ring—"

She took a kick at him, which he dodged. "I don't want your ring! I want cash! Now go get it!"

The young man kept his eye on her as he sidestepped his way out into the street, then turned, and jogged down the alley that he had appeared from only moments ago.

When he was out of sight, Barnabas leaned over the table and spoke in a low, urgent voice. "Listen to me, miss! That ring is worth more than that idiot thinks."

The whore startled. Looked at Barnabas. Then the ring. "Really?"

He nodded. Looked around, doing a good job of looking like the greedy trickster he was. "Miss, I'm an expert in jewelry, and if that is what I think it is…" he trailed off and held out a hand. "May I?"

The whore seemed reluctant to relinquish her collateral, but it was apparent that the thought of some profitable under-dealings was attractive to her. She handed the ring over.

Barnabas made an excellent show of it. He held it up to the light. He rapped it on the table. He scratched at it with his finger. He even bit it, which he immediately regretted, as he wondered whether the ring had recently been in contact with any of the whore's bodily fluids.

When he was finished with this show, he handed the ring back. "That idiot thinks the ring is worth five pieces. But, on my word as a professional jeweler, it's worth forty."

"Forty!"

"Forty. Whole. Pieces." Barnabas nodded in confirmation, still glancing about shiftily. "Or I cannot call myself a jeweler."

"Holy shit."

"Listen. The idiot thinks it's only worth five pieces. But, it seems to have some sentimental value. Do this when he gets back—offer to call his debt to you free, and further offer him twenty whole-pieces for the ring. He'll be flabbergasted. But he has no idea what the ring is actually worth. He'll take the deal. I guarantee it."

The whore was smiling now. "And then you'll buy the ring from me?"

Barnabas lowered his head. "I'm sorry, miss. I'm a poor man. I don't have that much cash on hand. If I hadn't already told you what it was worth, I might be able to make you a terrible offer, but since I am an honest man, I've already told you what it's worth. However, the jeweler down around the corner is richer than me. He'll recognize its value and buy it from you for thirty. You'll make a ten-piece profit."

"Yeah? I'll make a ten-piece profit?" The whore's smile was broad and earnest...

For about five seconds.

And then it soured, like sudden storm clouds.

Barnabas felt his stomach tighten.

The whore's smile turned to a snarl. She hurled the ring at Barnabas's face. "Ten pieces, huh? You sonofabitch! You two cooked this whole thing up to fuck me over, didn't you! Didn't you, you sheisty, shit-hocking motherfucker!"

"Hey!" Barnabas managed to dodge the ring, and then kept flinching, as though the whore's words themselves were projectiles. "Miss! Hey!"

The whore's eyes suddenly went wide. She took a step back. Looked up at Barnabas's empty pennant holder.

Barnabas felt faint.

The whore thrust her finger at him. "You! You're a godsdamned Light-sider! Just like that cheapskate! You two are in league together, aren't you?"

"No-no! It's nothing like that!"

303

"You knew that he was a dodger! You harbored him, and you planned to run this con on me! What? Were you going to get me to give him twenty pieces for the ring and then split it between you? You conniving, Light-sider, piece of shit!"

Once again, her voice rose.

Barnabas thought that most of the shops around him had probably heard her call him a Light-sider. He was practically begging her with his hands. "Miss! Please! Shut up! You'll cause trouble for me!"

The whore was savvy. He had to give her that. She glared at him, but she shut her mouth. Preserving Barnabas from a lynching—at least for now. She leaned over his little table of wares, and lowered her voice to a menacing hiss that sounded so much like a rock viper that Barnabas thought he was about to get bit.

"You Light-sider shits!" She snapped under her breath. "I wasn't born yesterday! You think people haven't tried to con an honest working girl before? I get that shit all the time! And now you're gonna pay! But I ain't greedy, like you are. You're gonna give me five whole-pieces to cover the work I've lost standin' out here in the hot sun, making my lady-bits sweaty. Five whole-pieces, or I swear to all that is good and holy, I will march straight off to the pontiff and I will tell him all about you two Light-side draft dodgers, and how you're tryna run a scheme on people! Five pieces, or you hang by sundown, you filthy cocksucking sonofabitch!"

Being called a cocksucker by a whore was almost more than Barnabas's pride could take. However, he knew that his position amongst his peers in town was tenuous already. The young man

304

and the whore were not the first to take notice of his pennant. There had been numerous grumblings about it already. If this whore went to the pontiff and told him that he had hidden a Light-side draft-dodger, then what she said was exactly right: Both he and the young man would be swinging by sundown.

Fearing for his life, but still conscious of his profit margins, he grabbed the ring from where it had fallen in the dust and held it up to the whore. "Here! Take the ring! It'll cover your debt. But for the gods' sake, keep your mouth shut!"

The whore slapped the ring out of his hand. It clattered across the table of homemade jewelry. "I don't want the ring. I want cash. Cash now, or I go to the pontiff. I'm done messing around, and you're wasting my time."

Fine. If the whore needed five pieces to get gone, then Barnabas would give her the damn pieces. Besides, he still had the ring, and he'd tell the young man on his return that the ring stayed with him to recoup his cost. If the young man didn't like it, he would be acquainted with the double-barrel scattergun that Barnabas kept in the shop.

So, really, he wasn't losing any money at all.

An unpleasant bit of business, but at least he wasn't any worse for wear.

"Alright. Okay." Barnabas reached into his cash box with jerky, irritable movements. Drew out five whole-pieces, and thrust these at the whore with a sneer. "Take them and get outta my face."

The whore snatched them from him. Gave him the evil eye. Then counted them meticulously. When she was satisfied, she gave him a final withering look and then turned her nose up at him. She turned around and walked across the street.

Barnabas muttered curses at her back.
What a disaster.
But at least he wasn't going to be hung.

CHAPTER 26

✿

HIDDEN FUNCTIONS

PERRY SAT IN THE SHADE at the mouth of the tunnel, staring at the clasp in his hands.

Behind him, the tunnel looked like nothing more than a shallow cave. But it was an optical illusion. The back wall of the cave had a small, offset gap. From the outside, it looked like a single, flat wall. Once you were inside, though, you could see the tunnel that the offset gap led to.

If you followed that tunnel, you would find that after a single turn, it lay straight, with a slight downhill grade, and if you continued on it, you would come to a little sandy shore and gently-lapping waters that glowed green.

You would also find a small boat, pulled up onto the shore.

Back at the mouth of the tunnel, Stuber lounged in the burning sun, reclined against a stone, with his Roq-11 in his lap. At intervals, he would raise his head, shade his eyes with a hand, and peer into the distance.

The landscape beyond them was scorched misery. But a small river shimmered its way across that hopeless scenery, issuing from the underground waterway they had just come from. On the banks of the river, a fuzz of sad plant-life clung to existence. Not green. More of a gray, as though it was bled out and already on death's door. And it never went any further than a few yards from the banks of the river.

In the distance, parked along the dusty confluence of this tiny source of life, you could just make out the huddle of civilization that was Lasima.

It was in that direction that Stuber would occasionally look, before relaxing back again.

Still laying, with his eyes closed, and hands clasped over his armored chest, Stuber spoke: "How long are you going to sit and stare at that thing?"

Perry glanced up. "I'm sorry, is there something better to be doing?"

"Yes. You should sun yourself. You've developed an unhealthy pallor."

"We've only been out of the sun for a day."

"The sun is healthy for the liver. Your liver needs sun every day."

"My liver isn't as corrupted as yours."

Stuber considered this for a moment. Then nodded. "You have a point there." He opened his eyes and glanced sidelong at Perry. "Fine. Stay in the shade then. Look like a nekrofage for all I care. But don't obsess over the clasp. Smegma will fix it for you."

Perry shook his head with a frown. "I'm not obsessing over it."

"It would be understandable. After all this time, and then to have the message be corrupted—"

"That's not it," Perry snapped.

A corner of Stuber's mouth twitched down. "Your poor temperament is likely a result of sunlight deficiency."

"It's not…" Perry rolled his eyes, growled under his breath, and then stood up and stepped into the sunlight. "There. I'm in the sun. Are you happy?"

Stuber gave a facial shrug. "I'm always happy. You, on the other hand, will need a few minutes for the sunlight to burn away your jaundiced distemper."

Perry stood there for a moment, looking at Stuber with a gauging expression on his face. His eyes squinted shrewdly. "You know, Stuber, it seems to me that half the shit you say is really just to get a rise out of me."

Stuber gave no response, outside of a small smile that crossed his lips, and then disappeared.

"Anyway," Perry said with a sigh. "It's not about the message. I've been…" Perry trailed off, not really sure how to articulate what it was that he perceived.

"You've been…?" Stuber prompted him after a lengthy silence.

"There's something else here," Perry mumbled. The sunlight was already making him sweat.

"How do you mean?"

"I mean…there's another function here."

"Like what?"

"That's the thing. I can't tell."

"Then how do you know it does anything else besides play messages?"

"Because I could feel it. When I was connected to it. I could feel the portion of it that operated the message function. But there was…this big…space…like a hole. Am I making sense?"

Stuber blinked a few times. "Let's just pretend that you are. Go on."

Perry began pacing. "I can't describe it any other way. It's like…it's like the block toy, when you were a kid. The one with the different shaped holes and the different shaped blocks. You have to put the round block in the round hole. The square block in the square hole. Right?" Perry glanced at Stuber. "You did have toys as a kid, right? Or did you just play with guns?"

"Don't be ridiculous. I wasn't allowed a gun until I was eight years old. As a toddler, I played with knives."

Perry nodded, as though such a thing was obvious. "I can feel the holes, Stuber—"

"I also like to feel the holes."

"—but it's like I can't figure out the *shape* of them. Do you get what I'm saying? Be serious."

Stuber raised his hands in surrender. "I will be serious. And, I must say, I don't completely understand what you're describing. But…did your Uncle Sergio say that it did anything else?"

"No. He never even hinted at it."

"What about the message? Do you think your father told you somewhere in the message?"

"Well, that would be helpful. If we could hear the whole message."

Stuber studied Perry with a careful eye. "What do you think he meant by that bit about the blood in your veins?"

Perry's expression became guarded. "I don't know. Won't know until we listen to the whole thing."

Stuber forced a flat smile. "Well. Maybe you take after your mother."

Perry bristled. "What's that supposed to mean?"

Stuber shifted his weight. Arched his eyebrows. Looked this way and that. As though waiting for Perry to connect the dots on his own.

Perry wasn't dense. It'd hadn't escaped him that he bore no resemblance to Legatus Cato. In fact, he'd particularly noticed it because he'd hoped that he *would* look like him, if not in stature, than at least in his face.

"You saying," Perry murmured. "That he doesn't think I'm his son?"

"Well." Stuber considered it. "He did call you 'my son' several times. But…"

He cut himself off.

Looked into the cave.

A few seconds passed.

Stuber held up a finger, as though asking for quiet. "Did you hear that?"

Perry felt his skin crawl. He hadn't heard anything. "Are you messing with me again?"

Irritation flashed across Stuber's face. "No, I'm not messing with you. I'm tempted to blame your peon ears, except that you aren't a peon, are you? Listen. Do you hear it now?"

"I hear wind."

"I hear whispers." Stuber shouldered his Roq-11. "Come with me, Shortstack."

As Perry and Stuber crept toward the back of the cave, and the tunnel that led to their boat, their backs were turned to the world beyond, and they did not see the flight of four skiffs ripping across the desert towards Lasima.

***

Sagum and Teran were huddled around the back of a brothel, two streets away from Barnabas's little shop of baubles.

"Five pieces?" Sagum said, sounding disappointed.

Teran gave him a look. "Five pieces is enough." She closed her hand around the gold pieces she had displayed for Sagum, and began walking down the street. "I wasn't trying to ruin the guy."

"He was an ass."

"Still."

"What was that ring worth anyway?"

"I dunno. It's a polished piece of metal. I still have ten of them leftover from when my dad and I would do this."

"You played a whore for your dad?"

She gave him a withering glance. "I never saw you complain when we brought supplies back to the caves."

"I have to say…"

She watched him.

"When you said that I came inside you…"

Teran punched him in the shoulder. "You're disgusting."

"I'm disgusting?" Sagum grinned. "You said it!"

Teran shook her head. "Just shut up."

Sagum rubbed his shoulder and followed after her, still smiling.

They went another two blocks into Lasima, and stopped at a general store.

"Stay out here," Teran told him. "Keep watch. I'll get what we need."

Sagum chose a post to lean on in the shade of the store's front awning, while Teran disappeared inside the shop. He squinted out into the bright, burning day. Watching the people shuffle along on the streets, going in and out of the shops.

The dust on the streets was so pale, it was nearly white. It puffed in little clouds underneath people's feet, and when a gust of dry, hot wind blew between the buildings, it stirred up little devils that whirled and then crashed, either into an unlucky person, or into the side of a building.

The white dust coated everything, and it reflected the harsh sunlight.

Sagum noted that a lot of the people traversing the streets wore cloths around their necks that they pulled up to cover their nose and mouth when the dust blew.

He rubbed the inside of a nostril with his thumb, and then inspected it. His thumb had a residue of dry, white crust. He sneered at it, and wiped it off on his pants.

Well. This place was unpleasant.

Then he started to think about the Glass Flats, and wondered how dusty *they* would be.

He fingered the scrap of red *sagum* bound around his neck, and figured it would work to keep out the dust...

In the midst of these thoughts, he became aware of a ripple of voices out in the street, and when he looked out, he saw that several people stood with their hands shielding their eyes, looking at something to the east.

Curious, he leaned out from under the shade and looked where everyone else was looking.

Down the street. Into the sky.

Four black objects, hurtling towards Lasima.

His stomach dropped.

The four black objects zoomed closer. The sound of them grew audible, building into a pulsing, rumbling noise, and the people in the streets cried out—not in shock, but in dismay.

One of the objects pulled into a hover over what looked like the eastern entrance to the town of Lasima. Two of them split off, to the north and south. The fourth ripped over Sagum's head, rattling windows and walls, and kicking up a cloud of dust in its wake that hung in the air like a pall of smoke.

Sagum's head snapped to the right, following the black skiff as it rocketed to the west end of Lasima, and then, perhaps two hundred yards away, pulled into a hover.

Sagum could still hear the rumble of the skiff's engines.

It lowered down to the point that it almost disappeared behind the roof line of Lasima's squat buildings. But not so low that Sagum couldn't see the four praetors descend, two from each side.

A deep, amplified voice roared through the town of Lasima. Sagum had yet to spot the town's jumbotron, but he recognized the blaring audio of it, echoed through the town by a hundred loudspeakers.

"By order of the paladins, the town of Lasima is currently under quarantine. There are Outsiders amongst you, and they must be purged. All loyal citizens will go to their homes immediately, lock their doors, and not allow anyone to enter who they do not know. Do not be alarmed. The heretics will be excised from your town shortly."

The people of Lasima disappeared from the streets like scattering cockroaches.

Sagum had the urge to run, but he had nowhere to run to.

The door to the general store slammed open behind him.

He glanced over his shoulder and found Teran standing there, looking pale. She held two

314

large, empty water bladders, and a canvas satchel filled with provisions.

Sagum still leaned up against the post, though his whole body had now gone rigid.

Behind them, they heard footsteps.

Sagum and Teran turned. Through the small screen window on the front door of the general store, the shop owner stood with wide and terrified eyes. He pulled the door shut, then locked it behind him.

They heard the security bar go across it with a very final-sounding *clunk*.

Sagum and Teran looked at each other.

"Well," Sagum said, his voice low. "This is a bit of a problem."

Teran shoved the two empty water bladders into Sagum's arms, then slung the satchel of provisions over her shoulder and turned. She walked three paces down the front deck of the general store, then stepped off and into the alley, cursing the whole way.

Sagum followed her.

They stopped in the alley.

Teran looked at Sagum. "You have any weapons?"

Sagum shook his head. "Even if I did, they wouldn't do any good."

"How'd you kill the legionnaire? The one whose *sagum* you're wearing?"

"Ah. Well…"

Teran glared at him. "Sagum, you sonofabitch…"

Sagum winced. "He may have already been wounded."

"You're such a bastard."

Sagum took her by the elbow, prodding her further down the alley. "That's actually true. But it's not helpful at this point. Do you have any idea how we're going to get out of here?"

"Yeah," Teran snapped. "We can hope that Stuber saw the skiffs incoming and is on his way to bail us out!"

CHAPTER 27

✿

QUARANTINE

S͏TUBER HAD NOT SEEN THE SKIFFS.

He and Perry were creeping into the entrance of the tunnel.

At the back of the cave, it smelled like desert—the singular aroma of burning sands.

But as they slipped around the corner of the offset wall, it was like passing through a membrane into the world of the underground. The temperature dropped twenty degrees in just a few steps, and the scent turned moist and dank and vivid.

Ahead of them, the passage dog-legged. Beyond that single turn, it would be a straight shot down to the underground river and their boat.

At first, Perry considered insisting that it was the wind. He had not dismissed the possibility that Stuber was messing with him. But as they approached the dogleg, Stuber's grip on his rifle tightened up, and Perry caught the first glimmers of what Stuber must've been hearing.

A quiet murmuring.

Like hearing a low conversation in the next room.

"Shit," Perry breathed. "You're serious. I hear it now."

Stuber gave Perry an incredulous look. "Of course I'm serious."

"Is someone down there?"

"I don't know."

"Maybe other Outsiders?"

"There wasn't another boat."

"They could've had boats stashed at different places."

Stuber didn't respond to this.

They reached the dogleg. Stuber peered around the corner. Determined it was clear. Then stepped around it. Perry followed, still gripping the clasp in his hand. The tunnel yawned before them, leading down into darkness. They couldn't see their boat from this vantage point. But towards the end of the darkness, the ambient glow of the underground glimmered on the walls of the tunnel.

Stuber's tread was very soft in the sandy floor of the tunnel. He kept moving forward.

"How much closer are we going to get?" Perry whispered.

"Close enough to make sure no one's stealing our boat. Unless you feel like walking to the Glass Flats."

Perry did not feel like walking to the Glass Flats. By Teran's reckoning, the trip overland to the Glass Flats was several days. By the underground river, it was only a day. The boat was their ticket out.

They'd moved forward another twenty feet or so when they heard a short, sharp, bark.

Stuber froze in place.

Perry did the same.

Perry's whisper was so low it was barely audible: "Do you think it's nekrofages?"

Stuber made a slight raspberry noise. "Fairy tales. I'm certain such things don't exist."

Then, by unspoken agreement, the two of them sank down.

Squatting on their haunches, they could just see the beginning of the sandy inlet where they'd parked the boat. Then they went lower, onto their knees, and then even lower, putting their bellies to the ground.

From that vantage, they could see the boat.

And the crowd of shapes around it.

At least two dozen of them. Vaguely human, though they crouched and hobbled about sometimes on all fours, like animals.

And, faintly, they glowed green.

Stuber and Perry stared at the sight for several seconds. Perry's heart thumped the inside of his chest.

"What the fuck do you call those?" Perry hissed.

"Well," Stuber whispered back. "Those appear to be nekrofages."

***

Teran and Sagum skidded to a stop at the mouth of an alley.

Sagum stuck the side of his sweating face around the corner of the clapboard building they stood next to.

Down the street, less than fifty yards from them, a pair of praetors stalked down the street.

Sagum jumped back behind the corner.

"Shit!" he wheezed.

"What?" Teran demanded. "Did they see you?"

"I don't think so."

Teran grabbed Sagum by the shoulder and hauled him back towards the other end of the alley that they'd just come from.

They were about halfway down the alley when an old man shuffled across the opening.

Stooped shoulders. Squinty eyes. Bristly gray mustache.

Teran hesitated for only half a second, then released Sagum and sprinted for the end of the alley.

"What…?" Sagum tore after her.

Teran hit the end of the alley and poked her head out from the corner where the old man had just disappeared. She looked at his back. But she was already certain who it was.

"Jax!" she called out.

The old man stopped. Turned around, confused.

Their eyes connected.

Recognition clouded his brow.

"Jax!" Teran said again, then dipped back into the alleyway.

She waited just inside the alley, until she heard the old man's soft footfalls on the planks, heard his mumbling voice, just above a whisper: "Teran? Is that you?"

She lurched around the corner, seized the old man by the shoulders, and hauled him back into the alley with her.

He moved fast for an old man. The second she slammed him up against the wall, he produced a blade from his right hip. It was pure reaction to being grabbed, and his eyes were still shocked. Teran seized his knife hand before he could think much about lashing out with it and in one lightning-fast movement, she stripped the knife out of his hand and held it to his throat.

"Whoa!" Jax breathed, flattening himself against the wall of the building, his eyes wide, his neck straining to get away from the edge of the blade. "Shit! Don't cut me, woman!"

Teran had her left forearm posted against the old man's chest, her right hand holding the blade to him. Her face close enough to smell his sour breath. "What are you doing here?" she demanded. "Is Hauten here? Is he the one that sicced the praetors on us? Have you been following us?"

Genuine confusion flashed across the old man's features. "What? No! What the fuck are you...? Could you take the godsdamned knife off my throat? I already shaved this week for godssakes!"

Teran was acutely aware of their position in the alley. It was only a matter of time before the praetors that Sagum had seen would clear this alley. And when they did, Teran didn't want to be in it.

Her brain was working overtime. A vague and misty plan started to coalesce in her head out of the panic.

"Is Hauten here?"

"Yes. He's right around the corner."

"What are you doing here?"

"I just got the boys set up in a crewhouse," he said. "Now I'm going back to meet up with Hauten before these praetors catch us on the streets!"

"I mean," Teran growled, pressing the knife harder against his throat. "What is *Hauten* doing here in Lasima?"

Jax strained the words through gritted teeth. "We're tryna find some new security muscle! And a few new greenhorns, since y'all lit out and left us high and dry!"

Teran took the knife away from Jax's throat. "Take us to Hauten. Now."

Jax looked unsure.

"Jax, I'll carve your fucking kidneys out."

The old man held up his hands. "Awright, awright. You don't need to be so cold-hearted, woman. Come on. Before we get gunned down."

Teran released her hold on Jax, and he straightened his ruffled shirt, and shuffled around the corner. She kept very close to him, their shoulders brushing, and the knife close to her body, serious about cutting Jax's kidneys out if he tried anything.

Sagum, wisely keeping his mouth shut through all of this, and knowing his place in the current food chain, followed closely behind.

"Are you the Outsiders they're lookin' for?" Jax asked them as they crossed in front of a building.

"No questions," Teran snapped.

At the next building over, a familiar voice reached her ears, in tones of argument.

"We've been doing trade for years, you sonofabitch! If you lock me out, the praetors are going to kill me, and then where will you get all your ammo?"

"There are other reloaders," an irritable voice replied.

"Other…? You wound me! Is that all I am to you? Just a means to an end? I thought that we had developed a friendship over these last dozen years! And now you're willing to feed me to the wolves!"

"We're not friends! You fucked my wife!"

"Oh, gods in the skies!" Hauten cried. "You're going to bring *that* up again?"

They cleared the corner of the building, and, at a side door, Boss Hauten stood in the dust, pleading with the owner of the shop to give him safe harbor before the praetors caught him outside.

The shop owner looked furious. He was loading a retort, but jerked when Jax cleared the corner, followed by Teran and Sagum.

Hauten followed his gaze, and for a brief moment, there was pure terror in his eyes, like he thought that it was praetors that had come around the corner. Then he saw Jax. Then he saw Teran. And he frowned.

"Teran?" he said, mystified.

Teran swung the satchel full of provisions—a few of which were heavy cans—and clobbered Hauten over the head.

Hauten went down like she'd chopped him with an axe.

The shopkeeper stared in wonderment.

Teran brandished the knife at the shopkeeper, to keep him agreeable. "Don't intervene," she ordered him. And given the fact that they had just been talking about how Hauten had screwed the man's wife, she didn't think he was going to give them much trouble.

"Gods, woman!" Jax expelled. Hands still up in surrender. "You didn't needa do that!"

Teran didn't respond. She felt the sweat dripping into her eyes, dripping down her back. The urgency propelled her forward. She looked at Sagum, and then gestured to Hauten, who was starting to groan and come awake again.

"Keys!" she said. "Get the key ring from him!"

Sagum shot down to Hauten and started pawing his pockets and his waistband.

Hauten's bleary eyes came into half-focus and he started trying to bat at Sagum.

Sagum reared back and gave Boss Hauten a straight right to the nose that laid him out again, but didn't knock him unconscious.

After another muffled groan, Hauten swore. "Brigands! Thieves!"

At the door, the shopkeeper smiled, despite the dangerous circumstances.

"Got 'em!" Sagum came up on his feet, triumphantly holding a ring of keys.

Teran gave the keys the once over, and saw what she was looking for. Then she turned to Jax. "Where's the buggy?"

Jax's jaw opened and closed, but no words came out.

Hauten struggled up into a sitting position, blood pouring out of his nose, coating his mouth and chin. "Don't you fucking dare!"

"We need it more than you," Teran said. "Now, tell me or I swear I will stick you. This is life and death."

"The hold's full!" Hauten cried. "That's the entire crew's wages!"

Teran, who had reached the terminal point of her patience, bent down and stuck him. One quick jab to the side of Hauten's thigh, opening a bloody hole in him.

Hauten seemed not to believe it at first. Like it offended him more than hurt him. Then he gasped, and clutched his leg, as the pain reached his brain. He had the presence of mind not to scream too loud.

"You bitch!" he rasped.

"Next time it'll be your belly!" Teran spat, waving the knife at him. "Where's the buggy, Hauten? Tell me or I'll perforate your fat innards!"

During this, Jax had retreated a few steps, as though he wished not to be remembered as being present.

"Alright!" A bit of saliva erupted from Hauten's mouth and wet his chin, along with the blood from his nose. "You evil bitch! It's two blocks down. At the back of the Johnston Five Crewhouses."

Teran raised the point of the knife to Jax and skewered him with a look. "Is he telling me the truth?"

Jax's head bobbed. "Yes, ma'am."

Teran wasted no more time. She turned on her heel and sprinted for the street beyond. She was familiar enough with Lasima to know where the Johnston Five Crewhouse was, and it was indeed just two blocks down from them.

She cleared the corner, found the street empty, and sprinted across.

She spared a look behind her to check that Sagum was keeping pace.

He followed, looking terrified, but somehow grinning.

Behind him, back in the alley, Jax helped Hauten up, and the shopkeeper stood aside, letting them into the safety of his building.

CHAPTER 28

✪

ESCAPE FROM LASIMA

PERRY AND STUBER stood in the sunshine again.

Each of them was on opposite sides of the cave mouth, so that they could at least keep the entrance of the tunnel in their periphery.

"Well, what are we supposed to do about the boat?" Perry asked, still fidgeting with the clasp.

Stuber frowned. He pulled the magazine from his Roq-11 and looked down into it. Reseated it. Counted two spare magazines attached to his armor. Looked at Perry. "I have to be honest with you, Perry, I'm struggling with the correct decision here. But I'm inclined to just kill them all."

"Do you have enough ammo?"

"Yes." A pause. "Maybe."

"What do you mean?"

"If more of them show up, I might not have enough."

"How many more could there possibly be?"

"I have no clue. Could be hundreds. Could be just the ones that are down there now." Stuber clucked his tongue. "There's also the possibility that I might shoot holes in the boat. Accidentally."

"You'll just have to be judicious with your aim."

"Yes, well, that sounds good in theory."

"Shit."

"While I don't want to walk to the Glass Flats, I want to swim there even less."

"Do you think they'll come up here?"

"I'm kind of hoping they avoid sunlight."

"But you don't know that."

"Ten minutes ago, I didn't think they existed. My breadth of knowledge on the subject of nekrofages is admittedly lacking."

At that moment, the two of them turned and looked out across the desert to Lasima, perhaps hoping to see Teran and Sagum approaching, laden with wonderful supplies and a ready answer to their questions about nekrofages.

What they saw instead were four black skiffs rising into the air above the little desert town.

Perry blinked. Hoping that his eyes were mistaken.

They weren't.

His breath caught in his chest.

"Stuber," he said. "You see those skiffs?"

"Yes," Stuber replied, flat as bedrock.

"Where did they come from?"

"Better question," Stuber said, as the four skiffs pivoted in midair and appeared to be pointing right at them. "Is where are they *going*?"

Perry's feet shuffled in the dust. His eye caught something else, rocketing out of the north end of Lasima. A rooster-tail of dust erupting behind it. He jabbed his finger into the distance. "There! What's that?"

In the air, the four skiffs seemed to converge on whatever was trying to escape from Lasima. And for a moment, Perry felt a wash of relief, thinking it was just some smugglers that were trying to make a run for it and were about to get waxed by the main guns on a skiff.

His relief only lasted a moment or so.

Whatever was hurtling out of the north end of Lasima cut a hard turn and began driving straight towards them. The skiffs pulled into formation and began to follow.

Stuber raised his rifle to his eyes and looked through the optic, twisting a dial on the side to magnify the image. After a moment, he lowered the rifle and pursed his lips.

"Well, this is odd."

Perry gaped at the other man. "What? What's odd?"

"The vehicle that's leading the skiffs towards us…it looks a helluva lot like Boss Hauten's buggy."

***

Teran clung to the steering wheel, because it was the only thing keeping her from flying out of the driver's seat.

The buggy roared across the uneven desert ground, and she didn't take her foot off the accelerator. They hit bumps and humps of sand and large rocks with reckless abandon, sending the vehicle into the air in giant plumes of dust, and rattling the shocks so hard it felt like they didn't exist.

She ramped them over a small dune, felt the buggy go airborne, and heard Sagum scream from the back, while her own rear lifted out of the driver's seat for a moment of weightlessness.

They hit the ground on the other side with a bone-jarring crunch.

"You okay?" Teran yelled into the back, and hazarded a glance over her shoulder.

Sagum clung to the rollbars with both of his hands, and a leg hooked around it as well. His mouth gaped open, catching sand and dust, but he didn't seem to care.

Teran jerked the wheel, skidding the buggy out of the path of a rock that was too big to jump. The move nearly sent Sagum flying out, but he maintained his deathgrip on the rollbars.

"Slow down!" he shouted.

"No! Get the case! The case in the back!"

"I'm gonna fall off!"

Teran let loose with the most vile questioning of Sagum's manhood that she could come up with. She found a section of flat terrain. Held the wheel steady, and turned to look in the back again, with pure venom in her eyes.

"Get the case, or we're gonna get blown up, you no-dick piece of shit!"

Cringing in terror, Sagum released his leg from the rollbar. He cast a look behind them, and spotted the four black skiffs roaring in their direction out of the searing, cloudless sky.

They had another few hundred yards of level terrain.

Sagum seized the moment.

He lurched off of the rollbars and fell to his knees on top of a large, black case that was secured to the rear of the buggy by two canvass straps. His fingers fumbled with the release. Managed to get one strap off. Then the other.

He glanced up, aware that he had limited time until the buggy was bucking again like an enraged bull.

He ripped open the case.

Saw what lay inside its padded interior.

In any other circumstance, he may have smiled.

Now, he was far too desperate.

He reached for the Boren LRG—

WHA-BOOM

The buggy lurched, a violent spray of fire and sand and super-heated rock washed over the rear of the buggy.

"They're shooting at us!" Sagum cried, looking behind them and seeing one of the skiffs taking the lead in a diamond formation, its two main guns still spouting smoke like dragon's breath.

"No shit!" Teran answered. "Hold on!"

Sagum did the only thing he could do—he grabbed the molded handgrip of the LRG with his right hand, and with his left hand he grabbed the nearest rollbar.

Not a second too soon.

The buggy hit bad terrain again.

And again, Teran didn't let up off the accelerator.

The buggy hit something on the right side and nearly flipped.

Riding on two wheels, close to the tipping point.

Sagum's body lifted into the air.

The Boren LRG and its case also lifted, no longer strapped in, and Sagum realized how heavy the gun was. It tried to fly out of his grip, but he held onto it, his arms now outstretched, while the case tumbled away from the LRG and vanished into the plume of dust they left in their wake.

The buggy crashed back into the ground.

Sagum hit the deck like he'd been body-slammed, the LRG coming close to crushing his arm underneath it.

The second the buggy had all four tires on the ground, Teran yanked it hard to the right.

Sagum slid across the deck, hit the wall, and the LRG rammed into him, the triple-barrel smacking into his face, and the heavy body of the gun knocking the wind out of his chest.

The earth to the left side of the buggy evaporated in another black cumulus cloud of debris.

Sagum gasped for air and got smoke and dirt instead.

"Get the gun up!" Teran screamed at him.

He hacked, then hauled himself up to his knees, still gripping the rollbar in one hand, and the LRG with the other. He turned his body to face the back and found himself staring down a black praetor's skiff, the main guns no more than fifteen yards from the tip of his nose.

Sagum wasn't a strong individual, despite what he liked to claim. He was a wiry sonofabitch, and he could run up and down desert mountains for hours without rest.

But not strong.

However, there is something incredibly motivating about staring down the muzzle of a 60-milimeter gun.

Screaming with wild fear, Sagum planted his feet and let go of the rollbar. He put both hands to the grips of the LRG, and hauled it up with every ounce of strength that he possessed, and in a serendipitous moment, Teran hit another small dune, and for a second, Sagum and the LRG he so desperately needed to lift were weightless...

He slammed the magnetic clamps onto the rear rollbar. They automatically locked.

He thumbed the red switch, and the Boren LRG that had once been named "Charlize," began to vibrate as the servos and motors inside began to spin.

The skiff directly behind them put on the brakes, and simultaneously lifted into the sky, trying to get out of his sights.

Sagum wrenched both thumbs down onto the butterfly trigger between the two molded handgrips, and Charlize roared.

***

Stuber's hand flew to his chest, like his heart had been wounded. "They're using Charlize!"

Perry was bobbing on his toes. "Who's 'they'? Is it Hauten?"

"Why do you think I always have the answers?" Stuber demanded. Then he lifted the rifle's optic to his eyes again, and looked through.

In the distance, the buggy roared across the desert and the back end sprouted a tail of fire, and a moment later the buzz-saw sound of the Boren LRG reached Perry's ears. At that same moment, the skiff that had been closest to them sparked, its underbelly exploded, and a gout of black smoke flew from it as it twisted off at an unhealthy angle, lost altitude, and nose-dived into a dune.

Stuber let out a strangled cry.

"What?" Perry yelled.

"It's Smegma! Dirty cocksucking bastard has his paws on my gun!"

"Sagum?" Perry exclaimed. "Is Teran with him?"

"She's driving!"

Perry felt a bloom of hope in his chest.

Then it was snuffed out by an eerie mewling noise from behind him.

Perry and Stuber both spun around. A ghostly visage peered at them from the back of the cave, lamplike eyes squinting against the harsh light of the outside world.

Stuber let out a three-round burst from his Roq-11 and splattered the phantom face against the back wall of the cave.

A terrible cry went up from the tunnel, a horrible ululation carried by a multitude of voices.

Stuber reached out and put his hand on Perry's chest, backpedaling them both away from the shadows and further into the burning daylight.

At the back of the cave, a tumble of pale limbs came around the corner, and then, as though they'd touched an electrical fence, they jumped back, howling and screaming. Five or six of them, clambering around at the back of the cave, spitting and gnashing their teeth, but unwilling to commit themselves further into daylight.

Perry looked over his shoulder.

The buggy, roaring across the desert.

The skiffs, backing off to get out of range of the LRG.

But they were still in pursuit.

They were only a mile away, and that mile was going to disappear fast.

Perry felt the clasp in his hands. He heard it, calling to him. Asking him to do what needed to be done, but he just didn't know what it was. He felt the depression, the space, the hole where his thoughts were supposed to fit, but he was still trying to cram that square peg into a round hole.

It wasn't right. Something wasn't right. He wasn't making a connection.

He looked at Stuber, still sighting through his rifle, but holding his fire. "Stuber, they're going to be here any second. There's no other way out of here. We need to get through that tunnel."

"Yes," Stuber nodded. "But the way appears to be blocked."

"We're just going to have to shoot our way through!"

Stuber's head swiveled, and a fierce expression overtook his countenance. "Godsdammit, Perry. That's the most hardcore shit you've ever said to me." Then he reached under his armor, drew out the small pistol he kept there, and shoved it into Perry's hands. "You got ten shots."

Perry shifted the clasp to his left hand so that he could hold the pistol with his right. He looked out at the buggy again, roaring ever closer, the skiffs still chasing behind it. "The second they get here, we're going in."

"Right," Stuber said, readdressing himself and his rifle to the back of the cave where the nekrofages were amassing. "If they don't get blown up first."

***

Teran realized that there was a reason that she'd never seen Boss Hauten run the buggy at full speed.

Three miles out of Lasima, and the battery indicator was already showing red.

Up ahead of them, she saw the terrain rising towards the crest of the jagged slopes. In among those tooth-like rocks, she saw the opening of the cave, and two small figures standing there.

She drove them recklessly uphill now. The battery indicator started to cry out an alarm.

"Did you see that shit?" Sagum screeched behind her. "I chewed them up! I musta killed five praetors! *Praetors*, godsdammit!"

Teran twisted in her seat, but she wasn't looking at Sagum. She looked at the sky, at the three remaining skiffs.

They were spreading out now. Keeping out of range of the LRG, but it looked like they were moving to flank them.

They knew that they were trying to disappear into the Underground.

The praetors were going to dismount. Cut them off and fight them on the ground.

The battery alarm reached a new pitch, and she felt the buggy slow, like they'd suddenly plunged into mud.

Teran whipped back around and looked at the cave. It was still about four hundred yards distant from them. And the grade was getting steeper.

She tried to let off on the accelerator, but that slowed them down too much, so she rammed it back to the floor.

"Why are we slowing down?" Sagum called out.

"Because we're running out of juice! You needa get ready to bail!"

"Bail?"

In her peripheral, she saw the black shapes of two of the skiffs, roaring ahead, far to her right and left flank. One skiff behind, to continue to push them.

Sagum clambered up, just behind her, clinging to the rollbar over their heads. "The battery is dying!" he shouted in her ear.

"That's what I just said!" Teran couldn't restrain herself, she whipped an elbow backward and caught Sagum in the chest with it. "Get back there! There's another case—it's got two shotguns and a pistol in it. Grab that! Now!"

Three hundred yards to the cave now.

She could make out Stuber and Perry, standing in the sunlight, outside of the cave. Stuber held his rifle up, pointing to the back of the cave, while Perry watched the buggy get closer, dancing on his feet and waving his arms as though he could cause the failing buggy to move faster.

Ahead of them, to the right and left, the two skiffs pulled into a hover.

The black shapes of praetors leapt from the sides and hit the ground behind the cover of the rocks.

She looked behind them and saw the third skiff, still trawling along behind them at a safe distance. And she realized that they were cattle, being herded into a corral.

That was when the batteries gave up the ghost, and the buggy slogged to a stop.

CHAPTER 29

✿

ROCKS AND HARD PLACES

A HUNDRED YARDS.

They could make it.

Teran sucked wind and scrambled up the rocky slope, towards the mouth of the cave where Perry stood, shouting at them to go faster. She'd had the presence of mind to grab the satchel of supplies and the water bladders—though one of them had fallen out of her grip twenty yards back, and there was no way in hell she was going back for it.

"Here!" Sagum gasped from beside her.

She turned, saw that he had ripped the second case open as they ran. Two shotguns inside. He seized one, and she the other, and the Mercy Pistol bobbled out and clattered onto the rocks where it was forgotten.

Sagum simply dropped the case.

They were fifty yards from the cave when something zipped by Teran's nose and smashed a rock to her left. She staggered to a halt and glanced to her right, where the bullet had come from.

A praetor leaned out from behind a rock, maybe seventy-five yards uphill from them.

Teran and Sagum dove for cover, hitting the sandy, pebbly ground on their bellies and skinning their elbows and knees as they writhed behind a jagged boulder.

The near edge of the boulder erupted in a clatter of bullet strikes, the whine and warble of ricochets piercing the air.

Sagum thrust his shotgun out and blind-fired a blast up the hill in the general direction of the praetor.

Teran elbowed him. "Save your rounds! Buckshot ain't goin' that far, you dumbshit!"

Sagum racked the shotgun, looked angry. "I'm just keepin' their heads down!"

Another long string of aggressive automatic fire chewed a chunk from the side of the boulder.

"Praetors won't fall for that." She turned her face uphill. She couldn't see the cave, but she hoped to the gods that they could hear her voice. "Stuber! We need covering fire!"

***

Perry felt it.

In his mind, rushing shades of red.

The fear was making it difficult to maintain his focus, but he still felt The Calm, there, at the center of himself.

He was almost there.

He was reforming his mind into a dozen different shapes, but it seemed that nothing fit that big, empty space that was in this lump of potential in his hands. The clasp remained inert.

His focus broke.

The red melted into searing white-hot desert heat.

"Sonofabitch!" he yelled at it, shaking it in his hands.

Down the rocky hill, far past where Teran and Sagum had disappeared behind cover, he saw the skiff that had taken up the rear guard, pulling into a hover over the defunct buggy.

A voice made it up to them over the din of the praetor's gunfire: "Stuber! We need covering fire!"

"Shortstack!" Stuber yelled. "You need to watch the tunnel!"

Perry spun around and pointed the pistol at the mouth of the tunnel with one hand. The nekrofages in the tunnel were angry. Swarming. But not brave enough to commit themselves to the sunlight. They kept jumping in and out of the tunnel entrance.

The second that Perry had the tunnel covered, Stuber spun on his heel and edged out around the rocks, sighting into his rifle and letting out a long rattle of fire at a target only he could see.

"Move!" Stuber yelled down the hill at Teran and Sagum, then resumed his covering fire.

Perry wanted to look behind him, wanted to see if Teran and Sagum were back up and running again, but he didn't dare take his eyes off the tunnel entrance. One of the nekrofages was getting bold, dancing around the dead body of its pack mate, making little jumps forward, and then retreating.

Perry's heart throttled in his throat. His finger was on the trigger. He got the sense that the thing was going to charge him at any second.

How many more were stacked up in the tunnel?

By their barks and snarls and cries, it sounded like a lot.

From out on the hillside, there came a walloping explosion. Perry felt the shockwave punch him in the chest—felt it in his sinuses. He snapped around out of pure reaction, and saw that the front end of Boss Hauten's buggy was smoking, fiery ruins. The skiff hovered over it, gray plumes billowing from its main guns.

Perry caught himself. Spun again. Back to the tunnel…

The nekrofage was charging him.

Perry let out a cry and fired without any thought to his aim.

The nekrofage's head snapped back. Its legs flew out from underneath it, like it had been clotheslined. It hit the ground, unmoving, less than five yards from Perry's feet.

"Great shot!" Stuber roared. "Don't get distracted!"

The pistol shaking in his hands, Perry stared at the tunnel again.

The savages pulsed out, then lurched back into cover, two or three at a time.

Around the corner of the cave, Stuber let out another rattle of gunfire, then his rifle fell silent. "Reloading!" he shouted.

The sound of scuffling feet. Gasping breath.

Out of the corner of Perry's eyes, he saw the shapes of Teran and Sagum stumble into the cave with them.

"What's going on?" Sagum cried out, when he spied the dead nekrofages.

"I'm back up," Stuber declared, then shouldered Sagum out of the way, and held his rifle on the tunnel. "I got the tunnel! Shortstack, brief the newcomers!"

Perry turned to Teran and Sagum, found that he was breathing just as hard as they were, despite the fact that he hadn't been sprinting uphill like they had. His wide-stretched eyes took in their sweaty, dusty figures. He jammed his hand towards the tunnel and, having no idea what to say, simply went with "Nekrofages!"

"I can see that!" Teran gasped out. She gestured all around them with the muzzle of the shotgun. "Praetors! Surrounding us!"

"How are we getting out of here?" Sagum demanded, his voice edging towards panic. "We can't get to the boat…"

"We're getting to the boat," Perry snapped. "We gotta shoot our way through!"

"There's too many of them!"

"You have no idea how many of them there are!" Perry had the urge to punch him in the mouth, but figured it wouldn't help the situation. "You wanna take your chances with the praetors?"

Sagum didn't answer, but the fear on his face was answer enough.

The stones near them exploded, peppering them with shards of rocks that stung and cut their faces. The three of them jumped further into cover, plastering themselves against the rock behind Stuber.

"Shortstack!" Stuber yelled. "We gotta move! You ready?"

"Yes!"

"You two!" Stuber said, keeping his rifle trained on the nekrofrages with one arm, while the other grabbed Teran and Sagum and yanked them up alongside him. "Shotguns with me! Teran to my left. Sagum, my right. Choose your shots! Perry, watch our asses and tell me if you see a praetor coming!"

"Got it!"

"We're moving!"

Perry wanted more time to plan. He felt like he didn't know what he was supposed to be doing. He felt like he'd been thrust onstage without knowing what he was supposed to say, except that, instead of booing him, the audience wanted to kill him.

None of that mattered. They had no more time.

They moved.

Stuber in the front, the tip of a diamond, with Teran and Sagum on either side, and Perry shuffling along in the back, still clutching his pistol and his clasp, still feeling desperately for what that other function was…

As he turned to cover their rear, he looked out, down the hillside, to the smoking ruins of the buggy, and it was through that image, rippling with the heat from the burning vehicle, that the mirage of a tall figure strode through, flanked by praetors, a paladin's longstaff in its hand, the helm of a demigod on its head.

The Tall Man.

"Selos," Perry said, but no one heard him, because at that moment Stuber's Roq-11 began to thunder, rocking the air around them. In the close quarters of the cave and tunnel, the sound of it reverberated off the rock and punched at their ear drums.

The shotguns roared.

Howls of fury and pain, and the mewling of the dying.

Sagum screamed and Perry couldn't tell whether it was from pain or fear.

The cacophony of chaos filled Perry's head to the brim and overflowed.

"It's Paladin Selos!" Perry tried to call again, but no one could hear him.

At the tip of the spear, Stuber blasted his way around the false back of the cave, and into the tunnel. The roar of the nekrofages reached an ear-splitting pitch, and it sounded like there were hundreds of them crowding the tunnel, but Perry still didn't dare to look around.

His eyes were fixed on the tall figure of the demigod.

The glowing red eye slits of the helm, staring right back at him.

The air shimmered around the paladin like a mirage.

Perry backed further into the cave, and yet somehow, he didn't losing sight of Selos. It was like Selos was growing taller before his very eyes, growing, growing…

And then Perry realized that Selos was gliding towards him, his feet not even touching the ground, like he commanded the very air that encapsulated him, and Perry's stomach did a flip-flop and then dropped, hard, like his belly was full of lead shot.

Selos's cape billowed behind him, and it was only at that moment that Perry realized that the paladin was hurtling towards the cave, leaving his praetor escort behind, his longstaff held low and ready in his hands.

Perry, stepping backward, nearly tripped on the headless corpse of a nekrofage. He staggered, regained solid footing, and just before disappearing into the tunnel, saw Paladin Selos land at the mouth of the cave with a rumble like thunder.

Perry backed into the tunnel and the rock wall cut off his view of Selos. But Selos was coming. He was coming to slaughter them all, and Perry only had a pistol and a clasp that did something he didn't know how to use…

The clasp, the clasp, the clasp!

Perry's feet found soft and unstable footing. He walked across a carpet of bodies, some of them still twitching, moaning, growling, reaching for him. He cried out and danced away from their clawing hands.

"There's too many of them!" he heard Sagum's voice cry out. "I'm out of ammo!"

Stuber shouted back: "Then beat the motherfuckers!"

Perry realized he had stopped moving his feet. He stood halfway down the dogleg of the tunnel while Stuber and Teran and Sagum plowed forward through the wall of bodies, the shotguns now silenced and overtaken by the dim crack of buttstocks on skulls.

Perry stared at the clasp in his hands. Trying to feel it. Trying to figure it out.

He was aware that the distance between him and his friends was growing, but he was locked into position. He couldn't move from this spot. He had to…*DO SOMETHING!*

But the more the fear came upon him, the further The Calm seemed to pull away from him. Which only made the fear stronger.

He was spiraling down.

His breath came in short, sharp gasps.

He heard his voice making panicked, uncertain noises: "Ah…ah…"

Paladin Selos rounded the corner.

Perry's vision constricted. He could not even see the ground, or the walls of the tunnel. All he could see was the helm of the seven-foot-tall demigod, the piercing crimson gaze, the bristling black crest of the helmet brushing the ceiling of the tunnel.

Perry thrust the pistol out, his last offensive weapon, and pulled the trigger as fast as he could.

Each squeeze of the trigger. The recoil of the pistol. A flash of light in the dimness.

The bullets lanced out.

Sizzled in midair, shattering against the energy shield that encapsulated Selos, causing it to ripple and shimmer.

With each ineffective impact, Perry's stomach sank further. In the span of those few short seconds as he cranked off his last few rounds, his brain scrambled for something, some forlorn hope to cling to, and he thought perhaps if he concentrated his fire it might break through the shield…

Paladin Selos stood there, unfazed, like Perry was a creature in a cage lashing out at the bars. Selos knew full well that the bullets would never touch him. So he watched without fear, until the slide locked back on the pistol, and Perry had nothing left.

Perry kept squeezing the trigger, though it was flat and dead. It was pure reaction. Pure panic. His breath was trapped in his throat.

He's going to kill you.

Selos raised the longstaff in his right hand and a green flame sparked from the cruel muzzle of the godtech, and it smashed into the empty pistol in Perry's hand.

The pistol flew apart in pieces.

Perry yelped, and horrible pain engulfed his hand.

He looked down and saw that his right forefinger had been mangled and hung at an odd angle.

Perry clutched the broken hand to his chest, his teeth bared, sweat pouring into his eyes and mixing with tears of pain. His mouth worked, but found no voice.

Paladin Selos still stood there, calm and placid.

He didn't need to destroy the pistol. He'd done it simply to show Perry that mere mortals could not stand against the demigods.

Perry started backing away. His last weapon destroyed, the only thing left for him was to try to create distance. His heels struck a mire of guts, stumbled over limbs. He was only dimly aware of these things. He could not take his eyes off the paladin before him.

Selos stepped forward through the mess and wreckage. Confident. Erect. He stretched out his hand, the gauntleted fingers opening. The palm facing up. A supplication. An invitation.

Selos spoke, and his voice rumbled and reverberated, filled the air, deep and powerful, like a serene mountain with a raging volcano at its heart.

"Percival," the voice shook the tunnel. Selos stepped forward again, his hand still outstretched. "This is the only chance I will ever give you. Kneel to me, and all will be well."

Perry reached for The Calm, for the only hope he had left. But it was gone.

Fear, like apocalyptic fire, had come down and burned away that flowing river.

The same old fear that had been pounded into him at Hell's Hollow.

He'd once been a fearless child. That's what Uncle Sergio had told him. But time and bad experiences build that up in us all.

Perry had been *taught* to fear. And now it was stealing from him the one thing that made him more than a runt.

Runt.

Shortstack.

Peon.

Perry.

In the tunnel, surrounded by carnage. In the darkness, bereft of hope. Alone, facing a being that could destroy him with a whim. Because he was small. He was insufficient. He could never be a warrior. He could never fill his father's shoes…

He faced Paladin Selos, and he knew these were the last few moments of his life.

Paladin Selos's gauntleted hand hung in the air. His voice rumbled again, lower this time. Haughty. As though it were all a foregone conclusion. "You have no chance of withstanding me. But I will grant you mercy if you kneel to me now."

Perry stared at the blazing red eyes of the paladin's helm.

If there was one thing in the world Perry hated more than anything else, it was being talked down to. If there was a second thing, it was when someone made him feel beholden.

So here was a nice one-two punch.

Perry realized he was getting angry, because that's what he did: he turned his fear into anger. He lashed out when he was terrified.

He had a chip on his shoulder.

And anger was a quick way to rid himself of fear.

Perry ground his feet into the sand. Knew he was about to die, and that was okay. The fear of death had bored holes through him, just like Stuber had said that it would. He had soaked in it. He had lived in it.

But…death waits in the wings, doesn't it? And there's not a damned thing you can do about it if it decides to descend on you today.

No more running.

Perry had decided to face his problems down.

"I'll die on my feet, thanks."

The paladin took a half step forward, and his grip on his staff shifted, and Perry prepared to feel the blade cut through him.

Instead, he heard Paladin Selos laugh.

Just a short, derisive chuckle.

"Such a pity you were raised by mortals. You've a simplistic understanding of a complex machine that keeps life on this planet going. Cato didn't understand its complexity. And neither do you." A pause. Selos's voice became lower. Grating. "I see nothing of myself in you. You're no son of mine."

Perry frowned in confusion.

No son of mine?

And then Selos lunged.

Quick as a cat pouncing.

The shimmering blade at the end of his longstaff cut through the air.

Perry watched it coming.

Watched his death rocketing towards him.

But that split second of confusion had blocked out any vestiges of fear that might've clung to him through his anger.

And that was all his mind needed.

That was the tipping point.

Red

The clasp

The dip

The place

His mind fell into the flow of The Calm.

Round peg—round hole.

A bright flash.

Perry cringed away from it.

Waited for the feeling of being cut in two.

But he only heard crackling, like a welding wire touching metal.

He opened his eyes and looked.

The blade of the longstaff hovered in the air, about a foot from his face. Around it, electricity seemed to sparkle and arc, and the air shimmered. It shimmered like it had around Selos. Except that now, it shimmered around Perry.

Energy shield, he realized. *That's what the clasp is. It's an energy shield.*

Through the veil of sparkling energy, Perry's wide-stretched eyes drifted to the piercing red gaze of Paladin Selos, a demigod that had wanted to kill him, and had just failed, not such a foregone conclusion after all. He watched the helm tilt, just slightly, as though Selos was reevaluating something that he found surprising and confusing.

The moment had shocked the hell out of Perry. But through that paralysis shot a very clear thought, and it had come from the clasp, and it had come from his mind—they were connected now, like a part of his body—and the thought was telling him *the shield won't last forever.*

As though to drive the point home, Selos jerked the backend of the staff upwards, so that the muzzle of the energy weapon was now facing Perry through the skein of sparking energy shield that surrounded him.

Green light flashed.

Perry felt a devastation, though he knew it wasn't his body.

The energy shield, an extension of his brain now, was telling him, just as if it were another appendage of his body, that it had been injured.

How much more could it handle?

Another blast?

Or would the next blast find Perry's head and disintegrate it?

Behind the hulking figure of Paladin Selos, Perry became aware of praetors, swarming into the tunnel.

Perry thought quickly, taking this bare moment and making it work for him.

There is something about smaller men—they can't rely on brute strength. If they want to win, they have to be clever.

They have to be faster and smarter.

He was aware of the massive energy potential of the shield. He was also aware of the giant weight of the mountain that hovered over his head, kept in place by the sculpted ceiling of the tunnel.

He thrust his hands upwards, and the energy shield followed his bidding.

The energy crashed into the roof of the tunnel, just as Selos fired another blast from his longstaff, but this time diverted upwards, so that it, too, smashed into the rocks above.

Perry knew better than to wait.

The mountain rumbled overhead.

Perry spun and sprinted away.

A cavalcade of stone rumbled under his feet. He felt the explosion of rock, bits and pieces chasing him, and heard them sizzle as they struck the shield that surrounded him, turning to molten splashes on the tunnel floor.

The cave-in turned into a violent roar, like standing under a waterfall…

And it didn't stop.

Perry suddenly became aware of chunks of rock raining from the ceiling ahead of him.

The entire tunnel was caving in.

Perry, tripping on broken limbs and bullet-blasted bodies, all faintly glowing like crushed lightning bugs, sprinted around the dogleg in the tunnel, gasping for air, tasting the dust and death of it. Rocks the size of his head were slamming into his shield, weakening it further by small but disastrous increments.

Ahead of him, perhaps fifteen yards across a landscape paved with green-glowing carnage, the three huddled figures of Perry's only friends stood in a tight formation, but it was only Stuber that fought. Teran held onto Sagum, whose legs were not operating correctly.

They were an island in a sea of inhumanity.

And they were about to be washed away.

Stuber howled like a rabid dog, crushing the nekrofages with his bare hands, raining hammer blows down on their skulls, kicking at them, breaking jaws with his elbows, but he was beginning to tire, and his limbs lashed out less effectively, finding less targets, moving slower...

Perry, with the clasp clutched in his left hand, and his broken right hand clutched to his chest, ran to his friends. Out of the corner of his eye he saw a black maw open up in the side of the tunnel—and the glimmer of daylight far beyond.

A way out?

He had the intelligence—or perhaps the instinct—to pull his mind away from the clasp, to extinguish the shield, before he rammed his friends with it.

Then he was beside Stuber, whose right arm was trapped by three nekrofages that clung to it, one of them whose teeth were sunk to the grimy gums in his forearm. As though his arm were only bait, Stuber hissed spittle through clenched teeth and drove a thumb through an eye of the nekrofage who was biting him.

It screamed and detached itself.

A boulder dropped from the ceiling and crushed the nekrofage flat.

Perry kicked one of the others in the chest, sending it stumbling back into the crowd of its brethren. "Stand back, Stuber!"

"What the fuck are *you* gonna do?" Stuber gasped, breathless, knowing nothing.

"Get the fuck back!"

Stuber ripped his arm away from the last nekrofage that had a hold of it, and gave the thing the boot, sending it flying backward. Stuber took a single step in retreat. The nekrofage gathered itself, caught and bolstered up by another dozen of its peers, and charged.

And turned into green mist.

Perry stood, at the apex of the small group of humans, the clasp held out in front of him, the energy field crackling and shimmering, creating a dome around them, while the nekrofage that had charged became a puddle on the ground with a few charred bones protruding from it.

Rocks continued to rain from the ceiling.

They were getting larger.

Perry took a single second to look over his shoulder at his friends, whose mouths gaped, their eyes affixed on him.

Even Stuber looked shocked.

And that felt best of all.

"I figured out the other function," Perry yelled, not able to restrain himself from smiling.

Stuber was the first to come to his senses, his eyes shooting upward to where rocks were smashing into the energy shield and turning to liquid. "We need to get out of this tunnel!"

The way ahead was still crowded with nekrofages, though they were beginning to retreat under the onslaught of the cave in. It would take too much time to push through them.

The energy shield wasn't going to last forever. And even if it did manage to last through the cave in, if they didn't get the hell out, they could be trapped.

Perry's mind fixated on the only way out that he could think of: the opening in the rock that had been exposed by the cave in. The promise of daylight beyond it.

"Come with me!" he shouted.

The four of them huddled close, shrouded by the energy shield. Perry pushed them back the way they had come, and for once, no one questioned him.

Perhaps they were all in too much of a shock, or maybe just too exhausted.

They scrambled through the corpses of nekrofages, dodging spots of molten rock.

Perry nearly passed the hole in the wall that he'd seen, but caught it only by the hint of light that shone from the other end.

"Into the hole!" Perry called, pushing them through one at a time until they were all in the tunnel. Here the tunnel did not seem to be collapsing, but it was tight, and it sloped steeply downhill.

Perry realized that, without any thinking on his part, the shield had formed itself to fit into the tunnel. Whether by instinct, subconscious control, or design of the device itself, he had no idea, and didn't care to ponder it at that moment.

When the roar of falling stone seemed to be behind them, Perry let the shield extinguish.

The part of his mind that was connected to that piece of god-tech told him that the shield was on its last legs. He wasn't certain if it would automatically recharge itself, but he hoped to the gods that was the case.

He had a feeling he might need it again, very soon.

CHAPTER 30

✦

LINEAGE

THE TUNNEL WAS LONGER than Perry had first thought. The daylight seemed to elude them until Perry began to panic, thinking that he'd led them into a dead end hole in the ground. He was just beginning to picture them starving to death or suffocating in a tomb of rock when a breath of fresh air hit him in the face.

They exited the tunnel, gasping from exertion and blinking into the stark white sun.

Teran and Sagum, who had been supporting each other, simply collapsed onto the dusty ground. For the first time, Perry looked them over and saw how bad they were hurt. Teran's arms had been bitten in several places, and they hung limp at her sides now. Sagum's right leg had been savaged and appeared to be unable to hold his weight.

Perry had the urge to try and help them, but rallied himself and forced his eyes to take in their surroundings. The tunnel had led them back out onto the hillside. For a moment, Perry was completely lost, until he saw the plume of black smoke that marked Boss Hauten's burning buggy.

It was close.

They were about a hundred yards back down the hill.

Shit.

"What the fuck do we do now?" Perry said.

Stuber knelt beside a boulder that hid the small mouth of the tunnel. His Roq-11 dangled from his chest, and Perry noted that the bolt was locked back. Stuber's arms bled profusely from multiple bites, dribbling red spots all over the rock and the ground.

"Does anybody have any ammo?" Perry asked.

Stuber looked back at him, teeth bared in a grimace. "I do believe we are categorically empty."

Perry belted out a multitude of curses. He sidled up beside Stuber. Smelled the man's sweat and his breath, huffing hard. The two of them peered around the boulder together.

The smoking ruins of the buggy were close. Maybe twenty yards back down the hill, and a little to their right.

To their left, they could see the cave that had been the entrance into the original tunnel. He could see no praetors around it, though. Had they all been smashed in the cave in?

Had Selos?

In the back of his head, his mind seemed to twist.

No son of mine…

The implications seemed too terrible to grasp.

His father's voice echoed through his head, right on the heels of Selos's.

No matter the blood that runs in your veins.

A glint of polished metal on the hillside caught Perry's eye and broke his train of thought. He squinted at it, then pointed. "There. Is that the Mercy Pistol?"

Stuber blinked a few times. "Gods in the skies." He put a heavy hand on Perry's shoulder. "That's pretty good for peon eyes."

Perry slipped back behind the rock. Looked at Teran and Sagum, who were still conscious, but looked like they were at the end of their rope. Then he looked at Stuber. "Well, the Mercy Pistol is better than nothing. Wait here."

Before Stuber could answer, Perry darted out from behind the rock.

He ran across the rocky scree, his eyes shooting up to the cave, looking for any signs of praetors—or Selos. There was nothing. Perhaps they'd all been crushed by the cave in. The way was clear.

He focused again on the Mercy Pistol lying on the ground.

Just a few more yards away.

He switched the clasp to his mangled right hand, so that he could use his good hand to scoop up the pistol.

He'd grab it, hightail it back behind the boulder and then…

What then?

Well, shit, he hadn't gotten that far yet. But it wouldn't hurt to have a pistol with at least a few live rounds in it.

It was right there.

He started to bend at the waist, reaching down for it.

The next thing that Perry was aware of was a bright green flash, and he felt himself flipping up into the air. He watched the world turn upside down, saw every terrible detail of it as a plume of dust and rock peppered his face and his neck, saw it all so clearly, like that microsecond of flight had stretched into infinity.

He hit the ground on his back, the air coming hard out of his lungs and not returning.

His ears rang from the blast.

His head was tilted to his left.

A cloud of dust was settling.

Through it, he saw a shape flying towards him.

A billowing cape, black against the sky, like ragged wings.

Longstaff held like a charging lance, ready to spear Perry to the ground.

Perry felt the clasp, still in his wounded right hand.

Almost reflexively, the shield activated.

Selos slammed into him with the sound of lightning striking. His own shield driving down into Perry's, the two energies spitting and sparking violently. Perry felt his back grind through the rocks, and he cried out through gritted teeth.

His shield's brief rest had strengthened it, but not far enough, and already he could feel it faltering like a candle running out of wax.

The glinting blade of Selos's longstaff hovered, just on the other side of those warring shields, just inches from Perry's face, pressing down on him with all of Selos's superhuman strength, waiting for his shield to gutter out.

But Perry was staring past the blade that was going to destroy him in mere moments. He was staring at Selos. He was staring into the face of a demigod.

The helm was gone.

Selos's skin was pale, glistening with sweat. Blood trickled from a cut on his forehead, starkly red on his flesh. The face was lean, the nose straight and equine, thin-lipped mouth twisted in cruel hatred, perfect teeth bared...

But the hair was brown and shaggy.

Just like Perry's.

And the eyes that stared down at him, full of malice—Perry had seen those eyes…every time he'd seen a reflection of himself.

—No matter the blood that runs in your veins—

—You're no son of mine—

Perry felt like his strength might suddenly leave him. His mind swirled, dizzy, the blood rushing out of his head. And it was only through monumental effort that he kept himself focused, kept the shield between him and imminent death, even as it continued to weaken under the constant pressure of Selos's might.

"So it's true," Selos hissed through his clenched teeth, and spittle flew from them and sizzled against the deadlocked energy shields. "A halfbreed *can* use the god-tech."

Selos shifted abruptly, as though trying to pressure Perry from another angle. Perry felt his shield shift to cover the new angle. It no longer had the energy to completely encapsulate him. It could only provide a barrier to the immediate threat.

Perry groaned with effort, trying to rise up from underneath the powerful weight that was on him. Trying to keep his mind focused on not dying, rather than chasing each permutation of this ghastly revelation as it began to connect the dots in his subconscious. But the knowledge began to well up in him like rising floodwaters.

"The others wanted you dead," Selos glared down at him. "I tried to save you. I arranged for you to attend the Academy. I wanted to see if you were anything more than a halfbreed runt. But you're not." One corner of his mouth twisted upwards in something like a smirk. "You're no godbreaker, little Percival. You're just an abomination."

"I'm the son of Cato McGown," Perry gasped, knowing even as he said it that it was not true. It was only a denial of the horrible thing staring him in the face right at that moment. The horrible truth that he didn't want to admit.

Selos's laugh was like steel dragged across rocks. "No. You're an unfortunate genetic mistake born of my seed and your mother's womb."

Perry looked desperately around him. Back towards the boulder behind which his only friends in the world were hiding. But he could not see them. They were not there anymore.

He saw the smoking wreckage of Boss Hauten's buggy…

"Give your mother her due, boy," Selos whispered, barely audible over the crackling of the shields.

Perry dragged his gaze away from the wreck of Boss Hauten's buggy. Stared into those malevolent eyes that were so much like his own.

Selos grinned savagely. "She tried to cry out, but I swore to her I would destroy everything that she loved if she breathed a word. And then I ravaged her. Again and again. While Cato McGown sat at a feast, one room away."

At first, he felt shock. Denial. But then Perry began to feel rage roaring through him, hot and destructive. It turned the red flow of The Calm into a river of lava. But it was impotent. It only burned himself. He didn't have the strength to push Selos off of him. He didn't have the power to get out from under him.

He looked to his left, desperate for anything in that moment, anything with which he could lash out.

The Mercy Pistol lay in the dirt, just out of arm's reach.

But what good would that do Perry with the shields still sparking between them?

He reached for it anyways.

Selos saw him, but didn't care. He knew as well as Perry did that the pistol would be no use to him. And he could sense Perry's shield failing. He knew it was only seconds from dying.

"I should've known nothing good would come of debasing myself with such filth as your mother. And look at what her peon genes produced? You should've been a great warrior. Instead you came out like this. A runt."

Clawing, stretching, Perry reached, and he tried to speak, but it only came out an unintelligible groan.

Selos's eyebrows arched. "What's that, Runt?" his voice was sanguine now, sensing victory. Almost gentle. "You have something to say, you bastard abomination?"

Perry's eyes met Selos's. He raised his head slightly off the ground so that his face felt the static of the energy fields, close enough that his grunted words could be heard.

"Watch your left flank."

Selos didn't move, but his eyes jagged to his left.

He saw what Perry had already glimpsed, moments ago, coming away from Boss Hauten's buggy, about fifteen yards away: a battered, bloodied, smoke-smudged ex-legionnaire, struggling to heft something very large at his hip.

The ex-legionnaire smiled beatifically at the demigod.

And leveled a tri-barrelled LRG at him.

Selos roared. But Charlize roared louder.

Three thousand rounds per minute splashed into Selos's shield, rocking his whole body off-kilter, and he only barely maintained his position of dominance on top of Perry. But it was enough of a shift in weight that Perry was able to stretch out an extra inch, and his fingers closed around the molded grip of the Mercy Pistol.

Perry felt Selos's shield shifting to cover the new angle. The battering of such an overwhelming volley of projectiles weakening it rapidly.

It no longer had the energy to completely encapsulate Selos. It could only provide a barrier to the immediate threat.

Selos strained under the withering fire.

And Perry raised the pistol. *Around* the shields.

Just before he put the muzzle of the Mercy Pistol to Paladin Selos's sweating, vein-bulging temple, Perry thought of all the things that he would have liked to say to this creature, this unrighteous god, this rapist, this murderer.

But in the end, he softly spoke the words that were always said:

"Accept this mercy and go to The After."

As the bullet passed through Paladin Selos's head, it snuffed his power instantly. His shield went down, and even as Selos's body was falling slackly to the ground, it caught a barrage of Charlize's sustained fire and turned to an unrecognizable liquid mass. Half of it disintegrated into pink mist, and the other half rained to the dusty ground in a shower of gristle.

All that blood. But it would never be enough to bring the earth back to life.

Perry collapsed back onto the ground, gasping for air. Feeling the warmth of blood on his legs, and not caring.

He stared up into a white hot sky, unblinking. His ringing ears were filled with the rush of his own blood, and the huff of his own breath. But he still heard the sound of something big and heavy clattering to the stone ground.

Perry turned his head to the right.

Stuber approached, limping slightly, the heavy LRG laid to rest behind him. "You alright, Shortstack?" Stuber stumbled to a stop, hovering over Perry, his eyes coursing across Perry's body, looking for injuries.

Perry frowned. "You could've shot me."

Stuber's eyes twinkled. "It was a chance I was willing to take." Stuber nodded towards the mess that cluttered the lower half of Perry's body. "You, uh…got something on your shoes."

Perry started to struggle to his feet, but Stuber grabbed him up, gentler than usual, or perhaps just too tired to be violent. Perry found himself leaning on the ex-legionnaire, catching his breath as he stared down at the mess on the ground that he'd just extricated himself from.

The lower half of Paladin Selos's body was still there. The black shin greaves and molded leather boots, coated in a fine layer of dust. The knee-plates scratched and scarred from their struggle. But the rest of him was gone.

Perry spat. But his mouth was dry. He only managed to issue a few flecks of froth that splattered bitterly onto the wreckage of the paladin that had betrayed his father—his *real* father, not just the one whose blood was in his veins. The paladin that had raped his mother. And murdered his family.

He hadn't even had time to come to grips with the depth of everything he had just learned. And yet...

"You know," Perry said, his voice raspy. "I've always heard revenge leaves you feeling hollow."

Stuber grunted, then blew a raspberry. "Well, I can't speak for every spineless peon out there. But for warriors like you and I..." He smiled, looking wistful. "Revenge is a beautiful thing."

Stuber bent down with some apparent effort and grabbed the longstaff from the ground. He held it out to Perry.

Perry shook his head. "I don't want that."

"The weapon doesn't make the man. And we need all the weapons we can get right now. This is a powerful one. And something tells me you might be able to use it."

Perry stared at the longstaff for a long time.

Was this the one that had cut Cato and Fiela in half?

Slowly, his hand closed around the grip of it. It was warm. Surprisingly light for its size.

He didn't bother trying to access it now. He didn't want to. His brain felt beaten and used up. He had no desire to solve another puzzle.

He felt Stuber's hand on his shoulder.

He looked up at the other man's soot-smudged face.

There was that rare glimmer of sincerity there.

"Teran was right, Perry. Your lineage only determines your starting point. You decide your fate."

CHAPTER 31

✿

THE LAST LEG

STUBER DIDN'T WANT TO LUG Charlize with him, so he took a moment to say goodbye, and Perry thought the ex-legionnaire might shed a tear. But he didn't. Instead, he stripped the half-empty box magazine from it, and hauled it onto his shoulder by a rubber strap on the side.

When Perry and Stuber rounded the boulder where they'd left Teran and Sagum, they found the two of them standing, leaning exhaustedly on the boulder. But they were both staring at Perry, agog.

Perry blinked a few times, not sure what to say or do.

Teran reached out and touched his arm gingerly. "I'm sorry, Perry. If any of what he said was true...I'm sorry..."

Sagum interrupted, his mouth split in an awestruck grin. "You killed a *paladin*."

Perry felt a strange mix of grief and satisfaction and embarrassment, and he deflected it by gesturing to Stuber. "We both did."

He expected Stuber to say something smart-alecky, but when he looked up, Stuber bore a queer expression of concern on his face. He waved Perry off. "Yes. Well. There might be praetors still in these hills. And there might be more coming." He patted the magazine he'd taken from Charlize. "We have some ammo now, but if it's all the same to you folks, I'd rather not stick around."

"Where are we going to go?" Perry wondered.

Stuber gestured to the hole in the ground beside Teran and Sagum. "The boat is still our best option to get the hell out of here unseen. If we can get to it."

No one appeared to relish the idea of going back into the cave that had just collapsed—and been riddled with nekrofages—but after a moment of silence and looking around, no one seemed to have any better ideas.

"Let me go first," Perry said, resignedly.

"Does your shield still work?" Teran asked him.

Perry still clutched the clasp in his injured right hand. He looked at it, but it was his mind that dipped into it to answer the question, and he found it odd and a little exciting that it was so easy now. It felt like the god-tech had somehow been hardwired into him now. It took almost no effort.

"Yes. It recharges. Or something." He frowned. "I don't know exactly. But it's still there. It'll be enough. I think."

Stuber used the weaponlight on his Roq-11 to illuminate their way through the dark tunnel. After a while of struggling on through jagging shadows and tight, claustrophobia-inducing turns, Perry found the way to the main tunnel blocked.

He considered using his shield to melt the rocks out of the way—not sure at all whether that would work or not—but Stuber and him strained at the pile of rocks blocking their way and were able to clear a passage that was big enough for them to get through.

The green glow of the underground greeted them.

All was still and silent in the passage where death now hung like a fog. Huge pieces of the ceiling had come down and the sandy path that led to the water was littered with great monolithic shapes. But the way wasn't blocked, and Perry could see their boat sitting on the small inlet, appearing untouched by all the calamity.

Around them, the shattered bodies of the nekrofages had gone dark. In the harsh spear of Stuber's weaponlight, their skin looked pale and translucent.

Out of the confines of the small tunnel, Stuber positioned himself between Teran and Sagum, supporting each of them with one of his arms around them. Though Sagum seemed to need supporting more than Teran.

As they picked their way through the wreckage, Teran spotted the satchel of supplies that she had dropped. They were kicked against the wall of the tunnel, half covered by a dead nekrofage.

Perry retrieved these, and they headed for the boat.

As they stepped into the inlet where they'd parked the boat, a glimmer of green caught Perry's eye.

Two nekrofages were crouched to the left, hunched over a third that was dead, and Perry wasn't sure, but in the instant that he saw them, he thought that they were feeding on it.

The two nekrofages jumped to their feet with a shriek.

Without having to think, Perry's shield activated itself. Damaged, but able to create a circle of energy, about the size of Perry, between him and the nekrofages.

The two unearthly creatures seemed to give Perry a half-second of consideration, and then perhaps something in their rotted brains recalled what had happened the last time they had seen this particular human.

They darted into the water, slipping through as though they were amphibian in nature. The crystal clear water showed their glowing shapes as they swam.

And it showed the wyrms stirring. Thrashing out of the deep dark places.

Perry realized he was standing still in the cool sand of the underground beach, just a few paces from their boat, watching as the fleeing nekrofages were attacked by what appeared to be three very large wyrms.

He trembled as he watched this, a chill going up his back as he recalled being in the water himself. He looked at Stuber, his face indignant. "They *will* eat you if you go in the water! I could've died when you threw me in!"

Stuber, already hauling Teran and Sagum around to the boat, tossed his voice over his shoulder: "But you didn't, did you?"

Perry stood rooted in the sand for a moment.

Stuber released Teran, who was able to climb into the boat on her own, and then tumbled Sagum in like careless luggage.

Stuber braced himself at the front of the boat, but stopped before pushing it into the water and looked back at Perry. "After you, my halfbreed friend."

Stuber pushed them free of the pale sand and the boat swayed in that disconcerting way that Perry was so unused to. Stuber thrashed through the water up to his knees and then hauled himself up into the boat, nearly tipping it, but then balancing it out once he had his bulk inside.

Clinging to the sidewalls of the boat, Perry took more careful stock of the three people in the boat with him.

Teran was bitten across both of her arms, in numerous places, but it was only the left arm that she favored. In the dim, green glow, Perry saw that most of the bite marks were shallow, but the one on her left arm, right above her elbow, looked like a chunk of her flesh had been taken with it.

It was difficult to determine her coloring in the low light, but Perry saw how dark and withdrawn her eyes were. She moved to bandage herself, but her motions were slow. Her breathing was still labored—more from pain, it seemed, than from exertion.

Sagum lay propped up against the side of the boat, like he'd tried to make it to one of the forward benches, but hadn't been able to get himself there. His arms, too, were covered in nips and scratches, but his right leg had been savaged, and he was trying now to tourniquet it to stop the bleeding, though his hands were clumsy and unsure.

At the rear of the boat, Stuber lay, collapsed across one of the benches, his tattered and bloody arms propped up, his wingspan so wide that his languid hands hung over each side of the boat.

He breathed hard, but marshalled himself—pulled in air through his nose and blew it out slowly through pursed lips. His dark and dangerous eyes lacked much of the fire that was usually in them, but they still watched Perry closely.

Perry expected the ex-legionnaire to spring up and seize control of the oars.

But he only shifted his feet and grimaced in pain.

Then he nodded to Perry. "You're gonna need to row us out of here. I'm..." It seemed the words were painful in their coming, but then Stuber finally smirked in resignation. "Well. I'm not sure I can pull an oar right now."

Perry nodded.

The inlet that led to the tunnel to Lasima was narrow, and already they were drifting towards one of the stone walls.

He grabbed a seat on the middle bench and hoisted first one oar, and then the other, letting them splash into the water and working them awkwardly—made worse by him having to grip the right oar without the use of his forefinger. He had none of the muscular grace that Stuber had. The big man had made the task look so effortless...

"Grip them in the middle," Stuber said, his voice uncharacteristically quiet. "Yes. There. At the end of each oar. Now pull them back. One smooth movement. Good. Now lift them out of the water. And return them to the original position." The voice became fainter as the instructions continued, to the point that, as Perry reset the oars for another pull, he became aware that Stuber's eyes had closed, and his head had lolled back. As Perry pulled the oars again, Stuber nodded, dreamily. "Yes. That's good for a peon."

Perry became aware that he was the only one among them that was physically whole. Except for his mangled right forefinger. But that was a small thing in comparison.

He had gotten used to depending on each of them—Stuber for his fighting prowess, Teran for her knowledge and quick thinking, and Sagum for…well, perhaps he hadn't yet relied on Sagum for much.

But now they were all relying on Perry.

Perry had managed to steer the boat away from the rock wall. He looked behind him as he pulled the oars once more. Saw the inlet opening up into the wide subterranean lake, rippling with gaseous green light.

Twisted in the bench seat, Perry looked to Teran, who was trying to rip what was left of her shirt into pieces of fabric for bandaging.

"Teran," Perry said, hearing his own sullen echo. "Which way do I go?"

Teran looked blearily around her, as though he'd bombarded her with a difficult question immediately upon her waking. The lake was long and narrow—they could see the far side of it, perhaps a hundred yards away. But, to the right and left, the lake stretched with no visible end in sight.

Teran nodded to their right. "That way. That should be it. Just follow the flow of the water."

Perry nodded, as though he understood, but he wasn't sure that he did. He leaned over—which made his stomach feel tight and worried—and inspected the surface of the water. Far below the surface, he saw glowing things writhing, and he had to force his attention back to the surface again…

It did seem to be flowing in the direction that Teran had indicated.

Figuring that would be enough to orient him, Perry gave the oars two more solid pulls, floating them out towards the middle of the lake, and then he pulled them back into the boat, stood up from his seat and wobbled on unsteady legs to Teran and Sagum.

Sagum's skin looked like the surface of the moon. The blood that was splashed across it stood out livid and almost black. Perry might not have the experience in battle that Stuber had, but he'd seen his fair share of violent death. And Sagum did not look good to him.

"Here," Perry said, interrupting Sagum's shaking fingers in their effort to secure a tourniquet. "Let me help you."

The tourniquet was a braided cloth belt that Perry figured had come from Sagum's own waistband. He affixed this to the man's thigh, knowing to go high on the limb until he could figure out where the bleeding was coming from and stop it.

Perry looked around for something to use as a windlass to tighten the belt.

Sagum held up a dagger that still glowed faintly green from nekrofage blood.

Perry took it, shoved the handle under the belt, and, careful not to cut himself, he used the blade to turn the dagger and tighten the tourniquet. Sagum grunted once in discomfort, but he didn't seem to have much left to give besides that.

Perry secured the dagger-turned-windlass with a piece of Sagum's shredded pants leg, and then grabbed the man's hand. Their fingers stuck together, tacky with blood. "Hey. That's gonna hold you for a minute. I'm gonna check on Teran and Stuber, and come right back to you, okay?"

Sagum didn't respond.

Perry moved to Teran. She was more with it than the other two, and she coached him through helping her bandage her arm in the places she wasn't able to do with one hand.

"That's fine," she said. "Check on Stuber. Then you can come back and clean us up."

Perry tended to the ex-legionnaire. Both the man's arms had been ripped up. He could see the muscles, exposed. Flaps of skin barely held in place. Perry didn't know what the hell he was doing. He needed Petra.

Perry frowned as he struggled through bandaging Stuber's thick arms. "Maybe we shouldn't try to hide out at the Glass Flats. Maybe it's a bad idea right now."

When he looked at Stuber's face, he found the man glaring at him in a hazy, tired way. "Perry..." his tongue touched his lips, looking dry and thirsty. "Don't be a bleeding vagina."

Then Stuber's eyes closed again. His brow still creased by a slight frown.

His lips moved, his breath a quiet susurration, as though speaking out of a dream, or from the depths of his cups: "Fuck th' beer. I'll drink th' liquor...gimme a whore...give 'er the sticker..." His voice trailed off.

Perry smiled, strangely relieved.

Floating out in the middle of that underground lake, the undulations of its slow current pushing them steadily towards an end that was far out of sight, Perry tended to his friends. He cleaned their wounds, and bandaged them as best he could with what they had. He filled the water bladders from the lake—Teran told him it was okay to drink—and he helped each of them drink as much as they could.

Last of all, he addressed his own broken forefinger.

There wasn't much to do for it, except straighten it out and hope for the best.

He hunched over it, gritting his teeth together and summoning his strength. He was determined not to make a noise. Not to disturb the others with his comparatively minor injury.

That turned out to be difficult.

But he managed to get the thing set, with just a minor groan that whispered out between his clenched teeth. "Set" was maybe too optimistic of a word. But it wasn't hanging askew anymore. And that seemed to be the best he could hope for at the moment.

The wounded lapsed into silence, and then sleep. Or at least the sleep of the injured, which is more like simply closing your eyes and trying to ignore the pain in your body.

Perry sat for a while on the middle bench, trying to think of other things that he might do to help them. Other ways that he might take care of them. He felt…responsible for them.

After a while, he realized that they were doing what was best for them—resting.

They'd been exhausted and bled out. Their bodies needed downtime.

So, with nothing else to do for them, Perry took up the oars, checked the flow of the water and started rowing.

***

He rowed for a long time.

When he was tired he took a break. Drank some water.

He often looked around at the others. Wondering if any of them had come awake. Occasionally one of them would grumble or groan, or in the case of Stuber, shout a curse that echoed all around them. But that was it.

Perry remembered his first days on Boss Hauten's crew. How the discomfort of his new life would cause him to wake before dawn, while everyone was still sleeping. And he would lay awake in his bedroll, longing for dawn to come.

That is what he felt like now.

He realized he was desperate for their company.

Even Sagum would do.

Time was indistinct on that underground lake. The green twilight remained the same at all times, so one hour looked the same as the next. It could be midday, or midnight, and Perry would have no idea.

He didn't know how long he rowed them along. Sometimes it felt like he'd been doing it for a full day. And other times, his mind would slip into the memories of the battle in the tunnel, and it would seem like they had only just shoved off from that beach.

The shape of Paladin Selos seemed to loom out of the shadows of the underground. He would think he saw movement, and when his eyes jagged to it, he would, for an instant, think he saw the glowing red glare and the high, haughty crest of the helm, the green spark of the blast from his longstaff...

The very longstaff that had cut his father and mother in half.

The very longstaff that now sat in the floor of the boat at Perry's feet.

But it was Selos's words that seemed to whisper to him, hidden amongst the quiet susurration of the underground waters.

...You're an unfortunate genetic mistake born of my seed and your mother's womb...

...And then I ravaged her. Again and again. While Cato McGown sat at a feast, one room away...

...You're no son of mine...

You're no godbreaker.

Perry took a break from rowing the oars. Breathing heavily, he leaned on them and stared out at nothingness, his mind filled with images from other times—things he hadn't even been witness to, but that were nonetheless clear and terrifying in his imagination.

In twenty years of his life, he hadn't thought of his mother.

Now, for the first time, he saw her.

He saw her in loyalty and love.

And his father—his *true* father?

Any normal man would have rejected a child that was not theirs, and they'd known had come from rape. And yet Cato McGown had given his life for Perry, as though he was his own flesh and blood.

They had *both* given their lives for him.

They had believed that he could *do something*.

They themselves had died *doing something*.

For the first time in his life, Perry knew his parents. One in blood, the other in spirit. But he knew them as they truly were. How they had lived. How they had died. How they had loved him in a way that he had never thought anyone ever had.

He put his head in his hands and wept silently for them.

***

Perry awoke to a bump.

He hadn't intended to fall asleep, and as he felt something hit the bottom of the boat he came up wildly, his arms seizing about as though looking for a weapon.

He looked about, expecting to see the glowing mass of a wyrm coming over the side of the boat to pull them all down into the cold depths…

Instead, he saw daylight.

He straightened in his seat, and saw that the boat had run aground on another sandy shore. This one very narrow, and very steep. The sand stretched upward in a sort of pyramid, narrowing as it reached a point far above them that appeared to be the end of a tunnel.

Shining down from that little opening, was bright, blinding sunlight.

Perry heard shuffling behind him, and looked to find Stuber rousing himself, glaring at the incoming sunlight as though it offended him. He looked about their environs blearily. "Is this where we're supposed to be?"

Perry shrugged. "I have no idea."

He rose from the bench and went to Teran, who was still asleep. He woke her with a gentle shake on the less-wounded arm. She started, and he had to lean back to avoid being punched in the face by a reactionary swing. When her eyes focused, she halted herself.

"What?" her voice croaked.

"Is this the place?" Perry asked.

Teran blinked several times, as though not sure what was being asked of her, and then she sat up and looked around. Saw the beach. Tracked her eyes up to the opening at the top through which the sunlight was blazing into the darkness.

"I think so."

"You *think* so?"

"I've never been to the Glass Flats."

"Then how do you know this is the right tunnel?"

She looked irritated. "Because I've been everywhere else on this lake. But I've never been here, and I've never been to the Glass Flats, so...see what I'm getting at?"

Perry smiled and nodded. He squeezed her shoulder. "Well, I'm glad you're feeling more like yourself."

A silent drama then played out in Perry's mind, as he looked around and saw that someone would need to pull the boat further on shore, and that someone looked like it was going to be him. Only problem being, it required that he get into the water. And, due to the steepness of the beach, he'd be up to his waist at first, until he could scramble up onto the sand.

He looked into the water behind them, hoping not to see any glowing wyrms in this particular area.

But no. They were there.

Lurking.

And now he knew they were dangerous. At least to the nekrofages. And if to the nekrofages, then why not to regular humans? They were approximately the same size. In fact, Perry was a smaller morsel still.

He hurled himself over the edge of the boat before he could think about it too much. He decided to seize on the fact that he did not glow like the nekrofages, and therefore wouldn't be as attractive a bait. He didn't know if this made sense, but before he could contemplate it too much, he had thrashed his way up onto the beach.

He looked behind him and did not see any wyrms in pursuit.

He was overcome with the urge to get out of this hellish underground and never see it again.

He seized ahold of the front of the boat and hauled backwards.

No joy.

His feet slipped through the sand.

He planted himself more firmly. Tried again.

Stuber watched him with a curious look.

Panting after several efforts, Perry leaned on the front of the boat and chose to look at his feet. "Stuber," he said, quietly. "If you're up to it, I could use your help."

"I was enjoying the show." The boat rocked as Stuber stood up, and then splashed into the water. It only came to mid-thigh on him. He waded ashore, his movements a little more stiff than usual.

Together, they hauled the boat up onto the sand.

Teran and Sagum staggered out, Sagum looking still half-asleep.

"Can you two make it up to the mouth of the tunnel?" Perry asked.

They eyed the distance. The incline. The soft sand that would impede their progress.

"I'd prefer not to leave you guys down here," Perry pressed.

Stuber put his arm around Sagum. The younger man stiffened at this, but then allowed himself to be helped. "I'll help Sagum," Stuber said. "You help Teran."

Paired up like this, the four of them struggled up to the top of the rise, Perry dragging the longstaff and the supply satchel along with Teran, and Stuber carrying his Roq-11 and the ammunition can from Charlize, along with Sagum.

There was no cave to shelter in, like there had been at the tunnel that led to Lasima. Here, there was only one opening, so small that they had to unlatch from each other and shuffle through, one at a time, stooped over. Stuber had to squeeze through on his hands and knees.

Scorching, dry air engulfed them like the inside of an oven.

The landscape beyond was so bright, it took a moment of fevered blinking for Perry to see any feature of it clearly. His eyes stung as they adjusted to the blinding world outside.

Everything was white.

The sky was a cloudless, dusty haze, the sun seeming to take up half the sky over their heads. It burned on his skin. He immediately began to sweat, and the moisture was immediately sucked off of his skin by a hot breeze.

Below the deadpan sky, a landscape of nothingness stretched out to where it seemed to boil into vapors on the horizon. All was flatness. There was no rocky slope for them to descend. They were already on a level with everything else in this gods-forsaken place.

As Perry blinked and his pupils contracted down to tiny pinpoints, a single feature in the landscape revealed itself.

A tiny hut stood in the midst of the barrenness. So small that Perry mistook it for a boulder at first, but then spied the door, and the single window, and the symmetrical, man-made aspect of its shape.

"What is that?" Perry asked.

"It appears to be a dwelling," Stuber responded, matter-of-factly.

"Someone lives out here?" Perry looked around. Saw no water source. Saw no plants. Saw nothing on which someone could subsist. But then, perhaps someone could use the underground lake as a water source. And perhaps they fed on the wyrm eggs, just like the nekrofages.

Perry shuddered and let his eyes skirt around their feet, looking for signs of someone else's comings and goings. But there was only a crusty hardpan around them. A thin layer of dust sat, undisturbed. No footprints, aside from the ones that Perry and his four companions had just made.

"Maybe no one lives there," Teran suggested. "Maybe it's just a stopping point. Like a hunting cabin. Maybe it's just there for whoever needs it."

Something in Perry's gut twisted up. Teran's suggestion was reasonable. And yet...wrong.

"Well," Stuber sighed. "If there were ever any poor bastards who needed a shelter, it would be us four."

Perry shook his head. "I don't like it."

Stuber pursed his lips. "It does look kind of small. And it's probably hot as balls inside..."

"I mean it seems…" Perry struggled for the right way to characterize it. "It just seems off."

"Perhaps one of us should go check it out," Stuber suggested, and roused himself as though he were about to set off.

Perry held out a staying hand. Looked up and met Stuber's gaze. "I'll go."

"You have no weapon."

Perry gestured to the longstaff in his hands.

Stuber shook his head. "First, you don't even know how to use it yet. Second, you probably shouldn't show up at a stranger's doorstep with a stolen paladin's longstaff."

Perry considered this for a moment and knew that Stuber was right. He shoved the longstaff into Stuber's hands. "Still," he said. "I have the clasp. The shield. I'm better protected." He smirked at Stuber. "And less threatening than you."

Stuber frowned. "Hmm."

"I'll go," Perry insisted. "You guys stay here."

CHAPTER 32

✿

THE PLACE AT THE END OF THE WORLD

PERRY STOPPED when he was about twenty yards from the door of the hut.

He stood there on dusty hardpan as white as tile. Looked all around the hut. But there wasn't much to see. It was made of mudbrick, just like Perry's childhood home on the farming freehold. Such dwellings were common on the outskirts and poor sections of many old towns.

But he usually saw them clustered together like they were inhabited by some sort of hive. This one sat solitary and alone, and appeared strange because of it.

Perry held up his hand to shade his eyes from the glaring sun, hoping to see something through the single dark window. But it might as well have been a portal into a cave. Nothing was visible from outside.

He looked around the entrance of the hut, and found that there was not a single trace of footprints coming or going from the door.

He looked behind him, wondering if the hardpan even held onto footprints at all, but he could see the trail of his own footprints across the bleak landscape, back towards the small protuberance of rock that he and his friends had exited. He saw them waiting at a distance, their images shimmering in the heat coming off the ground.

Perry turned back to the hut.

No footprints around it. Which meant it was uninhabited. Or the hot breeze that constantly blew had scoured them away.

He walked the rest of the way to the door.

The sun was directly overhead, so there was no shade at all around the hut.

Perry inclined his ear towards the door, listening. He heard nothing but the wind.

He took a breath, and knocked.

The sound of his knuckles on the wood was hollow and desolate. He wondered where the wood to make the door had come from.

No response came from inside.

He reached for the doorknob.

"Who is it?" a voice came from inside.

Perry jerked his hand back. Blinked several times at the blank face of the weathered wood. He realized he hadn't been expecting an answer—hadn't been expecting it to be occupied.

"Uh…Perry?" he answered, not sure what other answer to give.

From inside, he heard the shuffling of feet.

The rattle of a door-bar being removed.

A slight creak, and a wooden scrape. The door opened an inch.

A single eye peered out at him from the dim interior. Squinting.

He couldn't see much of the face that held that eye, but immediately knew it was ancient. The folds of skin around the eye were wrinkled and slack, and the eye itself was large and round and the iris was rheumy at the edges.

The old eye stared back at him. "Whaddaya want?"

Perry hesitated, not knowing what to say. Not knowing how much to reveal, if anything.

"Shelter," Perry finally said.

"Hrm," the voice grumbled. "You come alone?"

"No," Perry admitted. "I have friends nearby."

"Where are they?"

"They're at a distance. Until we determine that this place is safe."

"Hrm. Cautious then?" a wheezy titter. The eye wrinkled up in humor. "Good thing to be."

"Are we going to talk through the door?" Perry said, wiping sweat from his eyebrows to keep it from trickling into his eyes. "Or will you invite me in?"

The eye grew serious again. "You can come in when I determine what your purpose for being here is. I ask again: what do you want?"

"I told you. Shelter."

A huff of breath. "One doesn't travel to the end of everything to seek shelter. This is no one's shelter. This is no one's objective. This is no one's safe harbor. You didn't happen upon this place by mistake. What is it that you want? Tell me honestly, or be on your way and leave me in peace."

Perry shifted his weight. He felt himself getting irritated, thinking about simply kicking the door in on this old man's face. But the note of misgivings that slithered through his gut tempered him.

"We're hiding out," Perry said.

The eye regarded him for another few beats of Perry's heart.

Then the door slammed.

Perry was about to start pounding on it again, when he heard the sound of a chain being unlatched, and the door swung open again. Inside was only darkness. He couldn't see the man who held the door.

"Come in then," the voice said, more genial this time. "Be quick. You're letting the hot air in."

Perry touched the clasp in his pocket. Then he stepped into the darkness.

The door slammed behind him.

Perry spun, blinking his sun-dazzled eyes against the gloominess inside.

All he perceived was the shadow of a wraithlike figure, hitching away from him on stilt-like legs. Perry's heart sped up, but he perceived that the figure was unhurried, and that stayed Perry's desire to react defensively.

He stood there at the entrance, his eyes adjusting to the darkness.

The hovel that he found himself in was surprisingly cool. Or at least felt that way in comparison to the sweltering world outside. The mudbrick insulated it well.

It smelled…like nothing.

Perry had expected the stink of a hermit's hovel. He expected the smell of its unwashed inhabitant to be embued into every pore of the place. But this just smelled like dust. Like the inside of a cave that has never seen an occupant.

Gradually, his eyes perceived a dirt floor— no different from the hardpan outside. The hovel was square on the interior. Simply a cube. No rooms. Just one single space.

A single wooden table against the far wall, at which sat two wooden stools.

To Perry's left, a small bed that was little more than a jumble of sticks. No padding. No blankets.

There was no kitchen. No place to make a cookfire. No crockery in which to cook a meal. No skins or jugs to hold water. No items at all that might hint at a human need to sustain life.

Just the table, the chairs, the bed, and an ancient old man.

The old man had crossed to the table and he sat on one of the stools, facing Perry.

He was skin and bones. His hide stretched over his sticklike frame like suntanned leather. He wore a loose canvas shirt and a pair of tattered short pants that were the color of the dirt around them. A pair of ancient sandals were strapped to his gnarled old feet.

From his head sprouted a few gray hairs, while a wispy white beard clung to his jaw.

He hunched on his stool in a strange manner. The stool was small, so that his gangly legs were drawn up practically to his chest and his arms were clutched around his knees. He peered at Perry over the top of those two bony joints.

"So," the old man's voice creaked. "Fugitives. Heretics." A twitch of an eyebrow. "Outsiders? Deserters? No one comes to the Glass Flats to escape mortal justice. They only come here to escape the gods' justice."

Perry gave no answer to that. He glanced around the hut again. "You live here?"

"No one lives here, Boyo."

"This isn't your hut?"

"Yes, it is mine."

"But you don't live here?" Perry frowned.

The old man leered at Perry over top of his knees. "Do you know where 'here' is?"

Perry opened his mouth, then closed it. He didn't have an answer.

"In Pallesprek, they call this place Fiendevelt. That is the name of my castle. My estate. My manse."

Perry's jaw tightened. *He's insane. The sun's cooked his brains.*

The old man released his hold on his knees and leaned even further forward. "Fiendevelt, Boyo. Do you know what it means?"

Perry shook his head.

"It means 'the place at the end of the world.'"

An awkward silence passed, with the old man watching Perry like he expected this revelation to mean something. But Perry gave no response.

"You say you're hiding out. But no one *goes* to the Glass Flats. It is not a destination. Just like Fiendevelt is not a destination. It is a stopping point. And the Glass Flats, an obstacle. So tell me, Boyo, where is it that you're actually going?"

"My business is my own."

The old man thrust a wavering, bony finger at him. "Your business is my business!"

"I don't see it that way."

"I'm the gate keeper," the old man proclaimed, drawing himself up. "No one passes by Fiendevelt without first being allowed by me!"

Perry almost told the man he was a doddering, sun-maddened idiot, but held his tongue at the last moment. He still felt off-kilter. He still felt that there were aspects here that he was not seeing, and he did not want to delve into aggression before he knew what he was dealing with.

"Listen, old man," Perry said through gritted teeth. "My friends are wounded. They need a place to rest. And I don't see any other places but this one. So, are you going to help me or not?"

The old man lapsed into a sudden silence. He sat there on his stool without moving, his eyes affixed to Perry, although Perry got the distinct sense that he wasn't being seen. That if he moved to the left or the right, the man's eyes wouldn't track with him, but remain fixed on some far-off point.

Perry was about to snap his fingers to break the old man's fugue, when a voice came out of the old man's chest, and it was very different from what Perry had already heard. The timbre of it was too low. It seemed to echo in the small space.

"You will not leave this place," the voice said.

It was only the movement of the old man's lips that convinced Perry that it had come from his mouth.

The old man stood up, his fists held stiff at his sides, looking at Perry from under his wild white eyebrows. "There is nothing for you beyond Fiendevelt. There is only death and destruction beyond the place where your feet stand at this very moment. The gods have scorched the land beyond us. And even if you do manage to cross the Glass Flats, machines of terror and wrath will rip the life from your body, and that of your friends."

Perry swallowed on a dry throat. "No one said anything about crossing the Glass Flats!"

"Crossing the Glass Flats is forbidden!" the old man thundered.

Perry realized that his hands had begun to shake. He edged towards the door. "I'm fuckin' leaving."

"IT IS FORBIDDEN!" the voice punched at Perry's eardrums.

Perry lurched for the door.

The old man crossed the room in a flash.

Perry had barely touched the door when he felt an iron grip on his forearm, and the strength of it shocked him so much that he didn't immediately react to it as he should have. And then he was being hauled off his feet.

He felt his feet leave the floor.

Felt his body flying through the air.

He slammed into the wooden table and chairs, cracking and scattering them. The breath came out of him in a grunt of pain and he thought he heard a rib crack somewhere in his chest.

"IT IS FORBIDDEN! IT IS FORBIDDEN!" the old man thundered, scuttling across the ground again.

His hand, like a claw, outstretched for Perry again.

Protection, Perry's instincts called out.

The hand latched onto Perry's arm with a strength so unreal Perry thought it was going to rip his arm from his torso…

But his mind fell into place.

Round peg—round hole.

The air shimmered.

There was a shower of sparks.

The old man screeched.

Perry became aware of the pressure on his forearm and when he glanced down he saw the old man's hand still clutching him. Then his eyes jagged up to the old man again, and the old man had jumped back from Perry, clutching the stump of his arm.

Perry stared in shock at the old man's stump.

No blood came from it.

Only sparks, shooting and crackling.

Severed wires. Twitching servos. The glint of steel.

The old man began to screech, a horrific, warbling noise that caused every hair on Perry's body to stand on end.

Perry clambered to his feet. The old man's disembodied hand lost its grip on his arm and fell away. He glanced down at it and saw the same thing—sparks and black smoke and wires and steel.

The unearthly screeching did something to Perry's head. He didn't just *want* to kill the man. He *had* to kill him. It was almost a panic. He needed to stop the noise.

Perry rounded on the old man, who was now backed into the corner of the hut, near the head of the small bed. Perry advanced, his breath seething through his clenched teeth, his momentary fear turning into rage again.

The old man watched Perry coming, and somehow the screeching klaxon coming from his throat continued, but still more words came out simultaneously: "DEVIL! DIABLO! TEFFEL!"

Perry thrust his body forward, as though to grab the man. But the energy field that surrounded Perry struck the man first. Perry watched from the other side of his forcefield as it carved away first the tip of the man's nose, then his jaw, then his face, then his arms that rose to try to push Perry away, turning them all to smoke and sparks—

—the eyes still affixed to Perry, wide with terror—

And then they too were sheared off into smoke and ruin.

The screeching stopped.

The voice went silent.

Perry leapt backwards.

The body, now bisected from the top of the old man's head, to the bottom of his groin, tumbled to the ground.

Smoke billowed from the shattered corpse.

Nothing human was apparent. No blood. No organs. No bones. No muscles.

Only a cross-section of machinery stared back up at him, twitching and sparking.

Where the eyes had been, two round modules shown, and at their center glowed a red light, every bit as crimson as the glow of Paladin Selos's stare. They seemed to hold onto Perry's gaze for a long, horrible moment, and then they winked out.

And the body was still.

"What the fuck!" Perry shouted at whatever it was in front of him.

The door of the hut burst in, letting in light like a nuclear flash, silhouetting Stuber's massive form. The man skidded to a stop on the dirt floor, arms held out at his sides as though prepared to tackle and dismantle someone.

"What was that?" Stuber demanded, his chest heaving from sprinting to the hut. "What the hell did you do? And what is that on the floor? You kill a mech?"

Teran and Sagum tumbled in.

They peppered Perry with similar questions.

Perry, however, was still locked onto Stuber. "Yes, I killed it, whatever it was! What the hell is a mech?"

Stuber craned his neck to look at the jumble of half-human, half-robotic limbs that lay in a heap on the ground. "You never seen a mech before?"

"Obviously fucking not!"

"Okay, stop shouting at me."

"Is it a robot?"

"It's a mechanical man." Stuber seemed transfixed by it. But he managed to break his gaze away long enough to give Perry a sidelong look. "The paladins make them. I've seen them before. Just…never…you know…" Stuber motioned down the length of his body with his fingertips, as though imaginarily bisecting himself. "Cross-sectioned," he finished.

Perry thrust his hand at it, and glanced between his three compatriots. "Well, what the hell is a mech doing out here in the middle of nowhere?"

Stuber shoved it onto its side with the toe of his boot. "And why's it look like a saggy old man?"

Another question occurred to Perry. "Is it…I mean, *was* it alive?"

Sagum was the one who spoke up now. "No. It's not alive." He limped over to the heap in the corner on his bandaged leg, looking very interested. "It's just a computer and a program. A very complex one, but…still just a program. It can't think for itself. It can only do what it's been told to do."

Sagum, Teran, and Stuber, all looked at Perry with curiosity in their eyes.

"What did it do?" Sagum asked.

Perry worked some saliva into his dry mouth. Forced him to get control of his breathing. "It warned me not to cross the Glass Flats."

Stuber tilted his head. "Who said anything about *crossing* the Glass Flats?"

"That's what I said!" Perry shook his head. "I have no clue. It seemed pretty damn convinced that I was going to go. Kept saying it was forbidden. Then when I tried to leave, it…well, I'm pretty sure it was trying to kill me."

Sagum leaned over in front of the mech, studying it. "Weird, for sure." He turned and smiled at Perry. "But on the plus side, I've got plenty of spare parts to try and tinker up that clasp and play the full message."

CHAPTER 33

✦

THE SOURCE

LEAVING THE HUT turned out not to be an option.

It seemed very sudden when the sky began to darken. It was bright as midday one moment, and then, as though the sun had abruptly faltered, the day darkened, though there was still not a cloud in the sky.

Stuber stood outside the entrance to the hut and looked all around at the great expanse of white horizon, his hand shading his eyes. Then he seemed to focus on the east. Straight out across the Devil's Mirror, into a beyond that they didn't know.

Teran sat on the edge of the small, uncomfortable-looking bed, her back against the wall. She watched Stuber curiously.

Perry sat on one of the stools at the small table that they'd managed to piece back together. He held the clasp, and he was half-focused on Stuber, and half-focused on keeping the clasp open, while Sagum fiddled with its innards. The clasp seemed to be wearing a pathway into his brain: It required less and less effort every time Perry used it.

Perry's understanding of his own abilities was still in its infancy, but a lot of the pieces had come together for him as he'd had time to think about it. Uncle Sergio had described him as being a fearless child, and Perry was beginning to believe that this was a mark of the paladin blood that ran in his veins.

There was a connection there, between fear, and what Perry had come to call The Calm.

The Calm was the opposite of fear.

Fear was for mortals.

The Calm was something…divine.

When he controlled his fear, he was able to access The Calm more readily.

And why would it always seem to rise up in him when conflict with others occurred? Why was it that when trouble had brewed with Tiller, The Calm had been so readily available to him?

Well, he believed now that this was the one gift that he'd received from Hell's Hollow.

While the years of indoctrination had created a fear in him of legionnaires and demigods—a fear that, apparently, was not a part of his natural mindset—all those years of violence at the hands of his classmates had inoculated him to conflict with regular people.

Thanks to the near-daily beatings at Hell's Hollow, Perry was never afraid to fight mortals.

And he was learning how to overcome his fear of even the demigods.

Because they were not immortal, as he'd once believed.

He'd finally seen a demigod die. And he'd been the one to kill him.

At the door of their little shelter, Stuber ducked back in, his lips pressed to a line. He latched the door behind him. Looked at the others. "Sandstorm. Glad we have a shelter."

As he said it, a gust of wind, like the first battleline of skirmishers, rushed up against the side of the hut. The roof creaked. Particles of sand and pebbles peppered the exterior of the mudbrick. The door rattled menacingly.

"Perry," Sagum said in a warning tone.

Perry's gaze snapped around. He realized he'd lost his focus, lost the feeling of red momentum, and the multitude of metal flower petals on the clasp were beginning to close.

He refocused himself.

The petals stopped. Opened again.

Sagum gave him an irritated look. "Try to stay focused. Wouldn't want my fingers getting chopped off."

Stuber sank to the floor, put his back against the mudbrick wall, across from Teran. "We've got enough water. Just got to go to the underground to get it. And we've got enough food to last us for…I dunno. A few days." Stuber rubbed his face. "Suppose we could always eat the wyrm eggs like the nekrofages."

Teran frowned at him. "I'd prefer not to glow green."

Stuber shrugged. "I'd prefer not to starve. To each their own."

Stuber, Teran, and Sagum were all bandaged with clean white bandages from Stuber's medical kit. But that had exhausted his supply. He still had the ampoules of antibiotics, which he told them they would likely need. He said that the bites were probably going to get infected, given the foul mouths that they'd come from.

"How long do you think we need to stay here?" Teran asked him.

Stuber considered it. "As little time as possible. I don't like this place. I don't like that it was occupied by a mech. I don't like that it's sitting out here in the middle of nowhere. But…I'd like to be caught in a sandstorm even less. So…we should stay. Until we're healed. And the chances of infection on these bites has passed. Once that happens, we need to find another place." He looked at Perry. "And between now and then, perhaps we'll figure out what the hell it is we're supposed to be doing."

Perry watched Sagum's slender fingers at work. He recalled the garbled half-message that they'd heard from when they'd tried to play the clasp.

"At the end of my father's message, he mentioned something about The Source. But I have no idea what my father was talking about. Stuber? Does that ring any bells for you?"

"I can't say that it does."

Perry realized that he was still referring to Cato as his father. But that was how he thought of Cato. And though he knew the truth—though acceptance was still difficult—he would never see Selos as his father. Only ever as the demigod that had raped his mother.

He didn't know if the others thought it was odd for him to continue to refer to Cato as his father, but if they did, they didn't say so.

He guessed they understood the prickly mental space that Perry now found himself in.

And he appreciated them for not mentioning it.

It was something that he would have to come to grips with all on his own.

Sagum straightened, pulled his hands away from the clasp.

Perry leaned forward. "Is that it? Did you fix it?"

Sagum looked uncertain. "I replaced a coupler that looked a little corroded." He shrugged once. "I guess…try it and see what happens."

Perry took no offense. He folded his arms over his chest and rested there for a moment, thinking. Thinking about everything he'd heard. Thinking about his life up to that point.

But something burned inside of Perry. Something deep in his gut. It was almost a hunger. A desperation to find something. To find the pattern. To find some clue, some key that would decode everything. To find some *logic* in all this mess.

He didn't just *want* to know.

He *needed* to know.

He needed to know why his father had died. He needed to know why Selos had killed his family, hunted him down—and then forced him into the Academy. He needed to know if such a thing as The Source existed at all, and if it could be used against the paladins.

He needed to *do something*.

His father's voice forged a solid steel chain around his thoughts.

If you can find The Source, you can change things for the people of this planet.

Perry straightened up. Like the fire in his gut couldn't be held still anymore. Like it was jumping through his limbs. "I'm going," he blurted. "I don't care. I'm going to the East Ruins, and there's nothing any of you can say that's going to change that."

Teran gave him a quizzical arch of her eyebrow. "Why would we try to dissuade you?"

"Because it's across the Glass Flats," Perry said. "Because there are mechanical killing machines waiting for us on the other side. Because we'll all probably die. Just to name a few."

Stuber had roused himself from leaning back on the wall. He stared thunderbolts at Perry. "What a fuckheaded thing to say to us, Shortstack. To the three people that have been fighting and bleeding alongside you."

Perry threw up his hands, confused. "What do you mean?"

Stuber bristled. "After all of that! And you assume that a stroll across the Devil's Mirror and some centuries-old, rusted-ass killing machines are going to turn our guts to water and send us fleeing like a pack of peons? It's insulting."

Perry realized that a smile had come to his lips, against his will.

Damn that big, stupid animal.

"Stuber, I'd like for you to come with me." Perry looked at Teran and Sagum as well. "I'd like for *all* of you to come with me. I just don't want to force your hands."

Teran looked at Perry. "No one forces our hands, Perry. We make our own choices."

"But there's no backing out. If you're in this with me, you're in all the way."

Stuber made a gasping sound and clutched his chest. "You wound me again, Shortstack. I'm a professional warrior. Not some fair-weather peasant conscript like Smegma."

Across the room, Sagum drew himself up. "I'm coming, too."

Stuber chuffed. "If only you were half the man that Teran is, we'd almost have a whole squad."

"Stuber," Teran said, cutting off any further shots. Then she smiled knowingly at the ex-legionnaire. "It almost seems like you respect me."

"Hm." Stuber shifted around, as though uncomfortable at being caught. "Well. I suppose we're all getting quite friendly in this little sweat lodge." He snapped his eyes to Perry and raised a hand. "But I have a condition that needs to be met."

Perry quirked an eyebrow. "Oh?"

Stuber looked at him hard. "You're going to let me teach you how to fight."

"I already know how to fight."

Stuber rolled his eyes. "No, I don't just mean flailing around and hoping for the best. I mean intense and direct application of violence for the purposes of killing."

Perry gazed at Stuber in wonderment. Only Stuber could manage to flatter you so subtly and insult you so blatantly in such a short amount of time.

Surprisingly, Sagum came to Perry's defense. "Stuber, he killed a fucking paladin."

Stuber leaned back and looked dead serious. "Listen to me, Perry. You're great when it comes to hand-to-hand. And yes—you did kill a paladin. But what you need to realize is that you killed *one* paladin." He let that fact hang there for a moment, eyes locked onto Perry's. Then he looked at each of them in turn. "There are entire cities of demigods. Do you think that they're just going to stand by while one of their own is killed?" Stuber shook his head. "I hate to be the bearer of bad news, folks, but Paladin Selos was just the start. The demigods want you dead, Perry. They're not just going to let you go. With Selos gone, they're going to come after you with everything they have. And for that, Perry, you need to learn how to fight like they do."

The air in the cabin was still and tense, as each of them considered the ramifications of what Stuber had just said. Each of them testing it against their sense of truth, and knowing deep down that Stuber was once again right.

"Fine, Stuber," Perry said, before he had a chance to reconsider. He was letting his gut lead him now, he was letting that little flame pull him along. And he needed Stuber. He needed all three of them. "But you're not just going to train me." Perry drew a finger in the air, encircling Teran and Sagum. "You're going to train all of us."

Teran nodded in agreement.

Sagum gave an indignant cry.

Stuber simply smiled, his eyes filled with love and malice.

Outside, the sandstorm hurled itself at them, and the wind began to howl.

Translation of the *Ortus Deorum*,
complete 2nd Song:

[I] In the first days, human beings filled all the earth, and every part of land in it, from ocean to ocean, and from sea to sea. [II] And they built for themselves great cities, as monuments to themselves, for they did not believe that there was anyone else who would ever be as powerful as they were. [III] In those days, the gods watched humanity, and they said to themselves, "We will not trouble ourselves, for human beings are only a problem unto themselves."

[IV] But as the human beings began to increase in number on the earth, and daughters were born to them, and many sons, then they began to speak as one language, and think as one mind, [V] and the gods were troubled, for they saw that the intention of the human heart was to be greater than anyone else. [VI] And the human beings built for themselves great machines that took them into the skies, and they discovered powers of great destruction. [VII] Then they said, "Come, let us spread ourselves across all the stars, like seeds spread across fertile ground, so that no one may ever stand against us."

VIII And the gods perceived a great wickedness in humanity, and that every inclination of the thoughts of the human heart was only evil all the time, IX and that they would never be satisfied, and that they wished to swallow all the stars. X The gods saw what the human beings were building, and all that they had become, and all that they intended to become, XI and the gods said to themselves, "Come, let us go down to them and destroy everything they have built so that they will not swallow all the stars."

XII In those days there was the Paladin Primus who had seen that the daughters of men were beautiful, XIII and he had taken many of them, and they had born him sons, and these sons were powerful, and they were called demigods. XIV And Paladin Primus was the guardian of humanity, for he was good and trustworthy in the eyes of his fellow gods. XV And the gods came to Primus and told him, "The outcry against humanity is so great, and their wickedness so grievous that we will go down and destroy everything they have built."

XVI Then Primus said: "Will you sweep away the good and the bad together? For I have born sons with the daughters of men, and there are still some that are good amongst them." [XVII] The gods said, "If it is as you say, then we will spare some of the people, but their works shall be destroyed, for they are wicked in their hearts, and they seek to swallow all the stars." [XVIII] And Primus said, "Take my sons, who are born of both gods and men, that they might watch over those of humanity that you choose to spare."

[XIX] And the gods said, "We will take your sons, who are demigods, and we will make them paladins over all the earth, [XX] and all the people that remain in it after their wickedness has been destroyed. And the paladins will keep the people, and guide them, so that humanity will never again grow so numerous that they think to swallow the stars. [XXI] For if wickedness is found in them again, we will destroy every man and woman and child, and every bird in the air, and every beast in every field, and leave nothing living on the earth to remember them by." [XXII] And so it was that the gods decided to destroy the earth, and sweep away everything that humanity had built in their wickedness, [XXIII] and to leave the sons of Primus as paladins and demigods to watch over and to keep them from their wicked ways.

Hey, D.J. Molles here. Thanks for reading BREAKING GODS! Curious about what's coming next? You can get updates on my new projects, along with a lot of great deals and freebies, by signing up for my newsletter at:

http://eepurl.com/c3kfJD
(and if you type that in, make sure to capitalize the J and D).

You can also hit me up on my social at FACEBOOK.COM/DJMOLLES

I look forward to hearing from you!

ABOUT THE AUTHOR

D.J. Molles is the New York Times bestselling author of *The Remaining* series, which was originally self-published in 2012 and quickly became an internet bestseller, and is the basis for his hit *Lee Harden* series, which will release its third title in late 2019. He is also the author of *Wolves*, a 2016 winner in the Horror category for the Foreword INDIES Book Awards. His other works include the *Grower's War* series, and the Audible original, *Johnny*. When he's not writing, he's taking care of his property in North Carolina, and training to be at least half as hard to kill as Lee Harden. He also enjoys playing his guitar and drums, drawing, painting, and lots of other artsy fartsy stuff

You can follow and contact him at:
Facebook.com/DJMolles
And sign up for his free, monthly newsletter at:
http://eepurl.com/c3kfJD
(If you're typing that into a browser, make sure to capitalize the J and D)

Made in the USA
Monee, IL
22 June 2020